SPY WEDNESDAY

ALSO BY WILLIAM HOOD

Mole

SPY
WEDNESDAY

A NOVEL BY
WILLIAM HOOD

Spy Wednesday is the name given in Ireland to the Wednesday before Good Friday, when Judas bargained to become a spy.

W·W·NORTON & COMPANY
NEW YORK/LONDON

The text of this book is composed in Times Roman, with display type set in
Cheltenham Bold Condensed. Composition and manufacturing by
The Haddon Craftsmen, Inc. Book design by Margaret Wagner.

First Edition

Library of Congress Cataloging in Publication Data
Hood, William, 1920–
Spy Wednesday.

I. Title.
PS3558.O545S68 1986   813'.54   85–15390

ISBN 0-393-02250-1

W. W. Norton & Company, Inc., 500 Fifth Avenue, New York, N. Y. 10110
W. W. Norton & Company Ltd., 37 Great Russell Street, London WC1B 3NU

1 2 3 4 5 6 7 8 9 0

For Mary Carr

THERE is always the possibility that readers of any novel by an author who was once in the racket will assume that the characters, incidents, and situations are but lightly cloaked facsimiles of real people and actual secret operations. The people and the situations in this book are entirely the product of the author's imagination. There are no hidden clues or sly puns that might allow a canny reader to match the imagined characters to any person living or dead. However useful it might be, there is no element of American intelligence that much resembles "the Firm."

As for the story, well, it could have happened. . . .

SPY WEDNESDAY

1 NEW YORK

ALAN TROSPER pushed the canvas boat chair away from the desk littered with Poshcraft brochures, and turned to admire again the tapered bow of *Scat,* the thirty-two-foot racing sloop on the adjoining stand. From where he sat, *Scat* looked like a cutter, the mast stepped almost midships to accommodate the huge headsails.

It was eight-thirty and only a few hard-core window shoppers, their plastic tote bags bulging with brochures, were still trudging along the aisles. If the Cunninghams did not arrive in five minutes, Trosper decided, he would switch off the lights on *Seraglio,* the flagship of the Poshcraft line, and leave. Martha was at a gallery opening and would be late. It was excuse enough for him to have dinner alone. A drink and a bottle of wine would take the taste of the New York Coliseum and the annual boat show out of his mouth.

"Mr. Trosper," a man's voice called from the front of the stand. "Mr. Trosper?"

Trosper got to his feet and walked to meet the couple he assumed to be the Cunninghams who had telephoned from Sag Harbor. "Yes," he said. "Mr. Cunningham?"

"We're sorry to be late, the traffic was really rotten on the Expressway." They shook hands and Mr. Cunningham, who wore deck shoes, a Greek sailing cap, and a British warm, introduced his wife, Nancy. Her black mink coat was unbuttoned, revealing a yellow turtleneck sweater and gray flannel trousers.

"That's quite all right—the Coliseum is one place where we don't have to worry about the tide." Trosper noticed that Mrs. Cunningham's attention was fixed on *Scat*'s scarlet hull. "She's a flat-out racing craft, Mrs. Cunningham," he said. "Not the best thing for comfortable cruising."

Trosper gestured towards the white sloop with a foot-high Poshcraft logo embedded midships on the hull. "You were interested in our thirty-two footer?" he asked.

"Yes, indeed, that's what we drove in to see. I've been studying the magazines and looking around the Sound. Now that we've settled in Sag, I've decided to buy a real boat. We're shopping for something Nancy and our friends will enjoy, too. I read a good review of your boat in *The Weekend Salt.*"

"Right. It's always best to look around, to get the feel of things." Trosper gestured again toward the slab sides of the *Seraglio.* The more he looked at it, the more it reminded him of a panel truck.

"Of course, this is a view you'll only have when she's been hauled for winter," Trosper said. "You won't get the right impression until she's in the water."

Cunningham nodded, but his wife's attention was still on the crimson racing sloop.

Trosper unhooked the chain from across the gangway leading up to the deck of the *Seraglio.* "Let's step aboard and get a real look at her," he said, and took Mrs. Cunningham's arm.

The Poshcraft line had been designed to provide a maximum below-deck space and private sleeping quarters for all hands. A market research firm had determined that these were the qualities that sold sailing yachts. From the center cockpit where the binnacle and wheel were mounted, the *Seraglio* deck stretched out like a plastic patio. The only thing missing was a collection of molded leprechauns.

"Space and privacy," Trosper declared honestly, "that's what she's built for." And never mind how she sails, he thought.

He picked up a deck plan from the color-coordinated seat covers. "There's room for three couples to cruise in complete privacy," he said, pointing to the deck plan. "And headroom, there are damned few boats of any size with six feet, four inches of headroom."

It was then he spotted Mercer. He was, as always, unmistakable. Almost six feet tall, Mercer weighed about two hundred and twenty pounds. He thrust down the aisle between the exhibits like an aircraft carrier barging through a crowded canal. It had been three years since Trosper had seen Mercer.

Mercer stopped in front of *Seraglio,* shot a glance up at Trosper on the deck, and wedged himself into one of the canvas deck chairs alongside the polished hull. He pulled off his black Tyrolean hat and ran a handkerchief across his face. Bouts of malaria had left him bald as a honeydew.

"Can we go downstairs?" Mrs. Cunningham asked.

Trosper turned back to her. "Of course we can," he said. "Let's go aft . . . around the back, that is, and start in the owner's . . . bedroom."

Mercer began to study a Poshcraft brochure.

Cunningham asked about winches and made notes on the cost of optional equipment. Mrs. Cunningham sniffed at the galley and walked into the main cabin.

"There's not all that much room," she said. "I mean if you want to sit down and have a drink, you'd be like in the subway."

Cunningham helped his wife up the step and into the center cockpit. "It's not a liner, Nancy," he said. "Those days are gone. This is something we can cruise in. We'll be on deck most of the time. That's what sailing is all about."

"Does it come in red?" she asked, glancing across the deck at the racing sloop.

Trosper flipped open the Poshcraft catalogue. "I'm not sure. We have *Blanc de Blanc,* our special white finish. There's *Mojave,* that's yellow. And, of course, *Ginger.*" He wasn't sure what color ginger was, but suspected it would be brown.

"As far as I can see, there's no red. Maybe something could be arranged, but with all this freeboard . . ." Trosper hesitated. He was about to give up. "What I mean is, I'd recommend against red—with all this freeboard, you might be mistaken for a lightship."

Mrs. Cunningham gave Trosper an appraising glance. "Are you English, Mr. Trosper?"

Surprised, Trosper said, "Lordy no, although I've lived there from time to time."

"Nancy's always had a soft spot for Limeys," Cunningham said. "I think she's seen too many of those old movies."

Trosper helped Mrs. Cunningham down the gangway and handed her husband a card. He studied it for a moment and then took a last glance at *Seraglio.* "We've got a little more looking to do, Al," he said. "Chances are we won't make a decision until spring."

It was too late, Trosper decided, to mention the special Boat Show discount that Poshcraft was offering.

"I'll be here all week," he said. "Come around again if you have any questions."

WHEN he left the Firm, Trosper had turned his back on secret intelligence. Some of his friends who had been fired or eased into retirement had tried to keep abreast of things. This was a nostalgia he refused to share. Benched intelligence officers debating the Controller's decisions reminded him of émigré politicians arguing about who would be prime minister when they were summoned back to save the homeland. Trosper had made no effort to keep in touch.

Mercer struggled free of the deck chair. "You weren't as hard to find as I thought," he said as they shook hands.

"Isn't the telephone book still the case man's best friend?" Trosper asked.

"Computers, that's what we say now."

"I suppose you're here to pick up a boat," Trosper said. "The best plastic that money can buy?"

Mercer looked at *Seraglio.* "I've heard something about these things. *Poshcrap,* is that it?"

Trosper laughed. "It's good to see you."

"What about this boat business—are you really serious?"

"Of course I'm serious. It pays and it keeps me out of the house. I even get on the water from time to time."

Mercer ran his handkerchief over his glistening pate. Hairless and unwrinkled, he was heavier but seemed no older than when Trosper had last seen him.

"Did you just happen to wander in at eight-thirty?"

"I thought it was about dinner time," Mercer said. "The taxpayers are buying."

"That sounds fine to me," said Trosper, "but I have it on good authority that there's no such thing as a free lunch."

TROSPER took in the mournful surroundings of Kelly's and concluded that the case man's burden had not changed much since his day. In the experience of finance clerks, all French restaurants were an expensive waste of special funds. A case man could spend twice as much in a place with a down-home name and get away without a single question. But there was another, more legitimate reason to go to an American expense-account restaurant—businessmen on their third martini were not likely to eavesdrop.

As they checked their coats, Trosper glanced at a framed newspaper clipping beside the checkroom. The *Times* food writer approved of the meat, cautioned against the vegetables, and praised the decor, "redolent of a men's club." The writer was a woman.

"GENTLY, gently," Mercer said, as the waiter struggled with the cork. "Just twist it out."

The bottle open, Mercer waved the flustered waiter away from the table and poured a little wine into his glass. "Damn serving red burgundy at room temperature when the room's as hot as this," he muttered. "Cellar temperature, sixty, sixty-two degrees, that's what's called for."

Sometimes Mercer's relentless wisdom irritated Trosper. "What is it you want?"

Mercer poured wine into Trosper's glass. "The Controller has a problem. He thinks you can help."

"That's very flattering. But then, I never thought I'd live to hear Bates admit to a problem." It irritated Trosper to realize that even after three years, he still resented Bates having been appointed Controller.

Mercer smiled and ran his fingers across his bald head. "The truth is, your old chum Duff Whyte suggested he get hold of you. Were you ever cleared for 'Agate?'"

Trosper thought of the many special oaths he had signed, agreeing never to disclose, never to indicate any knowledge of one or another ultrasecret activity. Some of these sequestered cases died in infancy, others lived long enough to explode on the front pages of the world press. The best remained secret and continued to produce the bedrock intelligence that justified the Firm's budget. "If I was cleared, I've forgot about it," he said.

"I'm authorized to fill you in," Mercer said. "Incidentally, your basic clearances were never lifted—but sooner or later you'll have to sign a new oath."

Trosper took a sip of the wine. As usual, Mercer was right. At that temperature, even respectable burgundy tasted like grape juice.

"I don't think I'll be signing anything. I'm out of it. You and Bates should have figured that out."

"I thought you might say that." Mercer hesitated for a moment. "You know you didn't have to quit, even Bates would have agreed to your staying. You left to prove something, but I'm damned if I can see what it was."

"I left because I'd had enough," Trosper said. "I don't know if the President really told Bates to shake up the firm, to dump some of the old hands. But if he did, he should have given the job to someone who knew his way around. Maybe even someone who understands the racket."

"You miss the point, Alan," Mercer said. "No matter what impression Bates makes, he's no fool. He knows he's a new boy and doesn't fit the pattern Darcy Odlum set. But he's the best administrator the shop's ever had. My guess is that by now he's brought the outfit out of the horse and buggy days, and put paid to some of the attitudes OSS took over from the English in the forties. Most of those quill-pen routines should have gone over the side in 1945."

Trosper glanced around the room, grunted, and fixed his attention on the huge steak.

"Bates's problem with you people," Mercer said, "is that he's an outsider—the cruel stepmother. You blame him because Darcy Odlum couldn't live forever."

This was true, Trosper admitted to himself. Odlum had created the Firm, chosen the staff, established the disciplines, and set the style. Until he was carried from his office on a stretcher, he was the only Controller the Firm had ever had.

Mercer put down his knife and fork and swirled the wine in his glass. He knew he had touched a sensitive point. "The problem now is to convince Bates that he can count on the Firm and doesn't have to go around looking for outside support."

"He's got the support he wanted," Trosper said. "The people who didn't think they could give it have left."

"There's more to it than that," Mercer said, "and you know it. There's the special loyalty that we all had for Odlum, that we had for the Firm. He knows he hasn't got that." He took a swallow of wine.

"What about that story the *Times* had on Bates making the Firm more responsive to . . ." Abruptly Trosper put down his knife and fork. He had long ago decided to leave the debate on the role of secret intelligence in a free society to TV panelists and the Op-Ed pages of the *Washington Post.* This was exactly the kind of gossip he had promised himself he would never engage in.

Mercer raised both hands to frame his cheeks and mimed a gesture of coquettish innocence. His gleaming bald head intensified the ludicrous picture. "You mean . . . dare I say it . . . the scheme to make the Firm more responsive to the White House? Perhaps even to shape our reporting to fit the President's political notions?"

"I'm sorry, Mercer, I should know better than to raise a question like that."

"Try the hash browns," Mercer said. "They're not exactly *Rösti,* but not bad. Nourishing, too—about five hundred calories a bite." He took another forkful, grinned, and said, "All right, I'll admit that I don't like Bates, either. But he's got the job." He took another mouthful of wine. Like a *tastevin,* he rolled the wine over the back of his tongue and seemed almost to gargle as he swallowed.

Just once, Trosper thought, he would like to see Mercer flub that performance, suck the wine up his nose, and choke. It was probably too much to hope for.

"You win," Trosper said. "What is 'Agate,' if that's what you're supposed to enlighten me on?"

" 'Agate' was Bates's code name for the Galkin follow-up investigation," Mercer said. "Now it's being used for something your friend Roger Kyle turned up in Vienna."

Trosper was confused. "What's Kyle got to do with it?"

"Bates seems to think Kyle's bought a dog."

It was old slang. When a case man bought a dog, he had recruited a worthless agent, a fabricator, or a con man, and had vouched for him. Trosper waited to see if Mercer would say more.

"Bates thinks it's a dog on a leash."

The only leashes worth talking about, Trosper knew, led all the way back to Moscow Center.

Mercer emptied his wine glass. "You haven't forgotten the Galkin case, have you?"

2 NEW YORK/VIENNA

TROSPER did not need Mercer to remind him of the night the Galkin case came unstuck. Every detail was as fresh in his mind as it was three years ago in Vienna, the night he wrote the meeting report.

HE HAD gotten up and walked across the room to where Kyle sat peering through an opening in the curtains that stretched across the double windows overlooking the Rooseveltplatz.

"All quiet," Kyle said. "There's no one on the street at all. The whole damned square is empty." Reluctantly, he eased himself out of the chair and surrendered the OP to Trosper.

The rain had been falling since mid-afternoon. The wet, cobbled pavement blotted the light from the street lamps and passing cars.

Kyle walked to the sideboard and the buffet of cold meat, smoked fish, and potato salad. Taking a slice of roast beef in his fingers, he reached for a bottle of wine. Then he put it back. Trosper had told him it was bad luck to anticipate a successful contact. He would not open a bottle before Galkin arrived. The Russian was two hours late.

"There's nothing can happen here," Kyle said. "They can't try any rough stuff in Vienna these days."

"Don't jolly me," Trosper said. "They'll do anything they think they need to do."

Kyle picked up another slice of beef. His throat was dry. "I've got to have something to drink," he said reluctantly. "You want anything?"

"Some coffee," Trosper said. "Make some more coffee."

Kyle went into the kitchen. He was glad to be busy.

There was a flicker of motion on the sidewalk across the square. A dark figure, hugging the wall, had slipped into the protection of a deep doorway.

"There's someone on the corner," Trosper called. "Maybe a woman." He eased the curtain away from the edge of the window and hunched forward, closer to the glass pane.

Kyle hurried back into the living room and peered over Trosper's shoulder. "Where?" he asked.

"On the corner, by the Volkswagen. Just there in the shadows."

Kyle inched the curtain back from the window frame. "Damn it," he said. "That's Galkin's wife, and she's alone. Something's happened."

Dropping the curtain, Kyle took the 7-mm Walther from his shoulder holster and jacked a round into the chamber.

"Is Galkin there anywhere?"

"She's all alone," Trosper said. "There's no one else." He strained to get a better view of the woman. "I should have brought binoculars."

"He was due at four," Kyle muttered. "He's been here before. Who needed glasses?" It was Kyle's responsibility to equip the safe house.

"She's just standing there," Trosper said. "Maybe she's confused about the address. You'd better pick her up."

Kyle slipped the pistol into the pocket of his trenchcoat and pulled a green Tyrolean hat over his modish long hair. "Is there anyone on foot, any traffic at all on the square?"

"There's nothing," Trosper said. "But step on it. And watch yourself."

From the window Trosper could follow Kyle's slim figure as he skirted the square. As he approached the woman in the shadows, Trosper saw him hesitate. Raising his hat, Kyle leaned forward as if to whisper. Then he took the woman's arm and steered her swiftly toward the safe house.

"That goddamned Kyle," Trosper mused. "Who else would think to tip his hat?"

Trosper watched the square until he heard the downstairs door open and the sound of feet hurrying up the stairs leading to the apartment.

When the apartment door swung open, Trosper dropped the curtain and turned. The woman wore a small, knitted hat, like a cloche. It was dripping wet. As Kyle closed the door and snapped the heavy lock, she pulled off the sodden hat and shook her thick blond hair. She began to rub her eyes. For a moment Trosper wondered if she was brushing away rain or tears.

She was younger than Trosper had expected, and slim for a Russian woman. Her hair was wet, but he could see it was cut to show off her high cheekbones and huge blue eyes.

"Aleksei couldn't come," she said as Kyle helped her out of the rain-soaked gray coat. "He was ordered back to Moscow. He'll be here in about four weeks. He said you'd understand my coming."

Trosper did not understand. He had never understood why agents ever told anyone anything about their secret lives.

THE MEETING at the safe apartment had not been scheduled. It was an emergency contact, the first in the fourteen months since Trosper had approached Galkin and solicited his cooperation in return for eventual asylum and resettlement in the United States.

Trosper had spaced his contacts with Galkin. Usually their meetings were two or three weeks apart. He knew the Firm would have preferred a more frequent schedule, but he had learned that overworking an agent in place—demanding frequent meetings, asking for information beyond the spy's reach—was poor craft. Almost as bad, these frequent contacts became routine, a habit for the agent.

There was no such thing as a routine meeting with an agent in place. A spy's existence was at stake every time he met his case man. Maximum precautions increased security and, for the spy, underlined the risks involved. This helped keep the agent wary. Trosper had little use for sanguine agents. Chirpy spies were careless. Careless agents were short-timers, hardly worth the turmoil that came when they were uncovered.

Earlier that week, Roger Kyle had seen the numerals 3–4–7 jotted boldly across the top of page 222 of volume two of the phone books ranged alongside the bank of pay telephones in the Vienna Central Post Office.

He had checked the telephone book twice a week since Trosper had given Galkin the communication system. Until he saw the message, Kyle begrudged the time spent going across town to the post office. He suspected it was make-work, Trosper's way of reminding him that he was just a caddy, learning field work.

Kyle fished a pen from his pocket and drew a line through the numerals. The emergency meeting would be on the third day of the week, Wednesday. At four, the next digit, in the afternoon. The safehouse was at Frank Gasse 7, the third number. It was a simple system, easy for the agent to remember.

"EXACTLY what was it Aleksei said I would understand?" Trosper asked. "What was it he said?"

Kyle flung Vera Galkin's wet coat across a chair. He slipped out of his trenchcoat and steered the Russian woman to a heavy, overstuffed chair in a corner of the room.

"He said it would be all right for me to come here," she answered, thrusting her chin forward. "He said he told you he had told me all about his work with you."

Then, rattled by Trosper's impassive look, she said, "It was only just. The children and I are as much involved as he is." She glanced first at Kyle, then turned to Trosper. "He said he told you. You do remember?" she said.

"Yes," Trosper said. "That's exactly the sort of thing I remember."

Trosper could not recall a Russian expression for "fair play." Vera Galkin had said *spravedlivo*—"just." But it was less than just, Trosper thought, for Galkin to have involved his wife in treason.

"Aleksei was called back to Moscow," Vera said. "He said to say it was for a training course on American armaments, missiles, new weapons . . ." Her voice trailed off. "He said he had warned you he would be leaving."

Galkin was a KGB officer, First Chief Directorate, assigned to the Soviet Embassy in Vienna. He had told Trosper that he expected to be called to Moscow for a briefing on American guided missiles. He did not know when the order would come though, but guessed he would not leave for some weeks. Trosper had asked urgently for guidance on the priority information the Firm would want Galkin to seek in Moscow. But headquarters seemed to have taken Galkin at his word and had assumed it would be some weeks before he was ordered back. Galkin's sudden departure meant that he had left without the specific questions the Firm would want answered.

"Here," Kyle said. "Have something to eat and a drink." Trosper seemed to him to be soured by the woman's unexpected appearance and in a surly, almost dangerous mood.

"Maybe a little something," she said, with a glance toward the food. "I walked from the Cottagegasse. I'd have been here earlier, but I couldn't get away from the apartment. Feodorova came in with her brat, and I had to make tea."

Vera Galkin helped herself to sturgeon and looked warily at the vodka and wine bottles on the side board. Trosper guessed she would have liked tea but was too timid to ask for some.

"Could I have some soda?" she asked. Kyle nodded and walked to the buffet.

"Did Aleksei tell you about Feodorova?" she asked.

"Just that she keeps dropping in on you," Trosper said. He was not in the habit of making small talk with the wives of his agents. "Did Aleksei have anything else to say before he left?" he asked.

"Yes," she said. "Lopatin has been here. He's the old fellow, the one who has something to do with Sitnikov in Moscow."

Sitnikov, a Moscow Center American specialist who had served in Vienna in the late 1950s, was reported to be in charge of what the Russians called active measures, a catchall for Soviet disinformation, deception, and black propaganda operations.

"Did Aleksei say anything else about Lopatin?"

"Just that he's involved in some big new project and that Aleksei will find out more about it when he sees Lopatin in Moscow." Vera stopped to take a sip of her drink. "He said Lopatin was here all during the war, a real hero with decorations. He's older than—"

"Did Aleksei have any other message for us?" Kyle interjected.

Trosper said nothing. He had told Kyle more than once never to interrupt an agent. It was not impolite, it was a mistake. If Kyle had a real instinct for the racket, he would have remembered. The trick was to keep an agent on one topic long enough to cover it fully. Random questions were the mark of an inexperienced case man.

The Russian woman put down her fork. "Yes, there was something important. He wanted me to tell you again that no one was to contact him in Moscow. No mail. No telephone calls. No contact man from an embassy," she said. "Nothing at all."

Trosper nodded. As far as Galkin was concerned, the KGB had Moscow wrapped up.

"Aleksei will stay with Babushka, my mother, at our apartment. At least he'll be able to see the children."

The Galkins had two boys, ten and twelve years old. In keeping with Soviet practice, they had remained in Moscow, cared for by Vera Galkin's mother. In Vienna the Soviet Embassy maintained a kindergarten for young children. But school-age children were required to stay in the USSR to be trained in the Soviet school system. And, more to the point, to serve as hostages against the possible defection of their parents. It was an effective system, one of the many leashes the KGB tied to Soviet officials working abroad.

"Aleksei said that they always keep a special eye on people who come home for a few days," Vera said. "I can write to him through the embassy here," she added, "but you are not to communicate with him at all." Like a child, she seemed pleased to have been given the responsibility for delivering the message.

Trosper had lost interest in the woman's comments. If the Firm had responded when Trosper first asked for the questions, everything would have been all right. His departure before Trosper could give him the questionnaire to be memorized raised the possibility that the head office, eager for the information Galkin might be able to uncover, would force a contact in Moscow.

Galkin was Trosper's last shot in Vienna. He had come close several times, but Galkin was his first major recruitment in three years. He knew that his reputation had eroded, that from being known as one of the most experienced and aggressive field hands, he had almost imperceptibly slipped into old-boy status. He suspected that he was considered too cautious and slow-moving, excessively taken up with tradecraft and security, criticisms that could hardly be raised against any of the new case men.

Maybe, Trosper thought, he *had* become too wary and was obsessed with Soviet countermeasures and security. Possibly his reaction to the fresh, well-educated young case men was sour grapes, an expression of his reluctance to see a new generation take over. The truth, Trosper realized, was that the new boys were quicker off the mark and did move faster than he was willing to.

Still, there were some consolations. The flood of intelligence from Galkin had attracted "higher level" attention. Trosper knew that his reports reached the President's desk. There was something else. Aside from Galkin's admission that he had informed Vera of his relationship with Trosper, the case had been free of security problems, the "squeals," as they were called, that flawed much of the work of the younger case men.

Damn Galkin, Trosper thought. And damn all spies who tell anyone anything.

BY THE TIME Kyle had helped Vera Galkin back into her coat and eased her toward the door, Trosper had thought through the cable he would have to write. It would not be easy to tell the Firm that Galkin would be in Moscow for a month, and to insist that no attempt be made to contact him. Galkin had a long-range potential, as good or better than any agent Trosper had handled. Galkin's own judgment could be trusted to tell him what to concentrate on uncovering in Moscow. No matter how important the new active measures plan was, it would keep for a month. Galkin's future was too important to risk for any short-term gain.

Trosper went to the sideboard and poured scotch into a glass. He hoped that Duff Whyte would be in Washington. With Odlum dead, Whyte was the one man who had the reputation and seniority to make the overachievers keep their hands off Galkin for the next few weeks.

IT WAS almost a month after Vera Galkin had briefed Trosper on her husband's sudden departure that Kyle spotted another signal for an emergency meeting. This time Vera came directly to the safe apartment. Galkin had telephoned from Moscow, she said. His orders had changed and he was to remain in Moscow for at least a year. After that, he would be sent to the Soviet Embassy in Washington. Vera would return to Moscow on the weekly courier flight from Schwechart Airport.

Trosper, his anger barely muffled, was even more distant from Vera than before. It was Kyle who made the small talk, asked after the children, and gently offered Vera money for last-minute needs. Trosper's interest seemed to have vanished.

Only when Vera prepared to leave the safe apartment did Trosper shake off his preoccupation and ask her to tell Galkin that he looked forward to seeing him in Washington. Then he wished her Godspeed.

Kyle took Vera to the street.

"What the hell was that all about?" Kyle demanded when he returned.

Trosper turned his back and poured another scotch.

"You know damned well there's something wrong," Kyle insisted. "That story's too pat. There's no reason why Galkin shouldn't have come back to Vienna, at least to turn his agents over to another case man."

"You've got a point," Trosper said softly, "but not the main point." He swirled the whiskey in his glass and took a deep drink. Then he walked across the room to the window and pulled one of the heavy draperies aside. He stared out the window at the quiet square. "Along with worrying about that foolish woman, there's something you should have caught."

He closed the curtain and turned to face Kyle. "Even if Galkin had been authorized to telephone his wife, why would he have told her that he was being transferred to Washington? That's classified information, and the international lines aren't exactly private."

Kyle started to speak but Trosper cut him off.

"That was a message from Moscow Center to us," he said. "If Comrade Galkin is going to Washington, we're supposed to think he can't be in any trouble."

Trosper emptied his glass. "Galkin's been arrested," he said. "He made the call under KGB auspices. That's the sort of thing you're paid to notice."

Kyle flushed. "You're really something, Alan," he said. "As far as you're concerned it doesn't matter a damn what happens to any of them."

Kyle went to the sideboard and poured himself a glass of the soft Austrian wine. "Even if you didn't want to question her, to try to sort it out, you could at least have explained that something might have gone wrong. You could have given her an option, maybe offered her asylum."

Trosper put smoked salmon on a slice of dark bread.

"You may not believe it," Kyle said. "But there's such a thing as being too goddamned professional. Just because you think Galkin never should have told that poor woman anything, there's no reason for you to treat her like a bloody fool."

Trosper took a deep breath. He didn't owe Kyle an explanation of what he felt when an agent was lost. Instead he said: "Do you really think she'd have left Aleksei and the children just because I told her I *thought* her husband *might* be in trouble? If I said anything at all, it would just make her frantic. As it is she won't be able to stand fifteen minutes' interrogation. There's not a prayer she could stick to whatever story Galkin told her to tell."

The room had grown dark. The only light came from floor lamps near the sideboard. Trosper snapped on the overhead light, a cheap reproduction of a crystal chandelier. The room looked washed out, faded like an old photograph.

"When Galkin told her what he was doing," Trosper said, "he killed them both."

"This business stinks. We just sit here and that woman walks right into an inferno." Kyle slammed his hand down on the buffet.

Trosper took a sip of his drink. "You're right about one thing," he said.

Kyle looked across the room at him.

"It *is* a business," Trosper said. "It's not the Red Cross. Not even the Boy Scouts."

"All the same," Kyle said. "You shouldn't have let her go. There must have been something we could do."

Before Trosper drafted the cable he decided to reserve his speculation as to Galkin's fate until he could discuss it with someone he trusted. Someone like Duff Whyte. All he reported was that Galkin would not return to Vienna; he would be out of touch until he was posted to Washington; it would be about a year.

The Firm's answer was succinct. There was no problem. Contact had already been made with Galkin in Moscow.

IN APRIL that year, Reuters wire service reported a Soviet news item. A former military man, A. Galkin, had been found guilty of treason and executed.

A few days later, Trosper was called back to Washington for reassignment.

3 NEW YORK/WASHINGTON, D.C.

THE RESTAURANT had nearly emptied before Mercer signaled the impatient waiter for the check.

Trosper refused Mercer's offer to share a taxi. "I'd better walk off a few of those expensive calories," he said. As the cab pulled away, Mercer waved once, like a salute. Trosper turned and began to make his way uptown along Third Avenue.

I've been out of it more than two years, he told himself. Galkin's dead and there's nothing Kyle could have turned up that will change that. It's stupidity even to think about going back and trying to work with Bates.

With his rolled umbrella, Trosper flicked a crumpled cellophane candy wrapper from the sidewalk and slashed at it with a short saber stroke. He missed. The wrapper dropped into the gutter.

For months he had scarcely given a thought to the racket. Now, after two hours with Mercer, it was as though he had never left.

Memories jostled for his attention. It wasn't the drinks, or casual shoptalk that sparked his reverie, Trosper realized. It was the artful Mercer who had left him with a sense of unfinished business, the sort of business that Odlum would have expected him to deal with. Darcy Odlum, the man Trosper respected more than any.

It was Odlum who had called him back from Vienna for consultation a few weeks after the Galkin recruitment. No matter how heavy the other pressures might be, the Controller had always kept close to the case men who were developing important agents, the spies who delivered the hard intelligence that paid the Firm's way in Washington.

IN WASHINGTON, he had gone directly to the Controller's office. The young security man in the outer reception room had waved him into the inner office where Odlum's secretary, Blanche, sat. He paused at her desk with its bank of telephone equipment, interoffice scramblers, unlisted outside lines, and direct—cryptosecure—lines to the White House, Secretary of State, and CIA. He often wondered which line Odlum used for calling home.

He had handed Blanche a square cardboard box tied with a crumpled red ribbon.

"It's a *Sachertorte*," he explained. "I was going to get it at Dehmel's but then I thought you'd want the real thing. This is from the hotel, Frau Sacher's own recipe."

"*Danke bestens*," she said.

Blanche had never been stationed abroad, but rarely missed the chance to accompany Odlum on any trip that took him to Austria. She pushed a button on the intercom. "Alan Trosper's here." A small green light flashed above the door to Odlum's office.

Trosper pushed the heavy door open and stepped into the oak-paneled room. Odlum looked up from the desk. He rose to shake hands. Behind his oval, rimless glasses, the Controller's eyes were blurred with fatigue. His complexion, usually tanned from year-around tennis, was gray; his tangled white hair, a Washington trademark for so many years, had turned wispy and lay lifeless against his skull. For the first time Trosper realized how much the Controller had aged.

"You must be tired after that trip," Odlum said. "All I've done is spend the morning with those budget whizkids and their computers, and I feel as if I'd been run over."

Odlum glanced at his in box, piled high with dispatches and cables. Then he looked across the desk at Trosper. "Still," he said, "it's good to talk a little business after a day like today." Odlum's smile twisted slightly. "Particularly this kind of business." He pulled a foulard square from his breast pocket and began to polish his glasses. "How good is your new man?"

Trosper knew that Odlum had read every cable and studied the dispatches. He began slowly to give the evaluation he had rehearsed on the plane. "I think he's the only agent I ever handled who has the potential to step beyond the intelligence services and into the inner circle, the place where policy is thrashed out."

Odlum stuffed the silk back into his pocket. "How serious is the squeal?"

Trosper took a deep breath. He understood that Odlum had made his mind up about Galkin's potential, and that he had made his own precise judgment of the security problem.

"It's serious," Trosper said. "But there's nothing we can do about it, not now anyway."

Odlum pushed himself back from the desk. Obviously irritated, he seemed about to speak, and Trosper braced himself for a lecture. If Aleksei ever came under suspicion, Vera Galkin would be arrested as well. They would be held and worked upon separately until each would be told that the other had broken. Each would be promised a form of amnesty and rehabilitation for the family in exchange for confession. It was one of the oldest techniques in the book. And it was not something Trosper felt he needed to be reminded of.

Odlum sighed, and shook his head. "Why do they do it," he said slowly. "The best man we had in Berlin in 1943 did the same stupid thing. 'To make things easier all around,' was the way he put it. Three months later, he and his wife were hanging on hooks in a Gestapo cellar." Odlum picked up a pipe from his desk and began to fill it. "What did Galkin say when you challenged him?"

"He said, 'She hates them as much as I do.' That was when I told him that hating wasn't worth a damn, and that the GULAG was full of haters. This made him mad. He jumped up, struck some silly pose, and said that he would trust her with his life." Trosper cleared his throat. "I told him that was exactly what he had done."

"I've never understood," Odlum said, "why any agent ever tells anyone anything, ever."

In the library of his Georgetown house that night, Odlum poured brandy. "I'm really tired, Alan," he said. "There's so much nonsense these days, so many peripheral things. If it's not the budget, it's some damned administrative snarl. It's no wonder the President wants me out."

For months the rumor—leaked by General Paul Foster, the President's security adviser—had circulated that the President wanted a change and was looking for a younger man. The gossip had even reached Vienna. Trosper was surprised to hear Odlum confirm it.

"That damned security adviser of his would like to put the Firm directly under his office," Odlum said wearily. "That's all we need. We'd be a private political spook outfit with a new controller every time the administration changed. You can't run secret operations that way."

One of the reasons Trosper had preferred to work abroad was to keep a distance from the churning politics of Washington. Odlum, who knew how political pressure, even the rumor of it, rotted morale, rarely mentioned domestic politics to anyone in the Firm.

Odlum reached for a box of cigars. "It's a good thing I've got Duff Whyte and Walter Bates to take some of the load."

Another surprise. Trosper had never heard Odlum link Walter Bates with Duff Whyte. Whyte was Odlum's Assistant for Operations, the senior operations man in the Firm. Bates—who had confined his service to the Washington headquarters—was Executive Officer, more an administration and personnel man than an operations hand.

A LIGHT rain had begun to fall. Trosper pushed the memories out of his mind. He unfurled his umbrella and quickened his pace along Third Avenue. But his thoughts reeled back to the Firm.

It had been more than a decade before "the trouble"—the long season in which the press and Congress had combined to disembowel the intelligence services—that the Director of Central Intelligence recommended to the President that a small, ostensibly privately funded unit be established and separated from its parent organizations.

As the Director had seen it, the conglomerates—the Defense Intelligence Agency, the National Security Agency, and CIA—had no choice but to remain in full public view. "Bureaucratic sparklers in the tiara of big government," he had said with heavy irony. Under the right controller, the Director told the President, the new organization could hope to fade from sight. He admitted it was an imperfect solution. But in an untidy world, the Director had said, even an accommodation like this was more appropriate for a secret intelligence organization than the comfort of official status and the suffocating embrace of the civil service.

When Research Estimates, Incorporated, an independent think tank, bought the small office building on Wisconsin Avenue, even publicity-prone legislators cooperated in keeping the polite secret. It was then that a few insiders began to refer to it as the Firm. Aside from occasional shrill suspicions published by the intelligence critics, press coverage of American intelligence operations had, to Odlum's relief, remained focused on the public organizations, the conglomerates.

The rain had eased, but the lighted notice on the few empty taxis cruising Third Avenue proclaimed the drivers to be Off Duty. Wrapped in memory, Trosper was glad to walk.

IT wasn't the airline food, Trosper now recalled, that had soured his stomach the day he had come from Vienna for his reassignment interview with Bates. It had been the prospect of seeing Bates behind Odlum's desk. Before facing Bates, he had decided to stop at K Section.

"Hello, Gunny," Trosper said. "Is Mr. Severs still hiding out back there?"

Retired Marine Gunnery Sergeant Rines shot to his feet and reached across the desk to shake hands. "Glad to see you back, sir. I'll just ring to see if he's free."

Gunny Rines controlled all access to K Section in the restricted area on the fourth floor of the Firm's Washington headquarters. Only visitors with a K Clearance were allowed through the electronically locked door, and each was logged in and out. The red-bordered Top Secret briefing book on the guard desk contained the names and photographs of everyone holding a K Clearance. But Gunny Rines never consulted it. He had total recall for faces.

Otto Severs had two abiding interests in Vienna—the restaurants and the opera. He had kept up an amiable interrogation until Trosper said, "I'd like a peek at the Galkin file. I'm seeing Bates at four, and it may come up."

Severs hitched uneasily in his chair. Only the files in the Controller's Registry were more restricted than those of K Section. He glanced at a computer printout at the side of his desk and flicked an intercom button. "I guess you're entitled, Alan," he said quietly. "But you'll have to read it here."

"No problem, I only need to check a couple of points."

Trosper's guess had been correct. Scrawled across the file copy of his cable on the last meeting with Vera Galkin was Bates's directive. "Disregard field recommendation in paragraph 6. Implement Moscow contact soonest. B/C."

He closed the file and handed it back across the desk to Severs. "In this instance, am I correct in assuming that 'B/C' doesn't mean Before Christ?"

"You've got it," Severs said. "It means 'Bates/Controller.' A bit Napoleonic, but I suppose it saves time."

Trosper had not bothered to read the analyst's speculation on whether the contact man had been spotted mailing the letter to Galkin, or whether Galkin had been detected emptying the dead drop. What mattered was that a potentially priceless agent had been wasted.

ONCE the ritual pleasantries, made more difficult because Trosper had neither wife nor children to ask after, were over, Bates confessed that he had spent an hour studying Trosper's personnel file.

"It's impressive, Alan," he said. "Damned impressive. I've never seen more favorable comments on anyone." Letting this observation hang in the air, he reached across the desk to take a cigarette from a Chinese lacquer box. "And you know as well as I do that we've got some damned fine men here."

Trosper's attention wandered to the art work Bates had added to the controller's office—a pair of handsome African masks, bronzes from India, stylized Japanese prints, and a posterlike painting from Bangkok. A white porcelain elephant from Vietnam held the ashtray beside Trosper's chair. It was with an effort that he brought his attention back to Bates.

"What I mean," Bates intoned, "is that these comments were made by people who knew what they were talking about."

Trosper wondered if he was supposed to perceive the past tense —people who *knew* what they were talking about. Not people who *know.*

"I had to read your file twice before it struck me—the one thing, the key, something I hadn't tumbled to."

Trosper doubted that Bates had ever underestimated his capacity for insight. If it had taken him two readings to plumb whatever truth might be resting in the worn file, it was indeed obscure.

"In all the time you've spent on operations," Bates said, "you've never really been involved in covert action."

Pausing to let Trosper grasp the enormity of this observation, Bates took a deep drag on his cigarette.

Trosper shrugged. "I've always thought it difficult to work both sides of the street, to handle political action while trying to keep out of sight and work quietly with agents."

"That's exactly what I mean," Bates said. "From everything the President has told me—and certainly General Foster agrees with him—we're going to be doing much more of this in future. We'll all be walking on both sides of the street." To emphasize his point, he added, "And carrying water on both shoulders."

Trosper, in imagination straddling the street and hefting the water, glanced around the newly redecorated office. Relegated to one side was General Donovan's desk, the one from which he had directed OSS operations. It was a worn and scratched piece of furniture, but it had been used by each of Donovan's successors in CIA.

When the Firm was formed, the DCI shipped the desk across the river, gathered a few OSS veterans and presented it to Odlum.

Bates's desk was new, the same sleek walnut and steel model that had been approved for presidential appointees.

"What I'm going to ask you to do," Bates said, "is to broaden yourself, to get some new experience to go with that expertise you've spent so much time building up."

Trosper had learned to wait a few seconds after an interlocutor had apparently finished before allowing himself to speak. Silence usually encouraged others to keep talking, to elaborate on what they had said. The nervous pressure that pushed agents to fill in the quiet spaces sometimes led to surprising blunders. He had read of the "gift of silence." It was not a gift. Silence was a skill that had to be cultivated.

"I've spent a lot of effort on this and now I know what's right for you." Bates's smile contracted slightly.

"I suppose it is difficult to see these things for oneself," Trosper said pleasantly.

Speaking slowly, as if he were choosing his words with more care than usual. Bates said: "We simply can't afford the luxury of keeping so many of our best men tied up with the Russians any longer. Not that I'd ever say anything against Odlum—he was a great officer and we'll not see his like again. But his fascination with the Soviet Union was bending the shop out of shape. We were neglecting the important areas. Look at Africa, the Caribbean . . ."

Trosper wondered if Bates had listed these areas in order of importance.

"What I've got to do is take some of the experience the men in Asia, in Central America, have been piling up and put it to use against the Russians. New blood, different techniques," Bates said heartily. "It could make all the difference."

"Some of the tradecraft that works in those places will surely surprise Moscow," Trosper said with conviction.

"That's right," Bates said. "I've got to get some of our wise men, you fellows who've been toe to toe with Moscow all these years, and put you into covert action. It's all a matter of balancing the equation."

Bates got up from his chair and peered through the curtains at the enclosed courtyard.

"What I'm going to ask you to do is to go out where the action is and to learn the ropes," he said, and turned to face Trosper. "I'm sure you'll be just as keen on the new assignment and a different area as you have been on all your other jobs."

"It's not so much the area involved," Trosper said. "It's just that I've always thought that spying is an urban activity. There's not much need for spies in areas where they're still using a pointed stick to scratch their secrets in the dirt."

Trosper stopped. Perhaps he was being unfair. "The problem in those areas is social as much as political. Most of those poor bastards are hungry, and they've been hungry for a century. Reshaping their lousy governments is not my line of work. It's for specialists, and largely the sort of thing embassies and aid programs are supposed to handle. There's little need for a secret apparatus in many of those places. A few scouts can pick up all the intelligence that's needed to flesh out the embassy reporting."

"You've got it exactly," Bates said. "The market for spying and counterintelligence is drying up. We've got machines—and God knows they cost too much to be called gadgets anymore—that take care of ninety percent of what we used to get from spies."

Still standing, Bates leaned across the desk toward Trosper. "Not that spies ever came through with a fraction of what the White House really needed," he said.

Satisfied he had made his point, Bates sat down. With a nervous gesture he pointed to a slim plastic-bound book at the side of his desk. "I'm sure you've heard that all we need are a couple of slight technical adjustments and we'll have broken right through. Just a modification or two and we'll have the Soviets at their own game."

Trosper had no idea what Bates was talking about. "Stirring times," was as much as he could say.

"But maybe you haven't been cleared for . . . 'Bounder.' " Bates had hesitated, as if even mentioning the cryptonym for his technical wonder might have violated security. "I'll see about getting you cleared."

With a flourish, Bates reached across the desk and made a note on a pad. "We've been keeping this one under wraps," he said. "General Foster and the President are the only ones outside the shop who've been briefed."

In Odlum's time, Trosper reflected, no one outside the Firm was ever briefed until the new agent, the new gadget, the new whatever, was working and productive. The magician's vault was stuffed with beautifully handmade prototype devices that would revolutionize secret intelligence—as soon, that is, as a few kinks were worked out.

Technicians had been known as magicians ever since President Truman was shown a captured Soviet camera that had been built into a pocket wallet. "It's magic," he exclaimed, thinking it to be a product of American ingenuity.

With an effort, Trosper dispelled his reverie. Bates droned on. "That's a long way of getting around to it, and believe me I appreciate your patience," Bates was saying. "I've ticketed half a dozen terrific assignments out there for some of you fellows on the Soviet side. I've kept the whole slate open until I could offer you a choice. You can take your pick. You deserve it."

Tradition called for Trosper to say that he appreciated the offer and would take whatever assignment the Controller thought best. All Trosper said was, "That's very considerate of you . . ."

As Trosper got up to leave, Bates walked around his desk to shake hands. "It was rotten luck, that Galkin matter."

"Luck had nothing to do with it," Trosper said.

Moral indignation is not a quality that secret intelligence operatives wear on their sleeve. Years of working with political zealots, sly do-gooders, con men, and traitors had cut deep into his own share of outrage. Still, Trosper had not trusted himself to confront Bates over Galkin.

He closed the door. Then he stopped to say good-bye to Blanche.

Trosper spent two days cleaning out his files, had a boozy lunch with an unsuspecting friend, and took the Metroliner to New York. Then he mailed his building pass and a polite, one-paragraph letter of resignation to Bates.

It was Blanche, Trosper remembered, who had sent him a postcard when she spotted his name as navigator on *Biff* in that year's Bermuda race.

THE RAIN had stopped. Trosper turned east and hurried along Seventy-Ninth Street.

4 NEW YORK

TROSPER touched the bell as he turned the knob and pushed the door open. As long as Martha had lived in New York, she rarely remembered to secure the door when she was in the apartment alone. Snapping the bolt shut, he hung his hat and topcoat in the hall closet and walked into the living room.

Martha rose from the sofa behind the coffee table. She thrust her half-frame glasses into her heavy, ash-streaked hair and walked over to Trosper. She kissed him lightly on the cheek.

He never ceased to be embarrassed by casual signs of affection. Pushing her gently away, he looked admiringly at her housecoat and fleece-lined slippers.

"You look wonderful."

Martha smiled and reached out to touch his cheek. "And you're late. What happened?"

"I got taken to dine."

"And a drink or two?"

"A couple of martinis, some burgundy, nothing serious."

For a moment Trosper's glance lingered on Martha. Sometimes he caught a trace of uncertainty in her dark eyes. "Anyway, you said you'd be late—how was the opening?"

"The paintings were nothing special, but a lot of people were there. I had dinner with Freddy and Patricia. He's stopped eating —except for one meal a day, or something like that. He looked just as fat as ever, and was sloshing down white wine."

A few weeks after Trosper moved to New York, a friend had invited him for drinks. Martha Prynne's date did not arrive and Trosper took her to dinner. She was a striking New York woman, chic and intelligent. Her life revolved around her partnership in a midtown art gallery. Paintings were important, a new novel or play might be interesting. But politics and all that went with it was something that existed only in the pages of the *Times* that she rarely read. Martha Prynne and her friends opened a new life for Trosper, something far removed from what he had known, and mercifully unencumbered by the discipline and constraints of secret work.

Their affair developed casually until the night Martha plucked a worn copy of *Moby-Dick* from a bookshelf in his apartment. The middle pages had been cut to conceal a packet of ten- and twenty-dollar bills.

"What *is* this?" she demanded, dangling the packet like a fish by its tail. "How come it's stuck together like this?"

"Christ almighty," he said, jumping to his feet. "I've shipped those damned books half a dozen times. It's a bloody miracle no one ever found it."

"What *is* it?" she insisted.

"It's my mad money," he said quickly. "And it's not stuck together. If you press each bill with a steam iron, they don't take up so much space. It's an old trick."

Martha stuffed the money back into the book. "I just can't believe you," she said.

"There's a lot of housebreaking in Europe," he said. "But they never think to look through books."

"You must think I *am* a fool," she said.

Trosper jammed the book back in the shelf. He remembered now that the Controller, running an operation he did not trust to regular channels, had sent the cash by courier to Berlin. Trosper was to hold the money until he got a signal to cache it for an agent. The signal never came, and Trosper had forgot the incident. And so, he realized, had Odlum.

"If you ask me," she said, "it's getaway money . . ." Her voice trailed off.

Invent something, you silly twit, Trosper told himself.

"It's just that I forgot all about it," he said. "It's a miracle it's still there."

"I *hate* being lied to," she said, her face flushed with anger.

Reluctantly, Trosper began to explain. It was the first time he had ever discussed his work with an outsider. Martha wasn't impressed. "It must be awful," she said, glancing at the book, "to live your whole life as if at any minute you'll have to go over the back fence when the cops break down the door."

Martha's only questions were about the people Trosper had worked with. "Do they have children in your subculture?" she asked. "What does Dad tell the tots?"

Instead of being relieved that she showed so little interest in his work, Trosper finally realized that he was miffed by her reaction. "So much," he had told her, "for all of those espionage memoirs and exposés."

"*WHAT* about your dinner?" Martha asked. "Is the yacht business so good the customers are taking the salesmen to dinner?"

"This was a friend."

"Short, dark, and sexy?" Martha was five feet eight and knew Trosper's taste ran to angular blondes.

"About two hundred and twenty pounds and stone bald. An old friend."

"A voice from the past?"

"Just an old friend," he said.

"Do you want me to pry it out of you, or am I to wait until you decide to tell me something?"

Trosper walked to the bar in the far corner of the room and poured scotch into a tumbler. He opened the ice bucket. It was full. Martha rarely drank spirits. She had gotten the ice when she made herself hot chocolate. No matter how much she ate, Martha's weight never changed. It infuriated him.

"His name is Mercer. I used to know him pretty well. We did some work together in—"

Trosper stopped before he said "in the old days." He had promised himself never to use that expression.

"—in Rome. That was the last place. Mercer's one of the good guys. It's hard to see why Bates didn't deck him, too."

"I suppose he's decided there's no future in spying and wants to get into the yacht trade—give up the glamorous secret world?"

Trosper dropped ice into his glass. "Apparently something has come up," he said.

"And you're the only one with the answer?"

"They seem to think I might be able to help—the boss wants to talk with me."

"Damn it, Alan, I really think you're crazy." Martha turned and walked to the radio in the far corner of the room. She spun the dial to a Newark jazz station. Jazz was the only music Martha ever listened to.

Trosper picked up his drink and walked over to Martha. He knew it was more difficult for her to argue at close quarters.

"From what you've said, you have spent half a lifetime poking around in rat holes," she said. "Did it ever occur to you to wonder if anybody else gives a damn about any of it?"

She walked back to the sofa and sat down. Kicking off her slippers, she tucked her feet beneath her housecoat. "The trouble is that you've never stopped playing toy soldiers. What you don't understand is that there are real people under the rocks you like to turn over. When your games are finished, there are real widows left, and none of it matters a good goddamn."

"It's not a game," Trosper said. "And I don't know anyone who thinks it is. If it's done right, it can be important."

Trosper walked to an easy chair across the coffee table from Martha. He remembered the story of the Poles who had recruited the German sergeant who brought the first pieces of the German Enigma machine to Warsaw, two years before the Nazi invasion, and wondered if the German had survived the war, or if any historian would record his name. It was that German and a handful of intelligence officers who had made it possible for British cryptographers to break the Nazi cipher traffic. If it had not been for them, it might have been a different war.

Martha looked at him over the rims of her reading glasses. "When you told me about what you call 'the racket,' and said you were through with all that, I more or less believed you. Now someone whistles and, like old dog Tray, you're all atremble. I don't know which is worse, playing I Spy or that ridiculous yacht thing. One is a hair shirt you're not willing to peel off. Selling boats appeals to you because it makes you feel like some czarist general larking around as a taxi driver. If you were honest with yourself you'd recognize that it's just an excuse not to compete for a real job."

Trosper took a long drink. This was a real quarrel, made more serious because he knew Martha was right. He missed the the old life more than he would admit. Peddling shoddy yachts was a game he played against himself.

"Maybe you're right. Perhaps I should try to find something more fitting—a position like the ones they advertise in the *Wall Street Journal,*" he said.

He walked back to the bar. "It's just that I wonder what I could tell anyone I can do."

"One thing you can do is pay some attention to me. Perhaps even to us. I thought maybe we had something going, something worth working on. Now, all at once you walk in here sealed up like a damned drum. It takes an interrogation to find out who you had dinner with . . ."

Martha's eyes filled. She tossed her book onto the coffee table and turned away from Trosper.

"Where is it going to be, these fun and games?"

"I don't know," he said. "Maybe in Europe."

"And I'll just stay here," she said, her voice rising. "Maybe I could roll bandages. Isn't that what you men at the front expect from us?"

"Please, this isn't something I reached out for. It began a while ago, when a man was killed. As far as I know, it wasn't my fault. But he's dead, and his wife and children were probably destroyed— not killed, just left with half a life."

Trosper swirled the whiskey and ice in his glass. "The man wasn't a mercenary, he was fighting something he knew was wrong. In a way we let him down and I feel I owe him something."

"I wonder, darling, if that's really why you want to get involved. Are you sure you don't think of it as something to be *solved?* Like a chess problem, but with live pieces?"

He had spent a lifetime probing the motives of others, looking for the pressure points which, when played upon could move a passive spectator to run risks, to resist, perhaps even to fight. But he had seldom pondered his own motives.

When confronted, he had always been able to come up with an ideological justification for his work. Only after he quit the Firm had he begun to suspect that the secret authority and the challenges of espionage were as much a part of his motivation as ideas and politics. What he missed had nothing to do with ideology; it was the pressure, the occasional excitement, and even the companionship spawned by the bruising, secret war.

For a moment Trosper felt as if he had caught himself out.

Martha got up. She took her book from the coffee table. "It's late, darling," she said. "It's time for bed."

She began to turn off the lights.

5 NEW YORK

THE ADDRESS Mercer gave Trosper was a townhouse on Seventy-Seventh Street, between Park and Madison.

It was nine twenty-five, a blustery February night. Trosper crossed Lexington Avenue at East Seventy-Sixth Street and paused to catch the reflections in a liquor store window. At Park Avenue he stopped, as if deciding whether to cross against the flashing DON'T WALK signal. Then, as a cab driver gunned his taxi forward to jump the light, Trosper sprinted across the north-bound traffic lane to the center strip. On the island between the streams of traffic, he turned as if to admire the Pan Am building, like a giant domino, spoiling the sweep of the avenue. His eyes flickered back and forth over the busy intersection. No one had jumped across with him. He was clean.

"I *am* a fool," he thought. "Playing games with myself on Park Avenue."

The light changed and he crossed the south-bound lane. At Seventy-Seventh Street he turned west. Across the street, almost directly opposite the safe house, a black Chevrolet was parked in front of a fireplug. As uninterested as the two men in the front seat appeared to be, it was a gross violation of practice. Any little old lady walking her poodle would be sure to notice two men in a parked car.

No Loitering was the title of Henderson's famous lecture on surveillance at Fort Mudge, Mercer's name for the Firm's training center.

"Do something," Henderson would implore the plebes. "Play hopscotch, solicit women, skip rope, eat a banana. But don't *loiter.* It takes a generation of practice to loiter. None of you will ever have enough experience to get away with it."

Trosper wondered if Henderson, the invisible man, was still teaching.

When he was a few strides from the safe house door, the man in the passenger seat lifted his hand as if to rub his nose. Trosper could not see the palm mike or the wire leading up the sleeve, but he knew his approach was being signaled to a security man waiting inside the safe house door.

Because Mercer would not have given Trosper's name to the security detail, he wondered how Mercer would have described him. "Six feet, clean shaven, about fifty, tightly rolled umbrella, brown trilby," he guessed.

Mercer would have enjoyed making the security man ask what a trilby was.

It was exactly nine-thirty when Trosper touched the bell. The door swung open. As the security man stepped aside, his vest rode up, exposing an inch of white shirt and a stout belt with a Browning automatic in a soft leather holster.

"I see I'm expected," Trosper said with a smile.

"Yes, sir. I'll just take your things. You can go right up."

As he mounted the stairs, Trosper glanced through the open door of what seemed to be a ground floor dining room. Another security man looked up from a portable receiver-transmitter and stole a glance at Trosper's reflection in the mirror across from the stairs.

At the top of the stairs he turned and walked into a long formal drawing room. Heavy, ceiling-high damask draperies were tightly drawn to muffle the street noise and conceal any hint of activity within the house. The room had a decorator look, a comfortable mixture of expensive period furniture and modern, glass-topped tables. The discreet, indirect lighting was controlled by a dimmer beside the door. Over a marble fireplace, a huge mirror reflected the gentle gray tone of the fabric-covered walls.

A tall blond man rose from a brocaded armchair near the fireplace and dropped a sheaf of papers into an attaché case on the floor. With his foot, he nudged the leather case shut. Trosper guessed he was about thirty.

"Hello, Alan," he said as they shook hands.

Perceiving Trosper's failure to recognize him, the man stepped back.

"DeGrasse," he said. "Mike DeGrasse. We spent three days in Brussels—Rooster, the randy Rumanian, favored us with a meeting."

"Of course," Trosper said, embarrassed. Rooster was a Rumanian diplomatic courier Tim Cassidy had picked up in a gin mill in Rome. He had been in agent status for almost a year when he signaled that he had six rolls of Minox film for which he wanted five hundred dollars each. Odlum decided it was time for someone to take an independent look at Rooster and to check out Cassidy's judgment of the man.

While DeGrasse, fresh out of operations school, was working on the negatives, Trosper had put Rooster through the wringer.

Diplomatic couriers from Eastern Europe are almost as tightly reined as cipher clerks. But Rooster, as he finally convinced Trosper, was an old hand and had contrived to establish a pattern that allowed him at least one night on the town every time he was in the West. Cassidy's assessment of his agent was confirmed.

As it turned out, Trosper recalled, only one roll of the film was a dud. The others contained the Foreign Minister's file of privacy-channel cables from the Rumanian ambassadors in Moscow and Washington. Trosper remembered that the film was worth several times Rooster's asking price.

"What happened to the Rooster?" Trosper asked.

"Cassidy ran him for another two years. Then he spent one too many nights in a strip joint in Paris. His chums got wise—Rooster skipped, one step ahead of the goons. He's quieted down now, running an Italian restaurant somewhere around Chicago. He piled up quite a stake before he defected."

Trosper smiled. He had a warm spot for mercenary agents. Sometimes cash-and-carry spying was so matter-of-fact that it seemed almost wholesome.

"You've prospered," Trosper said with a glance at DeGrasse's suit.

"More luck than smarts, I guess. A few days after Mr. Bates took over, he got interested in a case I was handling and asked for a briefing. He was looking for someone to hold his horse and here I am." DeGrasse glanced around the room. "It's not the best job in the racket, but I do get my nose under some interesting tents."

"What's with all the security?" Trosper asked. "Two-way radios, a car across the street . . . ?" Too many toys, he thought to himself.

"Mr. Bates thinks it keeps people on their toes, and ready for the real thing," DeGrasse said.

"And helps to reinforce the image?"

DeGrasse laughed. "He knows you're here," he said with a gesture to an open door leading into what appeared to be a library. "You'd better go in."

6   NEW YORK

THERE were floor lamps at opposite corners of the book-lined room and a brass lamp on a Queen Anne desk. The light from the green glass shade of the lamp reflected a soft glow from the dark, red-leather top of the desk.

As Trosper came through the door, Bates rose from a high-backed chair behind the desk.

"Alan, it's good to see you again. It's been too long, too damned long." Bates extended his hand. "And it was good of you to give me the time. Especially at this hour."

Trosper mumbled a greeting, shook Bates's hand, and slipped into one of the deep leather chairs facing the desk.

With some satisfaction, Trosper noticed Bates was heavier. His dark, single-breasted jacket hung open and was probably too tight to button.

"It's no trouble," Trosper said. "I only hope I'm not wasting your time."

"That's the least of the problem. Actually I've got two things to take up. If you don't mind I think we'd better get right to it."

Trosper nodded. He had no stomach for Bates's version of small talk.

Bates stepped from behind the desk and took a chair facing Trosper. "First some good news," he said. "You remember the budget pressure we were under about the time you left? The finance people were at our throat—cut this, cut that?

Trosper nodded.

"Well, about six months ago I finally convinced General Foster —he's still the President's special security man—that it had gone too far. In less than two years we'd trimmed almost forty percent of our staff."

"I hadn't realized."

"Three weeks ago I got the President and Foster to agree to let me form a kind of active reserve, and to use some of the old hands when we needed to cash in on their experience without jamming up our new personnel program. I think I got us a damned good deal."

Trosper nodded.

"Actually Duff Whyte helped me set it up," Bates admitted softly. Then he called for DeGrasse. "It's time for a drink. I'm having brandy. What about you, Alan?"

"A scotch, please," Trosper said. "A scotch and soda."

"Before we get started," Bates said, "I'm afraid you'll have to sign another oath." He picked up a leather folder and extracted two printed forms.

"It sounds like a good scheme, Walter," Trosper said. "But as far as I'm concerned there's still one problem."

Bates raised his eyebrows.

"I'll sign on, but only with the understanding that I have the right of refusal. If the job doesn't make sense to me I won't take it."

Bates blinked but could not control the irritation that flashed across his round face. Then he nodded. "It's a deal. It's not my style to ram an assignment down anyone's throat." He stopped long enough to adjust his expression. "This work is tough enough without expecting old-timers to take on something they don't want to do, a job they won't give their best shot."

Bates handed one of the forms to Trosper. "After you sign this, we can get down to business. You can finish the paperwork tomorrow."

Trosper glanced at the paper. For a moment he thought it was the same security oath he had signed when he first transferred into the Firm. But it had been reworked; instead of an oath, it was a contract in which Trosper agreed forever to keep secret any information he learned in connection with his work for Research Estimates, Incorporated.

"It's much the same as the oath Odlum wrote," Bates said. "All I've done is change it to a contract. In the event someone decides to go public, it will be easier to go into court with a contract than something quite as medieval as an oath."

Trosper read through the three paragraphs. He signed the document and Bates scrawled his signature at the bottom. When De-Grasse came back with the drinks, he signed as witness.

Bates raised his brandy glass. "Welcome back, Alan."

Trosper took a sip of his whiskey.

"Now let's get down to business," Bates said. "Mercer's upstairs. He's got your pal Kyle in tow."

IF ANYTHING, the gray tweed suit, boldly striped shirt, and heavy foulard tie made Kyle look even more elegant than he had when Trosper last saw him.

"Hello, Alan," Kyle said. "I wondered if you'd be here."

"Roger, this is quite a surprise."

Bates remained seated behind the desk, and Mercer sank into a tufted leather club chair across the room from Bates. In the absence of a gesture from Bates, Trosper motioned Kyle to the remaining chair. DeGrasse stood, leaning against the doorway.

"It's late," said Bates, with a cool glance at Kyle. "You'd better begin."

"A few months after you resigned, Alan, I was transferred home. The management had big plans for me, something about country-building, teaching the Third World how to vote."

Bates looked up from the desk. "It was an effort to bring you into the twentieth century. But that hasn't much to do with why we're here tonight. Please get on with it."

Kyle ignored Bates. "I'd already seen how the wind was blowing and figured that whatever I might have been able to do for the Firm, I wasn't likely to be much of a wet nurse for developing countries. So I told Mr. Bates that I'd rather quit. I picked up my exit papers and termination pay, and stayed in the States just long enough to get a grant. Then I went back to Vienna."

"Get a what?"

"A grant, Alan. You may forget, but I'm a bit of an academic. For a well-qualified, fluent German-speaking scholar, it was easy to pick up enough money to keep me for a couple of years in Austria. I'm writing a history of the Austrian resistance in World War Two."

From his chair at the side, Mercer snorted. "That should be a short book. You could interview every bona fide anti-Nazi in Austria in thirty-six hours."

"Let him get on with the story, Mercer," Bates said.

"When I got back, I took a small flat in the Second District. I'm not much of a housekeeper, and I'd gotten into the habit of having breakfast at the Cafe Geiger two or three times a week—just to break the monotony of eating at home every morning."

Kyle shuffled in his chair and signaled DeGrasse. "Is there an extra drop to drink, a scotch and soda?" DeGrasse nodded and stepped into the next room.

"About two weeks ago, I spotted old Frau Hofer threading her way between the tables at the Geiger. Do you remember her, Alan?"

From the sofa Mercer interrupted. "Let's be accurate, Roger. What was the date?"

"It was January nineteen, zero nine-fifteen hours, Mercer," Kyle said sharply. He turned back to Trosper. "Do you remember her, Alan?"

Trosper shook his head. "Did she have a pseudonym?"

"I called her 'Oma.' But when you caught me up on it, I had to agree—it wasn't the best of pseudonyms, she really does look like a Viennese grandmother."

"Of course," Trosper said. "She was a letter drop. You recruited her two or three weeks after Galkin came aboard."

"That's because you insisted Galkin have alternative ways of reaching us. He had a safe telephone number and the written signal in the telephone book at the central Post Office. If for some reason he couldn't use either, he could write to a live drop—Oma, Grandma Hofer."

Trosper said, "I remember Oma."

"A few weeks after you left, maybe two months after the *Izvestia* piece on Galkin's execution, I got a message from the home office. Along with closing out the safe house we'd used with Galkin, I was told to terminate Frau Hofer forthwith. I went around to her apartment and thanked her for the help. All she'd done was to pass along the letters that I'd sent to make sure she had the signals straight, but I remembered your advice about always leaving an agent with a smile. I gave her a termination bonus and closed the file. We had given her a safe telephone number, but it was canceled after I closed her down."

"Had you ever seen her again? At Christmas, her birthday, or anything like that?" Trosper asked. Keeping in touch with agents who had been on the level, but who were no longer of any immediate use, was good practice. It was impossible to tell when they might be useful again, or even when they might stumble into something of interest.

"No, I was told to close her down."

"I see," Trosper said.

"Well, on this morning," Kyle continued, "I'd just ordered breakfast and begun to leaf through *Die Presse* when I looked up and saw Oma headed straight for me.

" 'Hullo, Herr Peters,' she said.

"My work name with her was Peterson, but she always called me 'Peters' and I never bothered to correct her.

"I jumped up, gave her a big *'Grüss Gott, Oma.'* When we shook hands, I leaned over and gave her a kiss. She was grinning like a schoolgirl. All bundled up in a heavy coat, ankle boots, and one of those hats that looked as if she got it in a men's shop. I got her to sit down, and ordered coffee and a *Krapfen* for her." Kyle glanced at Bates. "A jelly doughnut."

"For a while I thought maybe she was just being sociable. Then, because she was so nervous, I thought she was getting ready to ask for something."

Kyle stopped long enough to reach for the tall whiskey and soda that DeGrasse passed to him.

"I liked Oma, and I think she had a warm spot for me. But all the while she was fussing and apologizing for having bothered me. I guess she remembered the catechism—no recognition on the street and all that crap. Anyway, she didn't mention a bit of shop until the coffee came and she had taken a bite of the *Krapfen.* Then she began.

"A week, maybe five days earlier, she had had a caller. He was a small man, togged out in an old loden cloth coat, Steier hat, heavy shoes, the whole bit. She said he didn't *look* Austrian. He looked *like* an Austrian.

"He introduced himself as Herr Kinzl, said he was only in Vienna for a few days, and that he wanted to talk to her. Then, suddenly, he called her 'Oma.' This made her think he was with the Firm, and she invited him in for coffee. But by the time he had taken off his loden coat and was sitting in her kitchen, she realized that although his German was fluent, there was a frosting of an accent. It took her a while before she decided it was a Russian accent. Now she was frightened."

Kyle had been speaking directly to Trosper. When he paused, Trosper glanced around the room. Bates's head was down, and he was doodling on a yellow pad. Mercer was fussing with a tobacco pouch and pipe. DeGrasse had pulled a chair from the drawing room and was sitting just inside the door.

Kyle continued his story. " 'Frau Hofer,' Kinzl said. 'This is important business and I haven't much time. I want you to put me in touch with Mr. Johnson. It's urgent. I must speak with Mr. Johnson.' "

Kyle took a swallow of his drink. "You remember Alan, that I called myself 'Johnson' with Galkin. It was the only time I used that work name. But Oma only knew me as Peters. She'd never heard of any Mr. Johnson. But she did remember that I always called her Oma. Now she was really frightened.

" 'Herr Kinzl,' " she said. 'I don't know any Mr. Johnson. I think you have the wrong person.' "

Kyle leaned forward toward Trosper. "Of course she pronounced it 'Yohnson.' But by now she was so upset she told Kinzl to finish his coffee and to leave.

" 'But Frau Hofer,' he said. 'I know that Johnson called you Oma when you were working for him. It's very important you put me in touch with him.'

"Flustered as she was, Oma stuck to the rules. 'Lots of people call me Oma,' she said. 'Half the women in Vienna are called Oma.'

"Now Kinzl was beginning to show his nerves. She could see his hand shaking as he picked up the coffee.

" 'Forget Johnson,' Kinzl told her. 'Never mind what his name is. I must get in touch with the American you're working with.'

" 'But I'm not working with anyone, Herr Kinzl,' she said.

"This infuriated Kinzl. He shouted he had no more time for games. It was urgent that he get in touch with the people Frau Hofer was working with. If they didn't pay her, Kinzl said, he would make it worth her while.

"Finally she decided to take a chance. She asked what he 'really wanted.'

" 'All I want,' he said, 'is for you to tell your friends that I want to meet them. I have something very important for them. I guarantee they will appreciate what you have done for them.' "

Trosper interrupted Kyle. "When you closed Oma down, did you brief her about any future contact? You must have figured that sooner or later Moscow would come mousing around, checking Galkin's story?"

Kyle glanced at Bates. "No. I was told to chill her. She was not to have any means of getting back to us. It seemed pretty dumb to me, but we were under head office direction on everything to do with Galkin. Hamel—the office chief in Vienna—didn't think it worth fighting about."

"That's just a detail, Kyle," Bates said. "Please get on with the story."

"Finally Oma admitted that there was a young fellow who dropped in to see her once in a while. But she had no way of getting in touch with him.

"This was all Kinzl needed. After rattling on again about how important this was, how grateful her young friend would be when she told him, Kinzl got her to admit that she had seen me in a cafe once or twice since I stopped coming by her apartment.

"Kinzl pulled out his wallet and handed her five hundred schillings. He said she was to go to the cafe and find me. Meanwhile, he would telephone her every day until she had some news for him. Before he left, he reminded her that he had only a few days in Vienna."

"Did she give him the name of the coffee house?" Trosper asked.

"Hell, no," Kyle said with another glance at Bates. "She's an old woman, but she's got a better sense of conspiracy than half the hotshots treading water in Washington."

"I suppose she kept an eye out for surveillance when she left the apartment and started hanging around the Geiger," Mercer interjected.

"If she did, it wouldn't have been necessary. She told me she had seen me three or four times. I never caught a glimpse of her. It wasn't for nothing that I called her Oma. She looks exactly like every other woman her age in Vienna."

Bates looked up from his pad. "Can't we just stick to the damned story."

"She began checking the Geiger every morning. Then she'd go back to the apartment and wait for Kinzl's call. It was three days before she spotted me.

"I was completely out of touch with the Vienna office. I knew they had moved, but I didn't have any idea where they were or what cover they were using. I hadn't even seen anyone I recognized on the street for a year or so. There was no one I could get hold of in a hurry. Oma was convinced that Kinzl really was under some time pressure, so I decided to meet him myself. If there was anything in it, I would find a way to get in touch with the office later.

"Oma said that Kinzl usually called her apartment at about two, so I went there to take the call."

"Did it occur to you that the good Frau Hofer might have been setting you up?" Mercer asked.

"To be honest with you, Mercer, it did not. I've been out in the real world for two years now. You'd be surprised how easy it is to forget all that mumbo jumbo. You ought to try it sometime."

Trosper glanced at Mercer and suppressed a smile.

Kyle took a sip of his drink and turned to Trosper. "But I still remember what you said about meeting people on their own turf."

Bates looked up, about to speak. . . .

"You said the first rule is never to meet anyone you don't know at a place they choose," Kyle said. "After the night we met 'Nestor' at that kosher restaurant in the Twenty-Second District, I decided that the second rule was to remember the first rule."

All Trosper could remember about the Nestor incident was that he had taken Kyle along as shotgun on the first meeting. As they drove toward the restaurant on the distant outskirts of Vienna, the area became more desolate. Finally Kyle's nerves broke and he muttered, "Vienna hell, another three kilometers and we'll be in the sub-Carpatho-Ukraine."

With an effort, Trosper brought his attention back to Kyle.

". . . when the phone rang I answered in German, '*Hier* Hofer.' "

" 'Herr Johnson? Mr. Johnson?'

"I saw no need to admit I was Johnson, so I asked who was speaking.

" 'This is Kinzl. I must see Mr. Johnson. This is important, very important.'

"I explained that Johnson wasn't available, that I was speaking for him. I asked what he wanted.

"I guess Kinzl hadn't expected this. He may have thought his credentials—the fact he knew who Oma and Johnson were—meant that he would reach Johnson. Whatever the reason, he seemed flummoxed and it took him a few moments to make a decision. Finally he said he could meet me at four that afternoon. On the chance he was bluffing, I refused. But he wouldn't be put off. He insisted he had only a few hours left in Vienna and that if we couldn't meet by four that afternoon, the contact would be broken. Finally I said the hell with it, I'd meet him and find out what the scam was."

"You'd better have another drink, Alan," Bates said. "We've still got a lot of ground to cover."

Trosper shook his head.

"Then let's break for coffee."

7 NEW YORK

THERE was a rattle of china as the burly security man backed through the door to the drawing room. With the tray at waist level, he steered the precarious passage to a coffee table in front of the fireplace. The ugly china coffee pot, nondescript cups, and stainless steel spoons were proof that although the owner had rented out the town house furnished, he was too prudent to have left good porcelain or silver for his tenant.

Trosper caught Kyle's eye, looked around the drawing room, and then fixed his attention on the shirt-sleeved security man, who had bent over to spill coffee into the cups spread on the low table. The holstered Browning automatic dangling from the security man's belt punctured the muted, formal atmosphere of the room. Kyle laughed aloud.

Mercer took a sip of coffee, blanched, and quietly put the cup to one side.

Bates poured the coffee that had splashed into his saucer back into the cup and, motioning the others to follow, led the way back into the library.

Kyle hunched forward in his chair as if straining to remember where he had left off. Then he said, "I told Kinzl I would meet him at the Cafe Mozart at four.

"I arrived exactly on time. The place was filled with *Gesellschafts-damen* who'd spent the afternoon on the Kaerntnerstrasse shopping. You could put on weight just looking at the *Schlag* they were packing away.

"The cafe turned out to be a pretty good place for a *Treff.*" Kyle turned to Bates. "For a meeting."

"There was plenty of coming and going, and even enough men so that I wasn't conspicuous. In fact, it was about the last place I would have expected anyone to meet an agent.

"Kinzl hadn't given me a recognition signal, and all I had to go on was Oma's description of him. He arrived about five minutes after I sat down. It was an easy make—he was still wearing the loden coat, and had the Steier hat in his hand. When he spotted me, he came right to the table, stuck out his hand and said, 'Mr. Johnson?'

"Kinzl's short, about five six and thin, maybe about a hundred and forty pounds. He had an odd, almost bohemian look about him. Underneath the green topcoat, he wore an old tweed jacket, and a soft blue shirt and tie. There was nothing Russian about him at all. If anything, he looked like a journalist, maybe someone connected with a university. He might even have been an actor.

"Almost as soon as he'd said hello, he asked why I'd bothered to deny I was Johnson. He said I fitted the description perfectly.

"I was a little pissed to have a total stranger claim to have such an accurate description of me, so I skipped the small talk and asked what it was he wanted in such a hurry.

" 'Look,' he began. 'I'm from Moscow, already here a few days. My time's almost up. Before I leave there are a few things I have to get straight.'

"He spoke good German but, as Oma said, there was an accent. I couldn't place it at first, but after he began his pitch, it seemed to me he was Russian all right.

"I told him I didn't have any time either, that it was in our mutual interest for him to say what he had to say so that we could both be on our way.

"Right off the bat he said he was from the Second Chief Directorate—and even explained this meant counterintelligence." Kyle grimaced as he remembered this gratuitous information. "Then he said he had all the details on Aleksei Galkin's interrogation in Moscow, and that was how he had learned about Oma and me.

"Just to stall him a bit, I pretended not to know what he was talking about. I said I was a friend of Frau Hofer's, but that I didn't know anything about Galkin or Moscow. This didn't slow him down at all. He said he wanted a contact with the Firm—'a line to the Firm' was exactly how he put it. Once he had the contact, he said, he would meet us whenever he came abroad."

Kyle shook his head. "I've heard about cold approaches, but this was the first time anyone ever came on quite this way with me.

"Then he said that if I couldn't handle it, I should report to 'Mr. Warner, the man with the fancy shoes.' " Kyle glanced down at Trosper's hand-made shoes. "You remember you used the work name 'Warner' with Galkin?"

Trosper nodded.

"When I asked him how often he planned to be in the West, he was just as matter-of-fact as before. He said he could arrange to be in Austria or Switzerland five or six times a year, and that he would have no trouble meeting us whenever he came out."

From the corner, Mercer muttered, "A likely damned story."

"Then Kinzl got down to business," Kyle said, ignoring Mercer. "He said he wanted a fixed fee of five thousand dollars for every meeting, and a bonus for everything he reported that was particularly hot.

"The last thing I wanted was to talk money with him, or to let him think he could get a commitment from me. So I asked him to prove who he was.

"He said something to the effect that I should know damned well that he was on the inside. How else could he have known about Galkin's arrest, or Oma, or Johnson, or Mr. Warner, the boss?

"This made sense, but I'd been outside for so long I had no idea how much the Moscow press might have printed on Galkin's arrest after that first *Izvestia* story."

"That's just another of the fifty reasons you should have got in touch with the Vienna office and not be sitting around with some Moscow provocation artist," Bates interjected. "There's no reason for you to be sticking your nose into our work."

Kyle glanced at Bates and then turned back to Trosper. "So I took a chance and told Kinzl that the Galkin story was well known, that it had been in the American press. This seemed to put him off a bit. Perhaps he didn't know if the story had got any play over here, or if the Center had released any details to the foreign press.

"Then he said he could tell me exactly how Galkin was caught, and why he broke. At that point I just shrugged, leaving it to him to convince me that he knew what he was talking about.

"This irritated him. His voice rose and he said he wasn't surprised, that I was probably too constipated—he actually said *verstopft*—to react. He said any service that would mishandle Galkin the way we did was probably too incompetent for him to deal with anyway.

"In that case, I said, we really were wasting our time, and I made a motion as if I were going to leave. Then I thought maybe I was being too cute, too hard to get. So I asked him to tell me more about Galkin.

" 'Simple enough,' he said. 'Galkin said you had promised not to try to contact him in Moscow. Then, a week or so after he was there, you signaled him to pick up a dead drop. Even if you didn't know it, you should have believed him when he said we keep an eye on everyone who is in Moscow on temporary duty. As it happened, you just had bad luck. There was a class of candidates in the Second Directorate school, about halfway through their counterintelligence course. As part of the training, each class is given a live problem.'

"He gave me a sly grin and said 'It was Galkin's luck that about twenty of them were assigned to tail the five officers who had been called back for the briefing Galkin was attending. It was just an exercise, but three of these apprentices were told to take Galkin right around the clock—to sit right on his tail. It didn't matter how close they stayed, they weren't to lose him. They were on Galkin for about thirty-six hours before he made the pickup.

" 'They weren't even trained,' he said, 'just students. Galkin should have spotted them in thirty minutes. But he didn't—maybe he'd gone sloppy in Vienna. In the end they followed him right into the restaurant. He ordered vodka, looked around a couple of times, and headed fcr the men's room. One of these half-trained experts followed him.

" 'Galkin went into a cabinet and took a piss. Then he made his second mistake. He left the limpet in place. He just took the message and replaced the limpet. Are you people short of magnets? Did you tell him to do that?

" 'When Galkin left the cabinet, the kid went in and looked around—just like they told him in training. In a minute or so he found the limpet.'

"By this time," Kyle said, "Kinzl was really wound up. 'Of course it might have been a coincidence,' Kinzl said. 'Galkin might have wanted the vodka he didn't even bother to finish. He might really have had to take a piss, was too shy to stand outside, and went into the booth where no one could see his organ. Maybe the limpet had been left by someone else. Maybe it was all just a coincidence. But the geniuses in the Second Directorate don't believe much in coincidences.

" 'When the trainees got back, they reported what they had seen. If they hadn't brought the limpet, I'm not sure old Petkov, their instructor, would even have believed them. But he took them straight to Colonel Mantsev. By midnight they'd convinced him that they had a case. He took a squad and hit Galkin's apartment about six-thirty that morning. Galkin was there, and the old woman—his mother-in-law—and the two children. They cleared everyone out and went over the apartment with microscopes. Everything was clean. There wasn't a trace of anything.'

"At this point," Kyle continued, "Kinzl gave me a funny, prissy sort of smile and said 'From here on you're going to have to pay.'

"Pay for what, I said. You haven't told me anything yet."

Kyle took a final sip of his cold coffee. "And that's where we left it. Kinzl absolutely refused to give me anything more."

"What about re-contact?" Trosper asked.

"Kinzl said he'd be back in three or four weeks and would call me through Oma. Unless Mr. Bates wants someone from the Vienna office to take over, I can keep in touch with her."

Bates stood up from behind the desk. "Well, Alan, that's about the story." Turning to the others, Bates said, "Now if you'll leave us for a while, there are one or two things I'd like to go over with Alan."

Mercer heaved himself up from the low chair and, like a lumbering sheepdog, herded DeGrasse and Kyle out of the library. From the doorway, Kyle turned back to Trosper. "There's one more thing, Alan." he said. "There's something odd about Kinzl, something I can't put my finger on. He was nervous—who wouldn't be, throwing himself at me like that? But he didn't seem concerned that I might have brought a shotgun or two."

"Shotgun" was old slang for an outrider, who from a little distance could check for surveillance while the case man concentrated on the agent. In some circumstances a shotgun might be used to detain a flighty agent.

Kyle lingered in the doorway. "I'm convinced he's a Russian. By Moscow standards, he was first class—excellent German, good costume. Almost anyone would take him for an Austrian. But there was something about him that was askew. I can't place it exactly, but it was almost theatrical, as if he were playing a part."

"Okay, Roger," Bates said. "We've still got some things to discuss."

Before DeGrasse swung the door shut, he handed Trosper another drink.

WELL, Alan, what do you think?"

Trosper took a swallow of his drink. "If Kyle is convinced Kinzl is a Russian, chances are he's right. But I can't believe he's from the counterintelligence directorate. Those fellows rarely ever go abroad. When they do circulate, they don't use nonofficial cover. Moscow simply would not risk any of their counterintelligence hotshots getting arrested without diplomatic immunity.

"As of now, I'd guess that Kinzl is a leg man, probably working out of Moscow on special assignments. If I'm right, he learned about Galkin from someone else, someone who *is* on the inside."

Bates nodded. "There hasn't been any publicity at all on Galkin, except for the one story about his arrest and execution."

"If you want me to get involved," Trosper said, "I think I'd better go to Vienna and meet Herr Kinzl. Provided, of course, that he comes back."

"That's agreed," Bates said. "There's just one more thing, Alan, and this is for your ears only. I've got something pretty good going now, a line that reaches close to the top in Moscow. The last thing I want is something that might upset it."

For emphasis, Bates tapped his knuckles on the leather top of the desk. "There can't be any blowback, no broken crockery. I've got too much riding on this other case—the Firm's got too much at stake for any flap at all with this Kinzl fellow. I'll have to insist that you be careful."

There was no operational guidance quite so infuriating to Trosper as to be told to be careful, or to proceed with caution. Being told to be careful was like being instructed not to catch cold.

One of the lessons Trosper had learned from Duff Whyte was to handle every agent as carefully as he would a spy in place in the Kremlin. It was good professional discipline to keep the security fences high. And besides, there was no telling when the most humdrum spy might stumble into something important, or discover an access that had to be kept open at all costs.

With what he hoped was a manful tone, Trosper said he would do his best.

"I'll need a communications channel direct to the head office," Trosper added. "And if you want to keep the Vienna shop out of it, maybe Mercer could come along and handle any contact I need with

Hamel, or whoever is in charge there now."

"That's right," Bates said. "I want the Vienna office out of it. Mercer can use a little fresh air. He can give you the support you may need from Hamel. I'll have DeGrasse handle things on this end."

" 'Tis done," said Trosper.

8 VIENNA

"WE'VE already got a problem," Mercer said. "The ancient plumbing went haywire in the safe house. We've had to move to a place near the Sohottenring." He had met Trosper's plane at Schwechart Airport, and they had taken a taxi to Vienna.

"I hope it's not on the Kolingasse," Trosper said. "That's the address they told me to use for any mail I have forwarded from New York."

"The very place," Mercer said.

It was a comfortable two-bedroom apartment. The well-stocked linen closet, color TV, and daily maid meant that it was one of the places each local office held in reserve against the day it might be needed for a high-security agent meeting, or as temporary housing for an important defector. Safe houses used for routine agent meetings ran to form—an abundant bar, dirty ashtrays, a collection of glasses that had been rinsed, not washed, a small radio to mask conversation, and a patina of dust. In these always musty apartments, a collection of lined yellow pads and the ball point pens used for notetaking could invariably be found in one of the drawers in the cabinet provided for silverware and china.

Until Kinzl telephoned Frau Hofer, there was little to be done. Kyle, busy with the research for his book, called Oma at three every afternoon. Mercer spent hours at what he called familiarizing himself with the city—in effect touring the museums. Trosper, resigned to a long wait, stayed close to the safe apartment, watching TV and listlessly plowing through a paperback edition of *Nostromo* he had found in the bedroom.

In Trosper's experience, spying was half waiting and another thirty percent report writing and record keeping. In a good month, a case man could count himself lucky to spend the few remaining hours dealing with agents and contact men. The time committed to stakeouts, peering out of OP's, waiting for a safe house telephone to ring, and typing reports is such a significant part of espionage that Trosper had never understood why even the novelists with some professional experience never thought to mention it.

IT WAS ten days before Kyle called. "Mr. Miller" had arrived. He would be free all evening.

From the outset, Trosper had assumed that "Kinzl" was a pseudonym. Still, he did not want the name used on the telephone. "Miller" was a useful all around cover name, and like "Johnson," was a favorite of case men. There are six pages of Smiths in the New York telephone book, and five pages of Browns—enough to make these names cliché pseudonyms. But few remembered that there were also six pages of Johnsons, and four pages of Millers. It had been a long time since anyone in the racket had used Smith or Brown as a work name. Even Jones was better, and there are only three pages of Joneses.

KYLE made the introduction in German. Kinzl bowed slightly as he pumped Trosper's hand. "Of course," Kinzl said. "It's Mr. Warner, I recognize you. Comrade Galkin liked you."

"We'd better sit down," Kyle said, and steered Kinzl to the sofa in the corner of the living room. Trosper took a seat in one of the armchairs facing the sofa, and across from the low coffee table.

As he sat down, Kinzl glanced slowly around all four walls of the room. It was the spontaneous reaction of an agent experienced enough to know that when he steps into a safe house controlled by an intelligence professional his conversation will be recorded. Trosper had observed it frequently. He guessed that although Kinzl knew full well that the microphones were concealed in the walls, he was so aware of the recording that, subconsciously, he expected to see the devices dangling in plain view.

Kinzl's casual reference to Galkin's regard for him angered Trosper, and he wondered if the Russian had said it intentionally. "Before we get started, Herr Kinzl," he said stiffly, "I will need to know who you are. Will you please show me some ID?"

Kinzl shook his head. "No, I will not identify myself. What I have to offer will speak for itself. When you hear what I have to say, you won't have to worry about my birth certificate or even my passport."

Kyle interceded. "Will you have something to drink, before we get started, Herr Kinzl?"

"A small brandy, a cognac please."

"Exactly what is it that will speak for itself, Herr Kinzl?" Trosper asked.

"It's just as I told Mr. Johnson at the café. I'm here from Moscow. I am in a unique position to supply information direct from the Moscow Center—current data from the counterintelligence directorate. That's all there is to it." He glanced from Trosper to Kyle. "No intelligence service in history has ever had an offer like that."

Trosper leaned back in his chair and crossed his legs. There was nothing to be gained by correcting the Russian's apparently limited view of espionage history. For a moment he seemed to study the carefully polished instep of his shoe.

"Certainly that should be more than enough to make you agree with my terms," Kinzl continued. Flustered by Trosper's lack of response, he began to speak rapidly.

"As you know, I expect to be paid for my information. In case you have any question, I expect five thousand dollars every time I meet with you. And, I'll insist on appropriate additional payment for any special information I turn over." He hesitated, as if to think of another argument to bolster his case. Then he said, "After all, I am the only one taking any risks."

Kyle handed a small snifter of cognac to Kinzl and put an ashtray on the table.

"If you're as well informed as you say, you know as well as I do that any such money is out of the question—the more so if you won't identify yourself," Trosper said.

"You won't have to pay me any bonus for this meeting, but I do want five thousand dollars," Kinzl said. "In future, I will only come with the understanding that my terms have been met."

Money, Trosper knew, was one of the most important tools of his trade. But like fertilizer, it was necessary to use it prudently. Too much money at the outset could kill a promising case just as surely as an overdose of manure will smother an orchid. Too little cash, and a canny agent might be moved to look elsewhere for additional funding.

Trosper had four thousand dollars in greenbacks, two thousand Swiss francs, and five thousand Austrian schillings in a briefcase beside the coffee table. He did not plan to give Kinzl more than two thousand dollars. It would be enough, he hoped, to convince the Russian that money was available, and to leave him thirsty for more. He had brought the various currencies on the chance Kinzl would not want to carry a large amount in dollars, or could somehow justify a larger payment.

"You Americans are supposed to be businessmen, but you disappoint me, Mr. Warner," Kinzl said. "If I came to you as a defector, you would accept me at once, all I would have to do is sign a little piece of paper saying I wanted asylum. Then you would check on my story. Everything would come out just as I say, and you would give me a big payment for a few weeks of interrogation and some more cash to see to my resettlement. Then—if I agreed—you would give me a salary as a consultant. If I worked at that long enough, you would even give me a pension, just like your civil service. All this would cost much more than what you must pay me now. As far as I can see, I'm offering you a bargain."

Trosper did not suppress his smile. Kinzl, whoever he might be, knew how defectors were handled. Moreover, the logic of his argument was sound. Defectors were valuable, most of them worth much more than the costs of their resettlement. But defector information was finite, and dated quickly. Data from an agent in place remained current, and information from the right agent in place could be priceless.

There was another important difference between an agent in place and a defector that Kinzl had neglected to mention. Few defectors ever refused to answer questions. It was already apparent that Kinzl intended to deal with the Firm on his own terms. For the moment, Trosper did not intend to force a showdown with the Russian. This would only come after Kinzl had imparted enough sensitive information so that there could be no question of his making a unilateral decision to terminate the relationship.

"You told Mr. Johnson something about the arrest of a Russian officer, an Anatoli Galkin," Trosper said.

"*Aleksei* Galkin," Kinzl said. "Not Anatoli. He was *your* agent, Mr. Warner, and you know his name as well as I do. There's no point in our wasting time fencing like this. Galkin was arrested after we spotted him emptying a dead drop. That was a silly mistake. You should have known better."

"You've already told Johnson about that. For all I know, that story could have been in the Soviet press," Trosper said.

"It wasn't, Mr. Warner, and I suspect you know that too. Between your embassy and CIA, your government reads every publication in the USSR. Surely you don't expect me to believe the Agency would have failed to inform the Firm of a news break like that?"

Trosper watched as Kinzl picked up his glass, sniffed the bouquet, and took a small sip. He was as small as Kyle had indicated, no more than five feet six. His face was so narrow it seemed like an extension of his long thin neck. His gray hair was cut short and brushed forward on the top and sides. It was a hair style the Berliners called an *Idiotenfrisur,* a cross between Julius Caesar and a village simpleton. The deep lines in his face seemed to accentuate his pale blue eyes.

Beneath a weathered gray tweed jacket, Kinzl wore a light blue shirt with a soft, rumpled collar, and a narrow, dark blue tie with small, red figures. Trosper guessed the shirt had been made to be worn with stays and that Kinzl had lost or discarded them. It added to the Russian's vaguely bohemian appearance.

Taking another sip of brandy, Kinzl began to talk. His account of Galkin's arrest, interrogation, and confession was straightforward and cogent. With no evidence but the surveillance team's report on Galkin's behavior in the restaurant, and the limpet in the men's room, the interrogator had little to work on. Although Galkin had been arrested and jailed in circumstances that would have terrified most Russians, he had maintained his composure. Only when Galkin made the telephone call to his wife Vera in Vienna, did the interrogator—who was at Galkin's elbow—notice any nervousness.

Vera Galkin returned three days later and was arrested at the airport.

"She was so frightened," Kinzl said, "she seemed almost paralyzed. But she was pretty good. At the time, no one knew for sure if Galkin really was an agent. And even if you people had recruited him, he seemed too smart to have told his wife anything about it. So no one knew how much pressure to put on her. As it turned out, all she was really interested in was the children. She kept asking where they were, who was taking care of them. But she wouldn't admit a thing.

"About this time, the interrogator decided to take a chance. He got Amstov, chief of the American section, to agree that he could tell Galkin that Vera had been arrested, that she was in bad shape, calling for Galkin and telling the questioners an unbelievable story.

"For the first time, Galkin was shaken. He asked to see Vera. The interrogator refused. Galkin kept trying to learn what Vera had said. The interrogator laughed at him. To make sure the prisoner had nothing to do but wonder what had happened to his wife, and what might happen to the children, he ordered Galkin left alone for three days in a lighted cell. He was fed at irregular hours, and had no way of knowing whether it was day or night, or even how long he had been held. Maybe a little amphetamine was slipped into his food, something to keep him from sleeping too much. After seventy-two hours of complete isolation—even the guards were forbidden to speak to Galkin—the interrogator came back.

"At first the interrogator began to go over the same ground he had covered when Galkin was first arrested. Then, abruptly, he tossed his papers aside. In return for a full confession, he said, he could recommend amnesty for Vera and the children. Then, if Galkin cooperated in a double agent case, and if the operation went well, he might be able to get get off with a few years' rehabilitation.

"It's odd," Kinzl said. "No matter how smart they are, amnesty and rehabilitation are magic words. Galkin came around right after that—he told us everything. That's how I heard about you, Mr. Warner, and your splendid shoes, and about Mr. Johnson, and the old lady, Frau Hofer—Oma, as you called her."

Kinzl stopped to take another sip of his brandy. "In the end, Comrade Galkin was sitting at a small table, with a guard facing him. For hours at a time, he scribbled away with stubby little pencils, writing on those numbered sheets of paper they make prisoners use. Even if you hadn't known, you might have guessed he was writing for his life. Not that it mattered—he'd been a dead man from the moment those trainees saw him go into the toilet. It really is quite sad when you think about it."

Trosper had thought about it. He had thought a lot about Galkin and his pretty, young wife. And he didn't like being reminded of it by a smug little Chekist in second-hand clothes. Abruptly, he thrust himself up from the chair. His knee hit the coffee table, rattling the glasses and ashtrays.

Sensing Trosper's fury, Kyle said, "A drink, Mr. Warner—I'll get it."

"Thank you," Trosper muttered as he sat back down. "A scotch and soda will do." He turned his attention back to Kinzl.

"What you say is interesting enough. It may even be true. Certainly it squares with what has been published about the way you handle prisoners," Trosper said. At this point he was not willing to admit that he had ever read a secret report, let alone that he knew anything about Moscow Center. "But I don't quite see why you have gone to this trouble—and, as you put it, some risk—to tell us about it."

"Of course," Mr. Warner. But I haven't got to the point of my story. The point comes later, during the interrogation—*after* Galkin agreed to talk. It was two days before the interrogator was satisfied that he had the whole story. Then he told Galkin to write a complete autobiography, and to fill in all the conspiratorial details concerning his recruitment and agent work for you. This is the usual procedure, Mr. Warner, a way to double-check things. Often the written story opens new lines of questioning. It also gives the interrogators time to complete a preliminary report for the big bosses. It was only when Galkin began to write that he mentioned that while he was in Vienna, Mikhail Lopatin—a visitor from Moscow—had offered him a job in a new active measures program, code name 'Phoenix.'

"The interrogator paid little attention to this—he merely noted in his daily report that he planned to question Galkin on it at their next session."

Kinzl stopped. "You know about 'active measures,' Mr. Warner? It's what you people call 'covert action'—black propaganda, deception, disinformation, all that sort of thing."

"Yes," Trosper said. "I think I understand what you call active measures."

"When the transcript of Galkin's written report got to General Veselkov, he asked immediately to see the interrogator. The Galkin arrest was considered so important that General Veselkov had been reading the draft reports, even before the interrogators had them in final form.

"I'll spare you some of the detail, but after the general had posed a few apparently random questions, he began asking about Lopatin. He wanted to know precisely what Galkin had said about Lopatin, what Lopatin had said about 'Phoenix,' what job Lopatin had offered Galkin.

"At this point the interrogator wasn't even sure if 'Phoenix' was the code name for an operation, or for some agent. His only information came from Galkin's written notes. All he could do was to tell Veselkov that he would question Galkin on 'Phoenix' and Lopatin that night."

Kinzl took another sip of brandy and looked at Trosper as if to measure his interest in the story.

"But Veselkov had other plans," Kinzl said. "That afternoon, Colonel Amstov, chief of the American CI section, called the interrogator into his office and told him he had been taken off the Galkin case. No reason was given. For a while the interrogator thought maybe Veselkov had a favorite he wanted to put on the case. Later, he knew different."

"When was that?" Trosper asked.

"It was a few days later—when he learned that Galkin had been executed the day after the interrogator had been taken off the case. He knew something had happened. While he was working on Galkin, the interrogator was told several times that Galkin was to be used as a double agent against the Firm, that no matter what happened, he was not to do anything that might upset the possibility of doubling Galkin against the Firm.

"Suddenly it seemed absolutely clear that something to do with 'Phoenix' or Mikhail Lopatin was immensely important to General Veselkov," Kinzl said.

"It became absolutely clear to whom?"

"To the interrogator, or course."

"And what is his name?"

"That's not important. He's of no interest to you."

"Don't you think that I'm the best judge of that?"

"Of course I do," Kinzl said. "But that's one of the things we must get straight. General Veselkov, Colonel Amstov, any of the big men, I will talk freely about. But I do not want to identify the lower-ranking comrades for your files, Mr. Warner. It would be easy enough for me to call this man *Sniffpuffkin,* some nonsense name. Your analysts would add the name to your indices, and you'd be happy. But I would have told you a lie that you believed. I'd rather put our talks on the basis of truth, Mr. Warner. When I don't want to tell you something, I won't. But on the other hand, you can trust me to tell you the truth. That will be a better working relationship for us both, Mr. Warner."

Trosper could not remember the last time he had assumed any stranger had told him the truth.

FOR more than an hour Kyle listened as Trosper went quietly through a series of questions which had been tailored by the head office for the walk-in from Russia. With no apparent hesitation, Kinzl rattled off details of the organization and personnel at Moscow Center that could only have been known by someone with inside knowledge of the Center. But Kinzl calmly refused to tell Trosper why he was in Austria, or where he was assigned in Moscow. He also refused to discuss any of his past assignments or to give any biographical data on himself. Trosper did not press.

Finally he asked how much money Kinzl wanted. The Russian repeated his earlier demand for five thousand dollars per meeting. Trosper offered him two thousand in cash. The Russian refused. He did not want to carry large sums. For the present, he said, his fees should be deposited in his Basel bank account. If the money was not deposited there would be no further contact. Kinzl gave Trosper the account number and the code word "Avocado."

"Don't bother to have your analysts try to puzzle out the meaning of 'Avocado,' Mr. Warner. It doesn't mean a thing. It's just a code word the bank suggested."

"I don't give a damn about 'Avocado,' " Trosper said. "But I do want to know why you have approached us this way. Why are you telling us these things?"

"There'll be time enough for that," Kinzl said. "I don't think this is the moment for you to probe very deeply into the question of my motives."

AFTER Kinzl left, Mercer came in from the bedroom where he had been monitoring the tape recorders. He poured himself a drink. "He's not the most forthcoming chap who ever walked in," he said.

"He's a smug little bastard," Trosper said. "I shouldn't let him get under my skin that way, but it irritates the hell out of me to have him think I was responsible for that Moscow incident."

Trosper began to scribble on a yellow pad—Bates would be waiting for a preliminary cabled report. He wrote for a few minutes, and then stopped. "He reads us a lecture on truth, and how we can believe whatever he tells us. Then he does his best to convince me there was only one interrogator involved in the Galkin case. That's nonsense. On an investigation and interrogation as important as that, they would use three or four senior case men. Kinzl's protecting something, or someone."

Trosper tossed the pad aside. "All the same," he said. "it's never done any harm to let people think they've outsmarted you—particularly early on in a case. There'll be time enough to find out who's doing whom before we're through with Herr Kinzl."

IN THE *Controller Only* cable to Bates, Trosper outlined his tactics. Because it was more important to keep Kinzl's information coming, and to begin to explore his access to the Center's current operations, it would do no harm to let the Russian think he had the upper hand, and could bend Trosper and the Firm to his demands. The time to exert operational control would come later.

Meanwhile, Trosper asked for another, more extensive search of all records for any trace of Kinzl. There could not be many fluent German-speaking Russians who appeared completely at home in Austria, who had a Swiss bank account, and who were five feet, six inches tall.

Finally, Trosper recommended that Kinzl's financial terms be met. Unless the money was deposited promptly, Trosper was satisfied that there would be no further contact with the Russian.

9   VIENNA

KYLE hitched himself forward, bringing his chair closer to the table where Trosper sat studying notes he had penciled on a sheaf of yellow pages. Across the room, Mercer fussed with a tape recorder.

They had spent the morning replaying and discussing the tapes of last night's meeting with Kinzl. It would have been easier to work from a transcript, but they had no secretary. Even if an experienced transcriber had been available, it would have taken a day or more to make an accurate transcript of the meeting.

It had been almost an hour since Trosper had spoken, and then it was only to ask Kyle for a second cup of coffee.

In Washington, Bates had jibbed when Trosper told him he wanted to use Kyle in Vienna. But Trosper was adamant. Kyle spoke fluent German, good Russian, and he knew Vienna well. Mercer spoke French, but his German was only fair, and he had never worked in Austria. Mercer could maintain the necessary liaison with Hamel, chief of the Vienna office, and there would be other tasks for him as well. Surely, Trosper said, the Firm could afford two hundred dollars a day for a man as experienced as Kyle? Four hundred a week, Bates said, and not a nickel more. Trosper agreed. He knew he could keep Kyle busy enough to guarantee he would have the money for another few months in Austria to work on his book.

"There really is something odd about Kinzl," Kyle said, hoping to break the silence. "It's almost as if he were reading lines, and wearing a costume. He's not like any other agent I've ever bumped into."

It was the wrong way to stir Trosper from his reverie. As he began to weigh Kyle's remark, he was reminded of an incident in Rome. A prominent senator—on a European junket—thought he had encountered a hostile spy, and had demanded to see a counterespionage expert. Trying to sort out the account of what had obviously been a drunken night on the town, Trosper asked why the senator was so convinced that the man who had been cadging drinks from him was an agent. "Because he *looked* exactly like a spy," the senator thundered.

Nursing a hangover of his own, Trosper confessed sourly that he had never given much thought to the way spies look.

He recalled that after Kim Philby had escaped to Moscow, he had realized that the British traitor seemed, occasionally at least, to have used his stammer as a convenient distraction, a means of keeping his listeners at arm's length. Trosper also recalled that in spite of Philby's raffish mannerisms, the few times he had spoken to him, he had come away with the feeling that he had been patronized by a smug, English gentleman. But Trosper had never known any other spy who had a speech impediment.

Stig Wennerstrom, the Swedish Air Force colonel who as a military attaché had looted NATO, the Pentagon, and the Swedish defense ministry, had the eyes of a corpse. There was no trace of curiosity, no spark of humor, nothing at all to be seen in his eyes, or read from his face. Trosper knew several Scandinavians, but had never met another Swede, or even another spy, with quite the look Wennerstrom projected.

Heinz Felfe, the Nazi secret policeman who had clawed his way close to the top of the West German intelligence service, was a crude paradigm of ambition and self-interest. Devoid of any social warmth, without a whisper of taste, he had such contempt for his colleagues that he grew lazy and was tripped up as much by his own sloppy tradecraft as by skillful counterintelligence.

Finally, Trosper admitted to the senator that after twenty years in the racket, he hadn't the slightest notion what a spy looked like.

Later, in Washington, Trosper learned that the senator had written Darcy Odlum a furious note. The Controller never mentioned the incident to Trosper.

Kyle tried another tack, "It bugs me, being jerked around by that little bastard," he said.

Reluctantly Trosper shoved his notes aside. "For the moment he's in the catbird seat, just the way he planned it." He waved his hand in the direction of the tapes on the table in front of Mercer. "There's some good stuff there, it's more important to keep it coming than to risk a showdown with our friend."

Trosper folded his notes and handed them to Mercer. He would seal them in a double envelope, and take it to Hamel for safekeeping in the Firm's Vienna office.

"There's nothing we can do about Kinzl but to play along until we learn who else is in on the scam. Meanwhile, we'd better try to get a line on the mysterious Lopatin. He might be a different story."

"But we know damn-all about him," Kyle said. "All Vera Galkin said was that he was one of the old boys, a veteran of the great fracas, a hero who spent the war in Austria."

"Have we got any idea what the Russians had here during the war?" Mercer asked.

"Not really," Trosper said. "Along with the British, oss passed Moscow a lot of information, but they never gave us a damned thing. There was no cooperation at all. My guess would be that they had a considerable intelligence network in and around Vienna. There were two important German military headquarters and some *Abwehr*—Nazi intelligence—offices here. The Germans were trying to run operations into the Balkans and Eastern Europe. After the war, using captured files, we tried to sort it out. I doubt that we ever did much research on the ground. By that time the Cold War was on. Things were moving too fast, nobody had time for research." Trosper shook his head. If he had his way, research would have as big a budget as operations.

"For my book," Kyle said, "I tried to look into the Russian side of things in Austria during the war. But almost nothing has been published. I'm satisfied that they had no role in the military resistance. Oddly enough the real Austrian resistance was a combination of right-wing groups and Socialists. The most the Russians had here would have been spies, funneling military and political data back to Moscow. For this they relied on some of the old Party hands and *Schutzbund* survivors who were parachuted in."

Puzzled, Mercer glanced at Trosper.

"In 1934, Dollfuss, the Austrian chancellor, was more worried about the Socialists than he was about the Austrian Nazis," Trosper said. "He put so much pressure on them that the Socialist *Schutzbund*, an armed defense group, finally fought back. Dollfuss unleashed the police and some fascist paramilitary groups, and they began to shoot it out. Dollfuss won. Some of the Socialist military leaders escaped into Czechoslovakia with their families. Later, Stalin took some of them into the USSR. Many disappeared during the purges, but some survived."

"I doubt if anyone thought about it at the time," Kyle said, "but Stalin's charity gave the Center a good pool for recruiting. The children grew up bilingual in Russian and good little *apparatchiks* to boot. When Hitler invaded Russia, the survivors provided a natural pool of German-speaking agents. Some were sent to Austria, others to Germany. They even used some of the older children. The Gestapo called them *Schutzbundkinder.*"

Mercer brightened. "Stalin did something like that with some of the survivors of the Spanish Civil War. He took them in, and then sent some of the children back to Spain as agents after the war. They called them *Niños.*"

"Vera said Lopatin was 'older,' " Kyle said. "She was thirty-two. I suppose 'older' would mean anyone over fifty. If that's so, and with a good war record, and good connections with the old boys, Lopatin should be at least a colonel."

"Unless he was some kind of specialist," Mercer said. "In that case he wouldn't necessarily have much rank. He'd be kept around as long as he kept his nose clean and could do whatever it was they were paying him for."

"They don't have any mandatory retirement at Dzerzhinsky Square," Kyle said. "Most of them hang on as long as they can, at least until they're sixty-five or so. Then they try to grab something in another ministry. They don't have much choice. Outside the GULAG, there aren't any retirement homes for Center old boys."

"Fascinatin', all this history," Trosper said, "but I've got a bag to pack. Meanwhile, you'd better get started on the report for Bates. Every word, every scrap of information from the tapes is to be organized so that the analysts will have an easy time of it. Send it *Expedite,* and make sure their evaluation comes back the same way."

IN THE bedroom, he tossed a few things into a small bag and pulled on a wool-lined trenchcoat.

"I'm going to Salzburg for a day or two," he said from the door. "I'll telephone at eleven and at four. Please be sure one of you is here to take the calls."

If he could avoid it, Trosper never made a telephone call from a safe house. He knew that habits like this fueled his reputation as an operational mossback, but he could think of no telephone easier to tap then one in an unoccupied safe house.

Trosper would call Salzburg from the *Westbahnhof* before he took the train.

10   SALZBURG

TROSPER eased the rented Fiat into the lot alongside the Gasthaus Jaeger. The restaurant was only ten kilometers from Salzburg, but the heavy rain had slowed the night driving. He was a few minutes late. He hurried through the smoke-filled *Bierstube* alongside the entrance to the restaurant. A small, hand-lettered sign directed him to the private dining hall at the rear.

It was a long, low room, used most often, Trosper assumed, for wedding celebrations and septuagenarian birthday parties. Except for lights over a low platform and lectern at the far end, the room was dark. He guessed there were fifty people in the hall.

Groping for a seat, Trosper stumbled, almost falling into the lap of a woman seated on the aisle at the rear of the hall. As he brushed past her, a faint scent of rose water stirred a mnemonic hint of garden parties, watercress sandwiches, and the vicar's wife. This could only be the right place, the quarterly meeting of the Thistle And Sonnet Society. Trosper whispered an apology, but decided not to risk wriggling out of his coat until the echoes of his noisy entrance had faded.

At the lectern, a towering, gray-haired woman had begun to explain how much the Thistle And Sonnet Society owed to its own Colonel Douglas Brattle.

". . . and though Colonel Brattle will not admit that he too has put pen to sonnet and ballad, he stands second to none of us in his determination to see that our sacred Scottish muse is as cosseted here as she is in our own highlands." The woman punctuated each phrase by lifting both arms, as if a skein of wool were stretched across her wrists.

Trosper strained to scan the audience. He could not see his old friend. The speaker rattled on, her fresh accent strange in the antler-hung *Heimatstil* room.

". . . and now, though we know how he struggles to avoid speaking in public, Colonel Brattle has agreed to introduce tonight's program."

There was an encouraging flare of applause. Trosper stretched to see over the heads of the audience. From the side of the hall, a burly figure lumbered toward the podium. He was over six feet, and stuffed into a near-black, double-breasted suit—the prescribed camouflage for an overweight Englishman.

As Brattle moved toward the platform, the patchy, half light of the hall caught the rubbed lapels and shiny elbows of his suit like traces of moonlight on a lake. For most Englishmen, a new suit is a battle lost.

Brattle seized the lectern with both hands and dipped his knees, like a boxer flexing himself against the ring ropes before a bout. He lifted his eyes to squint at the audience and muttered something.

Trosper could not tell whether it was an imprecation or a Gaelic greeting.

Tossing a packet of file cards onto the lectern, Brattle plucked a pair of hornrimmed reading glasses from his pocket and cleared his throat. Trosper seized the moment to struggle out of his bulky trenchcoat. He was seconds late, and lost the first few words of the rich, whiskey baritone.

". . . and so we are fortunate tonight to have with us one of the —shall I say—great powers of contemporary poetry." Brattle paused and smiled at the audience. "Indeed, it would not be amiss to describe our guest as a superpower of contemporary poetry."

Knowing laughter acknowledged the hyperbole.

". . . and poets and readers alike can take heart that he has at last found a summit from which to speak for us all."

Over the rims of his reading glasses, Brattle scanned the audience as if challenging any pugnacious poetaster to rise up and contradict him. "I refer of course to *Whimper*—the magazine that more than any other speaks for today's poetry."

There was more applause.

"But our guest is not only an editor—and this will surprise no one in this audience—he has also described himself as 'a maker of poems.' "

With a slight smile, Brattle affected the manner of a schoolmaster as he began to riffle through the packet of cards on the lectern. He squinted over the half frame of his glasses. "Have we all read *Veneer?* Do we remember what R. R. Rune said about it?"

Pulling his glasses farther down his nose, he selected a card and paused to study it. Then, with another glance around the hall, and a serious mien, he continued. " 'To read *Veneer,*' Rune wrote, 'is to be spared little of life's agony.' "

Another scattering of applause swept across the hall.

"I see that we all agree with Rune on that," Brattle said with a smile.

"And now, as a member of the Thistle And Sonnet Society, and Acting Honorary Consul of Her Majesty's government, it is my duty to introduce our guest, Mr. Alfred Pewter—"

If Brattle had intended to say more, his words were lost in the applause that greeted the thin, balding man who stepped around Brattle to reach the lectern. After nodding thanks to Brattle, the poet dropped a thick, loose-leaf binder on the stand. With a confident glance at the audience, he began to thumb through the pages.

"There is such a feast of poetry to choose from," he began, "that I can think of no better way to get things started than to read one of my own modest efforts. I call it *Small Poem, Number One Hundred Twenty.*"

In the shadow to the left of Alfred Pewter, Trosper could see Colonel Douglas Anthony Farqhuar Brattle (Retired) ease himself onto a straight-backed chair.

LIEUTENANT D. A. F. "BUTCH" BRATTLE and an Austrian radio operator had parachuted into an orchard west of Wiener Neustadt in September 1943. The desolate area was as close to the intended Austrian drop zone as the nervous pilot and frightened navigator thought it prudent to fly. As on all special operations, it was easy for the jumpy flight crew to blame navigational difficulties for the failure to reach the plotted drop zone.

Brattle took three weeks to make his way to Vienna and to find the only Austrian contact London considered reliable.

"We'd had offices in Vienna since before World War One, for Christ's sake," Brattle had told Trosper. "Come Hitler and his war, and it's time to send one mission into Vienna. And what do we have on the shelf, what kind of resources? After twenty years, the best they could come up with was a card trace on an old man, the chum of a journalist who worked in Vienna before the war. Records Center didn't even know if he was still alive, or even in Austria. If he hadn't been there, we'd have been up that bloody creek you people are always talking about."

By the time the Red Army pushed into Vienna in April 1945, Brattle had been in place and funneling intelligence to London for sixteen months. He was twenty-one. After the war, the Brattle Mission, one of the very few wartime operations that came off as planned, had become something of a classic, and was part of the curriculum at the training schools. But like many behind-the-lines missions, its success depended entirely on the head agent—Butch Brattle.

After the war Brattle had remained on in Vienna until 1955, when the occupation finally came to term. Then, reluctantly, he accepted a transfer to Berlin. When he retired in 1975, he returned to Austria and settled in Salzburg.

TROSPER watched as Brattle conned his bulk through the crowded reception that followed the lecture. In twenty minutes, he had helped the poet sell a dozen autographed copies of *Pewter Poems,* sipped a little white wine, and chatted with each of the Sonnet And Thistle members. When he noticed Trosper watching his maneuvering, Brattle slipped casually across the room to his side.

"It's just a knack," he said. "I've always had it. I never forget anyone's name, and can usually remember one or two little things we may have talked about—you'd be surprised at the things they tell you. People like to be noticed. I guess everyone's a little lonely." Brattle fell silent, apparently contemplating his observation. Then he added, "I don't even do it on purpose anymore—just to make them feel better for a few minutes."

Then he eased away, already speaking to another guest.

It was a useful knack, Trosper thought, even if the Englishman wasn't in the racket any more.

"COME on back to my place," Brattle said. "I've done as much for the Queen tonight as I'm going to."

TROSPER thrashed the underpowered Fiat to keep the green Rover in sight as the Englishman threaded his way across the back roads to the immaculate, small chalet tucked against a hillside on the western outskirts of Salzburg.

"THE THISTLE AND SONNET SOCIETY," Trosper asked. "What the hell is that?"

Brattle poured three fingers of Smith's Glenlivet into Trosper's glass.

"Water?"

"A splash."

Brattle leaned back in the heavy chair. "I'm not a Scot, only my grandfather was. But these people have adopted me. They're a good lot. Harmless, most of them. Even that tonsured twit from London."

Brattle took a long drink. He had not put water in his whiskey. "You've been around for a long time," he said. "You know how it is, how it *was* anyway. I haven't got a single damned tie. No wife, no family except a niece—and she can't remember whether I came here in the fourteen-eighteen war or for the Hitler punch-up.

"So I'm back in Austria with a pretty good pension, and most of the cash I put away. I should be comfortable as hell, and in a way I am. This country gets to you after a while. Anyway there wasn't much reason for me to go back to England."

He glanced around the low living room. "I've got most of what I need hereabouts." He took another sip of the heavy scotch whiskey. "The funny thing is, that since I left the racket, I think I've gone a bit potty. I'm beginning to like doing things for people. It's getting to be embarrassing."

Trosper remembered Brattle as the toughest, most sardonic intelligence man he had ever known. Not for nothing was he called Butch.

Brattle shook his head in apparent disbelief. "It's probably just a hangover from all the years I spent trying to figure out what people —bystanders and that lot—could do for the racket. I hope the hell I can snap out of it."

The big man shifted in his chair. "I heard you were out, a row with the management?"

"I was out, more than two years. I didn't miss it much."

"The people are what I miss," Brattle said. "I miss some of the chaps."

He poured more scotch. "This was part of the final handshake," he said, gesturing toward the bottle. "When I signed out, they made some arrangement. I'm an honorary consul. All I have to do is wave the flag once in a while—like tonight—and they give me an occasional shot at buying a load of diplomatic, tax-free whiskey."

"This is pretty good stuff you're serving," Trosper said. He took another sip of the whiskey. "I wonder what Kim is drinking tonight?"

Brattle laughed. "I like to think about all of them getting together, maybe on the Queen's Birthday—Philby, Blake, and some of the others. Maybe they give a toast to their fallen comrades, Burgess and Maclean. I suppose those two chums of yours, the poofs from NSA, give a special drinks party on the Fourth of July.

"They must hate one another by now," Trosper said. "Think of the bickering that goes on, the jealousy—who's got the best apartment, the best job, who's sucking up to the boss. They're marooned in that godforsaken city, like being stuck on an island."

Brattle walked across the room to an elaborate high fidelity rig. "A little Mozart, for the listeners," he said, and dropped a record onto the turntable.

"You're here on business?"

Trosper nodded. "I'm curious about someone who was in Vienna when you first got there—and who stayed on right through the war. A Russian."

"That was a while ago."

"His name could have been Lopatin. He might have been one of the crowd that went back to Moscow after a long hitch abroad and was tossed into the Lubyanka by Stalin. If so, I suspect he was rehabilitated, along with some of the others, and was finally given the recognition he deserved. For what it's worth, I think he's still in the racket."

As the allegro came to a climax, Brattle lifted his arms like a conductor bringing the movement to a close. "When I first got to Vienna, I was too busy staying alive to worry much about what the Russians were up to. I always thought they were there in some strength, both on the military side, the GRU, and the NKVD. But my people stayed as far away from any of the Austrian Communist

Party types as they could. I figured Moscow had them all sewed up
—the ones who were still alive anyway."

"Lopatin, if that's his name," Trosper said, "would almost certainly have been documented as an Austrian, I suppose he might
even have been set up before the war. You remember that they had
Rado and Foote in Switzerland, and Trepper in Belgium before the
shooting started."

"Of course," Brattle said. "General Berzin, the old man you
admired so much on the military side, and General Abakumov for
the NKVD, had planned ahead. No matter how often Stalin told them
they didn't have to worry about his friend Hitler, they ignored him
and managed to put pretty good illegal nets in place before Hitler
attacked Russia and it became 'the people's war.' " He paused for
a moment. "I'm sure they would have had two or three agents in
place in Vienna."

Brattle poured more whiskey.

"The only Russian I ever heard anyone refer to by name was
someone who called himself 'Schneider.' I never knew his first name.
Just Schneider. I heard this in 1944, when the Gestapo were hot after
him. They had him pegged as the NKVD *rezident.* He probably was
a head agent, but only the Krauts with their passion for filling out
organization charts could have thought Moscow would have one
man in charge of everything in Austria. I never heard anything more
about Schneider. After the war, by the time London got around to
looking for him and some of the others, there just wasn't much of
a trail left."

"I can't imagine Philby would have let anyone push that very
hard," Trosper said.

"You can bet the beer money on that. Kim took over the MI6
Soviet section just at the end of the war, in 1944. That was when he
was still the golden boy, the man who would lead us all into the
bright new world. He was so bloody well connected, he peddled his
influence far beyond his own outfit. About that time, maybe 1946,
I had a hell of a row with my headquarters. I didn't have the brain
to realize it then, but I guess good old Kim was behind it."

Brattle stopped for a moment. "Now that I think of it, that might
be a lead for you."

He took a box of Havanas from the bookshelf, opened it, and shoved it across the coffee table to Trosper. Fishing a box of wooden matches from his pocket, he tossed it to Trosper.

"This was August forty-five, maybe as late as September, a few months after the war, and just before anyone got interested in the Russians. We were still allies, and the Yalta idiots—Churchill and Roosevelt—had agreed that we would send all the Russian POWs, displaced persons, expatriates, every former Russian, back to Uncle Joe."

Brattle bent forward to cut the end from his cigar. "It was murder, what we were doing then."

He began the elaborate process of lighting the cigar.

"Right here in western Austria, we were organizing repatriation trains full of Russians, all under guard. The poor sods were breaking windows and slashing their wrists with the broken glass."

Holding a match below his cigar, Brattle charred the end.

"It was the worst I saw anywhere, except the camps," he said. "And British and American troops were ordered to do it. I'm surprised we didn't have a mutiny."

Brattle struck another match and began gently to puff on the cigar. "I'd gone from Vienna to Klagenfurt, I can't remember why now, but I was there for a couple of weeks. One day we got a rumor there was a defector, a Russian captain, in the refugee camp just outside the city. It wasn't really my business, but I went out to have a look."

Brattle puffed gently. "He was there all right. Terrified, and with good reason. The other refugees, mostly Hungarian Jews—real survivors—were trying to protect him, working up some cock and bull story about his being a German, from Silesia somewhere—he spoke some German. It took a little while, but I finally got him to tell a straight story. He'd nipped out of a Red Army headquarters, somewhere near Baden bei Wien, and made his way on foot to the British zone. He figured he could get asylum from us. Damned little he knew.

"He claimed to be a paymaster, a simple Red Army captain. But there was a whiff of intelligence, just a trace of the racket about him. I don't remember why I thought so but I do recall that I had the impression he might have been in our business.

"I didn't have time to do any interrogation on my own, but I cabled the London office about him. I got the damnedest answer. 'Captain Anatoli Grachev comes under . . .' Then they cited some cruddy subsection of the Yalta agreement. 'If you satisfied he authentic Red Army deserter, Grachev to be turned over to Soviet Repatriation Commission forthwith.' How's that for balls on a blue plate?

"I know you were too young to have been around in those days, but things were different right after the war. You could get away with almost anything—everyone was trying to get out of the army. It seemed as if nobody held a job more than a few days before being demobbed. And of course the chaps closest to the mimeograph machines back home were getting out first. So I just ignored the bloody cable. By the time they caught up with me—in 1946 I'd guess —Grachev was long gone. There was one hell of a row—probably thanks to Comrade Philby. I suppose his NKVD contact man tore a strip off him for letting a 'deserter' get away."

"Did Grachev stay here in Austria?"

"Hell no. I knew the Russian repatriation team would piss up a fuss as soon as they got a line on him, so I slipped him out."

Savoring his victory, Brattle blew a series of smoke rings.

"There were a couple of Swiss cops here, looking for a trio of Swiss Nazis who'd been in Berlin during the war—training to be *Gauleiter* when Hitler took over the Alpine Republic. I knew your chaps in Salzburg had already found them, but I told the Swiss that if they'd take Grachev, I'd move mountains to track down their traitors for them. As it turned out, I wouldn't even have had to make a deal—they were only too glad to give asylum to any Russian who hadn't been a Nazi collaborator. Stalin hadn't sold *them* any of that Yalta crap."

"Do you know where Grachev is now?"

"If he'd come out just a year later, he'd have a chair at Oxford by now. Grachev wasn't that lucky. He came over at the moment when Philby had the most influence. At the time Kim was busy convincing everyone that none of the defectors was of any interest and might just as well be sent straight back to Stalin."

Brattle heaved himself out of the chair and crossed the room to change the record. "If my hunch is right, and if Grachev *was* in the racket, he might just remember something about what the Center had here during the war. I can't recall any other defector who could go back that far."

"Do you know where he is now?"

"My guess is that he's still in Switzerland. If Grachev is still there, I know someone who can find him. He's an old man, over eighty, and his memory isn't what it used to be, but he might help if I ask him."

Reluctantly, Brattle flicked the long ash off his cigar. "I take it this is serious business, and that you're in charge?" The question was as close as Brattle could come to asking Trosper for a commitment. It was one case man talking to another, trusting the other. It was not the sort of initiative that intelligence headquarters often approved. And in the secret world it was a rare happening.

"It's serious enough," Trosper said. "Before I left, we lost a good source, about as good as they come. Now something new has come up. That's why I'm back for a while. As for being in charge, I guess I'm about as much in charge as any field man ever is. You know what that's worth."

"Okay," Brattle said. "I had to ask. I knew it would be the same crap." He reached for the Glenlivet.

It would be a wet night.

11 LAUSANNE

IT WAS an old building, *sans ascenseur,* on the Avenue des Tilleuls. The hallway was dark, but clean as a Swiss kitchen. As Trosper approached 4–B, the door opened slightly, and a wedge of light fell across the polished floor.

"Mr. Johnson?" a voice asked in English.

"Yes, I'm Johnson," Trosper said. "Monsieur Lobanov?" Through the crack in the door, Trosper could see the old Russian bow slightly as he slipped the chain.

"Lobanov," he said, and extended his hand. "Victor Lobanov. Please come in."

Trosper followed the frail old man along the narrow hall to a sitting room at the rear of the apartment. The curtains were open. Across the quiet street below the window was a small park. Through the bare limbs of the trees, Trosper could see the narrow street leading down the steep hill from Lausanne to Ouchy on the lake.

"Some tea, Mr. Johnson," the Russian asked. "Or vodka? Vodka for this cold weather?"

"Tea, please."

"*Mais à la russe?* Hot, and with a little jam?"

"Perfect," Trosper said.

He could see an icon in the corner of the room, and shelves of books in Russian, German, and French. Newspapers and magazines were piled on tables at the side of the room. On a table beside Trosper's chair there was a small samovar. The old Russian excused himself. "I'll fetch the tea," he said.

From a doorway opening to the hall, Trosper heard the rattle of dishes. Carrying a small tray, the Russian pushed the door open.

"I should use the samovar, Mr. Johnson, but sometimes it seems like too much work. After all these years, I'm not sure the tea is any better than when I make it in the kitchen with boiling water right off the stove."

He poured the steaming tea into glasses set in metal holders. "We call these holders *podstakanniki,* Mr. Johnson," he said, and passed Trosper a pot of strawberry jam. Trosper spooned a little into his glass.

"And how is the Colonel, Mr. Butch?" the Russian asked. "How is he getting on these days?"

"He's fine. You know how Austria agrees with him."

The Russian nodded slowly, several times.

"That's what we called him in the old days," he said. "We all called him 'Mr. Butch.' I was never sure he liked it, but that's what we called him."

The old Russian wore a black suit, with a double-breasted waist-coat, and ankle-high black shoes. His shirt had a detachable, starched, white collar. His black knit tie had slipped down, and Trosper could see the gold collar button above it. The suit hung loose from the old Russian's shoulders, and the stiff collar was too large for him.

"On the telephone, the Colonel said I might be able to help you, Mr. Johnson."

The old Russian's face was unwrinkled, the clear skin drawn tightly across his high cheek bones and over the high, hawk bridge of his nose. His bushy white moustache was a sharp contrast to the thin white hair that lay flat against his head. He might have been a cavalry officer, Trosper thought.

"That's all he told me, Mr. Johnson," the old Russian said quietly. "Nothing more. You know how careful he is on the telephone."

"I know," Trosper said. "And I have to be careful, too, Monsieur Lobanov. I'm looking for a former Soviet officer."

The old Russian put down his glass of tea. He looked at his guest with new interest.

"He was in Austria in 1945. From what the Colonel said, you were in Austria as well, Monsieur Lobanov?"

"I had been there through most of the war," the Russian said. "Before that, Turkey, Italy, Prague—I actually had Czech papers when the war began."

"The man I'm looking for was a captain," Trosper said. "He was assigned to a headquarters in Baden bei Wien in 1945. When he escaped, he made his way to Klagenfurt, in the British occupation zone."

"More tea, Mr. Johnson?"

"Thank you." Trosper dipped his spoon into the jam, and swirled it in the tea.

"That was when the Soviet repatriation teams were combing the refugee camps," he continued. "But Colonel Brattle found him first. Some time later, Captain Grachev made his way to Switzerland. That's the last I know about him. I'm not even sure his first name is Anatoli. And I do not know his patronymic."

The old Russian sipped his tea. Then he changed the subject. "We knew Mr. Butch was a colonel, Mr. Johnson, but he usually wore civilian clothes. So we always called him Mister." The old Russian smiled again. "But I can't remember why we called him 'Mr. Butch.' Could it have been a *nom de guerre,* a *Deckname?*

"No, it wasn't a cover name," Trosper said with a smile. "It's a nickname, it means a tough fellow—I think you'd say *dubok* in Russian."

The old Russian laughed. "That's good, very good. He really was a tough chap when it counted for something. But he was the only one who helped us in those first days after the war. Later, there were the refugee agencies, UNRRA and others. But in the early days, when we Russians needed help, only Mr. Butch ever did a thing for us."

Trosper wondered how far the old man's attention would wander.

The Russian got up, walked to the book case, and pulled a thick loose-leaf binder from a shelf. "The Colonel was right, Mr. Johnson. I think I know your Captain Grachev."

IT HAD GROWN dark. The old Russian snapped on a floor lamp in the corner, behind a table piled with Russian newspapers. The newsprint exuded a musty smell that seemed to fill the apartment.

"I know Captain Grachev very well," the Russian said. "I got here in 1945, a few weeks after the war. My nephew had been in Geneva since the old days, with the League of Nations. He had arranged something with the UNRRA and the displaced persons people. It was he who made it possible for me to get in." The old Russian appeared to wander again. "I wonder, Mr. Johnson, how many people today know what 'DP' means?"

"Not many, I'd guess," Trosper said. "Now the expression is 'refugee.' It's more accurate for what happens today. Displaced persons were a phenomenon of the last war, when the armies were sweeping through hundreds of miles of territory."

"I don't know how the Colonel arranged it, but Anatoli Feodorovich was brought in by the Swiss themselves. I think it might have been the intelligence people. They settled him in the country, in a little inn. That's what they did during the war. When the tourists stopped coming, the Swiss simply put refugees into the resorts and country hotels. It was a good system, good for the refugees, good for the innkeepers.

"Anatoli was forbidden to engage in any political activity of course, but he was allowed—after a few months—to keep in touch with the emigration. We do nothing here in Switzerland, even our papers are printed abroad."

"The man I'm looking for was in the Soviet army, not one of the prisoners of war," Trosper said.

"There were a few Soviet POWs who crossed the Swiss border just at the end of the war," the old Russian said. "But they were Ukrainians, mostly scum who had worked for the Germans in France. They were mercenaries, helping the SS fight the French *maquis.*" The old Russian shook his head sadly. "Dregs they were, just filth posing as Vlasov men. They helped to ruin the reputation of all the anti-Stalin fighters who rallied to Vlasov." The old Russian took a sip of his tea. "But Captain Grachev was different. He was a good soldier. He hated the system.

"So of course I got to know him. He was one of the very few military men to have come here as a refugee. All I know is that he was interrogated by the Swiss, then finally allowed to remain. He stayed in the small village. A few years ago he married the Swiss woman whose family owns the hotel where he lived when he first got here. Even before he won citizenship, he changed his name. Better than any of us he managed to slip into the local life. Maybe being in a village helped."

The old Russian got up and turned on a table lamp.

"Now, Mr. Johnson, some vodka and a little piece of herring? Just for the weather?"

Trosper nodded. "I'd like that."

The Russian lifted his vodka glass. "*Na zdorov'e.*" He took a piece of herring, and a swig of the chilled vodka.

"It took many years," the old Russian said, "but Anatoli Feodorovich finally got his citizenship. Now he's proprietor of a *Gasthaus* in Worb bei Bern. It's the only place in Switzerland you can get real *pel'meni,* the little Siberian meat dumplings."

The old Russian took another piece of herring and sip of vodka.

"They even gave him a good German name, Anton Bergmann."

The Russian walked to a desk, strewn with papers. "I'll give you a letter of introduction and I will write to tell him a friend of the Colonel's is coming." Lobanov laughed. "Then he will telephone me, just to be sure I wrote the letter. He's a very careful man—but perhaps that's how he survived. This will take two days. If you call in forty-eight hours, I'll be able to confirm that he's willing to see you."

TROSPER folded the letter carefully and slipped it into his pocket. The old Russian took Trosper's coat from the hall rack.

"I appreciate what you've done, Monsieur Lobanov. You've saved me an immense amount of work, work that might not have had any result. May I offer you something for your time and help?"

"No, Mr. Johnson, I couldn't accept money for helping a friend of the Colonel. This is the least I can do for him."

Trosper pulled the trench coat over his shoulders.

"There's no need for the Colonel to worry about me now. I translate, Mr. Johnson," the Russian said. "I translate, and I teach Russian."

"Maybe something for the organization? I would like to offer that." Trosper did not know which splinter of the emigration the old Russian belonged to, but he knew there would be one group that had his allegiance.

"That is something else," the old Russian said. "I will not refuse a contribution to the organization."

Trosper had several hundred-franc notes folded in his pocket. As he said good-bye and shook hands, he gave the old Russian five of the banknotes.

12 MUNICH

THE FORTY-EIGHT-HOUR recess mandated by the old Russian's tradecraft would leave time enough, Trosper decided, to go to Munich. He had not been in Germany since leaving the Firm, and he had reason to go.

He telephoned Vienna from Cornavin, the airport at Geneva. Mercer answered. He sounded grumpy.

"Is everything okay?" Trosper asked.

"Of course," Mercer said. "We've been taking turns soaking up culture. That, and keeping house." He was silent long enough for Trosper to imagine him running his hand across his bald head. It was a familiar gesture, one that always made Trosper wonder whether it was a habit left over from the days when Mercer had hair, or if he was merely checking to determine if, by some miracle, hair had again begun to grow on his bald pate.

Then Mercer said, "I'm getting cabin fever watching this stupid TV set. I'd forgot what nonstop talkers these junior Germans are— if they aren't shouting politics at one another, they're standing around singing about Vienna."

"You'll get used to it," Trosper said. "You might begin by calling them Austrians."

Mercer snorted. "Just for the record, and in case you neglect to ask, our friend hasn't called."

"There's no reason to expect to hear from him for another couple of weeks."

"I know," Mercer said. "The little bastard probably planned to keep us cooped up like this. How are things on your end?"

"Not bad. I've picked up some bits and pieces."

On the assumption that the Devil had invented the telephone to lure case men into indiscretions, Trosper tried to keep his phone calls as arid as smoke signals.

Mercer brightened. "That's good."

"It looks as if my trip is stalled for a couple of days," Trosper said. "Will you people be all right?"

"Go ahead, enjoy yourself," Mercer said. "There won't be anything going on here."

"I'll call from Munich, about noontime."

There was a long pause before Mercer said "Okay."

"I was going to ask about the weather," Trosper said.

"Don't," Mercer said, and hung up.

TROSPER telephoned Emily from his hotel, the Eden-Wolff. He had not called from Switzerland because he knew that once he was in Munich it would be more difficult for her to refuse to see him.

The spurt of surprise and excitement when she recognized his voice pleased Trosper. But then she seemed to catch herself and, as if repeating a ritual, asked in a flat voice how things were going, where he was. Only once before had she sounded more English, more Sloane Street, and quite as chilly.

"I'm here, in Munich, and I'd like to see you," he said.

They talked for a few minutes before she invited him to tea.

EMILY BEAUFORT'S apartment looked out over the *Englischer Garten,* a park near the center of Munich. In summer, the sidewalks were banked with flowers and wound through masses of carefully tended shrubbery. Now, in the raw Bavarian winter, the park was barren except for the evergreens and patches of snow along the icy pathways.

As he hurried across the park, Trosper looked up at the apartment building a few blocks away. He wondered whether she was interested enough to glance out the window and, if so, whether she could see him.

Emily Beaufort pronounced her name "Bufford" and after they had become lovers Trosper called her "Buffy."

IT WAS a shameless nostalgia, Trosper realized, to sit watching as Emily moved about the flat, nervously busy serving the tea and asking about friends. She wore a white blouse and a pleated gray flannel skirt. As she moved, the skirt swirled, accentuating her narrow hips and long, slim legs. Her auburn hair, worn longer than Trosper remembered, was swept back, away from her face, and tied with a black satin bow. It complemented the graceful line of her shoulders and gave her a bonny, old-fashioned look.

"You know," Emily said suddenly, "it's like a parade, the way you people traipse through Munich. One of the reasons I went back to London after Tim died was to get away from all of you." She crushed her cigarette in a porcelain ashtray. "I'd only been here, on

this job, a few weeks when people began dropping by. Every month
or so there's a call from someone who says he's passing through."
"People are fond of you."
"Maybe so, but I feel as if I'd been mentioned in some guidebook.
'Fading widow offers tea and sympathy for certified case men and
families.' "
"For Christ's sake, Emily . . ."
"Anyway, I'd rather like seeing some of the people if they could
keep from acting as though Tim's corpse were stretched out in the
middle of the room. No one says anything about it, no one looks at
it, but no one can keep his mind off it. If it wasn't for that, I probably
wouldn't mind an occasional visitor."

THEIR AFFAIR had begun in Paris, almost casually. Emily's job
with an English film company was winding down, the rough cut
nearly finished. Trosper, on a temporary assignment, was maneuvering to recruit a sullen Polish intelligence man.

Spring was early that year, so beautiful that Emily called it a
cliché. "It's too pat to play—the weather, this perfect city, and our
carrying on." But it had played so well that Trosper remembered it
as the happiest time of his life.

In October, Odlum passed through Paris, en route from Berlin
and Vienna. Trosper briefed him on the moody, apprehensive Pole.
The Controller listened, asked a few questions and then abruptly
ordered Trosper to Vienna. At first Trosper wondered if word of his
affair had reached Odlum, and if the Controller had found an excuse
to interfere.

Trosper objected and said this was not the time to leave the Pole.
"There's something in the wind," Odlum said. "In East Germany, in Hungary, maybe even in Czechoslovakia. I don't know
what it is, but there's something, some kind of pressure building. All
I can do right now is reinforce the Berlin and Vienna offices. Turn
the Pole over to someone, or put him on ice for a few weeks. I don't
care how you handle it, but I want you in Vienna in three days."

"I should have another two or three weeks with him," Trosper
said quietly.

"This is a bad patch, Alan. There's also something on the boil about Suez—the Israelis, the British may be making a move. I don't know what it is, nor why everything has to happen at once." There was no use arguing. "Okay, I'll be in Vienna on Monday."

TROSPER had been sent to Paris as a consultant, ostensibly advising American clients on financial and political developments related to their business interests. It was a temporary cover, hastily stitched together, and intended only to serve the few days the Firm thought it would take to make the recruitment. Then he met Emily and was glad the Pole had proved balky and that the case had dragged on.

The tall English girl had been alone, standing in front of a small Paul Guigou, in the Jeu de Paume. "You know," Trosper said, "Guigou was thirty-seven when he died. He'd only been painting for twelve years." This was as much as Trosper could remember of what Mercer had told him about the obscure Provençal painter, but it was enough for his purposes. They chatted, and he invited her to lunch.

Once recruited, the skittish Pole clung to Trosper, and it was clear it would be weeks before he could be turned over to one of the case men stationed in Paris. Her job finished, Emily lingered on in Paris.

Thin as his cover was, it had one virtue. It was dull. Trosper avoided any masquerade with a touch of glamour or intrigue, and refused to wrap himself, even notionally, in any cloak involving the arts, high finance, journalism, even the wine trade. The best cover was something so boring, so profoundly boring that not even the most curious stranger would trouble to press for details. He envied morticians; no one ever questioned an undertaker.

Emily might have considered Trosper an unlikely business type, but he was the only consultant she had ever met and she thought little about it until in October he told her he was leaving Paris the following day and could not even be sure when he would return, or what his address would be. It was her first serious affair, Trosper was the first American she had known. She did not understand what had happened, and she was hurt.

If he had returned to Paris in a few days, he could have explained.

But on October twenty-third, enraged Hungarians knotted ropes around the sixty-foot statue of Stalin and toppled it. Only the great boots remained intact. Stalin Square became Bootmaker Place. Next morning, when the Hungarian army refused to fire on the demonstrators, the Hungarian Revolution began.

That Tuesday, the revolution three days old, Trosper folded a hundred Swiss francs into the passport he handed to the jumpy Hungarian border guard. The customs gate swung open and Trosper's Austrian-plated car was waved into Hungary.

In Budapest he organized ratlines—courier and escape routes—and recruited couriers to slip across the Austrian border with bundles of files from the looted intelligence headquarters and secret police buildings. In November, when the Soviet army rallied to smash the revolution, and the security police began mopping up the survivors from the provisional government, he used the same courier routes for the dozens of resistance fighters desperate to escape. Two wounded Hungarian militiamen vouched for by Butch Brattle were also passed along the underground route.

IT WAS three weeks before he was back in Vienna and could telephone Emily in Paris. There was no answer, and he guessed she had returned to London.

Trosper left Vienna that night, escorting Lieutenant General Laszlo Horvath to Washington. After consultations, and a round of conferences, he and the General left Washington to canvass the Hungarian officials still abroad.

From Brazil to Tokyo, Melbourne, Ankara, Rome, Bonn, Brussels, and Paris, General Horvath approached his former Hungarian colleagues and subordinates.

It was a good hunt, perhaps one of the most successful blitz attacks in intelligence history. The recruitments the general and Trosper made and the defections they engineered destroyed the remnants of the Hungarian intelligence service abroad and crippled the Hungarian diplomatic service. In a note congratulating the Firm on the operations, the Director of Central Intelligence speculated that it might be a decade before Hungary had effective intelligence representation anywhere in the West.

But it was too late for Emily. It was February before Trosper got back to Paris and could locate her in London. It was kind of him to call after such a long time, she said. But there was really no point in his coming to London. And Emily would not come to Paris. No, he needn't bother to explain.

The chaste fury of her response crushed Trosper. Like an actor offstage, he found himself reaching for bits of cover to disguise what he suspected might be his own empty center. He wished he could respond to Emily without excuses, without faking, but he knew he could not. He muttered a final apology and put down the telephone.

In the following days Trosper thought of things he might have said, honest, fitting reactions to Emily's choked outburst. By then it was too late. Pride interfered. If Emily didn't want an explanation, there would be none. Besides, there was work to be done, there was always a rush of work.

It was Mercer who told Trosper that Tim Gidding was getting married. "A real smasher," he said, lapsing into dialect, "that young English girl in Paris, the film editor—she works for Gaumont or some Limey film outfit." He caught Trosper's reaction. "Did you know her . . . Emily Beaufort?"

"I think I introduced them . . . in Paris a couple of years ago," he said. "I was cooling my heels on that Polish case. The office had spotted Tim, and asked me to look him over before they approached him. She had no idea what I was doing. The first time I had dinner with Gidding, I took her along as a beard."

"A class act," Mercer sniffed.

Trosper knew that despite Mercer's years in the racket, his old-fashioned, Victorian sense of propriety invariably rebelled against involving unsuspecting outsiders in operations. He had never even approved the practice of using outsiders to provide protective coloration in a social situation.

EMILY BEAUFORT had been married to Timothy Gidding for two years when he was fired from the Firm. They stayed in Paris, at Tim's flat on the Quai Voltaire. Tim went back to writing and, as

Mercer reported, full-time drinking. It was not a good match and by the time Tim stumbled out of a cafe and into a speeding truck, it was clear that the booze had won. After Tim's death, Emily returned to England. When Amanda was born, Emily began work again. Now she had taken an assignment in Munich, at the Bavarian film studios in Rosenheim.

SHE TURNED and walked to the window. "It's going to snow," she said absently, and crossed the room to turn on the track lights suspended along the wall.

"It was fun with Tim," she said abruptly, "the first two years while he was working and before he began to drink so much. I didn't realize it at the time, but it was exciting being around all of you, everyone so damned sure of himself. Like a good club, and the hell with people who didn't belong."

"Women never understand," Trosper said, "but there's a bonding that comes with shared experience. Hostages in a bank robbery have only one thing in common, but you read about them having reunions. Men who've been together in combat have a special relationship, something they never have with anyone else. The racket's like that. It's not so dangerous, but at times there's tremendous pressure. When you've shared it with someone a few times, it makes you close. I feel sorry for people who've never known it. It's like never having been in love."

"Tim said *you* got him in, and *you* put him out," she said. "Why did you take him in the first place if he was wrong? He was a good writer. If he'd stuck to it, he might have been very good."

He had forgot that Emily's conversation came in what she called "jump cuts."

"He was a natural, that's why," Trosper said. "He had everything, an easy way with people, no side at all, good Russian, fluent French. Beyond that he had an architect's eye for detail and a poet's imagination."

He hadn't come to talk about Tim, but he couldn't stop. "Tim had something else, maybe the best quality of all, common sense. The racket seems to nourish people who feed on fantasy and illusion.

But Tim never bought any of that metaphysical crap. He never saw himself as 'a lonely crusader, wrestling with the anti-Christ.' He was in the racket. He ran spies."

She thrust her hands into the deep pockets of her skirt. "It's so damned sad, the way it all turned out. Tim lost the only two things he really wanted—to work with you people and to have a child. I suppose he wanted a son, but he would have loved Amanda anyway."

She began to clear away the tea things. "Another cup?"

Trosper shook his head.

She walked across the room to a small bar in the corner.

"A drink?"

He shook his head.

"Before you got here," she said. "I'd made up my mind, I wasn't going to mention Tim at all. Then, the moment you came in, it all came back. . . . What Tim went through when he was sacked, his dying before he ever saw Amanda." She fished a handkerchief from her pocket and dabbed her eyes. "So much for British phlegm." She turned and walked back to the window. "Tim never mentioned it, but I think he guessed we had been lovers."

Trosper had hated unraveling the skein of circumstance that destroyed Tim Gidding. And he hated the drunken Russian with only his name to peddle who had started it all.

"Let's go out for dinner, a good dinner," he said.

THEY WALKED to Boettner, a small, sparkling restaurant near Emily's apartment. Trosper ordered a Tip Pepe for Emily and a martini for himself.

Emily reached across the table and touched Trosper's hand. "You know," she said, "it was nice of you to come here and to take me out to dinner."

Trosper smiled and cupped her hand in his. "It's a been a long time, I didn't know how you'd feel about seeing me again."

"You should have told me about your precious racket," she said. "If I'd known why you left like that and maybe just a little about your job, I wouldn't have been so hurt. At least I think I would have believed you and waited. When you made those stupid excuses, I was flattened. I didn't understand what happened and I couldn't handle it. I felt used and then jilted. That's why Tim, so different from you, appealed to me. You were my first real affair. Until Tim told me you were in the racket, and all that stuff about Hungary and the trip with the general, I really thought you'd used me for a jolly few weeks in Paris. I probably didn't know it then, but our little fling seemed to set me up for marriage."

"Emily, for God's sake it wasn't a little fling. We were in love and you know it. It was a marvelous six months."

Trosper wished he hadn't said six months. It reminded him of the all the TA's, the temporary assignments, he had been through. His life wasn't broken into chapters, it was more nearly paragraphs. A few anonymous weeks in Copenhagen, six months' liaison and research in London. Almost a year in Geneva, tied to the improbable schedule of a womanizing code clerk, and cultivating a Russian he finally decided was a lunatic. Brussels, Vienna, Mexico City, Seoul, and even New York. Along with the TA's there had been assignments—a long hitch in Rome, another in Berlin, three years in Vienna.

"You're right," she said. "It was a good time. Perhaps I used you, just for that."

"You didn't use me, I don't believe that."

"Do you know what I thought after Tim died? I thought that if you and I had stayed together, maybe married, that the same thing would have happened. That suddenly everything would have gone poof, just like it did with Tim."

"It makes no sense rolling around in the past like that."

"Who's living in the past? It's you who came to see me, it's you people who won't let go. Even after Tim died, when I went back to the UK there was a woman, Margaret something or other, who kept coming around to see me. I got the impression she was monitoring things. Then, after Amanda was born, she said there was a scholarship for her. Then checks started coming from some little bank in Atlanta. Why Atlanta, for God's sake?"

Trosper shrugged. "The bank belongs to Billy Forbes's family, he used to work for us. The scholarship comes from a fund we all contribute to. The racket's just like everything else—sometimes for no reason, people get chewed up. When that happens we try to take care of our own."

"Maybe, but that doesn't square things. It doesn't make up for my never knowing what really happened, why Tim thought you'd ruined him."

Trosper signaled the waiter for another martini. "It's not something for me to discuss, Buffy."

"It is, too—you're a card-carrying member, one of the fraternity. One of the old boys."

"What did Tim tell you?"

"All Tim ever said was that he had made a mistake, that it was his fault, that no one else was to blame. He said it was years ago. He never said you'd uncovered it, but I think that's what he thought."

Trosper knew that when Tim died, the file *Rabotnik//Timothy Gidding,* classified "Top Secret Ochre," would have been sealed and sent to the archive. With Tim Gidding dead, Moscow Center had probably tagged their records "Research Only" and consigned the file to Department Fifteen, the central records repository.

"Mercer was here a few months ago—he's one of my regular visitors—he said you and the great Duff Whyte were probably the only ones left who knew what happened. Unless you tell me, I'll never know."

"It's a stupid story," Trosper said, "not worth Tim's death. If he had wanted you to know, he'd have told you. It won't do any good, my talking about it."

They ordered clear soup, a rack of venison, and *spaetzli,* little egg dumplings. Emily had another sherry with the soup and Trosper ordered a Côtes du Rhône.

AFTER DINNER, when they stepped out into the swirling snow and Emily instinctively took his hand, Trosper knew they would go to bed. He had loved Emily as much as any woman he had ever known, but he had not planned this. He knew he wasn't good with women, and that no matter how thoughtful he tried to be, he always seemed somehow to hurt their feelings. He didn't want to wound Emily again.

SHE was a generous lover, passionate, and tender. He could make her laugh as they caressed each other and talked in the big bed.

"Do you know what Amanda calls this?"

"What Amanda calls what," he said, brushing her hand away.

"Making love, silly."

"Of course I don't."

"She calls it having a 'cozy.' It's the word they use for it at her school in England. Last month when she was here for holidays, she said it made her sad because I had no one to cozy with."

IN THE MORNING Emily went out to get fresh rolls for breakfast. Now she watched as he finished his coffee.

"I suppose you have to go now," she said.

"I must get to Zurich this afternoon."

Emily got up and walked to the window. With her back to Trosper she said, "I don't know what I was thinking of last night, throwing myself at you that way. I'm not like that at all. I'll blame it on being lonely—that's the usual reason, isn't it?"

"It wasn't my reason."

Emily came back to the table and sat down. "When Mercer was here, a few months ago, I asked about you. He said he hadn't seen you for two years, that you'd left the racket, and were in New York. He mentioned your girl."

Trosper blinked. "Mercer does like to keep up."

"I'm sorry," she said. "I didn't mean to sound bitchy."

"It's all right. I'm not even sure she likes me very much. She doesn't know a thing about the racket. Even though I'm on piece-work, she hates that, too. Maybe all of you resent things you can't share."

"There's one thing sure," she said. "Few of us like to share men."

"What about you," he said. 'It's been a long time since Tim's death. Aren't you involved, haven't you been seeing anyone?"

"I am . . . at least I was . . . of course I have been. It's just that nothing ever seems to be what I want. I took this job to be away long enough to break it up. I guess it worked, he doesn't even telephone anymore."

IT WAS time for Trosper to leave. "I'd like to meet Amanda," he said.

"I'll be going home in a few weeks. Come to London." She stretched her arms around his bulky trenchcoat and buried her face in his shoulder. "I don't know what happened to Tim," she said. "But if you were involved, it's all right. He trusted you, he said it was his own fault." She pressed her face against his and kissed him quickly.

Embarrassed, he pulled slightly away.

"I remember," she said suddenly. "I remember exactly. You always did that when you were standing and I kissed you. I never did get used to it." She laughed and pushed him through the door.

IT WAS only an hour's flight. The Alps were spectacular, like giant reefs thrust through the rolling gray clouds that churned beneath the plane.

Trosper ordered a double scotch. He had remembered something about the steel mills in Gary, Indiana. Tim Gidding had been a "cinder snapper," banking the furnaces so they would not overflow. "Not a classy summer job, like you guys teaching sailing," he had told Trosper, "but those crazy *muzhiks* liked me, and took the time to teach me Russian." But then, Trosper thought, everyone had liked Tim Gidding.

ZURICH AIRPORT is the most efficient in Europe. Trosper was through customs and had rented a car in less time that it would have taken to get his luggage at Kennedy.

13 SWITZERLAND

THE GASTHAUS ROESSLI is in Worb, a village eight kilometers from Bern. It is not far from Oberbipp, and quite close to Niederbipp. As far as Trosper could tell from the map, there was no 'Bipp,' only 'Overbipp' and 'Underbipp.'

TROSPER ordered half a carafe of Dole, game paté, and a small rack of hare. It was a heavy dinner, but no one cooked game better than the Swiss.

"WOULD you care for a dessert?" The waitress was young, about nineteen, Trosper guessed, and almost certainly from the village. Her English was lightly accented, but more than adequate for the restaurant. Swiss education was remarkable.

"No," Trosper said, "just coffee." The girl turned to go.

"If Herr Bergmann is free, would you ask if I may speak to him?"

The waitress flushed. "Is something wrong? The food, the service . . . ?"

"No, no, not at all. Everything is fine."

Relieved, the girl hurried across the room.

He was stocky, about five-ten. The traditional innkeeper's black suit added to the impression of bulk. His face was tanned, and the planes of his cheek bones gave it an open cast. His black hair was cut short, and shot through with gray.

"Mr. Johnson?"

"Yes," Trosper said, and eased his chair back from the table. "Herr Bergmann?"

"Yes."

The Russian's hand was as hard and smooth as polished oak.

"A digestif, Mr. Johnson? Kirsch, Pflumli, a cognac?"

"After that superb dinner," Trosper said, "a little scotch will suit me best."

The waitress brought the whiskey, a siphon, and a dish with ice cubes almost as small as dice. Bergmann poured two strong drinks, and offered Trosper the ice and siphon bottle.

"Lobanov telephoned," Bergmann said.

Trosper handed the old Russian's letter across the table. Bergmann plucked glasses from his pocket and scanned the single page.

"This is the first news I have had of the Colonel since 1945," he said. "I take it he's well?"

"He's back in Austria, retired, and he seems very well indeed," Trosper said. "I think he finds retirement better than he thought would be possible."

"I scarcely knew him," Bergmann said. "But he was very good to me." He glanced around the room as if taking inventory. "It's no exaggeration to say that he saved my life. I don't know what would have happened if he hadn't intervened. Did he tell you about it?"

"Not in detail, but he did explain how you got out of Austria."

"It worked very well for me. I only hope he didn't get in trouble."

"I think that's the sort of thing he could have handled," Trosper said.

The Russian laughed. "What is it that brings you to Switzerland?"

"It goes a long way back," Trosper said. "It's your memory I'm here for."

"All these years, and now that I'm a Swiss, someone finally comes with questions?" Bergmann leaned back in his chair, apparently studying Trosper. "But if you'd come earlier, before I had citizenship, I wouldn't have talked. So maybe this is the best time after all."

Trosper took a sip of his drink. It was strange to hear Swiss German with a Russian accent. "I'm trying to identify someone," he said. "A man who was on special service in Vienna when your troops took the city in 1945."

"I told the Colonel I was an administrative officer, an army paymaster," Bergman said. "Why would he think I'd know anything about what you call 'special service?' "

"The Colonel never believed your story," Trosper said. "But he figured that if he kept you in Austria long enough to find out what your job had been, that there could be trouble—from the Russians, or even from the Four Power military command in Vienna. You remember that the Western allies were under orders to turn all Russians back to the Soviet command?"

Bergmann looked around the wood-paneled dining room. It was after ten. Except for a Swiss couple, lingering over coffee, the room was empty. Bergmann pulled his chair closer to the table. Seconds passed. It was as if he was waiting for Trosper to speak. But Trosper remained silent. Then, hesitatingly, Bergmann began to speak.

"Of course he was right. Captain Anatoli Feodorovich Grachev was an NKVD man, a paymaster for the apparat." Bergmann sighed heavily. "It was a good job in those days. I got through all the war years without a scratch. I even learned a little about keeping accounts."

Bergmann shifted uneasily in his chair. "I told the Swiss what I knew. It wasn't much. All I ever dealt with were special funds and a few of the agents in the rear areas. After the war, when we got into Austria and settled down, it was different. The case officers were establishing agents for peacetime work. I handled most of the accounts. But there were no true names, everything was in pseudonyms. Even in 'forty-five, I doubt if I could have named five agents."

Trosper did not want the Russian to get into the habit of saying no. "Why did you decide to escape?" He disliked the word "defect" and avoided using it.

Bergmann pulled a handkerchief from his trouser pocket and dabbed at his nose. "That's a complicated story," he said. "Even now, I'm not sure that I know the answer." He turned to summon the waitress. "*Bitte,* Trudi, *Zigarren.*"

He turned back to Trosper. "There's never *one* reason why a man leaves. In my case, I'd seen enough of Austria to know that things were better there—even in the weeks right after the war—then they were ever likely to be at home. There was that, and my conviction that Stalin hadn't learned a thing from the war. I was sure he would go back to his old ways, to the same police system. I was part of it, but I hated it."

Bergmann examined the flat tray of cigars held by Trudi. "Try a *Punch,* they're my favorite." He handed Trosper one of the Havanas and a box of matches.

"I'm from Leningrad, I grew up there, a city boy. I never really knew my father, he died before I started school, before the war. My mother kept me alive. That was her whole life, keeping me alive and working. When I was called up, she stayed in Leningrad. In 1944, I was told she was officially 'missing.' Unofficially, I suppose that tired old lady starved to death during the siege."

There was a catch in the Russian's voice, and he blinked and turned away from Trosper. "It needn't have happened, none of it, not the famine, not the purges. If our 'little father,' that madman

Stalin, hadn't decided the General Staff were all traitors, there wouldn't even have been the early defeats by the Germans."

The Russian put his cigar aside, and drained his glass. "At least I wasn't wrong about Stalin." He poured two more drinks.

"What is it exactly that brings you to Worb, Mr. Johnson?"

"There's a Russian, now at least sixty, probably older, who was in Vienna through the war. He was documented as an Austrian. He may even have been one of the young officers General Abakumov sent to the university in Vienna under cover in the thirties."

Bergmann busied himself lighting his cigar.

"My guess," Trosper said, "is that if this man was in Vienna from, say from about 1937 to 1945, he would have stayed on for some weeks, maybe even months, after your troops occupied the city."

"Have you got a name, his rank, some kind of description?" The Russian spoke through a cloud of cigar smoke.

"The only name that might fit is Lopatin—possibly Mikhail Lopatin. But I have no patronymic."

"I've never heard of any Lopatin," Bergmann said.

"This man, whatever his name, probably came out of the war a hero, with excellent decorations."

"There's only one person I ever heard of who might fit that description," Bergmann said. He spoke slowly, as if he was withholding each word as long as possible. "He was in Vienna, living as an Austrian. He had been at the university, and he'd developed good military contacts with young, anti-Nazi Austrian officers. In the early days, I think his lines ran all the way to the Austrian General Staff."

"What was his name?"

"I never knew his real name. He was in Vienna when our troops took the city—he made contact a few days later. He was supposed to be in terrible shape, almost starving. For all I can remember, he may even have been wounded. Apparently he had been on the run from the Gestapo in the last few weeks of the Nazi occupation. I know that our people were anxious to do what they could for him. He was to have anything he wanted, food, money, liquor, medical service."

"Didn't you have his name, a pseudonym, or work name? How did you make payments to him or his sources?"

"Things were different right after the fighting. There was tremendous confusion, everything was in flux. We were paying our collaborators with captured money—stuff we had taken from Hungarian banks or had picked up in Austria. We even had some of your old bank notes, the big ones you haven't used since the thirties. But the accounting was almost nonexistent."

"You must have had to charge his funds to something?"

"Maybe there was an account. If so, I can't remember it. The general and one or two of the most senior colonels had their own private operations. Maybe this man was on one of those."

"But you must have heard a name? Someone must have referred to him by name?"

On the far side of the room, the young Swiss couple got up and were putting on their coats. Bergmann rose and walked across the restaurant. After helping the woman into her heavy black coat, he shook hands with them both, and held open the door leading from the dining room. It was a perfect imitation of a Swiss innkeeper.

He walked slowly back to Trosper. "You know, Mr. Johnson," he said, "those were bad times when I came over—'defected' as your people say. My comrades would have called it 'deserting.' It was terrible at first. I was drunk for weeks after I got here. And then I had a terrible depression, so bad I almost couldn't get out of bed. I couldn't remember things, even simple things. But even at the worst of it, I knew I had made the right decision. Maybe that was what saved me—that and the fact that someone was smart enough to put me in this village. If I had it to do again, I'd do it just as I did the last time. And I will never go back. My son is Swiss, my daughter is Swiss. The rest is all behind me."

Bergmann leaned back in his chair and blew a long puff of smoke toward the ceiling. Then he hunched forward, close to Trosper.

"Despite the act I put on about being Swiss, and no matter how hard I try to be Swiss, I know I'm still a Russian. I can't forget Russia. I can't even forget the war—there's not a day but what I think about my comrades who fought the damned Germans. I had it easy—I wasn't much more than an office worker in uniform. The real fighters froze, they were blown apart, starved to death in German camps. Then, after all the agony, the poor bastards, the survivors, went home thinking it would be better. But you know what happened—nothing had changed. Not a thing, nothing. I love my people, and I'll never do anything against them. They all deserve more than they will ever get."

Bergmann tapped the ash off his cigar, and finished his drink. He poured more whiskey into Trosper's glass. As he filled his own glass, he said, "Why is it that you're after this man, Mr. Johnson? What has he done?"

Trosper cleared his throat. "He knows something important. Maybe something very important. But I can't say until I talk with him. It might even be that he also wants to come over."

Bergmann seemed not to breathe at all. His eyes were fixed on the cigar. He had not removed the band.

Then he said, "We called him 'Schneider.' That's all I know about him."

"Bingo," Trosper muttered. "Bingo."

14   VIENNA

AFTER EMILY'S apartment and the Swiss hotels, the safe house air seemed stale, the apartment shabby and confining. Trosper was preoccupied and could scarcely keep his mind on the dispatch Mercer and Kyle had pecked out on the portable typewriter.

With an effort, he began again to check the details Kinzl had reported on the structure and staffing of the Second Chief Directorate in Moscow. It was no use, his attention wandered.

As far as Trosper had learned, espionage had produced few immutable rules—so few in fact that he thought he could write all the apothegms he had uncovered on a single five-by-eight card. One of these maxims postulated that in clandestine operations things can be done efficiently *or* secretly; that the greater the efficiency, the less secrecy. The art, of course, was to know when security was really at issue, when it wasn't, and when one could safely do things in a direct and uncomplicated way.

Before he left for Salzburg, Trosper had guessed that if he respected the rules and queried Bates before consulting Butch Brattle, Bates would waffle, and demand that Trosper prove why Brattle might know something, why he could be counted on for a straight answer, and why the Englishman might be expected to respect Trosper's confidence and not report it to his former colleagues in the British service. By acting directly, he had interviewed Brattle, Lobanov, and Grachev in less time than it would have taken to convince Bates that Brattle was worth consulting.

Trosper plowed through a few more paragraphs of the draft before his attention strayed again. There was one practice that defied the security-efficiency equation. The use of open sources—libraries, newspaper morgues, city directories, telephone books—was secure *and* efficient. It was even inexpensive.

Good spies are a precious commodity, too valuable to be used as anything but a last resort. For this reason Trosper never gave an information requirement to an agent until he was satisfied it could not be answered in the stacks of a public library.

Odlum had had the same idea, and often used a World War II incident to make his point. Early in the war, Bomber Command asked the intelligence services for the construction specifications of strategic factories in Nazi-occupied Europe. Once this information was in hand, the theory went, bombs and incendiary devices could be tailored to inflict the maximum punishment on specific targets.

About the time the agents in the field had deciphered their radioed instructions, an imaginative researcher remembered that the British had pioneered the insuring of property and shipping, and that for decades the headquarters of the largest re-insurance firms had been in London. Within hours she found that the architectural and construction details of most of the target buildings were on file within walking distance of her office.

Trosper nurtured a wry respect for agents who, usually without troubling to tell their case man, would begin—and sometimes complete—their mission in the stacks. No spy in history had ever been arrested in the reference room of his local library.

He initialed the dispatch and tossed it to Mercer. Turning to Kyle, he said, "It's time for some research."

TAKING a copy of *Die Presse* from the newspaper rack, Kyle made his way to one of the marble-topped tables near the front of the Cafe Landtman. The Staatsbibliotek could wait. There would be time for a quiet *Gabelfrühstück*, a second breakfast of coffee and a hard roll, one of the many congenial Viennese customs Kyle valued.

If he got to the library at ten, the pack of professional researchers who spent their days ferreting through the stacks would have drawn their material, and settled down at the long, polished wood tables. As soon as these favored regulars were taken care of, there would only be a short wait before a librarian was free to bring Kyle the bound copies of the newspapers he needed.

AS HE sipped the coffee, Kyle remembered the dinner he had with Trosper, the night before Trosper had returned to Washington for his reassignment interview with Bates. Late in the evening Trosper asked, "Are you going to stay in?" No, Kyle had responded, "It's not really my line."

"Then get out," Trosper said. "You've got a good enough file, you can always come back, even on piece work. If you stay too long you'll find it hard to shake our attitudes. You will find yourself seeing things our way, a little skewed."

"What I hate," Kyle said, "is trading on people's weakness, and the endless probing for hidden motives."

Trosper had smiled and said, "I've always thought that it's a mistake to try to exploit weakness—the trick is to recognize it, and then to use people for their strengths. That's something Moscow has never gotten straight."

THE HELL with it, Kyle thought. At least I can show him that I know a thing or two about research.

He had agreed with Trosper's hunch that some of the agents in Schneider's wartime net would have been drawn from the slim ranks of the Austrian Communist Party. But he was less convinced by Trosper's corollary—that, in the burst of pride that followed the victory over Hitler, the Party's rigid security code might have been set aside long enough to permit some public recognition of their underground heroes. Kyle knew that the Austrian Communist Party had played little role in the resistance as such. The underground apparat had functioned in support of the Red Army, transmitting military intelligence to the Soviet forces. Whatever their achievements might have been, it seemed unlikely to Kyle that any of these agents would have been surfaced and given public recognition. Even in the heat of victory, Stalin would have remembered that good spies would be as useful in peace as in war. Secret recognition was proba bly as much as the Party agents could hope for.

Even if Schneider and Lopatin were identical, there were no other leads. Even Kinzl was still an unknown. No matter how slim the odds, it would be worth a few hours checking the postwar newspapers. Besides, Kyle reminded himself, Trosper's ability to follow even the faintest spoor was positively eerie.

By mid-afternoon, Kyle was bushed. He had spent hours scanning the *Wiener Kurier*. Now, red-eyed, he was leafing through the brittle, graying pages of the *Österreichische Volksstimme,* the official newspaper of the Austrian Communist Party. It was boring work, and he could scarcely keep his attention on the pages crowded with stilted news stories applauding the heavy-handed Soviet occupation policies, and slanging the efforts of the Western Allies.

As he turned the page, Kyle's attention strayed from the propaganda-charged news to the sports coverage. He had lived in Austria long enough to have contracted the national passion for soccer, and he was amused to see how quickly, almost as the fighting died out, the teams were re-formed, and the leagues came back to life.

Because newsprint was scarce, the *Volksstimme*'s sports news was slight—in April 1945 there were only a few lines of soccer news in the eight-page paper. But by June, a scant two months after the liberation, there was more newsprint, the soccer coverage had doubled, and in the Friday edition, room had been found for a chess column. The board diagram was almost too small to decipher, but the musty annotation had achieved the requisite pedantry.

Kyle's eyes drifted from the blurred diagram to a small notice between the chess column and the few inches of classified advertisements.

Karlheinz Zeller,
Rechtsanwalt,
Karl Lueger Ring 22, Wien.

He snapped forward to read the notice again.

Except when opening a new office, or changing their address, Austrian lawyers do not advertise. Any lawyer who broke the custom, and who made the effort to advertise in the *Volksstimme* in 1945 was either a very proud Party member, or a come-lately opportunist scouting for Soviet support. If Zeller was a Party member, and a practicing lawyer in 1945, Kyle began to reason, he had probably taken his degree before the war—it being unlikely that any student could have escaped some form of military service between 1939 and 1945. This would mean that the lawyer Zeller would have been at least thirty years old in 1945 and that he had somehow survived the Austrian fascist police and the Gestapo.

The chance was remote, he knew, possibly one in ten thousand, but Zeller could have been a prewar Party man, perhaps even someone who had gone underground to escape persecution.

Quickly Kyle thumbed back through the pages to mid-May, a few weeks after the Red Army had punched across the Hungarian border and the broken Wehrmacht had stumbled back, away from Vienna. There, alongside the Friday chess column, was Zeller's discreet notice.

He turned to the 1946 file of the tabloid newspaper. There were more photographs now, and more pages. The chess column was there, and alongside, lawyer Zeller's announcement.

Then he began to check at random—1946, 1948, 1950, 1953. Each Friday, Zeller's notice continued to appear, his ideology apparently unmoved by the Soviet consolidation of power in Poland, the takeover of Czechoslovakia and the timely "suicide" of foreign minister

Masaryk, the Soviet refusals to agree with any of the Western allies' proposals for a peace treaty that would restore Austrian independence, and even the anti-Soviet outbursts in East Germany. Karlheinz Zeller had a strong stomach for power politics. Nothing seemed to shake his Party loyalty.

There was one last possibility. Kyle opened the file for 1956. Turning to October, he began to scan the first twisted stories of the Hungarian Revolution. On each Friday until mid-January, lawyer Zeller's notice continued to appear. Then, in January 1957, the notice vanished.

In November 1956, the spectacle of Soviet tanks in pitched battle with lightly armed Hungarian civilians in Budapest had riven the Western communist parties and shaken the faith of many Party zealots. In the Western world, hundreds of Communists broke with the Party. Not since 1939, when Stalin signed his pact with Hitler, had there been such turmoil.

Could the date be a coincidence? Had Zeller died, retired, or as Kyle began to hope, had his sympathy for the tens of thousands of refugees who swept across the Austrian border at last broken his loyalty to the Party and to Moscow?

Whatever the reason, the lawyer's notice had ceased to appear in the *Volksstimme* at the time rumors had begun to circulate that the leaders of the revolutionary Hungarian government had been executed without trial. It was Khrushchev's ambassador and future head of the KGB, Yuri Andropov, who lured the Hungarians to the negotiating table where they were seized by the Soviet secret police.

Kyle left the heavy volumes of bound newspapers on the table and walked quickly out of the reading room to the telephone booths at the end of the corridor. Karlheinz Zeller's telephone number was in the book, his address still at Karl Lueger Ring 22.

Perhaps Trosper's hunch had produced a lead. If so, Kyle would buy him lunch. Some boiled beef, a *Tafelspitz*, at Sacher's hotel would be appropriate.

"*JUST BECAUSE* he's all you came up with doesn't mean that Comrade Zeller knows a damned thing," Trosper said. Kyle's enthusiasm for this slight lead had irritated him. "It doesn't even mean that he'd be willing to talk to us."

"He's a lawyer, for Christ's sake," Kyle said. "Lawyers will talk to anyone."

"Sorry, Roger," Trosper apologized. "We're all getting a little cabin fever."

He knew Kyle was impatient and anxious to keep moving. But serious cases had a rhythm, a beat of their own. It did no good to force the tempo. "Forcing" was one of the cardinal sins. It meant crowding an agent, pushing him to try so hard to collect intelligence beyond his grasp that he risked attracting attention by breaking the normal pattern of his daily life. It also meant rushing things, developing an agent too quickly, demanding too frequent meetings.

"Just because we're holed up in this apartment, and Comrade Kinzl is all we've got to deal with doesn't mean that we can force this case," Trosper said. "If we were working out of an office, with in trays, secretaries, and a dozen different cases to worry about, you wouldn't be in such a rush. The fact we haven't got enough to keep us busy every day simply can't enter into it."

Trosper waited, expecting Mercer to remind him that he had questioned Brattle, a former British agent, and interviewed two Russians without having asked for head office permission, or even for a file search to see what the Firm might already know about any of them. But Mercer kept quiet.

When Duff Whyte was in Washington and monitoring the Firm's key operations, he would, it seemed at least twice a day, scribble "WTR?, paras 9, 16? PSM" on the routing slip attached to an important cable or dispatch. As soon as the message reached the desk man responsible for the operation, he would check the paragraphs Whyte had cited, brace himself, and call Whyte's secretary to say he had a "Please See Me," and was ready to explain "What's The Rush."

If Whyte was more agitated, he would scrawl "WTFR?" on the buck slip. When a young secretary asked for an explanation of the added consonant, Whyte thought for a moment and said, "Foolish —it means 'What's the foolish rush?' " She was not convinced.

"We've got to remember what we're doing," Trosper said. "We're trying to identify Kinzl, a walk-in who appears to have tapped something hot in Moscow. His story doesn't add up, but the material he's given is solid, inside stuff. Kinzl says he'll keep it coming, at least as long as we keep paying for it. He's told us what may be a cock and bull story about something called 'Phoenix' and that our man Galkin was yanked out of a maximum security cell and shot because he remembered someone having mentioned "Phoenix" to him.

"If Phoenix isn't something Moscow has dreamed up just for us, it could be important. Perhaps very important. But even if it is, our first job is to keep Kinzl coming back to us. If he gets frightened, if he thinks we're crowding him, or trying to make an end run, he could simply drop contact."

Kyle snorted. "And lose all the money we're prepared to pay him?"

"It wouldn't be the first time something like that happened."

Mercer interrupted, "You remember in Berlin, when . . ."

Ignoring Mercer, Trosper said, "While we sweat what we can out of Kinzl, we've got to work on identifying his Moscow source. I'm absolutely certain there's at least one person in on this with him."

"Why?" Mercer asked.

Trosper got up from the lounge chair and walked to the heavily curtained window overlooking the street. "He doesn't feel right—and that's not just because of that costume someone fitted him out with."

"I agree, Alan," Kyle said. "That's what I thought the first time I met him in the cafe."

"Until we've got some line on who's helping him, and have sorted out his motives, Bates can't even disseminate the reports we're sending back. He'll have to pass them around with a little note saying the material is from 'an untested source of unproved reliability.' That's like asking Bates to admit he doesn't know what he's doing."

"What about Lopatin," Kyle asked. "What can we possibly find out about someone who's in Moscow, and whom the Firm has no record of?"

Trosper shrugged off the question. "Before we do anything

more," he said, "Mercer will have to check with Hamel. Maybe the Vienna office has a trace on ex-Comrade Zeller. And if the office doesn't know anything, Hamel will have to send an 'Expedite' query to headquarters."

He turned to Mercer. "You'd better get moving. All things equal, I'd like to have some answers by tomorrow. Let's say right after breakfast."

"What's the rush, Alan," Kyle asked with a smirk. "What's the foolish rush?"

MERCER stuffed his coat into the closet beside the door. "We should have sent Kyle," he called to Trosper from the hall. "He's the one who comes back with the bacon."

Mercer came into the living room where Trosper and Kyle were finishing breakfast and tossed his briefcase onto the sofa. He poured himself a cup of coffee. "I crapped out completely," he said to Trosper. "Hamel and I checked every file in the office. There's not a thing on Zeller. And there's nothing in Washington either."

Trosper turned to Kyle. "You win. You'd better see how willing lawyer Zeller is to talk to an American historian about the Austrian resistance movement."

15 VIENNA

HIS FACE was broad and flat, as if molded in anticipation of a snub, Asian nose. But Karlheinz Zeller's hooked beak was alien to the flat Oriental cheekbones through which it thrust. Thick, round glasses bound in black plastic rims drooped across his face. His long hair was white, and brushed back without a part. At the sides, strands fell forward, masking his ears, and making his round face seem even broader.

"Mr. Connors," he said in English. "You are very prompt. Two o'clock precisely. Punctuality—*'die Höflichkeit der Könige,'*—the courtesy of kings, as we say." They shook hands. The lawyer's hand was thick, bulky as though he wore a fur-lined glove. He motioned his visitor to step into the apartment and snapped the heavy lock. Helping Kyle out of his coat, Zeller hung it on a rack beside the door.

Then, as if inviting Kyle to waltz, he bowed slightly, and said, "Let me lead." He walked ahead, taking small steps, his feet splayed outward, like a skier struggling up a snow-packed slope. He wore a double-breasted jacket of heavy black tweed, the only such cloth Kyle had ever seen. His shiny black trousers were gabardine or mohair, and reached only to the top of his black ankle-high shoes. The toe caps were high and rounded, like old-fashioned ski boots. A long, English schoolboy scarf was loosely wrapped around his neck.

They sat in straight chairs, on opposite sides of a long table in a room that had been Zeller's law library. The walls were lined with books, thick volumes in dark, uniform bindings. The old lawyer poured coffee into delicate white cups and opened a flat tin of miniature Dutch cigars.

"You said on the telephone that you are writing a book on the Austrian resistance to Nazi Germany, Mr. Connors?"

"There's almost nothing published in English," Kyle said, "I managed to get a small grant—a bourse—enough to let me do the research. I've pretty well covered a lot of it, but there doesn't seem to be anything at all, at least in open sources, on what the Austrian Communist Party and the Russians did here."

"But why me, Mr. Connors, what brings you to me?"

Kyle explained about the *Volksstimme,* and his guess that the Hungarian revolution in 1956 might explain the abrupt disappearance of *Rechtsanwalt* Zeller's notice in the Austrian Communist Party newspaper.

Zeller laughed. "A very shrewd guess, Mr. Connors. Out of the whole Party, only a few of us—all veterans—spoke up and quit. For twenty-four years, through Dollfuss, the *Heimwehr,* the Nazis, the Cold War, I was loyal to the Party. Then, after I watched a hundred and fifty thousand Hungarians give up everything they had to flee from Rakosi's Marxist paradise, none of the comrades even cared enough to ask why I couldn't put up with the hypocrisy any longer. No one even came around to say good-bye."

"You were in the Party during the Nazi period?"

The old lawyer nodded. "In February 1934, after Dollfuss shot up the Socialists in Vienna, he cracked down, and declared all political parties illegal. The Austrian Communist Party was quite insignificant. We were badly organized, and had few members. Those of us who stayed in Austria—some escaped to Czechoslovakia, others to Russia—simply dropped out. For a while there wasn't any Party, then slowly they started organizing again. When they told me I wasn't qualified for secret work—too conspicuous maybe—I was angry. But after I thought about it for a while, I decided they had done me a favor. I spent a year in England, learned a bit of your beautiful language and pretended to study law. Then I made a mistake, I came back. I missed my sweet Vienna."

The room was cold. The old lawyer hitched his scarf tighter around his neck. "Have you tried to contact the Party here?"

Kyle shook his head. "No," he said. "There didn't seem much chance they would help an American writing about Communist activity, even forty years back. I take it for granted that they'll think I'm a CIA snoop."

"Are you, Mr. Connors? Are you just that?"

"No, I'm not, Herr Zeller, but in truth I don't know how I can convince you or anyone else that I'm not."

They talked about the Austrian resistance, the national committee, the POEN, the o-5 military group in touch with Allen Dulles in Switzerland, Fritz and Otto Molden, the Messner Circle, Lieutenant Brattle, the *Weisse Kreis, Rot Weiss Rot,* and the French and OSS paramilitary groups in the South Tyrol. Having established his credentials, Kyle risked a direct question, "Where were you during all this?"

The old lawyer plucked another cigar from the tin.

"Not among the heroes, not like Karl Kramer and Fischer-Ledenice, Mr. Connor, I can promise you that. Not that there were so many—it's sad to admit it, but almost until the end, Austria was

Nazi." The lawyer leaned back in his chair, plucked a small box of wax matches from his pocket, and lit the cigar.

"It's a long story, and I'm sure you know it, but Austria never recovered from the 1918 debacle, the loss of the empire, and the monarchy. Then came the years of bickering between the parties and the politicians, the one less competent than the next. I think we just gave up hope for the future, any future. It's no wonder that Hitler held such magic for Austria."

Zeller's eyes seemed to swim behind the thick glasses.

"Hitler offered hope, and easy solutions. He filled the emptiness left by our own politicians. And, even better, he knew exactly what most Austrians wanted. He played the right tune every time. So Austria welcomed him, fought for him, and never gave a thought to what he was, to what he was doing. Anti Semitism wasn't born here, Mr. Connors, but at times we Austrians have nourished it.

"Hitler put an end to all the puerile bickering, except of course among the émigrés, and in the *Widerstand,* the resistance. The antagonisms between the factions blocked the support the resistance should have had.

"We're not a brave people, Mr. Connors. We're good enough soldiers—we even fought well in Russia—but to work secretly, to work against real authority, that's not our nature."

Zeller went to the kitchen and brought more coffee.

"Officially, I'm a *Mischling,* a 'mongrel,' as Hitler called us, and I still have a Gestapo document to prove it. My mother was Japanese, my father Austrian."

Zeller explained that he took his law degree in 1933, the year Hitler came to power in Germany. "A few years later, I would not have gotten it. We mongrels were not allowed higher education."

"In 1939, when the war began, what did the Communist Party do?" Kyle asked.

"We had been decimated. Even before the *Anschluss,* Dollfuss cut us down. There was clandestine Socialist activity, but nothing on the Communist side until Hitler attacked the Soviet Union and the 'imperialist war' became the 'Great Patriotic War.' Then the Communists began again. Of course it was too late."

"Wasn't there any clandestine Soviet organization, any espionage net in Austria before the war?" Kyle asked.

"There were spies, some at the university, others in the Army, I am sure of it. But I knew nothing about it."

Despite his political record, the old lawyer explained, he was called for military service in 1942. "I was thirty-three, too old for regular duty, politically suspect, and a *Mischling* as well. So they assigned me to what the Wehrmacht called a *'Magen-Einheit,'* a 'stomach company.' We were a front-line service battalion, made up of limited service troops, men with ulcers, bad feet, half-blind. They also sent petty criminals and men with shaky political records to the 'stomach troop.' We were cannon fodder, completely expendable. We got every dirty or dangerous job in Russia. Sometime we even went ahead of the healthy troops to clear mines, to dig tank traps, that sort of thing. Because we were suspect, we were not even issued weapons."

Zeller served seven months until, in the fighting before Leningrad, both feet were frostbitten. "One of the ironies on the Eastern Front was that it was a court martial offence to freeze," Zeller said. "Too many soldiers deliberately let their feet get wet and freeze— better to lose a foot than to stay on the *Ostfront.*

"It was just chance that I survived. As long as I could walk, I didn't dare report my feet. Then, when I could scarcely move, the Russians gave us a thunderstorm of rocket fire. I was wounded in both legs—that's the only thing Comrade Stalin ever did for me. A few hours later, an Austrian doctor stuck on some patches and slipped me onto a hospital plane.

"I got back to Vienna in the summer of 1943. That's when I decided to fight. I'd have done anything to smash the SS animals. I had hated Hitler and fascism from the very first, but even I couldn't have imagined what I saw those swine doing in the Ukraine and in Russia."

In Vienna, Zeller made contact with a former comrade, and through him with the underground. "I already had this apartment and office, so I thought I could keep a K.W.—a *konspirative Wohnung,* a hideout—something not too strenuous. But it turned out they wanted more than just a housekeeper."

Zeller leaned back in his chair. "The toes on my right foot were gone, neither leg had healed, I was still on crutches." He laughed. "I must have been the slowest courier in the whole movement. But at least I had cover, no one suspected me."

The lawyer laughed again and slapped his leg. "You know," he said, "I still wear long stockings, opera length. It's embarrassing to buy them, but if your legs and feet are bad, it's the only thing. I learned that at the front—keep the upper body warm, wear light trousers, stout shoes, two pairs of cotton socks, and full length lisle stockings. Summer and winter, that's what I wear."

Kyle nodded.

That winter, Zeller made two courier trips to Munich. "I carried crystals for W/T sets, and some documents. Not bulky and easy to hide in my old Wehrmacht greatcoat."

"What about the Russians in Vienna," Kyle asked. "Did you know any of them?"

"As far as I knew, all the radio operators were Russian. Young fellows, tough enough to come in by parachute. Even then they took terrible losses. I remember one time, maybe January 1944, our funds were gone, there wasn't any money at all. Finally Moscow agreed to risk a resupply. When it got to Vienna, the money—American bank notes and Swiss francs—was bloodsoaked. The courier was all smashed up in the jump—it took two days to find the body. We couldn't get the blood off the money, and had the devil of a time getting the Hungarian black market people to give us any reichsmarks at all for it.

"Aside from handling the W/T sets, the radio men were almost useless. They couldn't speak any German, we had to hide them all the time. It wouldn't have been so bad if they could have stayed in one place, but because of the Gestapo radio direction finders, we had to move them every few days. In the winter of forty-four–forty-five, the Germans had roving patrols, checking papers of everyone on the street. Two W/T men were arrested just moving from one safe house to another. When that happened, there was the devil to pay. Even in the safe houses, the radio men would get crazy from the confinement and fear. There was at least one suicide."

"Aside from the radio operators, were there any other Russians here?"

Behind the thick lenses, Zeller's eyes seemed small, as if Kyle were looking at them through reversed binoculars.

"You know, Mr. Connors, although I left the Party, I am still loyal to my old comrades, loyal to what we went through together. Most of the comrades were good people—idealists fighting for something they believed in, something better than Hitler's filth, better than the shabby politics of the old Austria. Aside from the Party, there didn't seem anywhere else for us leftists to turn. Stalin was as big a monster as Hitler, but he put a better face on things. That's one reason I hate him so. He squandered the idealism of some of the best people of my time."

The old lawyer hesitated, apparently savoring the memory of the struggle against Hitler. "I suppose it always happens, but the best men seem to go first. It was even true in Russia, in my company of cripples. The ones who had some political judgement, who might have helped to rebuild things, they always fell. Here, in Austria, most of those who should have lived, who were bravest, were lost."

"Was that true of the Russians here?" Kyle asked. "Did they take casualities?"

"I only knew two Russians. They were, as our British friends say, 'a mixed bag.' The one real agent was an expert. He seemed as Austrian as I am, maybe more so—at least he wasn't half Oriental," Zeller said.

"Tell me about him."

"I don't know all that much," Zeller said. "I know he was in Vienna before the war. He had some story about being from Poland, Silesia, or something like that—probably to cover his accent. Though by the time I knew him, there wasn't any accent at all. He went to the university here, then when the war began, he just dropped out of sight."

"Did he survive, was he one of the ones who made it?"

"He was the exception to my rule. He was dreadfully sick at the end, stomach trouble, ulcers, maybe tuberculosis. I doubt if he weighed more than sixty kilos. He could scarcely eat, and of course there was almost no medicine by then. Late in the game, when the Gestapo were hot after him, he kept on the move, a different spot every few days. He was here in this apartment four or five days. This was in March 1945, just at the end of things. The Gestapo had gone mad, they were hanging deserters from lamp posts—I've got pictures of the corpses hanging at the Waehringer Guertel. They were arresting people on the street for no reason, shipping them off to Germany."

"What was his name?"

Zeller took a deep breath. Kyle guessed the old lawyer was remembering the promises he had made forty years ago, and the oath he had sworn never to break security. "The war's been over more than thirty years, Herr Zeller," Kyle said softly.

The old lawyer shook his head. "He was the best of the lot, Mr. Connors. A real secret agent, a man who sacrificed everything to his task. When he was here in these rooms, he was exhausted, completely spent. I tried to make him stay, at least until he could get back some strength. I told him the war was almost over, that there was nothing more that could be done here. He wouldn't listen. He asked me if I knew how many people were dying every hour. Then he said that if he could shorten the war by seconds, perhaps even fifteen minutes, then all of the sacrifices, all of the losses in the local apparat would have been redeemed."

"What name did he use, Herr Zeller?"

The old lawyer turned away from Kyle to stare at a broken leather couch beneath the book-lined wall at the back of the office. Kyle wondered if this was where the agent had slept.

"Schneider . . . that was all I ever called him, all I ever heard anyone else call him." The lawyer's voice had dropped to a whisper. "But I doubt very much that this was the name on his papers—if, at the end, he even had any papers."

The room was quiet. There was no noise from the street. Kyle could hear a clock ticking. He counted twenty before he broke the silence with another question.

"What about the others, Herr Zeller, you said you knew another Russian?"

The lawyer turned to face Kyle again. He leaned forward, peering through his thick glasses, striving to bring Kyle into better focus. Then he shrugged his shoulders, as if shaking off the memory of Schneider. "Yes, there was one young fellow, he was sent from Moscow, dropped by parachute into the Burgenland."

For the first time Zeller smiled. "I told you they were a mixed bag, Mr. Connors. We called this man *'Tänzer.'* If you can believe it, he was from the ballet, the Moscow ballet. A real ballet dancer."

The lawyer explained that Dancer had told him that when the war was young, and the Red Army still reeling back before the invading Nazis, the Soviet intelligence services began to train agents who would be left behind, to be overrun by the advancing Wehrmacht.

"Among the agents picked to stay in place were service personnel —waiters, barmen, cooks—inconspicuous people who could speak a little German and make themselves useful to the Nazi occupation forces. They even trained a few dancers who were to become cabaret entertainers," Zeller said.

"It was a good scheme," he continued, "the trouble was that by the time Moscow had selected the agents and trained them, the German advance had been halted. There was no longer any place where the agents would be overrun by the Germans. So they broke up the stay-behind unit. A few of the agents were infiltrated through the lines to work with partisan groups, some were dispatched by parachute to work behind the German lines in Russia. Dancer came here, to work with Schneider."

Dancer was fearless, Zeller explained, and had a flair for operations. Schneider liked him. But Dancer had only been given a few weeks of German language training before being dispatched to Austria. Schneider asked for another agent, someone who spoke fluent German.

"Have you heard of what we called the *Schutzbundkinder?*" Zeller asked.

Kyle nodded. "The children of the Socialists who escaped to the USSR after the *Heimwehr* put down the Socialist uprising here in 1934?"

"Yes," Zeller said. "There were a hundred or so Socialist families who escaped into Czechoslovakia after the uprising, when the armed

Socialists—the *Schutzbund*—fought Dollfuss's troops and the *Heimwehr.* Stalin agreed to let them come into Russia. He butchered some of them in the purges in the late thirties, but there were survivors. The children went to Russian schools, but the families still spoke German at home. I suppose the older children still remembered Austria. By 1941, when Hitler invaded the USSR, the older boys were young men, and like their fathers, perfect candidates for operational work in Austria. I suppose several were sent here during the war, but the only one I met was 'Walther.' That's the way I knew him, I never heard his last name."

Because Dancer spoke so little German, Zeller continued, Walther worked closely with him, first as an interpreter, and then as Dancer's German improved, as an assistant, handling sub-agents, meeting with Schneider whenever Dancer could not make the rendezvous.

"Dancer was handsome," Zeller said, "high forehead, large, deep-set eyes, and a curious, rather candid expression."

Zeller looked sharply at Kyle. "That expression is a great asset for any secret agent, Mr. Connors."

Kyle glanced down at his notebook and nodded.

"Walther was about the same age, maybe twenty, not nearly so good-looking," Zeller said. "But he was shrewd and in a short while knew his way around Vienna almost as well as I did. Dancer and Walther shared quarters somewhere—for security reasons we never knew where any of the Russians went to ground. I don't know how it started, perhaps it was because of Dancer's background, the ballet and everything, but the story was that these two—certainly among the bravest and most exposed members of the entire Vienna apparat, were . . ." Zeller paused. "Even with all our real problems toward the end, there was still time for gossip," he said. "Some of our people who saw them together were convinced they were . . . er, homophilic, Mr. Connors."

Kyle looked up from his notes, surprised by Zeller's use of the Victorian expression. "Homosexual?"

"It was wartime, Mr. Connors, many strange things happened. These were young men, under great pressure, with no social life at all. If the gossip was true, I can't hold anything against them.

Whatever their personal life was, they more than did their part. That's more than I can say for many of us."

They talked for another hour, until Kyle, noticing how tired the old lawyer seemed, snapped his notebook shut. "You've been an immense help, Herr Zeller."

"I'm an old man, and I've talked too much," the lawyer said. "But I like to speak English and some of these things needed saying."

Zeller reached across the table for another cigar. Abruptly, he shoved the tin aside. "My doctor says only five of these a day, Mr. Connors. You've already made me use up three fifths of my ration. What will I do tonight?"

IN THE HALL, Kyle pulled on his coat. As they shook hands, the old lawyer pulled Kyle closer and said, "I don't believe a word about your research project and the book. But it's a good *Deckung*—cover, as we used to say."

The old lawyer laughed as he unlocked the door. "Not to worry, Mr. Connors," he said. "Your secrets are safe with me—at least for thirty years."

16   VIENNA

"A SMALL BRANDY, cognac, please," Kinzl said. "Good cognac is something I miss in Moscow."

Masking a grin, Kyle moved to the sideboard to pour the cognac and a scotch and soda for Trosper.

THAT MORNING Trosper had glanced at one of Mercer's expense chits. " 'Safe house supplies, $52.' What the hell is this?"

"It's Martell's Cordon d'Or," Mercer said. "Probably the only bottle in Vienna." When he noticed that Kinzl drank brandy at the first meeting, Mercer had searched Vienna for the best cognac he could find.

"You're out of your wig."

Mercer ran his hand over his bald head and shrugged. "I've always proceeded on the assumption that the best available would have to suffice."

"If our friend asks for beer this time, you've bought yourself a fancy bottle of booze," Trosper said. "I can't justify his retainer—five thousand dollars an appearance—and you're topping him up with Cordon d'Or?"

Because most agent meetings are in safe houses—usually small, inexpensively furnished apartments, and often in shabby neighborhoods—experienced case men liked to lighten the atmosphere with expensive food and good liquor. If the agent was a valued source, such small luxuries were a token of appreciation. Mercenary agents were reminded that, however modest the environment, money was available. The buffets served other purposes, like giving the case men an opportunity to indulge their own expensive tastes.

KINZL SWIRLED the brandy in his glass. He had on the same blue shirt, narrow blue tie, and tweed jacket he had worn at the first meeting. "I am glad you found our financial arrangement satisfactory, Mr. Warner. The bank has confirmed your deposit. To tell the truth I was a little worried about your attitude."

Trosper nodded. He did not want to begin the meeting haggling about money. "How much time do we have tonight?" he asked.

"I should leave by ten, maybe a few minutes later."

Trosper picked up a clipboard and yellow pad.

"Perhaps the best thing is for me to talk first," Kinzl said. "Later we can deal with the questions your firm wants answered."

Trosper nodded. Kyle eased himself into a chair at the end of the coffee table separating Trosper and the agent.

"I have some details on our friend Galkin, perhaps even the answer to the puzzle."

Kinzl took a sip of brandy. He looked expectantly at Trosper. Trosper said nothing.

"It is sad, don't you agree," Kinzl said reflectively, "to go to your death not even knowing why?"

Trosper nodded impatiently. "What was it Galkin didn't know?"

"It's about 'Phoenix.' He didn't know what Phoenix meant, he had no idea what was involved."

"We haven't much time," Trosper said. "Can't you just give me the story straight out?"

"Have you heard of Boris Kudrov?"

Trosper shook his head. "No, tell me about him."

For a moment Kinzl seemed flustered. Then, with a slight smile, he inclined his head in a suggestion of a bow and said softly, "Of course." He was ruffled. For the first time his pose as sophisticated operative had been challenged.

It was not for Trosper to tell Kinzl he remembered a year-old news story, that a second secretary of the Soviet Embassy in Paris had defected and asked for asylum in the United States. There were probably ten thousand Boris Kudrovs in the Soviet Union—it was Kinzl's responsibility to identify Kudrov and to tell Trosper what he knew about him. And so Trosper reminded Kinzl that he was the agent, and Trosper the case man. It was his first step in taking control of the agent.

"Boris Kudrov—I don't have his patronymic—First Chief Directorate, KGB, was assigned to our embassy in Paris. It was his second field assignment. Before that, he'd been in Geneva, some job or other with our delegation at the UN. In Paris he was under diplomatic cover, maybe second secretary. Kudrov is one of the new young men. He'd been given a good education, was bright enough to wear Western clothes, could probably have passed as a European diplomat. In the service, he had a good reputation.

"A year, maybe fourteen months ago, he defected to one of your people, a man he'd supposedly been cultivating in Paris. There were news stories on the incident. Everyone assumed that Kudrov was in CIA hands, but it was the Firm's case from the outset."

"What had Kudrov been working on in Paris?"

"All I know is he was assigned to the Domestic Line, probably working with agents on active measures, influencing French political matters, reporting on party politics in France, that sort of thing."

"How does Galkin come into this?" Trosper asked.

"It was just an accident, Mr. Warner. A simple matter of bad luck." Kinzl glanced at Kyle and took a sip of cognac. "Someone told him something about 'Phoenix.'

"Kudrov was dispatched from Moscow. He was sent to Paris to make contact with your people and then to defect. And that's what he did, a few months after his arrival in Paris."

"What about Galkin?" Trosper asked. He tried to control the tone of his voice. "From what you say, Galkin was executed in Moscow some time before Kudrov defected."

"Exactly—Galkin was executed after he gave the interrogators the impression he knew something about 'Phoenix.' 'Plan Phoenix' was supposed to start a few weeks after Kudrov arrived in Geneva, almost three years ago. He was to defect in Geneva. But just at that moment, we uncovered Galkin. Then, when he mentioned 'Phoenix' while writing his confession, we had no choice but to postpone the operation until we knew for sure exactly what Galkin knew about it, and what he might have passed along to you."

Trosper put his clipboard beside the chair. "There have been other false defectors dispatched from the Soviet Union," he said. "I know you consider these cases sensitive, and I suppose most of them are. What's so special about Kudrov? If he was sent by Moscow Center to defect, what was his goal? What was he to deceive us about?"

"Kudrov was the opening gambit in 'Phoenix,' a new strategic deception plan, maybe the most important since the German invasion," Kinzl said. "That's why there was such concern about Galkin. If he knew anything at all about 'Phoenix,' and had reported it to you, the operation would have to be canceled, all those months of preparation would have been squandered. Even worse, your analysts could probably have learned what was behind the deception, why the Secretariat wanted to deceive you."

Trosper leaned forward in his chair. "This is an interesting story. But before I can put any credence in it, I'll have to know how you learned about it. You say the operation is so closely held that Galkin was killed because someone *thought* he *might* know something about it? And that your service was afraid that even in a high security jail, he might have talked about it with another prisoner or even a guard? But then *you* claim to know all about it. Until I know who you are, until I know something about your access to information, your own sources, the story's not worth a *Groschen*—as we say, a plugged nickel."

Kinzl put his empty glass on the coffee table, and as if washing, rubbed his hands together. His fingers were long and slim, the nails well cared for.

"You remember, Mr. Warner, when we first talked, I told you I would not identify myself, would not inform on anyone whose name was not essential to your records. This is our second meeting. You can scarcely expect me to have changed after only a few hours with you?"

"I'm not asking you to change," Trosper said. "I'm telling you that your information is useless until I know who you are, and who your sources are. You seem to be a professional, surely you understand my position."

Without touching the arm of the heavy overstuffed sofa, Kinzl rose slowly to his feet. He moved gracefully, his back straight but not rigid, his stomach drawn in, his shoulders square. It was the movement of an actor, or, as Trosper now realized, of a dancer.

"We have a problem, Mr. Warner," Kinzl said. "A real problem. There are precise limits to what I am prepared to disclose. I've already given you priceless information—enough to keep your service from falling more deeply into the deception we are creating for you, enough for you to take action on."

Kyle got quickly to his feet and motioned toward the buffet. "Let's have a little something to eat," he said and steered Kinzl toward the sideboard. Kyle's slim figure seemed to tower over the agent.

Trosper heaved himself up from the deep chair. The little spy made him feel heavy and clumsy. He was glad that Kinzl's attention was on the food spread out on the sideboard.

"I'll have some cheese," Kinzl said. "It looks like camembert, and that's something else I miss at home. Russian cheese is a joke. Hundreds of cheeses in Europe, and even in our special commissary there is never anything but some imitation Emmenthal, probably concocted in East Germany. Our allies make good machinery, but their cheese is like *ersatz* rubber."

Kinzl cut a wedge of cheese, took some pumpernickel, and walked slowly back to the sofa. Trosper brushed some paper-thin slices of smoked salmon onto a plate and went back to his chair.

"Some wine," Kyle asked, "or a little more brandy?"

"Cognac, please," Kinzl said. "I think it's the best I've ever had. Quite delicious."

Kyle poured the brandy and mixed a scotch and soda for Trosper.

Neither Trosper nor the agent was ready to resume the argument about sources. They ate in silence until Kyle asked Trosper if he wanted the questionnaire for Kinzl. Trosper welcomed the initiative.

"Should we go over some of the material I have from home?" Trosper asked. "My office has sent a ream of specific questions for you." It was a bluff. He wanted Kinzl to offer more detail on Kudrov.

"Yes, of course . . . but then . . ." Kinzl paused, ". . . we can handle those at any time. My information on 'Phoenix' is important, very important."

"I dare say." Trosper shrugged. "But I need names, dates, even the objectives of your deception will help—something tangible to help prove your point about the defector Kudrov."

Kinzl pushed his plate aside. "Now, Mr. Warner, I *am* embarrassed. I will not give you the names of my sources, and as of now, I cannot give you a single operational detail. I know nothing about 'Phoenix' except what I have told you—Kudrov is a false defector, and a key person in a deception operation known as 'Phoenix.' The best I can do is to promise that I will try to learn more. Even so, I am not sure that I will be able to learn anything more. It is an extremely sensitive matter, and any mistake on my part will be fatal."

Trosper dropped his clipboard beside the chair and took a deep swallow of his drink. If Kinzl was faking, it was an effective routine. As irritating as the spy's manner was, his admitting he knew no more about 'Phoenix' was a good sign. Trosper could not recall any other agent as pretentious as Kinzl who would have admitted there was anything he could not uncover. A spy's promises are as plentiful as a suitor's. And worth a little less.

They talked for an hour before Kinzl pointed to his watch and said he must leave.

KYLE SNAPPED the lock on the safe apartment door and hung his coat on a rack in the hallway. He had taken Kinzl to the street. As he passed the bedroom where Mercer was monitoring the tape recorders, he knocked sharply on the locked door. "All clear, come on out."

In the living room, Trosper hunched over the coffee table, scribbling notes on a yellow pad.

"Not a bad night's work," Kyle said. "This will scramble the home folks' eggs a bit, maybe even spoil Bates's breakfast. Just imagine how our leader will feel when we tell him he's bought a pup, that Comrade Kudrov is a dog on a leash."

Trosper scrawled a few more words on the yellow pad. "You're crowding your fences, Roger. Who says anyone has bought Kudrov's story? All we know is that a fussy little fellow who says he's from Moscow, who says he's party to all the secrets in Dzerzhinsky Square, has told us he thinks Kudrov was dispatched from Moscow Center to deceive us. But all we've got is his word for it. If there's anything to his story, it may be that Bates has already uncovered it and is playing the deception back against Moscow."

Mercer was at the sideboard, eyeing the food. "And I, for one, don't even know our source's name—'Kinzl,' that's a phony if ever there was one." The earphones he had worn while monitoring the tape recorders had left a narrow red mark across the top of his head, as if a brain surgeon had marked the quadrant for an incision. "I'll give odds he's not even a Russian."

"He's answered every question we put to him, except about himself and his sources," Kyle said slowly. "He's not your everyday fabricator."

Trosper tossed his notes aside. "I'm not going to cable this," he said. "I want you to draft a complete report, every detail, just as close to a transcript as you can make it. There's no need for a lot of speculation about what it means. Have the report wrapped up in a couple of days. I'll let you know about transmitting it."

"Are you leaving us?" Mercer said. "Another bit of rest and recreation, in Munich maybe?"

There were times when Trosper had to remember that he liked Mercer. "No, damn it, I'm going back to talk with Bates. I'll leave in the morning if I can get a plane."

Mercer poured himself a heavy tot of cognac. "You know one of the sad things about good cognac? Once the bottle is open, and air gets to it, the brandy begins to fade. Cognac should always be drunk up promptly."

17   WASHINGTON, D.C.

"*THAT'S* an absolute crock," Bates said. "I can't believe you're serious, flying here from Vienna with a story as foolish as that."

The Controller sat rigid behind the sleek steel and walnut desk, his face flushed.

"I'm dead serious," Trosper said, "and I strongly recommend that you take this information very seriously indeed." He had barely outlined Kinzl's report on Boris Kudrov when Bates exploded.

"There are a few things you'd better get straight, and right now, Alan," Bates said. "Kudrov is the most important opportunity the Firm has had in years. His reports have gone straight to the White House. There aren't ten people in this town who even know what we're planning with Kudrov. That's how hot a case we've got."

"What you've got," Trosper said, "is an *alleged* defector. If what Kinzl says is true, it's Moscow that's got the case."

Bates shot up from his chair and began to pace in front of the window behind his desk. "What you say isn't true, it's a shot of poison, straight from Moscow—just a crude attempt to discredit a man they know can hurt them. It's one of the oldest tricks in their repertoire—so old, I'm surprised you'd fall for it. There's never been a defector they haven't tried to discredit—they've charged them with everything from murder and grand larceny to child molesting." The Controller walked back to his desk. "You know, Alan, Kudrov himself told us that someone would be sent out to discredit him. I'm just surprised that it took Moscow so long to come up with a story as patently phony as this."

"We *all* know Moscow attacks its defectors," Trosper said. "But just because they tinkle on someone isn't proof he's bona fide."

"You've been away a long time, Alan, and there's been a lot of water over the dam since the old days," Bates said. "We've interrogated Kudrov for months and we've learned things we never even dreamed of. He's given us hundreds of pages of reports. Every word he's said has been checked, everything has been confirmed—dozens of his reports have gone to the President. But that's already history. Now we're organizing to move ahead, to hit Moscow where it hurts."

"What about CIA? What has the Director said about Kudrov's material and your plans?" Trosper asked.

Bates pulled his chair closer to the desk and leaned forward toward Trosper. "That's been a bit of a problem," he said slowly. "General Foster, the President's security man, has ordered us to hold this case very close. All I've been able to send the Director— and this for his eyes only—has been our summary reports. As you can imagine, his nose is completely out of joint. He's said that he won't certify Kudrov's bona fides until the agency analysts have studied all the interrogation reports."

Bates sniffed and shrugged his shoulders. "And there's a fat chance of that ever happening. The President and General Foster don't want the CIA's 'experts' picking nits in a case that's already proved itself. Maybe they're afraid the evaluators would be more interested in trying to prove that the agency is the only outfit that can handle a case as important as this than they might be in giving it an honest evaluation."

A light blinked on the elaborate telephone panel at the side of Bates's desk. He picked up the telephone, listened a moment and said, "Unless it's the general or his boss, please hold the calls." He dropped the receiver onto the cradle.

"It's not like the old days, Alan," he said. "Sometimes I wonder how Odlum, at his age, managed to keep it all hanging together. Most of the time I feel as if I'm piling up water. When the DCI called to complain about the Kudrov reports, it was the first time I ever heard him lose his temper. He actually asked who was running the Firm, me or General Foster. Then he read me a lecture about keeping the racket completely independent, keeping the operational decisions and the evaluation of our cases within the family."

As if he had forgotten Trosper's presence, Bates began absently to riffle through a sheaf of cables on his desk. Without looking up he said, "The Director even offered to come to the White House with me, and go to the mat with General Foster, to force him to get off my back."

"That's not such a bad offer," Trosper said.

"Maybe so, but I can't have him fighting my battles." Bates fished a crumpled handkerchief from his pocket and dabbed nervously at his nose. "Besides, he might not be much help. Foster has begun to refer to him as 'that overage preppy.' "

"It's too bad we weren't all lucky enough to have been born in a log cabin," Trosper said.

Bates laughed and picked up the cables and tossed them into the out tray at the corner of his desk. "I really shouldn't do this, but I'm going to," he said. "What I want you to do is talk with David Barlow. He's handled Kudrov from the outset. After he's briefed you, come on back here and we'll decide what to do with your man in Vienna."

THE office was on the top floor, at the end of a corridor. The door was marked "Restricted Entrance." Barlow was tall and thin, with thick black hair. His heavy handlebar moustache contrasted with his Ivy League clothes and languid, professorial manner.

Barlow told Trosper what he'd expected to hear about Kudrov, a lot of what he'd heard from other defectors. Life in the Soviet middle level was boring, frustrating—every initiative precluded. The hierarchy was mired face down in the outdated Marxist-Leninist theology. Old men, sick old men, clung to power as if it were an amulet against death.

Trosper listened, nodded, stiffled a yawn, and looked for escape toward the closed door of Barlow's office.

"Does the story sound familiar?" Barlow asked.

Trosper nodded.

"We'd been questioning Kudrov for almost three months," Barlow said, "and it had been easy going. He was arrogant, but cooperative enough. Most of what he said, at least as much as could be expected, checked out."

Trosper waited.

"The first trace of trouble came when Kudrov asked to see the President. I thought this was just an expression of anxiety, worry about what would happen to him when the interrogation was over. I tried to reassure him, but nothing worked. He was adamant—he had information for the President only. We talked for hours before, a step at a time, I managed to lower his demands from the President, to General Foster, to the Director, and then, finally, to Bates."

"And Bates saw him?"

"They were closeted for four hours," Barlow said. "Kudrov said he represented a group of middle-level Soviet officials—a mixture of military and intelligence men—officers who had either gone through the Military Diplomatic Academy or military colleges together, and who, in a sense, had made their careers in government side by side. According to Kudrov, their objective is to return the Soviet Union to what they say were 'the ideals of the social democrats and the men who had led the revolution against the czar.' "

"How are they going to make the change?"

"Kudrov said that at first they hoped the evolutionary process would make the coup unnecessary," Barlow said. "But after they saw one geriatric apparatchik after another take over the Kremlin, they became convinced they must move on their own."

"Why did it take Kudrov so long to admit he had been sent?" Trosper asked.

"He was supposed to satisfy himself that we were serious and competent. Only then was he to ask to see the President."

"Why did they pick Kudrov?" Trosper asked. "They could have found a higher-ranking man."

"Because of his intelligence background and fluent English," Barlow said. He stopped talking and fixed his eyes on the ceiling. "Does it sound familiar?"

"It sounds like that refrain from the 1920s," Trosper said. "It sounds like the famous Trust operation."

"This time it's called 'Iskra.' "

"Lenin's old newspaper? Lenin's old *Spark?* How nice to know it's still lighting the way."

"But the Trust was something different," Barlow said.

"Yes, of course," Trosper said. "They were presented as a bunch of enlightened monarchists, striving to bring Russia back from Godless Communism to some polished up version of the czar's empire. Sixty years ago that is what the British and the others wanted to hear." He laughed. "Now we are given Iskra, miracle workers who will lead the Soviet Union into the future, a new world without the GULAG, with high ideals and only a handful of missiles. Just the thing that every American president yearns to hear."

"Just the thing," Barlow said.

"Do you remember that Lenin said the key to deception is to tell people what they want to hear."

"I remember," Barlow said.

"Kudrov, is he supposed to be one of the idealists?"

"There is that side to him."

"It's bullshit, you know," Trosper said. "The Trust was bullshit and this is bullshit."

Barlow stopped talking and reached into his desk drawer. Pulling out a bowl of chocolate-covered peanuts, he offered the dish to Trosper. "I've stopped smoking," he said.

Trosper would rather have had coffee, but he took a few pieces of candy.

"Iskra's first step," Barlow said, "will be to retire the old men. Once Iskra has power, they will establish a federation of states, with competing political parties. Russia, the Ukraine, Turkestan, Belorussia, and most of the other ethnic and geographic entities, will elect governments which will function as states within the new Soviet Social Democratic Federation, itself governed by a new form of their old congress, the Duma."

"Rather like the American model?"

"It's not such a bad idea," Barlow said.

"A federation of democratic states," Trosper said. "After sixty odd years of Big Brother's iron fist?"

"It could be made to work."

"How many do you figure are in Iskra?"

"Kudrov has given us fourteen names. I would guess there are at least that many he hasn't named."

"Perhaps even more?"

"Perhaps."

"And all of them are keeping the secret," Trosper said. "No private ambitions, no jealousies?"

Barlow pushed the bowl of candy across the desk to Trosper. He shook his head.

"Bates has got the operation tagged for God's Eyes Only," Trosper said. "But in Moscow forty comrades are privy to the secret?"

"We've got to give them a chance."

"Is that all they want?"

"Iskra has pinpointed ten high-ranking generals and security officials as essential to their plot. Kudrov was sent to persuade us to give them breathing room. If we do that, Iskra is convinced it can win the support of its own defense establishment. The generals must be convinced that we will not strike at the moment the old men are nudged aside."

"Let me guess," Trosper said. "We're to initiate a real détente?"

"Something like that."

"Cut back on the military budget? Be a little more responsive to their trade initiatives? Ease the diplomatic pressure?"

"More or less."

"The Trust," Trosper said. "That oft-told tale. The same hook, a slightly different bait, and we're ready to swallow it again."

"I'd better let you read about the other proposal," Barlow said.

Trosper took a handful of candy and thanked Barlow for the briefing.

IN A SMALL room opening off Barlow's office, Trosper took the first dossier from the mound of files classified "Top Secret Enamel/6." "Enamel" was a new code word, established after Trosper had resigned, and was applied only to operations run from the Controller's office. No decisions could be taken on Enamel cases without Bates's express consent, and the Controller initialled all cables and dispatches to the field. Incoming messages were delivered unopened to Bates.

"Enamel/6" was Bates's code name for Kudrov. The files contained copies of all the Kudrov interrogations, and a detailed biography and psychological assessment of the defector. There was nothing about Iskra, and no one reading the dossiers would have known Kudrov had ever mentioned the Iskra group.

When Trosper returned the bulky files to Barlow, he was handed a thick, red bordered dossier classified "Top Secret Enamel/6 PLATINUM." In it was Kudrov's account of the Iskra group, and its scheme for the coup. In return for cash and commo gear, Iskra also offered to pass intelligence collected from Iskra adherents to the Firm. The planning was projected over a three-year period.

"WELL, ALAN, what do you think? It's impressive, don't you agree?" Bates ran his hands over a leather-bound notebook on his desk. Trosper guessed it was Bates's personal copy of the Platinum dossier.

"Of course it's impressive," Trosper said. "More impressive than the file on Kudrov's interrogation."

"What do you mean, 'more impressive?' "

"Kudrov has told us a lot about Moscow Center. But some of it looks familiar to me. He's confirmed some things, added a jot and tittle here and there, but not much of it seems new. You'd better have someone make an audit of Kudrov's reporting—Platinum excepted of course—and see just how much of it is unique with him, and which can be confirmed."

"I thought Barlow had put someone on that," Bates said. "We've been so damn busy with the Iskra aspect that some of the donkey work and details have been neglected."

Trosper groaned. Details are to a case man as water in the pool to a high diver.

"What about Iskra?" Bates asked. "Are you convinced?"

"I'm convinced we'd better be sure we've checked out Comrade Kudrov before the White House begins swapping changes in policy for the *promise* of a coup in the Kremlin."

"Since I'm sure you agree that the Firm *can* do that," Bates said with a smile, "I don't see the problem."

"The problem is that Kudrov has been denounced as an agent dispatched from Moscow, a provocateur under Moscow control. Beyond that, Iskra reeks of deception."

"Damn it, Alan, you're missing the issue. This isn't some rinky-dink secret intelligence caper. What we've given the White House, perhaps for the first time in history, is a chance for this country to *move* the USSR, to ease it back into the family of nations. Along with the diplomatic gestures that the President has almost decided to make, the Firm has the opportunity to buy—and for not much more than the cost of a couple of those planes the fly-boys bang around —what promises to be first-rate intelligence reporting right from Moscow."

Trosper studied Bates as he spoke. For all of his enthusiasm, the Controller looked tired, his face was puffy and his complexion sallow.

"I don't know much about 'the family of nations,' " Trosper said, "but Iskra sure sounds familiar. In fact it sounds exactly like a replay of the Trust operation. You remember that bit of history, don't you, Walter?"

"Of course, I recall it. As a matter of fact, David Barlow brought me a couple of books on it. I'm going to look into it as soon as things quiet down around here."

"It's not surprising that Kinzl claims that Moscow calls the Kudrov operation 'Phoenix,' " Trosper said. "It's just Trust, risen from the ashes." He longed for a handful of Barlow's candy.

"Trust was sixty years ago," Bates said incredulously.

"It began in 1921," Trosper said, settling himself in his chair. "When Lenin told 'Iron Felix' Dzerzhinsky, the man who created the Cheka and the OGPU, that the Bolsheviks needed time to consolidate their government. There were one and a half million Russian émigrés abroad—some of them still doing military drill, most of them ready to fight to take Russia back from the Communists. The French, Poles and British were pumping money into the émigré organizations and threatening more armed intervention against the Bolsheviks."

"It's nothing like that now," Bates said. "The pressure comes from inside, from the new generation that is close to the throne."

"But wait. Dzerzhinsky sent an agent, to give the émigrés a rosy picture of the monarchist group—well organized throughout the USSR, good contacts in the military, even in the secret police. The problem wasn't the Bolsheviks, he said, that government would be brought down before long anyway. The problem was the uncoordinated activity of the Western powers and the émigrés attempting to work in the USSR. Because these agents knew nothing of the Soviet scene, he said, they worked at cross purposes, and, in their ignorance, were upsetting the serious work of his monarchist group."

"Kudrov has made no such . . . "

"The British and their allies latched onto Dzerzhinsky's agent as if he were carrying the Holy Grail. Within months the Trust—that was an acronym, rather an ironic one as it turned out—had established itself as the dominant counterrevolutionary group and was actually passing Western agents into the USSR along its own courier routes."

"Wrong again," Bates said. "Kudrov has offered us intelligence from Iskra men *in* the USSR. Nothing has been said about their sponsoring our independent work."

Trosper's eyes were fixed on Bates's pretty leather portfolio, as if it were a bomb. "Skeptics scoffed at the ease with which the Trust agents slipped around in the Soviet Union, and at the whole idea that the Bolsheviks were about to be overthrown; but they were hooted down. In 1925, when the critics were more vocal, Trust invited French and British representatives to come along—to accompany the couriers across the border and to Moscow."

"Nothing at all has been said about our meeting any of their people in the Soviet Union," Bates said.

Trosper ignored Bates's comment. "Sure enough, the Trust couriers got them across the border. They were whisked from safe house to safe house, halfway across Russia. They had secret meetings with the leadership and got back to Estonia as easily as they had slipped in. Of course Dzerzhinsky was in complete control, and the OGPU ran the whole trip was as carefully as if it had been stage-managed by the Bolshoi."

"But it wouldn't be difficult for us to meet some of their people inside," Bates said.

"By this time, the Russian emigration was honeycombed with OGPU agents, its ability to strike against the USSR was destroyed, and whatever chance there had been for a counterrevolution, or even armed intervention, had vanished. As frosting on the cake, the money the British and French had pumped into Trust was enough to pay for all the OGPU's unilateral operations during Trust's halcyon years."

"We haven't put a penny into Iskra," Bates said.

"Later, Trust operatives snatched two White Russian generals—key figures in the anti-Communist emigration—off the street in Paris. Scattered remnants of Trust were still active when World War Two broke out—German intelligence hired some of them, and with about as much success as the British had had earlier."

Trosper paused to catch his breath. "It was one of the most successful operations in intelligence history. A classic example of penetration, manipulation, and deception."

"I do plan to look into what you see as the parallels in Iskra and Trust," Bates said. "But that will take a while. Where does this leave us now?"

"It leaves us with no choice but to keep after Kinzl until we can evaluate his report on Kudrov. That will take time, but if we can keep Kinzl on the string, we will get to the truth."

"I really don't believe this," Bates said. "You're asking me to trust a walk-in—a little fellow who won't even tell you his name—rather than Kudrov, a man we've worked with for some time now, and whom we have every reason to believe?"

"You can do both—appear to go along with Kudrov here, and let us work on Kinzl in Vienna. Just tell the President we're checking further into Kudrov's bona fides."

"Do you think I'm going to tell the President that I've got an anonymous agent who says Kudrov's feeding us deception, stuff packaged in Moscow by the grandchildren of the chaps who pulled the same trick sixty years ago? Christ, Alan, it's been all I can do to keep the President from inviting Kudrov to the White House for a press conference. You haven't any idea what it's like around here these days."

"Give me two, maybe three, more meetings with Kinzl and I'll have the proof about Kudrov, one way or another."

Bates began to light a cigarette. His hands shook.

"You surprise me, Alan. You're supposed to be a stickler for security. Don't you realize the risks involved in letting Kinzl or anyone else investigate Kudrov in the Soviet Union? Iskra has friends in responsible jobs in the KGB, but even these people couldn't be sure of stymieing an investigation if something like that were to blow. Iskra is too important. I'd be out of my mind to agree to a field investigation of any part of it."

Bates ran his handkerchief quickly across his lips.

"The only reason I called you back from New York was to find out what happened to your friend Galkin, a hotshot agent who couldn't even keep a secret from his wife. Now, a few weeks later, you're on the verge of destroying the best opportunity the Firm's ever had to make a name for itself. Keep at it and you'll blow us all right out of the bloody window."

"That's the point, Walter. They've rigged the operation so that we won't dare to investigate it."

Bates smashed his his cigarette into the ashtray. It skittered off the desk onto the rug. "God damn it, Alan, I *have* investigated it," Bates shouted. "I've investigated it in every way I can without jeopardizing the operation, and the equities of the Firm."

"In that event, what am I to do with Kinzl?"

"Go back to Vienna and fire the little creep. Kiss him off. Tell him you know he's a fraud—that shouldn't be too hard." Bates reached into a lacquered cigarette box for another cigarette.

"After you've convinced him that we know he's a phony, tell him that if he continues to suck around or tries to get in touch with CIA he's likely to have a serious accident."

Bates bent to pick up the ashtray. "If the little bastard wants to defect, bring him the hell back with you. You can bet your ass I'll get the story out of him here."

"It's a mistake to call him off," Trosper said, struggling to keep his voice down. "It's an unnecessary and damned dangerous mistake."

"It's not a mistake," Bates said evenly, "but it is an order. You're to drop contact with Comrade Kinzl at the next meeting. And you're not to give him a nickel. He's one little creep that I don't want left with a smile."

Trosper tried a final tack. "Will you come with me to CIA and let the Director read the Platinum material?"

"No, I will not. And even if I weren't under White House orders to keep this case completely wrapped up, I still wouldn't agree with you."

Trosper stood up. He had lost. "I have no choice but to play the good soldier," he said. "I'll keep my mouth shut. But only on one condition."

"Nobody makes conditions to me in this office," Bates said.

Trosper ignored him. "I'll follow your rules on one condition."

"What's that?"

"Under no circumstance is Kudrov to be told anything about Kinzl," Trosper said.

"Of course no one's going to say anything to him," Bates said. "I may not have been present at the creation, but I've learned a few things about operations."

"Let's be damned sure, that's all," Trosper said.

"There won't be any problem."

Trosper walked toward the door. Bates rose and followed him. "Alan, I'm sorry to have yelled like that. But there's so much damned pressure building up in this case that it gets to me sometimes."

"These things happen, Walter."

As they shook hands, the Controller said, "It's the right decision, I'm sure of it." It was as if he were speaking to himself. He turned and took a few steps toward his desk. He called after Trosper.

"Look," he said. "You can handle Kinzl any way you want. Just as long as you rid me of him. Platinum comes first, I can't let anything upset it."

The promise to protect his security was all that could be done for Kinzl. It wasn't much. But if Bates kept his promise, Kinzl might at least live to spend the ten thousand dollars already in the Basel bank account.

18   NEW YORK

"*WHAT* in God's name went on in Washington? Or was it Vienna?" Martha Prynne's voice was husky and she cleared her throat before taking a sip of kir. "I may not be the most interesting date in town, but this is ridiculous. Out of the blue, you telephone from Washington to tell me you'll have twelve hours in town. You rush into the apartment like a sailor on shore leave. Then you whisk me off to dinner. We get here, you order drinks and then act as if you'd been struck dumb. You haven't said a word for five minutes."

"I'm sorry, Martha," he said. "I've had a hell of a time. I don't mean to appear so preoccupied."

"I seem to remember that before the charades began, we were lovers, Alan," she said. "You remember, don't you?"

They had gone to Parma, a noisy Italian restaurant on Third Avenue. He chose it because Martha liked the food, and the tables were close together. Too close, Trosper hoped, for her to continue to press him.

It had been almost ten weeks since he packed and said good-bye to Martha. Her first letters were tender and affectionate, and lightly scored with admissions of loneliness and concern for his safety. Unable to say anything about his work, Trosper resorted to travelogues and chat about the books he churned through in the safe house. After returning to Vienna from Munich, he had written only once.

"I'm sorry," Martha said. "Perhaps if I had a better idea of what was going on, just what you're up to, I could make more sense. As it is . . ." Her voice trailed off. She motioned toward her empty glass. Trosper ordered another kir and a martini for himself.

"There's nothing I can tell you that would help, you know that," he said. "I haven't accomplished what I hoped to, that's for damned sure."

"I don't think I'm cut out to sit and wait," she said. "I have to share things. For me that's an important part of being together."

The waiter came and they ordered—a shared portion of *trenette,* delicate, thin noodles with a sauce flavored with Black Forest mushrooms. After the pasta, they ate thick, pink veal chops with a hint of truffle in the creamed sauce. It was Martha's favorite meal and she ordered it every time they ate at Parma.

It was raining when they left the restaurant, a New York rain, oily and clotted with soot.

WHEN they reached the apartment, Martha snapped on the radio and went into the kitchen. Trosper mixed himself a drink and sat at the corner of the long divan. When she came back from the kitchen, Martha put down her cup of chocolate, kicked off her quilted slippers and curled beside him. He started to speak, but she gently shushed him. For a few moments she listened intently to the radio.

"You know, he died not far from here, at the Stanhope," she said. "A reporter is supposed to have asked the doctor what he had died of. The story goes that the doctor thought about it for a while and said, 'Everything. He died of just about everything.' "

"You've bewildered me again," Trosper said.

Martha laughed and pointed toward the audio rack. "On the radio—Charlie Parker, the alto saxophone." She took a sip of chocolate. "Just imagine, inventing a whole new music and dying before you are thirty-five."

"It was before your time, kitten, but I used to see him on Fifty-Second Street," Trosper said. "In the fifties, whenever I had a layover in New York. There was a girl I used to see. She liked those places, the Onyx, Three Deuces, and two or three others. Parker used to be there. Fat, and so drunk—maybe drugged—that I wondered how he could keep from falling off the stand. That was when the Bop musicians wore dark glasses—on the stand, stumbling from joint to joint along the street—everywhere. When Parker took the glasses off, you could see his eyes, huge and sad. He played beautifully, but like a frantic man who knew he was going to die before he finished his work. Sometimes he was friendly enough, making jokes and talking to the hangers-on."

"I'll be damned," Martha said. "Another unplumbed depth. Why didn't you ever mention it?"

"I never thought of it until now," he said.

"You know, Alan, I always used to think there were two of you. One, sort of gallant and old-fashioned, with some good talk and fun to be around. Then, every now and again, through a little crack in the surface I'd see something else, not a person at all, just a collection of secret panels and crazy-house mirrors."

He decided there was no point in asking if she would have had the same impression if she thought he had been a shoe salesman, rather than in the racket.

"I don't think I can live with that," she said. "I want to have it all, not always feel shut away from the secrets that have chewed up so much of your life."

"There's not much I can do about the past, not now anyway."

"It's up to me," she said. "It's my problem. I realized that when you stayed away so long—two months and nothing but those letters. Long letters and never a word about yourself, about you. It was as if you were being elaborately courteous to some stranger and not talking to me at all." She took another sip of chocolate. "And then you seemed to stop writing all together."

"It's difficult for me to write when I'm working."

Martha got up and walked to the telephone stand. "I almost forgot. I've mailed all your telephone messages. But a couple of days ago, when I checked your answering service, a Mrs. Cunningham had called. She left her number and I telephoned her. She said you had talked to her husband about a boat."

Trosper laughed. "They live in Sag Harbor. He actually seemed to be interested in one of those damned Poshcraft—don't tell me they've decided to buy one?"

"She said her husband was still shopping around, but they wanted to talk to you again. You must have made quite a hit with her—she did her best to find out if I was your secretary. She sounded quite lively."

"She's got more gumption than her husband."

"When I told her you were in Vienna for a few weeks, she said they were going to Europe and would be in Vienna and Budapest. I gave her your address."

"Jesus, Martha, we're *working* there. I can't have visitors dropping by."

"I don't think she'll pass it along to the Commies, if that's what you're worried about."

"It's not that . . ."

"What the devil is it then?" she said, her eyes moist. "All I said was that you were in Vienna for a few weeks. Is that such a big deal?"

"No, of course not. It's just that I don't like having people know things that don't necessarily mean anything to them."

"Really, Alan! Surely spies have people who ring them up? Doesn't it look funny if people can't do that?"

He said nothing.

"You make me think you've tossed my life—our life—onto a storeroom shelf, just canceled it because some little man in a black hat scurried out of a crack and slipped you the grip. I'm old enough now to need something permanent, someone I can spend my life with. I don't think I can do that with a man whose address is Top Secret—I really mean this, Alan."

"I really hate being crowded, Martha. Particularly about things I can't change."

He expected her to ask "Can't change, or don't want to?" But she waited until Parker's solo finished and switched off the radio. "You might at least have told me you used to know Charlie Parker. That can't have been such a big secret."

"I didn't know him, Martha. I used to see him. I was just one of the crowd."

19 VIENNA

"YOU'RE kicking at an open door," Trosper said. "It doesn't matter that I agree with you. What matters is following orders. Whatever you may think of him, Bates is the boss, and he's the only one who has the whole picture."

"This is one time I'm glad I'll be in the back room," Mercer said. "Kinzl is an irritating little bastard, but I don't envy you handing him the bucket of slops Bates sold you."

"Bates didn't sell me anything," Trosper muttered. "He just told me what was to be done."

"Damn it all, anyway," Kyle said and flung a copy of the *Wiener Kurier* into the corner of the divan. "I should have known better than to get caught up in this rotten racket again. I should have told Oma it was none of my business, and none of hers, either. Then Kinzl would have made his own way. By now he would have got to the British. Maybe they could have handled him."

BEFORE Kyle's eruption, Trosper had managed to say that Bates had complete confidence in Kudrov, that the Russian had been thoroughly vetted, and that he was to all appearances a straight agent. Trosper did not mention the White House enthusiasm for Kudrov, or the Iskra group and the possible coup.

"What reason did he give?" Mercer asked. "Or did he just give the order, 'Yours but to do and die' with no questions asked?"

"He said that Kinzl was to be dropped because his activity impinged on another operation, something more important than anything Kinzl was likely ever to come up with."

"It doesn't make sense, just to drop an agent cold like that," Mercer said.

"Bates is satisfied that Kudrov is straight, that Kinzl was sent to discredit him. Even if Kinzl wasn't sent to destroy our faith in Kudrov, Bates won't risk letting him attempt to find out anything about Kudrov in Russia."

"There's no damned reason we couldn't continue to work Kinzl.

It doesn't risk anything," Mercer said.

Trosper was in no mood to argue.

"It stinks," Kyle said. "The whole stupid business stinks." He went into the hallway for his coat. "I'll stay in touch with Oma, and I'll be here for the last supper. Meanwhile, I'll get back to work on my book."

"You know, Alan," said Mercer, when they were alone, "you sound like old Griffith giving an orientation lecture to the plebes. But I've been around for a while, I know all about 'the pyramid of knowledge'—only the man at the top knows everything. No matter how obvious the decision may seem, a case man may not have all the information on which to make a judgment. So, do as you're told, you're only a cog in the big machine. But on the other hand, you remember what Allen Dulles admitted in his book *The Secret Surrender?*"

Trosper nodded, but was uncertain of the drift of Mercer's remarks.

"He said, 'Only a man in the field can really pass judgment on the details' of an operation. Then, later, he said it was true that a man in the field was 'supposed to keep his home office informed of what he is doing.' But the old fox had reservations about that—he cautioned the field man against telling too much, against asking for too much advice."

"Dulles said that when he was describing his negotiations for the surrender of the German forces in Italy in 1945," Trosper said. "That was a wartime situation. It has nothing to do with us." Trosper shook his head. "It may be good advice, but when Dulles was DCI he would never have let a field man get away with anything like that."

"What do you think he would have done in our situation?"

"The first thing he would do is tell you to knock it off. After that, he would do exactly what I'm going to do—follow orders."

THAT afternoon Hamel telephoned and asked Mercer to come to the Vienna office at once. There Hamel showed Mercer an urgent instruction from Bates. No further support was to be given Trosper in connection with the "Agate" operation. Trosper and Mercer were to return to Washington after their next, and final, meeting with their agent.

20 VIENNA

"*LET IT* be Kyle," Trosper muttered piously as he hurried to the safe house telephone. "Please, Barabbas, let it be Kyle with news from Oma."

Without looking up from his book, Mercer said, "The patron saint of spies is Dismas, not Barabbas." He ran his hand slowly across his bald head and began absently to massage the back of his neck. "It's all in the Apocrypha."

Trosper signaled Mercer for silence and picked up the telephone.

It had been eleven days. Mercer continued to sulk but, except for occasional outbursts, had avoided railing against Bates's decision. Kyle had gone back to what Mercer called "the literary life." Aside from his daily check with Oma and afternoon telephone call to Trosper, Kyle had avoided the safe house.

Mercer put his book aside to watch as Trosper picked up the phone.

"Yes . . . yes . . . when? All right . . . of course."

Trosper dropped the telephone back into the cradle and turned to Mercer. "Kinzl's back, he's telephoned Oma. She told Kyle he said it was urgent. He even asked if she was all right. Oma thinks something's gone wrong."

"How much time do we have?"

"He'll be here in an hour, about six," Trosper said. "Kyle is on his way now. You'd better check the audio."

Mercer tossed his book aside and heaved his bulk up from the chair. "Damn and blast. There's never anything simple." He fished a handkerchief from his pocket. "The next time you invoke help, you'd better forget Barabbas and try Dismas, the 'Good Thief.' " He hustled towards the bedroom where the tape recorders were concealed.

"IT'S all quite clear, Mr. Warner," Kinzl said. "There's been a leak. A catastrophic leak." His face was haggard, the deep lines seemed to accentuate his light blue eyes.

"That's not very likely," Trosper said. "We haven't taken action on anything you've said."

Kinzl's glance flickered around the room.

"There's no problem here, Herr Kinzl," Trosper said quickly "The apartment has been checked inside and out for audio, and one of us has been here all the time since your first visit. There's no way anyone could have bugged this place."

Trosper knew it wasn't true. A good mike man could produce high-fidelity audio from almost any location and without having set foot on the premises. But it was not his task to educate Kinzl.

Kinzl shook his head. "That's not the problem. Mr. Warner."

Trosper remained silent, it was Kinzl's time to talk.

The little spy sat rigid in the corner of the sofa. Instead of the familiar tweed jacket and blue shirt, he wore a dark gray suit, striped shirt, and discreet dark tie. His light blue eyes shifted restlessly from Kyle to Trosper. Then he said, "You've betrayed me. Your service has sold me out."

Kinzl fixed his eyes on Trosper. The room was silent. From the street came the muffled throb of a motorcycle moving slowly along the rain-slick street.

"No one's been betrayed," Trosper said stiffly. He spoke slowly in an attempt to keep the anger out of his voice.

Kyle looked sharply at Trosper, who had not taken his eyes off Kinzl. "That's a very serious allegation," Kyle said quickly. "You'd better explain." He pulled his chair closer to the coffee table, as if preparing to thrust himself between Trosper and the agent.

"It was in Washington, not here," Kinzl said heavily. "Someone at your headquarters told Kudrov that Moscow has sent an agent to denounce him."

"That's not possible," Trosper said.

"Please, Mr. Warner," Kinzl said, "don't embarrass yourself. It's too late for you to cover up. Kudrov knows that an agent has told the Firm about him and mentioned the 'Phoenix' plan. Kudrov has already reported this to Moscow."

Kyle reached for the cognac and poured a drink. He handed the glass to Kinzl. He put the drink on the coffee table and pushed it aside.

Kyle turned to Trosper. "A drink?"

"Whiskey," Trosper said. He had overreacted to Kinzl's allegation, and appreciated Kyle's intervention. Kinzl had a knack for offending him. Kyle moved quickly to the sideboard and began noisily to mix the drink.

"It's clear," Kinzl continued. "You've betrayed us . . . I mean someone in Washington, someone in the Firm, has betrayed us."

"*Betrayed us?* What do you mean '*us?*' " Trosper asked. He turned to take the drink from Kyle. "You've never mentioned anyone else."

"It doesn't matter now, it's too late. It's just a fluke that I'm here at all."

"Maybe you'd better start at the beginning and tell—"

Kinzl interrupted. "There's an investigation in Moscow. . . . Right now they're tearing the place apart, looking for the leak. It's only a matter of days, maybe hours before they find something." His voice cracked. He spoke in a whisper. "I've got no choice but to go back. . . ."

"Before you do anything, particularly something stupid," Trosper said, "there's some explaining to be done. Give me the facts and maybe I can help. Keep up this silly masquerade and there's nothing anyone can do."

Kinzl picked up the glass and gulped the cognac. "I've told you everything I'm going to tell you. And you—someone—has passed it right along to Moscow." He drained the glass. "If I'd identified myself as you wanted, I wouldn't even have gotten this far." Like a chess player thoughtfully advancing a pawn, Kinzl pushed his empty glass slowly along the coffee table to Kyle.

"I suppose you won't think it very professional," Kinzl said, "but the least you can do is tell me *why* you played this rotten game with us. Why did you do it?"

"Why don't you stop this damned charade and begin telling me what you know?" Trosper demanded.

Kinzl shook his head. "I shouldn't even have come here. It's just that I wanted to face you and ask *why* the Firm sold us out."

"Have you forgotten that it was you who came to us, that you made some effort to find me? We weren't out looking for you. You walked in with a preposterous story about your position in Moscow. It was nonsense, but I played along with you. We've even paid you for a lot of second-hand chat about Moscow Center. Now you say you're in a jam and that it's my fault. Why don't you try telling me a straight story?"

Kinzl shook his head slowly. "Nothing more. I've already told you too much."

Trosper remained silent.

Kyle sat motionless, like a bass drummer silently counting the measures. Trosper tossed his yellow pad onto the coffee table that separated him from Kinzl.

"Perhaps it will help if I ask more precise questions," Trosper said. It was time to gamble.

Kyle poured more brandy and pushed the glass back along the table to Kinzl.

"It is past time for any more questions," Kinzl said.

Trosper took a long swallow of his drink. "What has Lopatin got to do with you? What was his connection with Galkin? Is Lopatin identical with 'Schneider,' the famous head agent, the man who was here all through the Nazi time?"

Kinzl blinked and quickly looked away from Trosper to Kyle at the end of the table. It was a spontaneous gesture, one of the few Trosper had seen the agent make. He seemed to be asking Kyle to intercede, to ease the pressure.

"I know you're not 'Tänzer.' But are you 'Walther,' the Dancer's leg man? Are you one of the *Schutzbundkinder?* Is that why you seem half-Russian, half-Viennese? If so, that's not exactly the right background for someone who says he's an *officer* in the KGB—it's been thirty years since Moscow gave anyone with your background a commission in their service."

Trosper did not take his eyes off Kinzl. The little spy shook his head. "Nothing more. Nothing."

"Were you here in Vienna during the war, an interpreter for the Dancer? Is that it? Is that part of the big secret you're trying to hide from me? Or are you sensitive about being an agent—one of the *privlechennye,* one of the agents who do so much of the work, but who can never be made officers?"

Kinzl cupped both hands around the brandy glass. Trosper could not tell if he was warming the cognac or steadying his long fingers.

"Nothing, Mr. Warner. Nothing more." He glanced at Kyle, as if he still expected him to speak, to intercede. Motionless, Kyle ignored Kinzl's mute appeal.

"If you *were* 'Walther,' it's nothing to hide. It was honorable service. Working right under the nose of the Gestapo is nothing to be ashamed of. It wasn't what I'd call a habit-forming line of work for a young man." Trosper smiled slightly and took a sip of whiskey.

The little spy turned to face Trosper. "Galkin said you were good, Mr. Warner. He gave your Firm high marks. But in truth, I hadn't expected this."

"Perhaps you'd better tell me what you did expect."

Kinzl inhaled deeply through his nose. As if to calm himself, he held his breath for a few seconds and then exhaled noisily. His eyes were turned down, avoiding Trosper's face. Then, again inhaling deeply, he shrugged his shoulders and leaned back against the sofa. He exhaled and said, "The game's over, we've lost."

"No one's lost anything, at least not yet," Trosper said.

Kinzl shook his head. "I don't care anymore." He seemed exhausted, and even smaller than he had before. He pulled a white handkerchef from his breast pocket and wiped it across his eyes. Then he blew his nose.

He began to speak. "My name is Radl, Franz Radl." He spoke softly as if he hoped the hidden microphones would not pick up his admission.

"My father was Peter Radl," he said, "one of the group leaders in the *Schutzbund,* the Socialist Workers fighting group. He was wounded in 1934 when the *Heimwehr* attacked the Socialist workers who had holed up in our apartment block, the Karl Marxhof. The Party managed to get us—my parents, my older brother, and me—into Czechoslovakia after our resistance collapsed and the Fascists began arresting our leaders."

"Did you go to Russia with the others?" Kyle asked.

"Some months later. In Prague, the comrades took care of my father until we could travel. In Moscow, at first anyway, we were heroes. I can even remember marching in a parade, my family were part of an 'Austrian workers delegation.' It was probably a May Day celebration. We were given an apartment—only two rooms—but as good as anything my Russian friends had. My father had a job, my brother and I went to school. I was only ten so the language came easily."

He looked up at Trosper. "It's a little late, isn't it, for anyone to care about the life story of little Franzi Radl?"

"It's a beginning anyway," Trosper said.

"I'd better eat something, I'm not used to your cognac," Radl said. He pulled the handkerchief from his pocket and dabbed at the sweat on his forehead.

"I'll get something," Kyle said and hurried to the kitchen.

"Tell me the story from the beginning," Trosper said. "And tell me how much time we have. We haven't lost anything yet."

"We have, Mr. Warner. We've lost Grisha."

"Has anyone been arrested? Surely it can't have gone that far yet?"

"No one's been arrested," he said listlessly. "At least not yet." Kinzl pulled himself erect on the sofa and took another sip of brandy. "There's time for one phone call. If Grisha is there, it means he has not been arrested. We arranged for me to telephone Moscow tonight. At eleven, he expects my call."

"Then we've got almost four hours, that could be time enough," Trosper said. "Not for any more games, but to try to work something out." He was impatient and eager for details, but it was still too early to push Kinzl.

He spoke rapidly, the words spilling from his mouth. "From the first my mother hated it in Moscow. She was *petite bourgeoise,* an innkeeper's daughter from the Salzkammergut. She hated politics, it was my father who was the activist. He was handsome, not like me. A tough working man, Viennese to his bones and a Socialist from the cradle. He met her when he was on holiday, hiking in the mountains. He filled her with stories of life in Vienna and carried her off—at least that's what she always told us. But the fact was, she had three younger sisters. I suspect my grandfather was glad to see her married, even to a Socialist from 'Red Vienna.' "

Kyle hurried from the kitchen, balancing a platter of cold cuts, potato salad, and a bottle of Moselle. Kyle began to serve the food. Like a headwaiter, he manipulated the large serving spoon and fork with one hand.

Radl began to pick at the food on his plate. "My grandfather— my mother's father—was probably a Nazi. I can't even remember him, but I always thought there were more Nazis in Tyrol than in Berlin. There still are, as far as I know."

Kyle poured the wine.

"In Moscow in 1937, the purges were at their height. Suddenly Stalin turned on the Austrians he had invited to Russia in thirty-three. He decided that the *Schutzbund* men, the 'heroic anti-Fascist Austrian workers' he had welcomed, were really enemies of the state —Nazi agents, Trotskyites, even British spies. Two or three disappeared every night. Then it happened to us. There was a knock at our door, and the police were there. Within minutes my father was hustled out. He had even packed a little bag—he knew what was coming. I remember him kissing my mother and telling us that it was all a mistake. Later, my brother told me that Father knew he would never come back. A handful from our Austrian group were lucky —they went to the labor camps. But eventually, most of them were murdered, along with the old Bolsheviks."

He started to take another bite of chicken. Then he dropped the fork and pushed the plate aside.

"But you know all of this, Mr. Warner. There's no point in going over it."

But there was a point to letting Kinzl, or Radl, ramble. When, abruptly, the agent began to talk, and the long-cloaked details of his life came tumbling out, it was like the breaking point in a fever. Each admission fueled his compulsion to keep talking.

"What happened to you, were you in school?"

"I was fifteen, spending half-time in school and half-time in training for the examination for the Bolshoi Ballet Academy. I would have been accepted, too, except that when my father was arrested, we were thrown out of our apartment and my brother and I expelled from school.

"During the day we scratched for a living and at night I tried to keep up with my training. But it was hopeless. In 1939, my teacher suggested I apply for the music hall school—the Studio of Vaudeville Art. It was a new school, maybe that's why I could squeak in. Suddenly I was a vaudevillian. I even learned tap dancing. I was still there when the war began. We all volunteered for the army. I suppose most hoped to be sent to an entertainment unit, but it didn't work that way. We wound up in a mortar company. A few weeks later, I was pulled out of my unit. It seemed the intelligence people were frantic for German speakers. I began training and then— halfway through the course—they picked me to go back to Vienna."

"To work with Schneider?"

The little spy sighed. "Not directly for him. I was to help Grisha, the man you know as the Dancer. It's ironic, but being with him is the closest I ever came to the ballet."

"What is Grisha's name?"

Radl ignored the question. "We were here almost two years. Schneider was fantastic, a great agent. It doesn't matter what happened to him afterward, he was one of the best in our service. Maybe too aggressive, but he got things done and he knew enough tricks to keep us alive. You wouldn't believe the risks we took." Radl shook his head as if to wash the memories away.

"Grisha and I worked for Schneider's respect. At the time this seemed even more important than what the Center thought of us. And maybe it was—nobody in Moscow gave a damn what happened to any of us as long as we continued to produce. The army was losing thousands of men every day—in the occupied areas, the Nazi extermination squads were butchering civilians. How could anyone at headquarters have time to worry whether a couple of spies lived another few hours? Schneider had the same notion. He was obsessed with time, he measured it in casualties. As he saw it, an hour wasted on operations meant dozens more casualties at the front."

With an almost effortless movement, Radl rose from the corner of the sofa and began to pace around the room. "Nobody else seemed to worry very much, the Center made blunder after blunder. But they were keeping the records—and as Schneider found out, all the mistakes were charged to the field men."

Trosper smiled. "It's not the first time that's happened."

Radl ignored Trosper's remark. "Thanks to Schneider we survived. That was almost more than he could do for himself. At the end, when our army finally pushed into Vienna, he was exhausted, completely spent. But he stayed on in Austria, piecing things together, making sure our survivors were taken care of. Then, a few days after the liberation, Grisha and I were evacuated. Back to Moscow and what we called a hero's reception—a handshake at the airport and ten weeks of interrogation."

"We can go into that later," Trosper said. "What happened after your release?"

Wandl snorted. "I was again found worthy to prepare for a career in vaudeville and restored to my status as student. By then the bureaucrats had elevated the school—it had become the All-Union School of Vaudeville Arts. I was twenty-two, an age when most dancers are beginning to perfect their form. But I hadn't had a dance class for four years. It's no wonder that the school wanted me to become a comedy dancer, maybe even work up a peasant clog routine. It was a joke."

"What about Grisha? What did he do?"

"He's a year older than I. He'd had three years training with the Bolshoi school, but hadn't danced at all for almost five years. He took class for a few weeks and quit. It was hopeless. He took what he thought was the easy road, and asked for a commission in the service. He had good German and, God knows, plenty of experience. It took a few weeks, but he was accepted."

"I take it you stayed in touch with him?"

Radl fixed his light blue eyes on Trosper. "He was about the only friend I had in Moscow. My mother had taken up with some lout from the Free Germany group. He was a real opportunist, one of the Germans who waited until 1945 to see the light and switch from Hitler to Stalin. My brother, our school friends, and the Austrians I had known had all disappeared during the war, dead or scattered."

He pushed his plate to one side. "I suppose I might as well tell you, not that it makes much difference now. . . ." He paused and stared at the floor. "During the war . . . I mean when we were here in Vienna . . . when we were working together, before Grisha had learned enough German to operate on his own, we had become quite close."

Trosper nodded.

"It wasn't anything we had planned . . . as a matter of fact, it was the first experience for both of us."

Trosper dropped the yellow pad onto the coffee table and took a sip of whiskey.

"Despite the ballet and everything, Grisha had avoided that sort of thing . . . even in the ballet it was bad form . . . 'dance like a man,' they were always saying. It was nothing we reached out for . . . I knew about it, but I had never known anyone who was that way."

Radl's voice had dropped to a whisper.

"We were lovers . . . that's the only word for it . . . we were in love. I never even knew it could happen that way to men. Not the way it was with us."

"Yes," Trosper murmured.

"Neither of us understood what had happened. We blamed it on the war, on the constant pressure to get the job done and to stay alive. That was what seemed to rot our discipline. We even swore to each other that we would separate when we went home."

Radl sniffed. "We might just as well have promised to stop breathing. There wasn't a thing we could do about it."

"Did the Center know about it?" There was no point in reminding Radl that the KGB considered homosexuality something to be exploited, not a permissible way of life.

"I think there may have been some talk in Vienna, maybe a little gossip. But the fact was, we didn't know anyone outside the apparat and almost no one but Schneider ever saw us together. Schneider must have suspected, but he never let on. Even when he was back in Moscow under interrogation and later in prison."

"How long did you stay with the academy?"

"A year, maybe more. I got to be fairly good again, but I had no interest in music hall dancing, prancing around for a lot of people who didn't have taste enough to appreciate real dance.

"I stayed in touch with Grisha, but we kept our distance. I doubt if anyone even remembered that we'd been friends. Finally he proposed that I apply to be reinstated in the service. He kept out of it, and I got in on my own. Despite what happened to Schneider, we came out of Austria with a good reputation and my German was letter perfect. As a former Austrian, I could not be an officer. I was classified as you said, a *privlechenny*, one step above a 'co-opted agent.' But it was enough for me, the pay was good, we had privileges and could use the special commissary in Moscow. We even got the same fifteen percent pay bonus given to the officers—the 'allowance for conspiracy.' "

"Where did you work?"

"At first I was in East Germany—in the early days, right after the war, some of the case men couldn't speak enough German to get by. I interpreted for them, it was a rotten system but in those days Moscow had no alternative. Later I was sent to West Germany, to Munich, posing as a refugee. I settled down there, but there was a defection, someone from the East German headquarters in Karlshorst jumped, and the Center ordered me home. I doubt the defector knew anything about me, but Moscow insisted. At the time I thought about coming over myself, but I couldn't do it. Not that I had any loyalty to the service—I knew what they had done to Schneider—Lopatin—and to others. But I couldn't face starting a new life alone in the West. I suppose the real reason was Grisha. I knew that if I left, I would cut myself off from him forever. I couldn't do that."

"What happened then?"

"I got a training job, helping to prepare agents for assignments in West Germany or Austria, there was even one couple headed for Switzerland. It wasn't full-time work, it came in spasms. Busy for a few weeks and then nothing for a month or more. I was lonely. I had been away so much I had no friends, my mother had died, there was nothing for me in Moscow. Except Grisha. Before we knew what had happened, it had started all over again. It probably seems silly when I tell it like this, but it is as real for us as any relationship can be."

"You know," Trosper said, "it isn't all that difficult to understand. At home now, people are changing their attitude about it."

"That's what we found out. And that's one of the sad parts of the story."

"Tell me about it."

"Grisha was a colonel then. He was a good linguist and had been studying English, the language of the principal enemy. You know we call you people the 'principal enemy'—in all our documents, every time there is a reference to you Americans we call you 'the principal enemy.' "

"Yes, I know," Trosper said. "I've read some of your documents."

For the first time Radl smiled. "And I've read a few of yours."

"What about Grisha?"

"Four years ago, he was sent on a temporary assignment to our consulate in San Francisco. It was partly for orientation, arranged to let him see something of the United States. But the real reason was to reactivate an agent, someone working in the electronic field near San Francisco. It was an important case, one of the best we had there. Like most of the big cases in California, the Center insisted that the agent go to Mexico City to meet his case man. The agent was a computer scientist, but he had dropped contact. There was no way for the *rezidentura* in Mexico City to reach him in San Francisco. Grisha's job was to find the agent, and put him back in business.

"He had the man's address. The funny thing was that no one had realized the man was homosexual. When Grisha went to check out the address, he discovered that the fellow was living in a homosexual community and sharing an apartment with a man who was obviously 'gay,' as the Americans call it out there."

Radl paused for a moment and then said, "How different it is in

the United States. You call it 'gay.' We have only two words—
pederast, or *pider.* The slang term *zhopnik* is too vulgar to translate." He pulled the handkerchief from his sleeve and brushed it
across his face. "In the service, they think homosexuality isn't Russian, that there is no homosexual activity in Russia. Little they
know." He stuffed the handkerchief back into his sleeve.

"Grisha had learned some English, and like many of our best
operatives, he constantly studied the United States. But this was his
first trip. He had read about San Francisco and the homosexual
community there, but of course he had never seen anything like it.
This is what started the whole thing."

"Started what?" Trosper asked.

"It started him thinking about our existence in Moscow. How we
were not able to live our own lives, always afraid that someone
would find out about us, that we would be destroyed if anyone even
suspected us. For the first time we began to think about getting out.
We began to dream about spending our remaining time in the open,
in a society that didn't care how we lived."

Kyle stirred in his chair. He glanced at Radl's glass, but the agent
had barely sipped the wine Kyle had poured for the cold supper.

"You'd better tell me more about Grisha," Trosper said.

Radl shrugged. "I guess it doesn't matter now. We've spoiled
everything." He pulled the white handkerchef from his sleeve.

"His name is Grigory Pavlovich Aksenov. He is Chief of Department Twelve, First Chief Directorate, Moscow . . ." Radl's voice
trailed off. He whirled around on the sofa to stare in the direction
of the hall leading to the apartment door.

There was a muffled knocking. For a moment Trosper thought
Mercer was tapping lightly on the locked bedroom door.

Kyle sprang to his feet. Before he reached the hallway, the door-
bell rang. A long, harsh ring.

Radl braced himself as if to spring from the sofa.

"Steady," Trosper said. "Steady." He got up and walked slowly
to the buffet. Opening a drawer, he pulled his Walther from beneath
a pile of linen. He jacked a round into the chamber, walked quickly
back to the coffee table and slipped the pistol under a pad of yellow
lined paper. Radl began to speak, but Trosper motioned for silence.

He was straining to hear Kyle's muffled voice.

"Yes, he's here . . . Whom shall I say is calling . . . ?" It was a parody of politesse.

There was a sound of footsteps in the hallway. As Kyle stepped back into the living room, his face was contorted, as if he had interrupted a sneeze.

"Alan," he said heartily, his voice pitched an octave higher than moments ago. "There's someone to see you. . . . It's Mr. and Mrs. Cunningham, and their friend, Mrs. Bristol, all the way from Sag Harbor." He spoke loudly as if to convince himself that he had not imagined the intrusion.

"Hello, Mr. Trosper," Mrs. Cunningham said. "I hope this isn't the wrong time to drop in." She strode into the room, her black mink coat open to reveal her white blouse and black silk suit.

From a step behind his wife, Cunningham boomed, "Look, Al, we were just on the way out for dinner. Barbara, Mrs. Bristol here, wanted some fresh air, so we walked over from the Hotel de France to stretch our legs. We just took a chance that you'd be in."

The striking blond woman beside Mr. Cunningham began to nod her head as if to encourage Trosper to say something. Her expression was slightly blurred, as if she had put on her makeup in the dark.

"I'm so sorry to bother you like this," Mrs. Cunningham said, "but we didn't have your telephone number. It was all I could do to get the address from your snippy answering service in New York. Since we were in the neighborhood, I thought we might just as well say hello."

"It's no trouble," Trosper said lustily. "No trouble at all. I'm delighted you thought to call." He smiled brightly and stepped across the room to shake hands.

For the first time Radl moved. He had pressed himself so deeply into the corner of the sofa that he shot up as if propelled by a coiled spring. His leg brushed the yellow pad. It spilled to the floor. The black pistol lay bare on the table. Startled by Radl, Cunningham stepped back, pulling Mrs. Bristol off balance. She dropped her handbag. "Jesus, Jerry," she muttered. "Let's be a little more careful."

"I'm so sorry," Mrs. Cunningham said. "We didn't know you'd have company." She stared at Radl.

"It's fine, just fine," Trosper blurted. "We were having some cold supper and talking a little business." He turned to Radl. "Let me introduce my colleague, Herr Kinzl." He paused, and added thoughtfully, "He's from Vienna."

Cunningham reached in front of his wife to take Radl's hand. "It's a pleasure," he said. "A real pleasure."

Radl shook hands with Cunningham and bowed politely to the two women. "Good," he said. "Quite good." It was the first time Trosper had heard him attempt to speak English.

For a moment Trosper wondered what Mercer was making of the scene.

"A drink," Kyle said, his voice cracking. "Shall we all have something to drink?"

"I could press down a small martini," Mrs. Bristol said.

"No, no," Mrs. Cunningham said. "We just stopped in to say hello." She paused for a moment and glanced at the coffee table. "We have to run along now, we've got dinner reservations at the *Drei Husaren* and we've got to find a taxi."

"Good," Radl said. "Quite good."

"We're leaving the day after tomorrow," Cunningham said. "We're going on to Budapest. We'll be at the Hilton," Cunningham said. He clapped Trosper on the back. "I'll be making a decision about the boat as soon as we get home."

"Good," Trosper said. "I've always recommended thinking over any purchase like a Poshcraft."

21 VIENNA

"*CHRIST*," Mercer said as he closed the bedroom door behind Trosper. "What a floor show—you've got the little guy, you may have 'Phoenix,' Bates has bought a dog, and the Sag Harbor Yacht

Club will never know what they stepped into. It's better than I thought possible."

Trosper had left Radl with Kyle ana was ostensibly headed for the toilet when he tapped on the door and slipped into the bedroom where Mercer was monitoring the tape recorders.

"Please, Mercer, don't start counting any chickens yet—it's Aksenov we're after, not this little fellow," Trosper said. "Besides, it's bad luck, like whistling on the foredeck. You know that."

Rebuffed, Mercer muttered "Sorry" and gestured toward the bed. "If Kyle had taken another five seconds to announce that it was the Sag Harbor crowd at the door, I'd have been out there with my noisemaker."

A sleek automatic shotgun lay across the neatly folded eiderdown at the foot of the bed. The gun had no shoulder stock, only a gently curved grip like a highway man's pistol, and a twenty-four inch barrel. Loaded with heavy shot, it was meant to be fired from the waist like a firehose, with almost no need to aim. It was Mercer's favorite weapon and ideal, as he put it, for "crowd control."

THE CUNNINGHAMS and Mrs. Bristol had left to look for a taxi to take them to the restaurant. Trosper guessed that Jerry Cunningham had not seen the pistol on the coffee table and that Mrs. Bristol was too drunk to have noticed it. But when Nancy Cunningham had shooed the others out of the room and said, "We'd best be getting along, so you can finish your . . . er . . . business," her wry expression underlined the probability that she had seen it.

"I suppose there's a simple explanation," Mercer said, "but I'd sure as hell like to know how your answering service could tell the Sag Harbor Yacht Club exactly where to find you in Vienna."

"It's because the plumbing went out in the first safe house we had here, and we had to move to this place—the address to which I was told to have my mail sent," Trosper said angrily. "Right now, we've got enough on our plate without worrying about that."

Trosper stepped to the monitoring equipment, picked up the earphones, and for a moment listened to Kyle attempting to explain the Cunninghams and Mrs. Bristol to the shaken Radl. Then, although he knew the answer, he turned to Mercer and asked "Do you think there's any chance that Hamel would help us—despite the orders he's had from Bates?"

"Help us *what?*"

"Help us try to get Colonel Aksenov out," Trosper said impatiently. "We've only got a couple of hours to work up a scheme."

Mercer ran his hand across his scalp. "Hamel's a decent guy and he knows what he's doing. But he hasn't been told a thing about what we've been up to in his territory and his nose is out of joint. Every station man hates operations run out of someone's vest pocket in Washington."

"Would he help us out?"

"He's under specific instructions not to give us any further support of any kind. You know that."

"What would he do if I asked for help?"

"Because there's no fixed deadline he would send an 'Expedite—Eyes Alone' message to Bates, and ask for instructions."

"And what would Bates say?"

"He'd cable a hundred questions, and then when he got our answer, he'd think the whole thing over for a couple of days or so. From what you say, he's got too much riding on Kudrov to act quickly. If Radl was telling the truth, it could have been Bates who told Kudrov he had been denounced. If Bates did that, it's because he trusts Kudrov completely. If so, he's not going to jeopardize Kudrov on the basis of any cable we might send from here."

"That's exactly what I think," Trosper muttered. He pointed to the earphones. "Will your mikes pick me up if I speak into the telephone?"

"Of course."

"Comrade Radl will be sleeping over. I'll go to the telephone and pretend to call you. When I do, stop taping, conceal the recorders, and slip out of the apartment for ten minutes or so. Then come back and ring the bell. I don't want Radl thinking he can leave any time he wants to, so do your Mr. Hyde act and come on a bit heavy."

Trosper stepped back into the hallway. He walked to the toilet, flushed it, and went back to the living room where Kyle was talking quietly to Radl. Trosper slipped back into his chair facing the agent. He listened for a few moments and said, "What about Grisha?" he asked. "What was your plan?"

Radl's long face was flushed, and his thin, nervous fingers fluttered as he spoke. "It was simple, probably too simple, but Grisha tries to keep things that way," he said. "Like anyone who's been on the run the way we were during the war, he gets frantic about security. He doesn't trust anyone. That's why we would never have identified ourselves to you. When we had enough money in Basel we were going to make a break—with the Center, with you, with everything. We planned simply to disappear and to be done with the whole business. Then we made our mistake."

Trosper knew what Radl meant, but asked, "What mistake was that?"

"We never should have said anything about 'Phoenix.' The operation was too important, too closely held. It was only after I had first mentioned it to you that Grisha realized there were only a handful of officers at the Center who know anything about it. If we'd known that at the start, we would never have said anything. We had plenty of material, good material for you. It was more than enough for the money we wanted. It's just that Grisha underestimated 'Phoenix' when he first said I could mention it to you."

There was more to "Phoenix" than this, but Trosper did not pursue it. Instead, he asked, "Where did you plan to go?"

Radl was silent. For a moment he glanced at Kyle and then turned back to Trosper. "You'll probably laugh, but it meant a lot to us." He shifted uneasily in the chair and pulled his handkerchief from his pocket. He dabbed at his nose and upper lip. "We planned to go to the United States—right into the fist of the 'principal enemy.' " He smiled uneasily. "It wouldn't have been all that difficult to get in. Once we were there, we planned to look around until we could find a place to settle. We thought about Key West, or perhaps near San Francisco. Some place where there isn't much winter and where nobody cares about the way other people live."

"How much money did you think you could get from us?"

"About a hundred thousand dollars," Radl said. "Grisha thought that would be enough to get us established. I wasn't so sure, but

Grisha makes the decisions. We knew that once we were settled
down we would have to work, to open a shop or something."

Radl now seemed older and smaller. It was as if the anxiety had
compressed him. The bohemian look of his hair, brushed forward at
the top and sides, contrasted oddly with the conservative dark gray
suit, and reminded Trosper of a businessman in a mod wig.

"What about papers, what did you plan to do about documents?"

Radl shook his head slowly. "Grisha's a senior colonel now, a real
nachal'nik, one of the big bosses. He was arranging everything.
We've been planning this for almost two years. With enough time,
he could have got most anything we needed by appropriating it from
other operations. Not many people ever question a senior colonel,
particularly one who has a reputation for handling a few operations
on his own. His passport would have come last, but I had already
begun to cache some of the things we needed in the Basel bank. All
of his notes are there, the details on how to regularize ourselves once
we get into the United States—how to get legitimate birth certificates, Social Security cards, even passports. He had already begun
to collect forged backup papers—the stuff you call 'pocket litter'—
club cards, the sort of junk that people carry in their wallets. Grisha's plan was to get an American passport for himself. I would
probably have used my work document, maybe even the one I have
now, a West German passport."

"Has the Colonel already got a passport?" This was not the time
to ask what else might have been cached in Basel.

"No, he was going to wait until later, a few days before we were
ready to jump. We figured it would take eighteen months, maybe
even two years—ten or fifteen more meetings—to sell you enough
to get the funds we needed. Now, thanks to your damned Firm, he
hasn't got anything and the investigation has begun. It's too late
now."

"Why?"

"Because he can't get out," Radl said loudly. "Don't you understand that?"

"I'm not talking about booking a first class flight to Paris," Trosper said softly.

"What are you thinking? That if he got to Leningrad, or Minsk, maybe you could send a limousine to pick him up? Perhaps a helicopter could fetch him from Volgograd? Use your head, Mr. Warner. We're talking about the Soviet Union."

"I want to know where he can go on his own authority," Trosper said.

Radl shrugged. "For two or three days, maybe a week—it will depend on how the 'Phoenix' investigation goes—he can probably travel anywhere he wants in the USSR. But there's no chance he could get out now. There are so few people who know anything about 'Phoenix' that it's only a matter of days before the security people close in."

"Then we've got a little time. . . ."

"We haven't any time," Radl said heatedly. "All I can do is make one phone call tonight. After that, I'll go back. Perhaps the two of us can piece together enough of a story to divert suspicion from Grisha when the time comes."

"What about Eastern Europe? Can he get to Hungary, or Czechoslovakia?" Trosper asked.

For a moment Radl's eyes flickered, then his interest died. "If he can leave soon enough, he might be able to issue orders for his own travel to one of the Socialist countries, Czechoslovakia, Hungary, Bulgaria—there's no point in talking about Poland or the DDR— East Germany. But that could mean he'd have to travel in uniform, maybe with some kind of military orders." Radl shook his head sadly, "There's one thing I can tell you—if he can't write the orders himself, he might as well ask to go to the moon."

"If he got to Hungary, would he be able to go to Budapest?"

Radl straightened himself on the heavy overstuffed sofa. He turned to Kyle, "Is there something to smoke, a cigar or cigarette?"

Kyle grinned and said, "Yes, we've got some good Havanas." He hurried to the buffet where Mercer kept his private stock of cigars.

"When Grisha goes anywhere in the Warsaw Pact countries," Radl continued, "he has to report to the military headquarters. In Hungary, I suppose he would have to report to the Central Group of Forces headquarters in Debrecen. After that he could go to Budapest to check in with the *rezident*—the chief of station—at our embassy. That is so he can get urgent messages from the Center."

Trosper asked a few more questions and abruptly went to the telephone on a table at the far side of the room. He picked up the phone and, with his back to Kyle and Radl, dialed six numbers. He waited a moment and then said, "Hello, Mr. Hyde, please." He waited again and said, "Will you please come over? We will need a sitter. . . . Yes, for a day or two. Yes, please bring a weapon." He wondered how much English Radl could understand.

"*I'M GOING* out for half an hour," Trosper said. "Mr. Johnson will stay here, and I've asked for Mr. Hyde to come along to help keep house."

As if to protest, Radl began to speak. Trosper cut him off. "Before I go, I want the details on your telephone call. Just what was your plan?"

"I think I'd like a little cognac . . ."

"You can have some coffee later, we haven't time for any more cognac right now," Trosper said firmly. "Just what is involved in your telephone call to Moscow?"

"Grisha will be at one of the operational flats his section keeps in Moscow. I'm to call him at eleven tonight. If he's not there, I'm to call again on the half hour until two. If he's not there by then, something will have happened. He might even have been—" It was as if Radl did not want to say "arrested." "He might have been detained."

"Can you call him at home?"

"Of course I can't call him at home from abroad. On the safe house phone, I'll pretend I'm an agent. We'll talk in German, in open code, the monitors will never understand what we are talking about. When their report is translated, it will go directly to Grisha's office. At least there won't be any trouble about that."

Trosper turned to Kyle. "When Mr. Hyde gets here, tell him to rig a monitoring device to the telephone and a tape recorder. I want every word on tape."

Kyle started to speak, but Trosper cut him off. "I think there's some gear in the back room."

Trosper got up and went to the hall for his coat. Pulling it over his shoulders, he came back into the living room. Speaking directly to Radl he said, "I'll be gone about half an hour. Meanwhile, you're not to leave here." He turned to Kyle. "Is that understood?"

Kyle glanced at Radl. "I think we've got it," he said. The door bell rang, stifling whatever protest Radl had started to make. There were three harsh rings.

"That will be Mr. Hyde," Trosper said. "Please let him in."

22 VIENNA

"*BUDAPEST*," Brattle said. "That's your only chance."

"I haven't been there since November 1956," Trosper muttered into the telephone. "Even then I scarcely knew my way around."

"Get him to Budapest," Brattle repeated, "and I think we can do something."

TROSPER had hurried from the safe house to the Hotel Imperial on the Ring. The busy switchboard would not notice one more cryptic telephone call in English. "It's come unstuck," he began. "That matter I mentioned to you a month ago has run right off the tracks . . ."

The Englishman snorted and muttered an obscenity.

". . . which leaves me with something of a problem," Trosper added.

"Can you give me a hint?"

"It seems it's about time for one of my clients to take a vacation, maybe a long vacation. About an hour ago, I learned that I've got forty-eight hours, maybe less, to arrange for his travel. The immediate problem is that I have to call him tonight to let him know about reservations and visas."

In his imagination, Trosper saw Brattle sitting in a cardigan, with a double old-fashioned glass of malt whiskey and water on the table beside his chair. A thick Havana would be balanced on a wedge-shaped crystal ashtray at his left.

"In about an hour," Trosper said, "I've got to tell him where he can best make the crossing. The fact is, I'm completely out of date on this sort of thing and there's no one hereabouts I can ask for advice."

"Is this the old fellow you came to ask me about?"

"Not that particular chap, but a very close friend. Potentially he's a very important customer."

"It's probably none of my business," Brattle said, "but what about your regular travel service?"

"That's part of the problem. There's been a slight misunderstanding. Given a little time, I might be able to clear it all up, but for the moment, they've washed their hands of this particular account. I'm afraid I'll have to service this one on my own."

The phone was silent. He could hear Brattle take a sip of whiskey.

"If you'll bear with me for a moment, Alan, there are two things I have to say."

"Of course, Douglas," Trosper said. As long as he had known Brattle, he had never called him "Butch."

"First, because I don't want to seem insulting, I will tell myself that you're sure you know what you are getting up to. Second, if I make any introductions for you, I want you to remember that sooner or later, I will have to send a minute to my old shop."

"That's understood," Trosper said quickly.

"Budapest," Brattle said. "That's your best bet. It's full of tourists the year around. It's even more crowded now that we're heading into the Easter weekend. It might even be that I still have a chum there. Someone who might be able to help with the transportation."

There was another pause, presumably for a sip of whiskey.

"What about visas," Trosper asked. "Do you know how long it will take me to get a visa?"

"The IBUSZ tourist bureau advertises forty-eight hours," the Englishman said. "From what I've heard, that's all it takes. But I've got a gimmick that might speed things a bit."

"I've got to pass the word tonight," Trosper said. "And I'll have to give him a rendezvous. Have you any idea where we could meet?"

"Will your chap be in mufti?"

"I don't know."

"Have you got anything against hiding in plain sight?"

"I haven't, but I can't imagine what he might think."

"Try the Cafe Vörösmarty either mid-morning or early afternoon."

"What if he's in uniform?"

"He'll get better service." Brattle chuckled, and then said, "It should be all right, I've seen a few Ivans in there, and it's got to be one of the least likely places anyone might expect any jiggery-pokery."

"That should do it, Douglas. If we need an alternate meet, I'll tell him to be at the railway station, the *Ostbahnhof,* alongside whatever track the trains from Debrecen pull in on."

"Look," Brattle said. "Maybe we should talk this over after you've spoken to your client. I'll drive down early this morning—maybe we can have breakfast, say about eight-thirty?"

"That's really not necessary, Douglas, but if you want to come down, I'll pop for breakfast at Sacher's."

Before Brattle rang off he said, "It looks to me as if you'll need some hand-holding inside. I'd better plan to come along on the rest of the trip as well."

TROSPER touched the bell as he turned his key in the safe house door. Kyle stepped into the hallway, and took Trosper's rain-soaked coat. The spy in the rain might be a a Hollywood cliché, but the fact was, that when there were things to be done, it usually rained. If Hollywood hadn't spoiled things, a trenchcoat would have been the most practical garment any case man could wear.

"How is our guest?" Trosper asked.

"A little windy, but all right. He was worried about your getting back in time."

"Have you closed the bar?"

"Yes, Radl wanted more cognac, but I told him it was coffee and tea from here in."

"How is he getting on with our Mr. Hyde?"

"All right. I think Mercer likes the part, coming on a a little severe." Kyle chuckled. "It's the first time I've seen him in costume."

Trosper glanced into the living room. Mercer's wig was dark brown, and fashioned long at the sides and in the back. Because he had no eyebrows, the hairpiece seemed to direct attention to Mercer's large brown eyes, and gave his face a softer aspect.

Radl stood beside the buffet table, a cup of coffee in his hand. Not sure how he should greet Trosper, he nodded expectantly.

"Let's sit down," Trosper said. "Now," he began, "how soon can you call Moscow?"

"My first call is scheduled for eleven."

"The best exit point is Hungary," Trosper said. 'I've arranged for Grisha to be met in Budapest. We will take over from there."

Kyle inhaled sharply and glanced at Mercer. Seated near the door and behind Radl, the burly case man rolled his eyes and shrugged.

The little spy put his cup on the table and bent forward as if to speak. Trosper headed him off. "What I must know is when Grisha thinks he can arrive, and how long he can remain in Budapest without causing suspicion."

Radl nodded. Kyle pulled a sheet of paper from his note pad and handed it to Radl. The agent fished a fountain pen from his breast pocket and began to scribble a note.

"We have two choices," Trosper said. "The first, is the Cafe Vörösmarty in Pest. Grisha can be met between ten-thirty and eleven-thirty. If this is not possible, he should be there between two-thirty and three forty-five in the afternoon."

Radl shook his head. "Don't your people even know the Vörösmarty is one of the most popular coffee houses in Budapest? It will be crowded at those hours."

"Yes," Trosper said, "I know that. If we had more time we might be able to find a place where our contact team could sit around until Grisha shows up. As it is, the Vörösmarty will damned well have to suffice." How nice it would be, he thought, if there really was a contact team—two scouts who knew Budapest, and a contact man with diplomatic immunity. He looked across the room to where Mercer, who had kept himself between Radl and the door, was still studying the ceiling. "Have you rigged the telephone?"

"The recording is set, and I've arranged earphones so you can monitor the call," Mercer said with a gesture toward the telephone and tape recorder.

Trosper turned back to Radl. "The alternate *Treff* is at the *Ostbahnhof.* At eight-fifteen, and at five-fifteen, on the platform where the train from Debrecen comes in. The station should be busy then. If Grisha does not like that, we can try again later at night. But he will have to set the time for that meeting."

"That feels better to me, either in the morning or late afternoon," Radl said, and made another note. "But it will be up to Grisha. He has his own view of things like that. He makes the decisions."

"If Grisha can get out on his own, he should feel free to take all of the decisions," Trosper said. "If he wants our help, some of the decisions will rest with us." Even in extremis, Radl had the ability to irritate Trosper.

"I must also have some idea how long Grisha can stay in Budapest before he is missed," Trosper added.

Radl shrugged. "I'll try, but there's only so much we can say on an open line."

"What about you?" Kyle asked. "Where were you staying in Vienna. How long will it be before you are missed?"

"I'm at the Hotel Stiffler, a little place in the Seventeenth District. It's my *Stammlokal,* I almost always stay there. They know me. I'll go back right after I call Grisha."

"You won't be going anywhere after you call," Trosper said carefully. "You'll be right here with us." He glanced at Mercer.

Radl started to protest.

"Is there anything you need there?" Kyle asked.

"Just my clothes," Radl said. "I can pick them up tomorrow, if that's what you want." He looked across the room to Mercer near the door. "That is, if it's all right with Mr. Hyde." Mercer shifted in his chair and raised his hand as if to run it across his head. He stopped, unwilling to risk disturbing the wig.

"Tomorrow, you can buy what he may need for the next few days," Trosper said to Kyle. "I don't want him to leave the apartment until we're all clear." He glanced at the empty coffee cups. "While you're making some more coffee, we'll have time to review the telephone business again."

TROSPER tossed the earphones onto the table. The call had taken four minutes. In as broad a Viennese dialect as Trosper had ever heard, Radl had flawlessly played the part of an anxious agent, frightened at talking directly to Moscow, anxious to make a good impression and querulously eager to get his instructions straight. In Moscow, Grisha spoke in a low voice and with brisk authority. His German was accented but fluent. While pretending to misunderstand Radl's almost impenetrable *Wiendeutsch,* he answered each of the questions Trosper had given the agent. There was no hint of emotion in his voice, no trace of concern, only the quiet authority of a senior operative talking to an anxious agent.

THERE were few things, Trosper admitted to himself, that gave him a greater feeling of well-being than breakfast in a good hotel. The sparkling white napery, glistening silver, spotless crystal, and attentive service gave him an almost childish sense of luxury. And in Sacher's, the fresh orange juice, scrambled eggs, sausages, bacon, and the profusion of hard rolls, toast, and croissants were as irresistible as the marmalade, jam, fresh butter, and coffee with hot milk.

Before Brattle pushed his coffee cup aside, Trosper had sketched the outline of the case and the leak in Washington, and identified Aksenov as the primary source of the information Radl had delivered. He described Bates's conviction that Kudrov was a straight agent and that Radl had been sent to discredit him. But he did not mention the Iskra group or Bates's conviction that it was a bona fide resistance organization.

"I can't see exactly why your headquarters is so convinced that Kudrov is straight, and that Radl is controlled," Brattle said. "It seems to me, your head office could have had it both ways—exploit Radl for what he is worth and run Kudrov as if he were straight.

You could have gone on that way until something came up to prove things one way or another."

"There are a couple of bits I've left out," Trosper admitted with a grin.

"I dare say."

"If we can believe Radl, Colonel Aksenov will be able to tie the can to Kudrov. Aside from that, he should be a damned good source on what Moscow Center has been up to for the last few years."

"And if your head office is right about Radl," Brattle said, "and if Radl is controlled by Moscow, he'll have put our weenie right into the wringer in Budapest."

Trosper laughed and said, "That's why I keep telling you there's no need for you to come along. I'll have enough to worry about without trying to keep you out of trouble in Budapest."

"We'll need a Polaroid camera," Brattle said, "and plenty of film. My guess is that city street plans and small-scale maps will be easier to get here in Vienna than in Budapest. We'll need as much cash as we can scare up. How are you fixed?"

"Kyle's already gone to buy the camera and maps, that's no problem. I've got about three thousand in cash of one kind and another and credit cards. I plan to put the money into Swiss francs and twenty-dollar bills."

"I've got fifteen hundred quid in the bank and credit cards," Brattle said. "I'll draw some of it in schillings, the rest in dollars. There are so many tourists in Hungary now, I expect they will take almost any currency."

"I don't know when I can put your account straight," Trosper said. "I'm doing this on my own, more or less ignoring Mr. Bates's orders. If I've bought a dog, the Firm won't pick up the tab. It may take me awhile to settle with you."

"If your dog is on a leash, settling accounts will be the least of our problems," Brattle said.

"I've got a cold passport," Trosper said, "but I'll have to cook the exit stamp from the States and some cachets showing my tourist travel in Europe. Mercer's with me and I've got him working on that now. What about you?"

"I'll go with my own passport, honorary consul and all that. It doesn't give me immunity, but it won't do any harm either."

"Haven't the Hungarians got a book on you?"

"I suppose they have, but it would be pretty old stuff. If I can get the visa in less than two days, I might be in and out before they can run traces on my visa request." Brattle reached for the heavy silver coffee pot and poured himself a final cup. "The only expression for my attitude is sanguine.'" He put down the coffee cup. "When you come to think of it," he said slowly, "it's that approach to things that's been at the root of my outfit's greatest disasters."

23   VIENNA

TROSPER pushed the door to the compartment aside, said *"Grüss Gott, gnädige Frau"* to the woman beside the window, and heaved his suitcase onto the rack above his seat.

Three pieces of leather luggage occupied most of the rack on one side of the compartment, and a camel's hair coat was thrown across the opposite seat. She had done as much as casually possible to make the compartment look as if it had been reserved for her use only.

She was slim and well turned out in an ageless suit of soft tweed, a silk blouse, and polished brown oxfords. Her aquiline features, carefully shaped rose-blond hair, and cared-for complexion made it difficult to judge, but he guessed she was nearly seventy. Old enough to remember the good days, when, he supposed from her appearance and the attitude she projected, her family had estates in Austria *and* in Hungary. Along with the good days, he wondered how selective her memories might be of the *Hitlerzeit*—the time when many of her class had welcomed the *Anschluss* with Germany and were convinced that once Hitler settled down, he would temper all that rhetoric and find accommodation with England.

The train was half empty. Aside from a noisy clutter of German tourists in the smoking compartments, there was only a handful of travelers in the first class section. Trosper hung his trenchcoat on the rack and dropped into his seat.

"Grüss Gott," she said, not certain if his choice of the shop-keeper's *"gnädige"* was meant to be ironic or was merely the awkward use of an unfamiliar language. Trosper pulled the London *Times* and Paris *Herald Tribune* from his coat pocket and tossed them onto the seat.

He watched the familiar scenery as the train pulled from the *Westbahnhof* and through Hietzing and Pukersdorf. Then, a few kilometers west, it veered from the main line and headed south across the rolling farmland towards the flat plain that stretched to Hungary.

When, over the loud, self-conscious voices of the Germans he heard the *Schaffner's* chanted demand, *"Fahrkarten vorweisen bitte,"* Trosper pulled his passport from his pocket. Folded in the notebook-size passport were the entry–exit documents issued by the Hungarian Consulate in Vienna and his rail tickets.

It was a cold passport, and in a way a souvenir of his school days. Harry Fessenden's father was a doctor and his grandfather had been a doctor. With any luck at all, Harry, who was Trosper's best friend, would also have been a doctor. But the summer before he was to leave for Tufts, Harry had earned enough money to buy the ancient Ford he called his jitney. Then, on a rain-slick September night, he slammed the Ford head-on into a beer truck.

In 1962, Trosper had signed Harry's name to a letter requesting a copy of his birth certificate. A few weeks later, with the birth certificate at hand, Trosper applied for Harry's passport. As far as the passport office knew, Harry Ryder Fessenden was alive and planning a trip abroad. It was a misdemeanor, but Trosper had a cold passport—a bona fide document, legally issued, and as far as any counterintelligence investigation might prove, quite untraceable. If Harry hadn't bought his damned jitney, Trosper thought, he would have been amused by the charade.

"Are you English or American?" the woman asked, her light accent bringing Trosper out of his reverie. "American," he said, tucking Harry's passport back into his pocket.

"I thought it was only the English who polished the instep of their boots." She gestured toward his crossed leg and the exposed sole of his shoe.

If the woman was as well-born as her manner suggested, Trosper guessed she had learned English from a nanny at a time when Austria was happy to forget the Great War and English nannies were more chic than French nurses in anglophile Vienna.

He smiled and twisted his foot to glance at the polished instep. "It is an English affectation, you are quite right. An old shoemaker once scolded me for not taking proper care of my shoes. You must be the only person who has ever noticed it." Trosper folded his newspaper. "The old man used to say that leather was alive and could be kept for decades if it was taken care of."

He had always thought of John Thomas as "old Mr. Thomas," although he could not have been more than fifty when Trosper first met him. Even after he had retired from the posh shop in St. James's, Mr. Thomas had been amused to continue to fashion the concealment pocket in Trosper's shoes. Opening from the bottom of the tongue, there was only room for a single sheet of flimsy paper. But in the minuscule diamond type that Trosper had taught himself to print, the single sheet was adequate for cryptic notes.

"There aren't many handmade things that anyone can afford these days," Trosper said. "About all I can indulge myself in is an occasional pair of shoes."

He would have liked to ask if she was going to Hungary to see relatives, or maybe friends she had been at school with. But he would not. He would be the one American she had ever met who did not ask questions and did not offer his life story.

"My father was so," she said, adding another prop to her image. "He wouldn't move a hand to do for himself except to polish his riding boots. He spent hours rubbing at them with an old bone. But he would never let anyone else touch them." As carefully as she spoke, the *w*'s came out as *v*'s, and like many German speakers, she had trouble with English prepositions.

"That's too much for me," Trosper admitted. "Aside from the work involved, once leather has been boned a few times, you can't brush it anymore." Satisfied he had held up his side in the gentry stakes, Trosper returned to his newspaper.

THE TRAIN slowed and then pulled to a halt at what seemed to be a bleak railway siding. There was no indication of a border, but he guessed they had crossed into Hungary.

"Sopron?" he asked, artlessly parading his knowledge by pronouncing the name of the border town "Shop-ron." Putting vanity before cover was a failing that Trosper knew he should have outgrown.

"Yes," she sniffed, and then, as if prudently to distance herself from Trosper, she lapsed into German. "We are entering the future, the People's Republic of Hungary." As the train moved slowly ahead to an apparently empty station, she began to fish for her passport and papers in a leather satchel from Hermès.

In 1956, when he escaped from Budapest with General Horvath, they had avoided Sopron, the westernmost city in Hungary. They crossed at Andau where, just hours before the Soviet armored units closed the frontier, the Hungarian border troops had shucked their uniforms and dashed into Austria.

Trosper stepped into the train corridor. The raucous Germans, momentarily subdued by the prospect of facing Communist authority, were leaning out the windows to peer along the track. On the track at the rear of the train, Trosper could see a soldier. With his feet spread, a machine gun slung across his chest, and the fitted tunic and baggy trousers of his Soviet-style uniform, he was the perfect caricature of a police-state guardian. On the platform alongside the locomotive another guard stood silhouetted. Trosper turned back into his compartment.

THE BLUE-UNIFORMED customs official checked each page of the passport, and then, staring ostentatiously, compared Trosper and the photograph in the document. He handed the passport to the security officer beside him.

The security man scrutinized each passport page, checked the photograph, and handed the document back to Trosper. After removing one copy of the entry–exit form, he held the photograph at arm's length, and like a portrait painter studying his subject before adding a final dab of pigment to the canvas, measured Trosper's appearance against the colored photograph. Apparently satisfied, he handed the paper to the customs officer, who repeated the ritual. Then both stepped aside and a young soldier, a submachine gun strapped across his back and flashlight in hand, dropped to his knees. He flashed the light beneath the seats and ran his hand along the upholstered underside.

"*Est-ce qu'il chasse des puces?*" Trosper asked, speaking softly to the Austrian woman. Less certain than Trosper that the officials did not know French, she glared back at him.

Apparently satisfied there was no secret sharer in the compartment, no hidden messages or bundles of propaganda tucked beneath the seats, the young soldier got to his feet, said something to the security man and stepped out of the compartment.

"*Schön. Gute Reise,*" the customs man muttered, and with a token salute, touched his cap and closed the compartment door.

The border controls were a bit of theater, pro forma and ceremonial, intended at the most to dampen casual smuggling by tourists. Trosper guessed that the exit procedures would be more demanding.

IT WAS as if he had fallen into a time warp. When Trosper had last seen the high steel-and-glass-domed Budapest West Station in November 1956, it was shabby but undamaged by the fighting. Now, it was in exactly the same state of decay. Only the few luggage trolleys, provided in lieu of Communist porters for capitalist tourists, had been added. But they had gone rusty and were coated with grime.

If the West Station was unchanged, much of the rest of Budapest had been swept clean, and restored.

The streets he had last seen cluttered with burned-out vehicles and strewn with the litter of smashed shopfronts were crowded with traffic. Even at intersections, where the buildings favored by snipers had been blasted by Soviet tanks until they spilled into the street like sand castles kicked by petulant children, the reconstruction had been completed. Well-dressed pedestrians churned along the side-walks, aggressively challenging the traffic at crosswalks.

Trosper threw his suitcase onto the backseat of the Fiat taxi and wedged himself alongside. "Hotel Flamenco," he said.

BRATTLE was flying from Vienna. He would stay at the Gellért. "The locals would be pissed if they didn't know where to find me," he said. "I stayed there before the war with my father. In those days the restaurant was worth eating in. Now it's so full of trippers from Stuttgart and Dusseldorf, the food's gone Boche. It's no wonder that your lot goes to the Hilton."

But the rush of tourist travel for the Easter holiday had relegated Trosper to the Flamenco, a huge new hotel, built back on the slopes of Buda by Spanish investors, and fashioned for the busloads of tourists flocking into the Communist capital.

24   BUDAPEST

IF THIS operation were to work, Trosper told himself as he pushed open the glass doors of the Budapest Hyatt Atrium hotel, the Category One Operations seminar would never be asked to critique it. The notion that two capitalist bachelors and a colonel on the run from Moscow Center could hope to knock around Budapest with less cover than the three balls on a billiard table would surely under-mine at least fifty of the hours devoted to denied-area operations planning. If it came unstuck, he realized ruefully, it would be rich training material—look what happens when you don't obey the rules.

In the far corner of the chrome-and-leather hotel bar, Butch Brattle's bulk loomed over the undersized cocktail table. It was the catbird corner, with a commanding view of the bar, and exactly where Trosper expected to find Brattle.

Spotting Trosper, he closed his guidebook and heaved himself to his feet. "Hello, Harry," he boomed. Trosper slipped out of his coat and shook hands.

"I can't understand it," the Englishman said, his hand cupped around an ice-filled tumbler of whiskey. "Every time I ask for whiskey without ice, I get an extra portion of ice. It's no wonder these people drink barack." He signalled for the waitress and Trosper ordered a scotch and soda.

"How's trade?" Trosper asked.

Brattle did not move his head, but behind the heavy hornrimmed glasses, the Englishman's restless eyes swept across the room. Trosper guessed that he was wearing cheaters, thick clear glass in a heavy frame. Although little use as a disguise, the glasses helped mask eye movements that might betray a nervous operative attempting to detect surveillance. For years, the magicians had tried to perfect miniature mirrors which, when built into eyeglass frames, would give a case man an undetected glimpse over his shoulder. But nothing had worked.

"I've walked past my chum's apartment," Brattle said. "The building is in good shape. His name is still on the post box."

The waitress brought Trosper's drink. "Would you like ice, gentleman?" she asked. Trosper glanced at Brattle and said no.

IT WAS dicey, they had agreed in Vienna, to go in with only tourist cover. But there wasn't any choice. "Our best chance," Trosper said, "is to get in and out before the local beavers have sorted through the visa applications and someone begins to wonder why two bachelor tourists should independently decide to spend a few days in Budapest. Then it will only be a few hours before they begin to look us over."

"It will be SQP all right," Trosper had muttered. "Business as usual."

"SQP?"

"*Sauve qui peut.*" It wasn't very funny, but they both laughed.

Trosper glanced around the bar which was beginning to fill with tourists. "Yesterday, last night, did you notice anyone off the reservation?" he asked. "Any Indians at all?"

Brattle shook his head. "There aren't even as many cops on the street as in Vienna," he said. "Certainly no sign of any Indians." He took a sip of his drink, frowned at the ice, and said, "Of course it's not the ones you see that do the damage. It's the invisible little bastards that wing you."

THAT AFTERNOON, Trosper had coffee at the Cafe Vörösmarty. Colonel Aksenov was not in sight. Trosper was not surprised. In Vienna Radl had guessed that the earliest Aksenov might arrive was Sunday. It was just as well. It might take more time than Brattle had figured to arrange things with his chum, Sandor Kados.

IN VIENNA, Brattle had told Trosper the story of Sandor Kados. For almost fifteen years, the widow Marta Kados had worked as a servant in the British minister's residence in Budapest. She reared her son, Sandor, in two small rooms in the servants' quarters of the residence. Until he was sixteen, and apprenticed to a printer, it was the only home the boy knew. By 1938 when she could no longer work, Sandor was a staunch Socialist and anti-Nazi. Despite his politics, and his resentment of the aloof young diplomats, Sandor Kados harbored a grudging regard for the milords. He envied their inpregnable self-confidence and would have liked to share a portion of it.

In 1941, a few hours before Admiral Horthy's government broke relations with Great Britain, the Passport Control Officer from the Consulate came to Sandor's flat. Although he could scarcely comprehend the jittery man's broken Hungarian, Sandor knew enough English to understand the proposition. He refused the code name "Lajos." He would be known as Frederick. He had no memory of Frigyes Kados, his father. But Frigyes translated as Frederick, and it seemed a fitting pseudonym.

In 1943, the first British team parachuted into Hungary. The printer Sandor Kados, code name "Frederick," was on their contact list. For twenty-eight months, Frederick forged identity papers, travel orders, and Gestapo passes for the British network. In 1946, after the war, the British Military Attaché visited Frederick's apartment. He thanked Frederick, presented him with the King's Medal For Valour, and wished him well.

Six years later, another Englishman visited Frederick. Yes, Frederick said, he would help the young man with documents, but no, he would not print propaganda. Aside from the danger of running a clandestine press under the nose of the Soviet occupation troops, he considered propaganda to be nonsense. The Hungarians did not need to be told why they should hate the Russians. The Hungarians knew why they hated the occupation force. Marked "uncooperative" by his impatient young visitor, Frederick was forgotten until November 1956 when the Hungarian revolution broke out and there were pitched battles between Soviet forces and Hungarian resistance fighters in the streets of Budapest. It was then that Brattle, who had dug Frederick's name out of an old file, appealed to him for help with identity documents. Before Brattle made his own escape, he offered Frederick asylum. The Hungarian refused, politely. He would not take his pregnant wife across the border. He would remain in Budapest. Hungary was his life; if the baby was a boy, it would be his son's life.

Kados would be old now, Brattle had told Trosper, but if anyone could cook a document that would see Grisha across the border, it would be Sandor Kados, code name "Frederick."

THEY dined at Matyaspince in Pest, near the Elizabeth Bridge, and lingered over their meal. They would walk to Frederick's apartment and arrive before the outer door was locked. "I'd better not telephone," Brattle said. "If the phone is spiked, a few words in German, even pretending to have a wrong number, will attract attention."

"What if they have visitors?" Trosper asked. "What if they are out for the night? What if they have gone away early for the Easter holiday?" He did not expect an answer.

"We should put the place under surveillance for a few days," Brattle muttered. "Maybe bring in a team, some of our own Indians, so we can establish their pattern—what time they leave the house, when the neighbors drop in, what time they go to bed." He stopped to let the irony sink in. "If it takes too long to get the team assembled, maybe we should do the watching ourselves." More irony. "I like the picture—the two of us, taking turns, loitering across the street until we see Frederick come in alone." He shook his head slowly. "It's been twenty years, for Christ's sake, I'm not even sure I would recognize him at a distance."

"Hard lines, Douglas, no Category One folderol, no phone calls by perfect native speakers, no surveillance, no equipment, just potluck at ten-thirty." Trosper smiled, "When you get right down to it, we haven't got much money either."

"I wonder what a passport, any bloody passport with photograph and exit paper goes for in downtown Budapest these days?"

"A bundle," Trosper said. He poured the rest of the Egri Bikaver into their glasses. "Or, as you would say, a proper bundle."

"Now that we've got that off our chest," Brattle said, "I think it's time for coffee and a walk to Frederick's."

25   BUDAPEST

THEY WALKED east along Kossuth to the intersection where, abruptly, the name changed and the avenue became the Rakoczi. As they crossed the broad thoroughfare, Trosper dropped back, and when they turned north on Kazinczy, Brattle crossed the street. Trosper, now fifty yards behind his friend, remained on the opposite side. It was dark, there were few vehicles, and the scattered, self-absorbed pedestrians hurrying along the empty streets paid no attention. As far as Trosper could see, there was no one behind Brattle.

At the second intersection, they repeated the maneuver, and Trosper took the point, almost eighty yards ahead of Brattle and on the opposite side of the deserted street. It was primitive, do-it-yourself countersurveillance, but as much as two men alone could manage.

When he reached Csanyi street, Brattle, hugging the wall, turned the corner so quickly it seemed for a moment as though the burly

Englishman had disappeared. Trosper continued across the intersection and crossed at the opposite corner. In the distance, he caught another glimpse of Brattle, walking slowly now. Then the Englishman swerved and stepped into the darkness of a tall doorway. Still on the opposite side of the street, Trosper continued past the doorway where Brattle stood, and on toward the intersection. There he crossed again and walked slowly back to Brattle. There was no sign of surveillance, no Indians anywhere along the deserted street.

"It's a big apartment," Brattle had told him, "three or four rooms. I suppose Kados got it during the war. Everything was cheap then. I know he was already there in 1945, when the Russians came in."

Brattle pressed the *minuterie,* the hall lights that switched off after thirty seconds, and they walked quickly up the broad stone stairs. When they reached the third floor, Brattle pointed to the end of the corridor. A faint light shone through a small, translucent glass panel in the heavy apartment door. He raised his clenched fist in a gesture of a job well done.

As Trosper bent to read the name on the brass plate above the white bell, the unmistakable, pounding beat of a rock record echoed from the apartment. He drew back and glanced quizzically at Trosper who bent down to check the name. No question, "Kados" was boldly etched across the brass plate.

Brattle touched the bell. For a moment, the sharp, harsh clanging blotted out the pounding rock music. There was no response. Brattle touched the bell again.

From within the apartment came a muffled shout and the sound of a door opening. Then steps along the hallway, a head silhouetted against the translucent glass, the rattle of a chain lock, and the door was eased ajar.

He looked about thirty, slim, long dark hair, turtleneck sweater, faded blue jeans, and running shoes. His deep-set dark eyes widened in surprise as he confronted Brattle, whose broad-shouldered bulk almost concealed Trosper standing a foot behind. In a quick gesture, he moved to push the door shut. Brattle leaned forward, across the threshold. He spoke in German.

"I am sorry to disturb you at this time, but my friend and I are looking for Herr Kados Sandor." Brattle's only concession to Hungarian was to reverse the family and given name. "I am John Miller." As he thrust his hand forward, he eased himself another few inches into the apartment.

"Kados Tibor," said the young man. As he reached to shake hands with Brattle, the door swung open and Brattle stepped into the apartment. "My friend, Mr. Johnson," Brattle said. Trosper extended his hand and slipped through the doorway.

ALONG the far wall of the square living room was a rack of audio equipment, a shining Sony amplifier, receiver, record player, and tape deck. In the corners of the room were free-standing loudspeakers, slim as Chinese screens. Although the young man had turned down the amplifier, the room seethed with sound.

"MY FATHER has been dead four years," Tibor explained. His German was fluent, but spoken with the unmistakable glottal Hungarian accent, each syllable carefully pronounced.

"I'm sorry," Brattle said. "He was a good man, I liked him."

"And my mother died in 1982."

Trosper mumbled his sympathy.

"How did you know my father . . . ?" The young man stopped, not certain how to finish his question.

"It was after the war, I was here in Budapest on a visit. Some of my friends had known him, they asked me to say hello."

It was not one of Brattle's most convincing fabrications.

"My father was a quiet man," Kados said softly. "I didn't know he knew any foreigners."

"My friends had known him during the war," Brattle said. "They had a high regard for him."

The young Hungarian glanced anxiously at Trosper, and then nodded.

"What about you?" Brattle asked. "Have you carried on his trade? Are you a printer, too?"

No, not at all, Kados said. He had won admission to the university, and had taken a degree in music. After that, he had completed his obligatory military service. "I am the least military of all the Magyars," he laughed. "After the military, another two year sentence, marriage." He shrugged and, as if remembering some long-ago caress, ran his slim fingers through his hair and along the side of his face. As Kados moved his hand, and the sleeve of his jersey pulled back over his wrist, Trosper could see a modish black wristwatch and black steel band.

"But that is also over. Now, I have a small position, a post in the State Recording Institute. I supervise recording sessions, pop and classic," he said. "Now, sometimes, when I'm lucky, I get to travel, and arrange for foreign artists to record with our people."

"Your father's work," Brattle asked softly. "Didn't he give you some training as a printer?"

Kados ignored the question. "When you rang, I thought you were the neighbors," he said. "That's why I shouted."

His dark, deep-set eyes were large and moist and girlish. Starlet's eyes, Trosper thought.

"The walls are thick in these old buildings, the windows double glazed, but the peasants down the hall still think they can hear my stereo. I suppose they have to have something to complain about— but they're better off with my music than if this apartment were turned over to someone else, some good Party functionary with six kids and a fat wife from the provinces."

"We thought it best to come a little late," Trosper said. "Just because the neighbors might have been curious about your father having foreign visitors."

"That's why we didn't telephone," Brattle said. "As I remember, he didn't like the telephone at all."

Kados shifted uneasily in his chair. It was a copy of an Eames. The black leather and moulded shape clashed with the heavy, dark furniture his parents had left for him. "Just what is it you want?" he asked. "What was it you came to see my father about?"

It was a moment of truth. When the next step was taken and disclosure made, there would be no turning back. Because Brattle shared some of the risk, Trosper turned slightly so that he could see his friend full face. The Englishman sat motionless, his hands folded across his massive chest. Then, with an almost imperceptible movement, he nodded. It was probably meant to signal that the decision was Trosper's. But Trosper could almost hear the Englishman speak —"In for a farthing, in for a quid."

Trosper would have liked to have the case file spread out on a desk. He would like to read the data again, to weigh the evidence, ponder the equities, to think for a moment about Galkin and his wife, the little spy Radl, and about Bates, Iskra, Dancer, and the unknown Colonel Aksenov. It was in moments like this that Trosper knew he had touched the heart of the racket. There were no gadgets to fall back on, no experts to consult, and no reams of printout, spun fresh from a computer chip. There was only a case man, on his own and at the end of the line.

"A friend is planning to make a trip," Trosper said briskly. "But first we need help with the papers. Perhaps even a little printing."

26   BUDAPEST

KADOS rose from his chair. "Your visit surprised me so, I have forgot my fine Hungarian hospitality," he said. "I haven't offered you a drink, not even a cigar." He picked up a box of Havanas. "They are the very best, you can't even get them in New York."

"It's not necessary . . ." Brattle waved his hand.

"A drink certainly," Kados said. "What would my father have thought." He got up. "Some whiskey? I like your Anglo-Saxon drink more than barack—the stuff's too sweet." He walked to a bar at the side of the room, his Adidas running shoes squeaking as he stepped from the rug onto the waxed, parquet floor. "Will this do?" He picked up a liter bottle of Johnny Walker Black Label. "It's the best there is."

Brattle grunted.

"You can get it in the Inter-Tourist shops if you have dollars or Swiss francs," Kados said.

"Soda or water?" Kados reached into a bucket on the bar and, before Brattle could object, dropped ice cubes into the glasses half filled with whiskey.

Kados took a long drink. "You'll have to agree," he said. "Things are not altogether bad behind the famous Iron Curtain?"

The muted thunder of the audio rig, the brash, framed wall posters—the Rolling Stones, Cream, and Heavy Metal—the Eames chair, blue jeans, and running shoes made a complete picture. Except for the heavy crystal whiskey glasses, tall and too slim for Trosper's taste, Tibor Kados, functionary of the Budapest State Recording Service, might have been entertaining his friends in London, Rome, or Paris.

"What about this printing—as you call it," Kados asked, his eyes darting from Trosper to Brattle.

"It is nothing special," Brattle said. "Just a few changes in a passport." He shook the ice in his glass like poker dice in a cup.

"What kind of a passport is it?" Kados asked. "Hungarian?"

"What would be best?" Trosper asked.

"Do you have so many to chose from?"

"Actually," Brattle said, "that's part of the problem. It may be that we will need a passport as well as a bit of cobbling."

Kados flicked the ash from his cigar, twisted sideways and hooked his leg across the broad arm of the leather chair. "When I was just a kid, I asked my father what he had done to get the medal he kept hidden. All he said was that he made shoes for the British during the war. When I was older, and realized how much the medal meant to him I asked again. He told me that 'shoes' were identification papers, passports, or the wartime identification cards the Germans made everyone carry. He said you people called him 'Frederick, the cobbler.' "

'Cobbler' was slang from the twenties, probably pinched from the old Comintern by some long-forgotten British agent, but Trosper saw no need to explain. "Given a choice, what passport is best for crossing out of Hungary?" he asked.

A slight smile crossed Kados face. "Why don't you ask your people, the famous CIA or the great British intelligence, what they think? Find out what passports they have on the shelf. I don't see why you think I can help you to do things like that."

"This is a private matter," Brattle said. "We're helping a friend, there's no one else involved."

"Samaritans," Kados said with a shrug. "A pair of NATO Samaritans." Trosper saw Brattle hunch forward in his chair. Irony was for friends.

"What passport would be best?" Trosper asked sharply.

"British, American, Spanish—even Austrian," Kados said. "Just so long as it is from a country that sends plenty of tourists here." He reached to touch his face, and for a moment tugged lightly at his ear. "I suppose you Samaritans know that your friend should be able to speak the language of the passport. It's no good speaking Hungarian when you've got Spanish papers."

"Yes," Brattle said. "We've figured that out."

"What language does this lucky man speak?"

"Time enough for that," Brattle said. "Am I correct—did your father teach you a bit of the trade—can you cobble something together for us?"

Kados pushed back the sleeve of his jersey and glanced admiringly at the black face of his watch. "I have a friend coming in a few minutes." His smile was nearly a smirk. "Because of the neighbors, she won't ring at this time of night. She has a key and will come right in. When she arrives, you just sit here. There's no need to get up, or to speak. She'll go into the other room."

"What about the papers?" Brattle asked.

"Look," Kados said. "It's very tough now, almost impossible. It will be better in summer. Why don't you Samaritans tell that to your friend?"

"We won't be waiting that long," Brattle said. "We plan to move along in a few days."

"Then it's out of the question."

From the hallway came the grating of a key in the lock and the sound of the heavy door swinging open. A throaty woman's voice called "*Salut,* Tibo, hullo."

Kados got slowly to his feet, called something in Hungarian, and strode toward the girl who had stepped into the room.

She was as tall as Kados and slim. She wore a black skirt and a white blouse cut like a man's shirt. The heavy gold link bracelet on her left wrist echoed the thick necklace visible beneath the unbuttoned shirt. She brushed her lips against Kados's cheek, pulled back for a moment and then, taking his face in her hands, pulled his mouth to hers. Without taking her hands from her lover's face, she twisted to look over her shoulder to where Trosper and Brattle were sitting. She turned back to Kados and still holding his face, kissed him again.

Kados said something in Hungarian, and taking her arm, led her toward the door leading from the living room. He began to speak in English. "Darling," he said, "my friends talk business," and then lapsed back into Hungarian. At least Trosper thought he said darling. It sounded like "dohlingh."

The girl brushed back her hair and, with a dismissive glance at the visitors, stalked out of the room.

"I suppose it's the paprika," Brattle whispered wistfully. "All that damned paprika makes them like that."

"Sultry," Trosper muttered. "Their mothers take them to gypsies for sultry lessons."

YES, Kados admitted, his father had taught him a few things. "Aside from this apartment," he said, "that was all he did for me. Except to say a thousand times that I was not to tell anyone, and only to use his tricks for a cause, for something I believed in." The Hungarian snorted, and stopped to relight his cigar.

"He never told anyone about his work in the war," Kados explained. "No one knew what he had done against the Nazis. Even the people he worked with didn't know his name. He said that was the only reason he survived. And that's probably why the AVO never bothered him. Only the milords, as he called them, at the embassy knew about him. After the war they came twice. Once he refused to do what they wanted. Then in fifty-six, before I was born, in the middle of the fighting here in Budapest, someone came again. This time my father helped, he actually thought we could get free of the Ivans. Even so, no one ever found out. Not the AVO, not even the Ivans. No one.

"But things are different now," Kados continued quickly. "Hungary has changed, people have made their peace. We live, we get by —some good food, a little travel, my music—it's not a bad life. No one needs politics anymore. All that danger for nothing."

It sounded like a practiced monologue, the kind of mantra jittery agents recite to themselves. Kados put down his cigar and picked up the glass of whiskey. Looking at Trosper over the rim of the glass, he said in German, "Of course it helps to have a little extra bread."

He might be able, Kados said, to cobble the right passport— change the photograph, alter the personal identification data and physical description, check the visas and the entry and exit stamps. The Hungarian exit certificate and photograph would be no problem, but would cost extra. He could give no idea of the time, until he learned what passports were available.

"How much will you pay?" he asked.

"Make your price," Brattle said.

"Depending on the work I have to do on the passport, it will be from a thousand to two thousand dollars. Half of it to be given me here in dollars, the rest to be delivered to my account in Vienna."

"What about the passport?" Trosper asked.

"It depends on what is available, but it will be a minimum of a thousand dollars here, and another thousand in Vienna."

"Where do you get the documents?"

Kados's eyebrows shot up. He shook his head, "That will be my secret."

"And if we supply the passport?" Trosper asked.

"If it's in good condition, my price will be the same. If not, I'll have to charge more. Maybe a lot more."

"You're too expensive," Brattle said. "Those prices are ridiculous."

Kados smiled. "Maybe you can do better. Try it. Try and get something from one of the embassies. They will laugh in your face."

Brattle shook his head. "We'll see, once we have had a chance to look at your merchandise."

"Look," Kados said. "There's one thing I can promise. If I don't think the passport and the exit certificate will pass, I won't let you have them. I can't take any more risks."

His glance flashed between Trosper and Brattle. His fingers drummed on the leather arm of the chair. He picked up the cigar. It was dead. He dropped it into the ashtray beside his chair.

"Look," he said. "The important thing is to stay in control. That's the way I do it. No one—at least until you two showed up here—deals with me directly. Everything goes through a friend of mine. He's the only one who knows me, and he handles all of the details on the business side."

Kados glared at Brattle. "You people . . . all dressed up and protected by a fancy embassy. Things would look different if you were taking the risks."

The young Hungarian gulped the last of his drink. His hand shook as he put down the empty crystal glass.

27 BUDAPEST

"THERE'S one thing sure, he's not the fellow his father was. The old man was like iron." Brattle put aside the menu he had been studying. "And he could keep his mouth shut. Young master Tibor is something else."

"Windy as hell," Trosper said, "and beneath the stupid posturing, he's wide open."

THEY had left Kados's apartment at midnight. By the time they slipped separately out of the area, it was too late to meet safely for a postmortem. Even in benign areas, hotel rooms were dangerous. Shop talk in a Budapest hotel, they had agreed, would be foolhardy. Without a safe house or access to an embassy, they had no choice but to meet in restaurants, the more expensive and tourist-cluttered, the better. On the stairway, after leaving Tibor Kados's apartment, they had agreed to lunch in Buda, at the Gellért.

Trosper didn't mind waiting a few hours before trying to sort out Tibor Kados with Brattle. The emotional unwinding triggered by the safe return from a dangerous meeting was notorious for skewing the judgment of even the old hands. A few hours alone would allow both of them to make an independent assessment of the meeting with Kados.

AS BRATTLE had predicted, the hotel was filled with German tourists. "*Wehrmacht* old boys," he snorted, "reliving their salad days, when the hotel was a Nazi *Stammlokal.*"

They looked like businessmen to Trosper but, knowing that time had scarcely dimmed Brattle's memory of the war or softened his view of the Nazis, he remained silent. The Englishman caught Trosper's reaction and apologized. "It's not your fault you were too young to have seen them in uniform," he said.

"That audio gear of his would cost a thousand bucks in New York," Trosper said. "Maybe more."

"Only 'the very best,'" Brattle said, imitating Kados's glottal accent. "Even the expensive girl friend."

"I guess we have to figure that Tibor gave her a complete rundown," Trosper said softly. It wasn't a question, he didn't want an answer.

"She wouldn't even have had to ask what he was up to," Brattle said. "He couldn't wait to remind her what an important fellow he is."

The waiter came and they ordered lunch.

"Perhaps it's because I'm four years out of the racket," Brattle said, "but it's hard to see how a young hustler can carry on like that. Things can't have changed that much."

"Some things have," Trosper said, "probably more so here than . . ."

Brattle shook his head. "I wonder."

"There's a whole underground economy in the Soviet Union, almost a subculture," Trosper said. "Food, clothing, liquor, even medical attention—the best of everything they have—is all available on the underground market. Andropov as much as admitted that the gray market was out of hand when he began his big crackdown in the Soviet Union. Given the Hungarian temper, it's done with more panache here."

When the waiter finished serving the paprika chicken, Trosper said, "They've introduced a little free enterprise, made local managers responsible for turning a profit, and uncorked the tourist industry. Now, for the first time in years, there's some money available. The hitch is there is almost nothing to spend it on. That's what nourishes the gray market and people like Tibor."

"That's as may be," Brattle said, "but it doesn't explain why our friend Tibor acts as if the security service had disbanded itself."

"I agree."

"You can't tell me the AVO—the security service—doesn't have a line on someone living like that."

"We can hope," Trosper said, his voice trailing off. Hope was a placebo. It had no place in operations.

Brattle raised his glass. "Cheers," he said, irony written large across his face. "You've made me feel much better."

"Damn it," Trosper said. "You know as well as I do that if we were stunting like this in Moscow, and one of us sneezed, two KGB Indians would catch a cold—they'd be that close to us twenty-four hours a day. It's different here, the paranoia isn't so deep, and they've got to protect a tourist industry that produces half their hard currency. Total security—a cop on every corner and a squad of Indians behind every tourist—just won't wash. Until the AVO has some reason to suspect one of us, we still have a little room to maneuver."

Brattle looked around the room. "I wonder where all the musicians go at noontime," he said. "It doesn't seem right, eating Hungarian food without some gypsy sticking his fiddle in my ear." He speared another piece of chicken. "Where do you think our friend can get a passport?"

"Probably right here in Hungary," Trosper said. "They're lifted from tourists, taken from hotel rooms, snitched in nightclubs or restaurants. A hundred bucks will see you a stolen tourist passport almost anywhere in Europe—ask any of the terrorist punks. It can't be much different here."

"The real problem is to find a good cobbler," Brattle said. "Someone who can wash a passport clean as new and reissue it—that's what I thought I had in old Kados."

There was no point in talking about what might have been. Trosper said, "Even if the AVO has some idea of what young Tibor has been up to, they will do what they always do when they uncover a scheme—they try to put in a window, an agent. Then they sit back and watch. When it gets too close to the knuckle, they bust it."

Brattle laughed. "I'm glad we're not up to anything they might object to."

The waiter cleared the table and served the coffee. Then Trosper said, "You know, Douglas, this is a first for me." Brattle looked up expectantly. "Not only are we working on a shoestring, but there are four people in the operation and I haven't the slightest idea who the hell any of them may be."

Brattle grinned. "Tibor, the fearless young man," he said. "His cut-out and pal, name not given. And, lest we forget, that man-eating bit of crumpet." He dropped a sugar cube into his coffee. "Who's the fourth?"

"Colonel Aksenov, our man in Moscow. All I know about him is what Radl has told me."

Brattle stirred the sugar in his coffee. "Thou shalt never work with persons unknown. Thou shalt always run name traces on those with whom you work." He took a sip of coffee. "And, thou shalt never rendezvous at a place of *their* choosing." He shrugged his shoulders. "That is the writ—in my service, in your outfit, and I suppose in Moscow." He glanced around the room, his eyes masked by the heavy cheaters. "I suppose there are some other rules we've broken, but I can't recall them right now." He drained his cup. "What about the AVO window?" he asked. "Is it the friendly cut-out, or Miss Budapest?"

"I'm not about to bet against us, but if I had to wager, I'd say it is the cut-out who's on the leash."

"To the AVO?"

"That, and maybe the foreign intelligence service, the AVH," Trosper said. "Any scam involving illegal border crossing is as interesting to the intelligence guys as it is to the AVO security goons." He emptied his wine glass. "You know what they say, 'any number can play.'"

"This has been a great lunch," Brattle said. "I hope we're both free for dinner."

THE Vörösmarty was on the northern side of Vörösmarty Ter, the square north of the Vaci Utca and a few steps beyond the pedestrian mall that once had been bordered by the best shops in Budapest. The small marble-top tables, banquette seating, and dingy, thirties decor, reminded Trosper of a Vienna cafe, Sacher's or Dehmel's, a few years after the war.

Trosper lingered in front of the *patisserie* counter, studying the pastry. Then he walked to a small, round table at the far corner of the cafe. He draped his coat across a chair and slipped onto the banquette.

It was three-thirty. He would wait forty-five minutes.

28 BUDAPEST

HE WAS taller than Radl, but walked the same way, erect, stomach tucked in, moving carefully as if taking care to balance his head squarely on the top of his spine. His heavy uniform blouse was well tailored, the burnished khaki cloth shaped to fit his trim figure. He moved slowly, threading his way between the crowded tables, until, near the corner where Trosper sat, he paused. Trosper rose a few inches from the upholstered bench. As he caught Colonel Aksenov's eye, he inclined his head in a tentative bow of recognition.

"Warner," he said, extending his hand in the German manner.

"Karpov," said the Russian.

Trosper smiled. "Greetings from Franz." He spoke quietly, in German.

Aksenov's expression did not change. "He is well?"

"In good hands, and impatient to see you."

If I've been set up, Trosper thought, they will wait until we have finished, and Aksenov has left. He scanned the room. If there was surveillance, he knew there was only a slight chance he could spot it. Working on their home field, the AVO would have flooded the cafe with its own people. The best he might do would be to spot a goon. The muscle men were harder to camouflage. His glance swept the room again. Nothing.

"I am quite alone, Herr Warner," Aksenov said, his brown eyes suggesting a smile.

Embarrassed, Trosper muttered, "Sometimes I feel that I'm a long way from home."

"I know that feeling."

A waitress came to the table. She said something in Hungarian. Aksenov spoke in Russian. Flustered, she shook her head in apology. In German, Aksenov ordered Baroque Torte and coffee. He took off his uniform cap and placed it carefully on the chair beside him. Trosper asked for another coffee.

"After liberation in 1945, our Hungarian allies made Russian-language study mandatory at all levels of school here," Aksenov said, glaring at the waitress as she took Trosper's cup. "Until our grateful hosts master enough Russian to serve coffee and a bit of cake, we have the choice of speaking German or learning Hungarian." He watched the waitress hurry across the crowded cafe. "For this we took three thousand casualties forcing the Germans back across the Danube."

"How much time do we have?" Trosper asked.

Aksenov's expression did not change. "Forty-eight hours, possibly three days. But not a moment longer. They had already begun the investigation of the leak on 'Phoenix' and Kudrov before I left Moscow. It is only a matter of days before they smell me out."

"What about clothing? Do you have civilian clothes?"

"Yes."

"Papers?"

"Nothing that will help at the border," Aksenov said. "If there had been more time, if we could have acted as I planned. . . ."

He was quite handsome. Thick, close-cropped black hair shot with gray, high forehead, large brown eyes, and delicate, almost aquiline nose. His face was unlined and, in the manner of a veteran case man, almost without expression.

"Before we go further, I will need something concrete, something I can present as proof of your identity." It would do no harm, Trosper reasoned, to let Aksenov think there was a team behind him, and a senior officer who would pass on the Russian's bona fides and make the decisions.

The Russian nodded.

"Who is Lopatin?" Always begin on the flank, and with easy questions.

The Russian studied Trosper. It was as if he were memorizing his face to describe it in a meeting report. Then he bent forward, closer to Trosper. "Mikhail Alexandrovich Lopatin is one of our men— from the old school. He was at the university in Vienna before the war, and stayed on until the liberation in 1945. You people may know him as Schneider. He was one of the best. Didn't Franz tell you about him?"

"Not enough," Trosper said. "How did he know Galkin?"

"The Lopatin story does no credit to my service, but it is very long. I told my driver I would be back in thirty minutes. I'm not sure that gives us enough time. . . ."

"Your driver?" Trosper did not conceal his surprise.

"Why not a driver? I'm here on official business. The least the *rezidentura* can do is provide a car so I can have coffee and a bit of cake."

Trosper did not suppress his smile. "This may be the first time your service has supplied a car and driver so that an officer of your rank can come to a meeting like this."

Aksenov smiled. "I will miss these privileges."

"How did Lopatin come to know a young officer like Galkin?" Trosper asked.

"After his release from prison Lopatin was too shaky for foreign work. He began to teach at our schools. Later, when he was better, and could go abroad again on temporary assignments, he would still lecture whenever he was in Moscow. He is very popular with the young men, and for good reason. He is one of the best from the old school, a living link to the past. Like Sorge in Japan, and William Fisher in Germany, he made a real contribution to our victory. A few years ago he was made a Hero of the Soviet Union. Our highest decoration. With it comes the Order of Lenin, and the Gold Star."

Aksenov shifted in his chair and turned to glance around the crowded cafe. The tables on either side had emptied. Even the nonchalant Hungarians kept a distance from a Soviet colonel in uniform.

"You know about Fisher, I suppose?" The Russian's expression changed slightly. Trosper guessed it was a smile. "Even after your people arrested him in New York, they still thought he was someone called Colonel Abel."

Trosper grinned. "If it makes you feel any better, I was on assignment out of the country at that time. But perhaps you can tell me what Mr. Fisher, or Colonel Abel, was doing in New York?"

"Of course," the Russian said, "I can give you the exact details of Willy Fisher's assignment in your country. But not now. That is one of the things that will wait until we have completed our arrangements, and Franz and I are in the United States."

"Tell me more about Lopatin?"

"In nineteen forty-five, when he got back from Austria the Little Father gave him the same treatment that they all got—long interrogation in Lubyanka, then prison. Because he had been successful, *and* managed to survive, *and* had been abroad for so long, Stalin decided Lopatin must have made a deal with the Gestapo or, even worse, allied himself with the British or Americans. It was nonsense, of course, but it happened. But Lopatin was very sick. After all he had gone through in Austria, he couldn't take the treatment he got. By the time he was released, he was half crazy."

"Surely he wasn't the only one treated that way," Trosper said.

"It was the same with Leopold Trepper from Belgium, and Sandor Rado, who came back from Switzerland in 1945. Only the Englishman, the one who was Rado's radio man in Switzerland, managed to avoid prison. He called himself Foote."

"And Foote defected the minute you sent him back to Berlin."

"We never told the Little Father—Stalin—about that, he would have had some heads."

"What was it that Lopatin did to gave him such a reputation?" Trosper asked.

"He did exactly what old General Abakumov told him to. Before the war he had spotted three young Austrians, good Austrians, but not Party men. They were reserve officers. He recruited them—one was killed early in the fighting. The other two went to the German General Staff in Berlin. They were the source of the best order of battle intelligence ever collected. It came right off the battle maps in the General Staff headquarters in Berlin, and was funneled through Rado in Switzerland to Moscow. The Nazis never identified either of our men. Even after the war, you people never did figure out the source of Rado's information. As a matter of fact, Rado never knew—all he did was send the stuff back to Moscow. As long as the operation ran, the material was almost as important to us as the German codes that you and the English broke. It was Lopatin who set up the entire operation. And because Stalin was convinced Lopatin had made a deal with the British, he threw him into Lubyanka. No wonder Misha is still a little crazy."

Ancient history, Trosper knew, but solid information all the same.

"Now, before I talk anymore, before I say anything about 'Phoenix,' it is your turn to speak. What are you offering Franz and me?"

While the waitress served the coffee and pastry, Trosper had time to frame his answer.

"I can make no promises," he began. "But the usual arrangements would call for both of you to be hired as consultants at the pay of your equivalent rank in our service. This will go on as long as you are active. When the interrogations are finished, you will have a choice. If you want to work, there will certainly be a job for you. If you prefer to retire or begin a new career, we will help you establish yourself. In either event, the pensions will be more than adequate to ensure a decent life for you and Franz."

"You said you can make no promises?"

"Not while I am sitting in a cafe in Budapest. The details will be worked out once you are free and clear and have asked formally for political asylum. It is a matter of routine, but you and Franz must have visas. Besides that, my many superiors back home must have a good idea of the value of your information, and be certain of your bona fides."

Like an actor miming astonishment, Aksenov raised his eyebrows. "Are these the same people who decided Kudrov was a bona fide defector?"

"Yes," Trosper said.

"That is not satisfactory," Aksenov said. "I will not subject Franz or myself to such a collection of simpletons. I am a division chief at Moscow Center. I will not deal with ignorant amateurs."

"I understand your feeling, but my service must operate under certain guidelines—"

"You ask me to leave one bureaucracy for another? Is that what I'm to do?"

"I haven't asked you to do anything," Trosper said. "It was Franz who asked *me* to arrange your escape. I am doing so at some expense and considerable effort. If this is not satisfactory, you should find other means."

Aksenov's expression hardened. In Moscow, only generals talked back to senior colonels. "Thanks to your service having told Kudrov that he had been denounced, I have no other means," Aksenov said.

"If that actually happened, it was a very serious blunder. It is not something that I can undo. But, as it happens, you will profit from it. Your plan simply to vanish was nonsense. It would only have been a matter of months before your friends from the Center caught up with you. With our support, you will have protection and a decent life."

Trosper took a sip of his coffee. It was cold. "We have to make plans. It is a waste of time to argue like this."

"You were fools to believe Kudrov. That was the oldest trick in our book—we pulled it on you in 1922, and we did it again in Poland in 1948, and later in Czechoslovakia." Aksenov took a bite of the cream-filled pastry. "At least these ungrateful bastards can cook."

"In the time we have left, tell me about yourself and your career —a brief curriculum vitae."

The Russian spoke rapidly, making no attempt to mask the pride he took in his steady advance from the wartime agent assignment in Vienna to case man status in postwar East Germany, and later at the Soviet Embassy in Bonn. It was after a year with the Soviet delegation to the United Nations in Geneva, Aksenov admitted with a phantom smile, that he began to climb the command ladder. "First I was a desk chief in Moscow. After that, a string of staff assignments in the First Chief Directorate, each one more important than the last," he said. "Then, finally, I came under consideration for posting to London." He shook his head slowly, as if to rid himself of an unpleasant memory. "I would have been the youngest officer ever to have been *rezident* in that country," he said slowly. "But it was not to be."

"Why?"

The Russian glanced around the room, his eyes lingering on the large windows opening onto the sidewalk. "The decision against me had nothing to do with my work. It was always of the highest order. I have the best recommendations."

"What happened?"

"It was quite personal, nothing to do with the service."

"Were you too well known, did the British Foreign Office refuse to accredit you?" It was a mistake to lead an agent, to supply answers for him. But Trosper wanted to keep the Russian talking.

"Not at all," Aksenov said. "I had perfect cover, and always served abroad as Konstantin Mikhailovich Karpov. No one ever identified my true name. Not even any of our defectors could give my real name to your people."

"What then?"

"It was not so important. I married very late, too late perhaps. She was a good woman, but after two years she decided our marriage was empty. She left me for an air force man, a real warrior. My service will not send a senior officer abroad without a wife."

Not true, Trosper knew. Officers *could* go abroad alone, although sometimes marriages of convenience were arranged between members of the service.

Aksenov did not look up from the table. "Perhaps my wife prattled. I know there was some gossip. Not much, but enough to end my hopes for another foreign assignment worth my ability." This, he said, meant that he would finish his career doing staff work in Moscow. "I had worked too hard, and accomplished too much to settle for less than promotion to general. I lost it all because of that silly woman."

"You had a much better career than most," Trosper said.
"That wasn't the only problem. I had seen too much of the West, too much of your capitalism. Perhaps if we Russians hadn't been promised anything, I would not have minded. But there were always the promises that things would change, that the system would finally work, that things would be better for everyone. During the war, the Little Father promised that things would change once we had beaten the Germans. But nothing did. Then came Khrushchev. At least he had the strength to admit that the Little Father was a monster, I'll say that for him. But even so, nothing changed. Then Brezhnev, now Yuri Vladimirovich—Andropov, a man from our own service. It's always going to happen 'soon.' But things go on the same way. Nothing ever changes."

Aksenov looked warily around the cafe. Trosper wondered if the Russian had ever talked this freely, even to Franz Radl.

"It was while I was on a temporary assignment in your country that it all came together for me. I decided to put aside enough money so that I could disappear, just slip away without any fuss. Franz had wanted to leave for years, and was ready to act as a cutout to you people. It was the least I could do for him. He had taken terrible risks for me in Austria during the war."

Again the Russian glanced around the crowded cafe. With a dismissive wave of his hand, said, "Even these Magyars have a better life than hard-working Russians." He took the last bite of his pastry. "I suppose it was the Hapsburgs who taught them to cook."

It was the other way around, but Trosper decided to let Aksenov have the last word. He finished the cold coffee and said, "It's time to make some plans."

29 BUDAPEST

"*CALL ME ISTVAN,*" he said in English. "I work with Tibor." The metal cleats in the heels of his shoes rang with authority as he

crossed the waxed floor of Tibor Kados's apartment to the carpet
where Trosper and Brattle stood. He shook hands and said, "I do
the details."

He was older than Kados, about thirty-five, and shorter. His head
was egg-shaped, small at the top, broad at the chin line. His eyebrows, like accent marks—acute and grave—suggested an inverted
V above his small, dark eyes. His long black hair was like a helmet,
and tailed down the back as if to protect his neck. Trosper decided
it was a wig. The dark green of his heavy Harris tweed jacket
reinforced the intense orange of a turtleneck jersey. Beneath metallic
gray trousers that flared like sailor pants, Trosper could glimpse the
square toes of his tan shoes.

THEY had come to the Kados apartment at eight-thirty. It was to
be a short meeting, a chance to examine the passport, to check on
the exit document and to arrange payment. Tibor Kados had met
them at the door and led them to the living room. Then, without
introducing Istvan, he disappeared through a door at the side of the
room.

As Istvan introduced himself, the sound of a quarrel, with Tibor
speaking sharply in Hungarian, could be heard from the study.

Istvan raised his eyebrows and gestured with his thumb toward
the closed door. "Tibo has trouble with the girl. If I was a nice-
looking boy like that, I wouldn't have trouble with the girls." He
winked broadly, as if to remind the visitors that they were, after all,
men of the world. "What is it you say in jolly old London?" The
Hungarian looked expectantly at Brattle.

The Englishman shook his head, "I don't know, it's been a year
now. . . . What is it we say?"

"Women," the Hungarian said, "we can't live with them, and
can't live without them. That's what they say."

"In New York perhaps," Brattle said loyally.

"Not once in this century," Trosper said.

The side door opened wide enough for Trosper to see into what
seemed to be a study. At the rear was a second door leading into
another room, possibly a bedroom. After a loud exchange in Hun-

garian, Tibor stepped into the living room and slammed the door shut. "Some drinks," he said, walking quickly to the heavy Biedermeier cabinet at the side of the room. "Whiskey, it's the best for business talk." He spoke in German.

"*FIRST,* we will want to look at the merchandise," Trosper said. He would have liked to swirl the whiskey, and to let the air at it. But the tall, thin glass made it impossible. It was like drinking out of a test tube.

"Of course," Istvan said. "It is always the best first step." He stood and peeled off his green tweed jacket. "Business always goes better when we are all comfortable together." The short sleeves of the turtleneck reached just below his muscular biceps. He reached into the breast pocket of his jacket and fished out a passport. Standing, he leafed through the document. "This is good, one of the very best." Still holding the passport, he glanced at Trosper. "You mustn't get the wrong idea," he said. "You are paying a lot for our help. It's not just a matter of our handing you a document."

"What is it, then?" Brattle asked.

"We are experts. It takes time to do our best work." Istvan smiled, and opened his arms slightly and then brought them together. It was as if he were trying to herd them closer together. "It is not good security to hurry things like this. We need more information to do our best work, the work you are paying us for."

"What is it that you want to know?" Trosper asked.

The Hungarian shrugged, as if it would be redundant to say more. "We must have a physical description of your friend, very accurate, for the document. We should prepare other papers to support your friend's legend. For this, we need to know his languages, his business, his status in life. These documents will come easily, once Tibo has the necessary facts."

"What else?"

"There must be two photographs, one for the passport, one for the exit document. You must take me to your friend. I will do the photography and make the necessary prints, exactly the right size. I am very good. When I am finished and Tibo puts them into the documents, everything will be perfect, absolutely professional."

"Anything more?"

"A detail," the Hungarian said with another broad wink. "Just a detail—about the money."

"How much will this cost?"

"That depends. Let's say two thousand dollars to be paid here for this passport and the supporting papers. Then, when your man is across the border, another two thousand to be paid to a friend in Vienna."

Trosper glanced at Kados. Prices had doubled in twenty-four hours.

"This is a pretty expensive bit of detail," Brattle said.

Istvan shrugged. "We are taking risks," he said. "We don't know you, we have no idea who it is you represent. All we know is that you claim to have known Tibo's father—and he's long dead. If anything goes wrong, if you or your friend talk, Tibo and I are as good as dead. No more girls, no whiskey, and no good life in Buda-pest. A few thousand dollars is nothing to the people you represent."

"We represent no one," Trosper said, "only our friend who wants to leave. If we had sponsors sitting in some embassy, this would be handled through the services. As you can see, we're quite alone."

"We see nothing but two strangers who dropped into Budapest from nowhere and who expect us to commit crimes that could mean our heads." The Hungarian picked up his jacket and stuffed the passport into the pocket. "If you want to know, I am quite satisfied that you are employed by one of the special services, and that this is a political matter. Since we are risking our heads, you people should be prepared to pay."

Tibor muttered something in Hungarian and went to the bar. He poured himself a large whiskey and drained it. He dumped more scotch into the glass and walked slowly back to his chair.

"I think we had better look at the document," Trosper said.

It was an Austrian passport, issued in 1973 to Walter Egon Taub, a businessman, born in Graz, 1923, resident of Vienna. Herr Taub was a much-traveled man, Trosper learned as he studied the document. In 1981 he had made three trips to Budapest, in 1982, he made four trips. There were border-control cachets showing frequent travel to Germany and one trip to France. The last visit to Hungary was in January 1983. As far as Trosper could learn, it was on this trip that Herr Taub had been separated from his passport. There was no exit cachet in the passport. He handed the document to Brattle. "This thing expired in March 1983," he said.

"No problem, no problem at all," Istvan interjected. "Tibo can revalidate it just as easily as he can change the photograph and the physical description."

Tibor started to speak, but Istvan cut him off. "There is no better document for Hungary," he said. "Hundreds of Austrians cross every week."

It would not be easy to revalidate a passport. Trosper wondered if that was what Tibor had tried to say. On the assumption that it would do no harm to add a bit of camouflage, he said, "I think a different document would be better. What about a French or British passport?"

"Of course, of course," the Hungarian said. "But much depends upon the language. Does your man speak enough French or English to handle the *Grenzpolizei?*"

"That will be up to him," Trosper said. "We will be gone long before he can wind up his affairs and leave."

30   BUDAPEST

THEY separated on the stairway leading from Kados's apartment. Brattle would turn to the right as he reached the sidewalk, and Trosper, a few moments later, would move off to the left. They had agreed to meet at the bar of the Castle Hilton in Buda. But it would take an hour or more before the two men completed the tiresome backtracking, abrupt street crossing, and the apparently innocent window shopping necessary to convince themselves that they were clean.

The Russians called these maneuvers "dry cleaning." It was as good a term as any, Trosper thought as he hailed a taxi.

ASIDE from two men standing at the bar, the dark room was empty. They spoke Spanish and were soliciting the barman's advice on Budapest nightlife as Trosper walked around them to a round table in the corner. He took a chair facing the doorway and had ordered whiskey before Brattle stepped into the room.

"We've got about thirty-six hours before our man begins to sweat," Trosper said. "As far as I can see, there's no choice but to go with Comrade Istvan's Austrian passport."

Brattle took a pretzel stick from the basket on the table. "There's no need to give Kados anything but a physical description of your friend," he said. "Until we've seen how good his work is, and how neat a job he can do on altering the passport, we don't even have to show him the photograph."

"We can do the photography last, the Polaroid will be good enough," Trosper said uneasily. "Good enough" was almost never good enough in operations.

There was a bustle of activity near the door, and the loud sound of American voices. Trosper looked up at the three figures silhouetted against the light at the entrance. "Jesus H. Christ," he muttered. "The Sag Harbor Yacht Club has just docked." He took a quick swig of his drink, but did not avert his glance soon enough. From the doorway, Mrs. Cunningham caught his eye and waved a greeting. She nudged her husband, who had his arm around Mrs. Bristol and whispered something. Cunningham looked up, recognized Trosper, and called out. "Al . . . Alan Trosper, I'll be damned. We bump into each other in the strangest places."

Trosper stood up and made a slight gesture toward the empty chairs at the table. For a moment it looked as if Mrs. Cunningham would move toward an empty table in the opposite corner, but Cunningham was already maneuvering Mrs. Bristol toward Trosper's table.

"We have to stop meeting like this," Cunningham said brightly. Then, chuckling at the joke, he said, "You remember Mrs. Bristol?"

"Yes, indeed," Trosper said, pulling a chair back from the table for her. Brattle rose, offered a chair to Mrs. Cunningham, and said, "Douglas Brattle."

"He's from Salzburg," Trosper added fatuously, as Cunningham introduced Mrs. Bristol. She was, if anything, more striking than she had seemed in Vienna. She was also drunk, just as drunk as she had been in Vienna.

"We just stopped for a nightcap," Mrs. Cunningham said. "Not that we couldn't have got on without one." She glanced at Mrs. Bristol and gave Brattle an appraising look.

"What are we drinking?" Cunningham asked loudly, "Scotch all around?" He signaled for the waitress.

"I'll just stick to another one of those teeny little martoonis," Mrs. Bristol said.

"Coffee," Mrs. Cunningham said. "*Café crème.*"

"And a round of whiskey for the gents," Cunningham added. He took a handful of pretzel sticks and glanced appraisingly at Brattle. "What's your line, Mr. Brattle? Something to do with boats, like Al here?"

"Douglas," Brattle said with an effort. "Please call me Douglas."

"Is that a touch of cockney I hear? Are you from the old country?"

Trosper winced. It had been a long time, but now he remembered that for some Americans all English accents were called cockney.

"Uh . . . ," Brattle stumbled for a moment before saying, "Cambridge actually."

The waitress served the drinks, poured a cup of coffee for Mrs. Cunningham, and left the silver pot on the table.

"While she's still here, Jerry, darling, why don't you order some more of these tiny little drinks," Mrs. Bristol said languidly. "You never can tell when one of these lazy girls will come back again."

Apparently intimidated by his wife's frigid expression, Cunningham said, "Later, Barbara, later."

Turning to Brattle, Mrs. Cunningham said quietly, "Barbara is celebrating her divorce. After six years with that nice guy, I suppose she thinks she's entitled to it. It's just that I don't see why she has to do it in every barroom in Europe."

They chatted until Cunningham said, "If it's all the same to everyone, I'm going to sign this bill and then we can go to the nightclub and hear some of that gypsy music, and maybe do a little dancing. Why don't you and Al come along with us?"

Brattle shook his head, "Alan and I have a pretty full card tomorrow, I think I'd better call it a night."

"That's right," Trosper said, "I'm afraid—"

Mrs. Cunningham cut in. "Alan and Mr. Brattle may have some business to discuss, Jerry. If we don't get started, we'll be in that nightclub all night."

Mrs. Bristol gulped the remains of her drink and delicately popped the olive into her mouth. As she pushed her chair back from the table and began to rise, her leather hand bag tumbled from her lap, and spilled beneath the table at Trosper's feet. Bending double, he began stuffing the cosmetics, travel brochures, money, handkerchief, back into the bag. In the dark beneath the table, he glimpsed the blue corner of an American passport. With a quick motion he swept a folder of travelers' checks and an eyeliner into the gaping bag and edged the passport under his foot. He sat up again, his face flushed from the effort, and handed the bag across the table to Mrs. Bristol. "There," he said, rising to say good-bye, "that should be everything."

Mrs. Cunningham glanced at Trosper and turned to her husband. "Jerry," she said, "why don't you and Barbara go along and see about a table. Like a good hostess, I'll stay here with my coffee, while Alan and Mr. Brattle finish their drinks."

Cunningham hesitated for a moment and said, "Okay, sweetheart, but don't be long." Mrs. Bristol waved a cheery good-bye and, taking Cunningham's arm, hurried him out of the bar.

Mrs. Cunningham took a sip of coffee, gave Brattle a quick smile, and turned to Trosper. "I don't know what the hell is going on here," she said evenly. "But if that drunken broad is ever going to get out of this workers' paradise, she's going to need her passport."

"I'm not sure I follow," Trosper said lamely.

"I mean, Barbara will need the passport that you've got your foot planted on."

"I say," Brattle murmured, "I think we should talk things over."

"That's just what I'm doing," she said, turning to Trosper. "First you're working the boat show, selling junk to unsuspecting Sunday sailors. Then we find you sitting in some bright young man's Vienna apartment, with a huge goddamned gun on the coffee table. Then a little pansy in a knock-me-daddy haircut jumps up and looks as if he's going to faint. Scene three, and you and John Bull are sitting big as life in the Budapest Hilton with your shiny shoe on Barbara's passport." She paused to catch her breath. "I think it's about time for you to tell me what's going on."

"I seem to have missed something," Brattle said softly.

Trosper bent over and picked up the passport. Folded neatly inside was the exit paper, complete with photograph of Mrs. Bristol. He put it in his pocket. "I think I can understand your confusion, Mrs. Cunningham—"

"At this point, you can call me Nancy."

"I suppose I should begin by saying this is a long story," Trosper said.

"In the time you've got, I think a synopsis will suffice," she said.

Trosper picked up one of the two drinks in front of him and took a deep swallow. "Douglas and I are here in Budapest to help a friend who wants to leave. It is very important that he get out. The problem is that he has no papers, and we have no time to arrange something for him. With luck, another friend should be able to, er . . . adapt your friend Nancy's passport for our man's use."

"I'll be damned," she mumbled, and reached across the table to pick up the untouched drink in front of Trosper. "I don't think I believe a word of that," she said slowly.

"It really is very important, Nancy."

"And just where would this leave Barbara?"

"I should think," Brattle said, "that all Mrs. Bristol has to do when she finds her passport is missing is to go to your consulate and explain. At the most she'll only be delayed for twenty-four hours or so."

"I'm sorry about that John Bull crack," she said. "Alan has me rather shaken up."

"Of course," Brattle said.

"Are you sure it will be all right, that she can get a passport in a couple of days?" she asked.

"I think so," Trosper said. "It happens all the time."

Nancy took another sip of the drink. "Actually, I don't give a damn. All she's done on this whole trip is drink and try to get Jerry into bed with her."

Brattle coughed politely.

"Then it's all right?" Trosper asked, "You won't say anything until we give you a sign?"

"I must be crazy." She turned with an admiring look at Brattle and asked "Is this something official, CIA, Bulldog Drummond, the Scarlet Pimpernel, and all that?"

"Not exactly," Brattle said. "But it is important. A man's life is in the bargain, and the information he has will mean a lot to the right people when they get it."

"I wish I could be sure of what you say," she said slowly, looking from one to the other.

"There is no proof of what we are telling you," said Brattle. "Not here, not now."

"I am positively out of my mind," she said slowly. "But it's a deal." She looked at Brattle again. "I'd better join the lovebirds before something happens. Are you sure you don't want to come along? I could use a little cheering up."

Brattle shook his head. "Next time, that's a promise."

31   BUDAPEST

"*HAS THERE* been any change in your situation here?" Trosper asked. "Do we still have time before you will be missed?" They had met in the bar at the Atrium-Hyatt Hotel, on Roosevelt Ter in the Inner City. The Russian had shed his uniform and wore a gray American suit. A blue button-down shirt and black knit tie flattered his deep-set eyes and fine features. Aside from the the dancer's discipline with which he carried himself, and the arrogance that Trosper associated with persons accustomed to command, Aksenov's appearance and manner gave no clue to his background.

"Colonel Sadovnikov, the *rezident,* has been told that I am here for a series of important agent meetings—what I actually do here is none of his business," Aksenov said. "This morning I changed into these clothes and Colonel Pokhomov, my man here, took me to a *malina,* a safe house as you call it." He sat straight in his chair, his right hand, with a cigarette between the second and third fingers, cupped lightly around a glass of Campari and soda. "As long as I am correct, and telephone old Sadovnikov each day to check, he has no choice but to keep his curiousity in hand, and give me any support I request."

The Russian took a quick puff of his cigarette. "The problem is in Moscow. I have no idea how fast the investigation will go, but I think I must leave Hungary within thirty-six hours."

He was slight and lithe, and the soft shoulders of the trim American suit made him seem smaller than when he wore the stiff uniform.

"Then it is time to move," Trosper said. "From here, we will go to an apartment for photographs and the preparation of your papers. After that, we will make arrangements to leave by train for Vienna."

"By train?" The Russian was surprised.

"This time of year there are fewer controls on the train, just the normal passport and security checks. At the airport they take extra precautions to guard against hijackers and terrorists."

"What papers will I use?"

"You will be given an American passport."

The trace of a smile flickered across the Russian's face.

And that is all the good news, Trosper thought.

"With backup documents?"

"No," Trosper said. "There isn't enough time, and the border control people do not do body searches."

"Never do searches? No questions ever?"

"They ask about currency. It is forbidden to take Hungarian money across the border."

"What about the photographs? Why can't they be done at your

embassy? You can easily drive me into the yard in one of your automobiles."

The Russian had done his own reconnaissance.

"We are not to have any contact with the embassy whatsoever. There is too much surveillance."

"That is stupid. I insist that we use the embassy."

"It is out of the question."

The Russian ground his cigarette in the ashtray. To be contradicted was still a new experience.

"What about the apartment where the passport will be prepared? Is it a diplomatic residence, occupied by an officer of your embassy?"

It would have been easier with an amateur, someone who had no idea how things were done.

"No," Trosper said firmly. "We will not use any diplomatic areas at all."

Aksenov drew in his breath sharply. For a few moments he remained silent, his eyes blinking like a boxer who has just taken a heavy punch. Conversation with the Russian, Trosper realized, was a form of contact sport.

"I suppose you will think this is a stupid question, but can you kindly explain why you are going about my evacuation in this fashion?"

"Does an explanation really matter at this point?"

The Russian's deep-set eyes blinked. "I think it is what you call a matter of life and death."

"I've already told you all you need to know about the evacuation. From here along, you will have to surrender yourself to our handling."

"You are blundering amateurs. Given three weeks, I could have crossed that stupid border without any risk at all."

"I would have preferred that," Trosper said slowly. "I'm not particularly thrilled to be sitting here talking about your escape with only a tourist passport in my pocket."

"I don't believe this," the Russian said. "Did Franz Radl know anything about this amateur arrangement?"

"Not a thing."

For a moment the trim figure seemed to sag. Trosper guessed that the Russian was reviewing his options. There were only two. He could return to the Soviet Union, attempt to talk his way out of any involvement in the "Phoenix" leak, and in due course, answer for the defection of Radl, his agent and wartime colleague. The other choice was to proceed with the escape, no matter what the risk.

"It's a very long story," Trosper said. "There's no point in my burdening you with it here. The plan is the best possible in the circumstances."

Aksenov snorted and began to speak. Trosper cut him off. "I will give you the background details when we are across the border. Meanwhile, there's work to be done here."

SMILING expectantly, the doorman opened the rear door of the tiny Fiat taxi. American business men tipped well, and in Hungary, unlike the Soviet Union, tipping was an institution untouched by the revolution. The bigger man squeezed into the backseat. His slight companion opened the front door, glared at the doorman, and took the seat beside the driver. It was as if he had stepped into the command seat of a staff car.

The doorman's smile faded as he touched his cap. The more these damned capitalists come here, the more they act like Ivans.

32   BUDAPEST

IT WAS after seven when the taxi dropped them half a kilometer from Kados's apartment. There was no point in attempting any countersurveillance, and they walked silently, side by side. When Aksenov spoke it was only to observe quietly, "They walk faster here, as if they are hurrying to get somewhere, and looking forward to something." As they neared the apartment, Trosper thought he heard Aksenov sigh, and murmur, "My poor Russia."

Trosper touched Aksenov's arm. "We turn here. From now on you must speak English or German. Not a syllable of Russian."

"Who am I supposed to be?" Aksenov asked in English.

"It doesn't matter," Trosper said. "You won't be introduced."

They hurried up the dark stairs to the third floor. "My colleague will be here," Trosper said softly. "He is coming with us to Vienna. The other man is Hungarian. He knows nothing. His only job is to help with the documents."

Reluctantly, Trosper touched the bell, surely the loudest in Budapest. The door swung open and Kados, shaking Trosper's hand, pulled him across the threshold. Aksenov followed closely. Kados mumbled a greeting. His face was gray, his eyes barely rested on Aksenov. He shook hands hurriedly.

In the living room, Brattle heaved himself up from the chair, bowed slightly, extended his hand and said, "Welcome." The Russian said hello and shook hands.

Kados turned to Trosper. "Some drinks? I still have plenty of whiskey."

Trosper shook his head. "No, there's too much to be done."

"Mr. Miller tells me you have procured a passport," Kados said abruptly. "That's best. No risks at all. Everything easy and in the open."

"Not quite," Trosper said. "There are the changes to be made."

"What changes in an American document? Why make changes?" The Hungarian's voice was high and tense.

"The passport was issued to a woman. You'll have to wash the description and the birth date. The photograph must be changed. I've got a Polaroid in my coat."

Kados's face was white. He ran both hands through his hair and said, "Look, I can't make a move without Istvan. We have a deal, he takes care of details."

"There are no details," Brattle said. "Just get started on the damned document."

Trosper pulled the passport from his pocket. "Show me what you have to do."

Kados took the passport. His hands were shaking. "Look," he said. "I'm more used to simple things, like changing the date on an identity paper. I don't want to take a chance and maybe spoil this document."

He pushed the passport back into Trosper's hand.

Behind Trosper, Brattle thundered, "Get your fucking equipment, you pretentious little twit." Later, Trosper recalled that Brattle had shouted in English.

Kados pointed toward the hallway, "In the kitchen," he mumbled in German.

"Show me," Brattle ordered, and followed Kados out of the room.

"You're nothing but blundering idiots," Aksenov hissed in Russian. "I should have known better than to trust myself to anyone, even on Franzi's word."

"Stick to German or English," Trosper said. "We've got trouble enough without you speaking Russian in front of that ass." He heard footsteps and turned to see Kados carrying a wooden box about the size of a case of wine.

"It was built into a panel behind the stove," Brattle explained. "A good job, about what I'd expect from the old man."

Kados put the box on a long library table behind the sofa in the middle of the room. With Brattle looking over his shoulder, Kados lifted the top. "If that's everything you need," Brattle said to Kados, "get yourself set up."

Followed by Aksenov, Trosper stepped to the table. Kados lifted a small tray of tools, like dentist's picks and modeling knives, out of the box. There were bottles of solvent, a variety of inks, cotton swabs, and a collection of blank rubber stamps with wooden handles. Kados unrolled a soft leather case of small wedge-shaped tools.

From the bottom of the box, the Hungarian pulled a hard leather pad with a pockmarked surface. Trosper guessed it was used as backing when the wedges were tapped against a document to simulate embossing. Several neatly tied bundles of hard rubber, which could be cut to duplicate almost any shape of rubber stamp, completed the collection.

Kados picked up a small can with a long spout, like a miniature oil can. "You heat this over a little burner, it makes a small jet of steam," he said. "It's just a miniature tea kettle, very precise, for opening letters." In slots on the cover of the box were thin slivers of ivory, shaped like letter openers. "To lift seals, or slip under envelope flaps that have been steamed," he explained.

"Is this all you need?" Trosper asked.

"Look," Kados said, "You have to let me explain." His brown eyes were moist, as if he was going to cry. "I don't know too much about this. I can do simple things, a driver's license, import certificates . . . " His voice trailed off.

Trosper, Brattle and the Russian were ranged around Kados, who stood with his back against the table.

"What kind of talk is this?" Brattle shouted. He waved the passport at Kados. "Can you do this or not?"

The Hungarian stammered, and said, "I've tried to explain, I've never worked on a passport. I don't know how."

"What about the import licenses, isn't that tricky work?"

Kados turned and bent over his father's box. "That's simple. We just make it look good. It's not even forgery—Istvan has fixed it with the customs people. He pays them, they will accept almost any piece of paper that looks good enough to throw into a file that no one will ever open." He ran his hands through his hair again. "I'm not my father. We're just small black market people. We've never got involved in any of this political stuff."

From the hallway, Trosper could hear the rattle of the door and a key turning in the lock. Aksenov whirled, his right hand thrust across his chest, beneath his jacket.

"It's only Marta," Kados said.

There was a murmur of voices and the door slammed shut.

"*Salut,* Tibo," the girl called, and a man's voice added a greeting in Hungarian.

"And Istvan," Kados whispered.

33 BUDAPEST

ISTVAN glowered at Kados. "A party, and I'm not invited? What kind of friends are you? Or is it a business meeting?"

Marta pulled off her tweed coat and slung it over an armchair beside the heavy cabinet Istvan used as a bar. She pulled open the doors and began checking the bottles. "Campari, Tibo? No Campari, Tibo? You promised, Tibo." Her German had a hoarse, throaty quality.

Kados said something in Hungarian and the girl picked up a plastic ice bucket. With a switch of her short black skirt, she strode toward the kitchen.

Istvan turned to Aksenov. "You are the traveler, the man who wants to buy this nice Austrian passport?" It was as much a statement as a question.

The half-light from the floor lamps caught the sheen of the Hungarian's wig. Parted in the middle, it covered only the top of his head, and clashed with the flat tone of the natural hair combed straight down to his ears.

The Russian turned his back and took a few steps across the room, away from Istvan.

"We've made other arrangements," Brattle said. "All we need now is a few changes in our own document."

"I *see,*" said the Hungarian, hitching his shoulders like a fighter about to throw a punch. "And what about all the effort I've made to get this passport?" He took the Austrian document from his pocket and waved it at Brattle.

"We appreciate that," Trosper said. "But it's too much to expect Kados here to revalidate it and make the other changes. We don't even have an Austrian passport that he could use to copy the validation from."

"So, so," Istvan said softly. Then, raising his voice he said, "But that's not the way business is done here. Not even by fine gentlemen from abroad. That's not the way we do things here."

"There's no choice, no choice at all," Trosper said. "This is the only way it can be done at this point."

"So, so," the Hungarian muttered again. "Poor Istvan takes all the risks and pays good dollars for a passport that doesn't suit the fine visitors." He whirled to face Trosper. "Istvan may be just a dumb Hungarian but he knows when he's being cheated."

Kados said something in Hungarian. Istvan, his eyes narrowed in anger, barked an answer. Kados started to speak, but fell silent when Marta crossed the room with the ice bucket. "Some highballs, fellows," she asked in English. "Scotch soda? *Mit Sprudelwasser?*" Kados followed her to the bar.

Aksenov walked back to Trosper. "This is vaudeville," he whispered. "You are fools to tolerate this behavior. It is not correct."

Kados handed Istvan a tall tumbler of whiskey. "What about it?" he asked Trosper. "What about me, my expenses and the risks?"

"I will cover your expenses," Trosper said.

"And the risks, the chance I took in looking for the document?"

"A little something for that too," Trosper said.

"A *little* something?"

"What do you want?"

"I paid one thousand for the passport, and I want five hundred for the chance I took in buying it." He flashed a grin at Aksenov. "And five hundred for my time, that rounds it off to two thousand dollars."

"I'll give you one thousand right now, and that is it. You can sell the passport to someone else."

The Hungarian's glance flickered from Brattle to Trosper. "You know that it was you people who started this, it was you who asked us to help you to break the law. We responded out of charity, to help someone. We took risks, and we spent time and money. Now you expect all of this for nothing."

"We have work to do," Brattle said. "I recommend you accept our offer and let us get on with it."

The Hungarian's glance shifted back to Brattle. "Your attitude makes me wonder. It makes me wonder exactly who you people are. It makes me wonder about your friend here, the man you are supporting so graciously." He turned, and walked slowly to the bar and poured whiskey into his glass.

"Just why is it," Istvan continued, "that your speechless friend has decided to leave Hungary?" He walked back to Brattle and Trosper. "At first I thought it was a charity case, some deserving family man who wanted to join his relatives in the West. Now I must begin to wonder. He doesn't look like a devoted son, someone who is anxious to make his old mother's final years happy." He drained his glass. "Now that I think about it, he looks more like a criminal, someone who is wanted by our police."

"No one is wanted by the police," Trosper said.

"If he is a murderer," Istvan said, "the police will have a reward for him." He tapped his finger along the side of his nose. "The reward is probably much more than what I have put into your little scheme to arrange his escape."

"That's nonsense," Brattle said. "If you take one step toward the police, you and your friend Kados will be in bigger trouble than either of you can handle."

Istvan turned toward Aksenov. "What's your big secret, my silent friend, why is it that you and your capitalist friends have to take such elaborate measures to help you escape?"

Aksenov loosened the button on his jacket and turned to Trosper. "You damned incompetent idiots," he hissed in Russian. "How could you involve thieves like these little fascists in an operation as simple as this?"

A broad smile crossed Istvan's face. "A Russian," he exclaimed. "That's the mystery. It's one of our beloved liberators, a Russian, all dressed up like a capitalist, who wants to leave." He gulped more whiskey. "That puts a different face on everything."

They were standing in the middle of the room, in a rough circle, Brattle, Trosper, and Aksenov ranged a few feet from Istvan, Kados, and the girl. Istvan handed his glass to Marta. She hurried toward the bar.

Still smiling broadly, Istvan said, "This *does* make it a matter for the police."

Kados, his face white, started to speak, "Istvan, for God's sake, don't make threats . . ."

Marta, the glass still in her hand, stepped to the tape deck and turned up the volume.

Aksenov snarled in Russian. All that Trosper could understand was ". . . rotten fascist hooligan . . ." The Russian pulled his hand from the shoulder holster concealed under his gray flannel jacket and leveled a small automatic pistol at Istvan's head.

Marta stopped. The glass slipped from her hand and bounced on the thick carpet.

It was, Trosper realized, a perfect shot. The 7-mm round hit Istvan exactly between the eyes and just a quarter of an inch above the bridge of his nose. Had it been a fraction higher, the bullet might have been deflected by the heavy bone in the Hungarian's forehead.

As the impact slammed Istvan's head back, his arms raised as if in a tardy effort to catch the bullet. His eyes, open wide in surprise when he glimpsed the gun in Aksenov's hand, bulged as if to burst as the shot smashed through his skull. His head rocked back until a whiplash snapped it forward again.

The violent passage of the bullet loosened the rear tape of the black wig. As the Hungarian's chin smashed down against his chest, the wig, still anchored above his forehead, stood straight up. Then it fell slowly forward until it hung upside down, the greasy backing covering the neat red hole between the bulging eyes. The long black hair fell across Istvan's open mouth and tumbled down over his chin.

Trosper read "Roma" neatly stenciled on the underside of the wig, and in that instant wondered if it was a trademark or if the wig had been bought in Rome. It was the irrelevant things that Trosper would remember.

As if he were falling in upon himself, Istvan's legs began to crumple. Then, bending at the hips, he pitched forward, face down on the carpet.

The hole in the back of Istvan's head was smaller than Trosper expected—about twice the size of a poker chip, but less perfectly formed.

As the Hungarian hit the floor, Aksenov crouched and, like the turret of a tank, turned slowly until the pistol was leveled at Marta's head. She inched backward until she touched the high wooden wainscotting. She spread her arms, and flattened her hands against the wall. It was as if she had been espaliered.

Brattle lunged toward Aksenov. With a quick karate chop, he smashed his fist down on the Russian's wrist. The pistol made a popping sound as the round buried itself in the carpet. Brattle dove to pick up the gun as it spun from Aksenov's hand. Trosper heard him mumble, "Oh, dear."

Like a puppet whose master had dropped the strings, the girl slid down the wall to the floor. She remained sitting, one long, thin leg thrust out, the other tucked beneath her. The short skirt was hiked up. Trosper could see the vaccination scar on her thigh and wondered irrelevantly if all Hungarian women were vaccinated on the thigh. Marta began to sob and made a dry, retching noise.

"Shit," was all that Trosper could say.

Brattle stuffed the pistol into his pocket. "This tears it," he said to no one in particular.

Cursing in Russian, Aksenov whirled to face Trosper. With his left hand, he held his bruised wrist close to his chest.

Trosper glanced at Kados. The young Hungarian had not moved. He stood a few feet from his late friend. His eyes blinked and his mouth was working as if to keep from vomiting.

"Sit down, goddamn it," Trosper said in English. Kados dropped into the Eames chair. He clasped both hands over his ears and began to rock back and forth, mumbling to himself.

Like the sulphur from a burning match, the sharp smell of powder almost masked the rising odor of urine and fecal matter coming from the corpse on the rug.

34 BUDAPEST

"*COULD* those shots be heard outside the apartment?" Trosper snapped.

Still staring straight ahead, Kados shook his head.

"The walls are pretty thick in these old buildings," Brattle muttered. "That and the stupid, thumping music should have taken care of it."

Turning to Aksenov, Trosper asked, "What the hell do you think that accomplished?"

"I will not be threatened," the Russian said. "That's something I learned a long time ago." Aside from his slighly flushed face, Aksenov showed no more emotion than if he had been on a target range. "This is not a business for amateurs," he said. 'If that little fascist had left here, we could not possibly have kept him from going to the AVO or the police." He bent over the body and began groping in the pockets of the green tweed jacket. "There's one thing cheap informers understand, and that's force," he said. "I would have thought you people might have learned that by now."

The Russian stood up. He had Istvan's thick wallet in his hand. "What's more, I'll guarantee you won't have any more trouble with that imbecile and his girl friend." Aksenov gestured toward Kados.

"Get a towel and wrap it around his head," Trosper said to Kados. "Then roll him onto a blanket. If you ever expect to get out of this, try to keep the blood and piss off your rug."

Kados shook his head.

"When you've finished, get Marta the hell off the floor and give her a drink."

When Kados shook his head the second time, Brattle bent over the leather chair and grabbed both lapels of the young man's jacket. Lifting him out of the chair, he shook him like a naughty puppy. "Now move, goddamnit." He turned to Aksenov. "Keep an eye on him. Don't let him near the hall doorway."

"Give me the pistol," Aksenov said.

"If you can't handle him," Trosper said, "call for help."

The Russian tossed Istvan's wallet onto a chair and followed Kados through the study and into the bedroom.

"The *next* time I deal with a Soviet defector," Brattle said heavily, "I'll remember something I learned when I was a recruit." Mimicking the rasping voice of a drill sergeant reading from a training manual, he said, " 'Take the time to search each prisoner. Never, I repeat *never*, assume that the man you are about to interrogate has already been disarmed.' "

Trosper forced a smile. "Douglas," he said softly, "this might be an opportune time for you to leave Hungary. You could take the morning plane, with no one the wiser. I can sort this out."

Brattle shook his head slowly, disbelievingly. "What is it that makes you Yanks so anxious to throw yourselves on the spears? It will be all the *two* of us can do to get out of here." He glanced toward the study door and lowered his voice. "Judging by his manners, I'd guess that our impulsive Russian is accustomed to a certain amount of authority. After all this bloody trouble, there's not much point in leaving him here."

"He claims to be chief of Division Twelve, First Chief director-ate," Trosper said.

Brattle whistled softly.

Still propped against the wall, Marta had stopped sobbing and was hitching at her dress. Brattle gestured in her direction. "Besides, there's not a chance you could make it on your own. The minute you turn your back that stupid girl will scarper. If she doesn't, Kados will." He walked to the bar. "Let's have a tot of his famous whiskey and try to figure something out." He splashed scotch into into the tall glasses. "Primitive goddamned Central European way to serve whiskey."

"I've got one last idea," Trosper said. "Let's get Kados and the girl into the bedroom and see if we can work it out."

Brattle stepped lightly over the body. "First, I'll just make sure there aren't any weapons in there," he said, as Kados and Aksenov came back with towels and a blanket.

"*I DON'T* like your plan at all," Aksenov said. It will be a problem for me."

"Nothing like the problem you'll have if it doesn't work," Brattle said. "If you've got a better idea, you'd better speak up right now. We've got to move along."

The Russian shrugged his shoulders. "It will be a problem for me, that's all."

"I'm off," Trosper said. "It's eight-thirty now. I'll be at the Hilton by about nine. With any luck at all, I can be back by midnight."

"A wig could be the biggest bother," Brattle said. "The rest might be easy."

"While I'm gone you three might give a thought to what we do with the late Comrade Istvan," Trosper said.

35   BUDAPEST

IT WAS exactly nine o'clock when Trosper eased himself out of the Fiat taxi and nodded to the doorman. It was too much to hope that they would be in, but he decided to call from the house phone beside the concierge's desk before settling down in the bar to wait. She answered on the fourth ring.

"Mrs. Cunningham?"

"Yes," she said.

"Nancy, this is Alan Trosper. I'm sorry to bother you this late, but . . ."

"Alan, how very unexpected."

"I wonder if I could talk to you for a few minutes?"

"Is something the matter? You sound peculiar . . . not that I'm surprised."

"It seems I have a bit of a problem."

"You and Douglas? Is he with you?"

"No, not at the moment. Could I see you for a few minutes?"

There was a pause. "Yes, I suppose so. Give me a moment to put something on, and then come up. I'm in 314."

"Are you alone? Isn't Jerry with you?"

"All alone. The young at heart have staggered out for dinner. They're at Gundel's, at least that's where they said they were going."

It was a suite, carefully decorated with expensive Hungarian antiques. The remains of a room-service supper were on a table in front of the window looking across the Danube to Pest.

"I don't know exactly how to put this, but Douglas and I really need some help," Trosper said.

"I should have known something would happen. Is Douglas all right?"

"Of course he is," Trosper laughed. "But we need your advice . . . and possibly to borrow some things."

"You'd better explain."

Never, Trosper thought, had he involved so many outsiders in an operation. And never, he promised himself, would he do it again.

"We've had trouble with the papers for our friend. Now it seems it will be easier if we use Barbara's passport just as it is. The only change we can make is to substitute a picture of our friend for Barbara's photo."

"Yes," she said doubtfully, dragging the vowel into a protracted diphthong.

"But our friend is a man. We need to dress him as a woman."

Nancy got up and walked slowly to the window. She stood silently for a moment, and then turned and walked back to where Trosper sat. Still standing, her arms folded across her chest, she said quietly, "You realize, I suppose, that I haven't the slightest idea who either of you really is. For all I know, you could be setting me up for some kind of confidence game."

"It would be a lot of trouble just for a few of your clothes, expensive as they are."

"I didn't want to come here in the first place," she said. "It's scary enough to be in a Communist country without you and that Douglas stealing passports and trying to involve me in some crazy charades." She seemed on the verge of tears.

"If it weren't important, I wouldn't keep asking favors. The fact is, a man's life is on the line."

She walked over to the window. "The last thing I need right now is more aggravation. I've got about as much trouble as I can handle." She turned and walked across the room to a bar in the corner. "Could you use a drink?" she asked. "You look a little frazzled."

"No, thanks, but if there's still some coffee in that pot, I'll have a cup."

He took a sip. It was tepid. "What we need is cosmetics, some clothing, and if possible . . . a wig."

"One of us is crazy."

"You can have it all back," he said. "Just as soon as we're in Vienna. Or," he added as an afterthought, "I can mail it to you in Sag Harbor."

She poured herself a cup of coffee and walked to the window. After a moment she turned and said, "There's one thing I can't understand," she said. "Don't people in your line of work have any facilities at all? Can't you get a fence or a mole or what ever you call them to give you documents and disguises?" Her expression softened into a tentative smile. "I mean, it's not much like all those books, the way you and Douglas behave."

Never again, Trosper promised himself. Never again. "If it wasn't important, Nancy—and this you really can believe—I wouldn't be badgering you like this."

She shook her head wonderingly. "Would it be breaking the faith if you were to give me some idea of what your friend looks like— how tall he is, how big around the waist, what size he might wear? What about shoes?"

"Christ, I forgot about shoes," Trosper said. Then, remembering to keep a commanding presence in front of the troops, he said, "He's medium height, about five-nine. Thin face, light complexion. He has deep-set eyes and short hair." He took another sip of the cold coffee. "That's all I can remember, except he has a rather delicate nose . . . fine features, I think you would say."

She laughed. "You'll need some pancake—probably a couple of shades—eye shadow, eyeliner and mascara, rouge, powder, lipstick, nail polish . . . and perfume."

Trosper groaned.

"What about his eyebrows?"

"I don't know," Trosper muttered. "It never occurred to me. But I think I would remember if he had bushy eyebrows."

"You may have to pluck and shape his eyebrows."

"What about clothing?"

"Slacks, blouse, sweater, hat, and maybe a raincoat. You should try to make him look a little casual, not too dressy."

"Could you possibly lend me some of these things?"

"I haven't even worn the wig I bought in Vienna," she said slowly. "They say the Austrians get the hair from peasant women. The wigs are supposed to be pretty good, and only half the price of the Italian ones. But the Italians get the hair from nuns. It's really a question of his head. Is he about my size?"

"I don't know."

"Then I've got most of what you need here. Except underwear . . . mine would never fit."

Trosper looked at her appraisingly. "There are some flat-chested

Americans, but I don't think we can hope to get our man through a body search."

She walked back to the bar and began to make a drink. "You know," she said slowly, "If Jerry had told me two days ago that I'd be mixed up in something like this, I'd have had him committed. Now I think I'm the one who's flipped out."

"Can you show me how to apply the makeup, and how to trim his eyebrows, paint the fingernails?"

"No," she said. "It takes the best of us about four years to learn how to make up."

"Just a few hints," Trosper suggested desperately.

"Where is your friend? If your hideout isn't in the woods somewhere, maybe I could do the job myself."

Not a chance, Trosper was about to say. But he caught himself. "What about Jerry?" he asked.

"I probably shouldn't be telling you all this," she said deliberately. "I haven't even told Jerry." She walked to the window, her back to Trosper. "The fact is, Jerry and I have come to a parting of the ways. When Barbara asked if she could come on this trip, I felt sorry for her, going through the divorce and all. Now, the way it's turned out, they've made me feel as if I were intruding on their affair. I must have been the only person in Sag Harbor who didn't know what was going on. He's been making a fool of himself with Barbara for months. And now he's made an even bigger fool of me. Imagine the nerve he has, bringing his doxy along on a trip like this."

"I'm very sorry to hear that," Trosper said.

She walked into the bedroom and opened the double doors of the closet. "I don't give a damn what he thinks about what I do. Anyway, I've got a seat on the train to Vienna in the morning. They can have the rest of this trip to themselves." She began to throw clothes across the twin bed. "You'll need a little jewelry. A chain or two and gloves." She pulled a canvas tote bag from the closet.

"Nancy," Trosper said, "There's something I'd better tell you now—up front—as they say. Our place is right here in Budapest, but it's a little messy."

"Messy hideouts I can put up with," she said with a catch in her voice. "It's matrimonial messes that bother me."

"It's more than that," Trosper said. "We've had an accident, a really bad accident."

"Not Douglas," she said quickly.

"He's fine, but someone else got shot."

"Shot?"

"Dead."

She tossed a cosmetics bag onto the bed.

"Look," Trosper said. "The more I think about it, there's no reason you should get mixed up in this. If it comes unstuck, we'll all be involved in aiding and abetting murder, and Christ knows what else. If you let me have the makeup stuff and some clothes, I'm sure we can do a good enough job of it."

She shook her head. "You can't, it really wouldn't be possible. It may not be possible anyway." She shoved a sweater into the tote bag. "Will I have to see the, ah . . . corpse?"

"No, of course not."

"Then let's get started."

Never again, Trosper promised himself. Never again.

36   BUDAPEST

"*JUST* remember," Trosper said on the stairway. "Do not call Douglas or me by name. And speak only to me and Douglas."

"Where will the body be?"

"I don't know," he said. "But it *is* covered up."

"This is scarier than I thought it would be."

"It's not too late," Trosper said, his finger on the door bell. "I can get you back to the hotel in twenty minutes."

"Push the damned bell."

Trosper touched the bell. The noise echoed along the hallway, masking for a moment the booming bass of Kados's tape deck.

"Lordy," she whispered. "If that doesn't wake him, he really is dead."

The lock rattled and Brattle, his bulk blotting out the faint light from the hallway, pulled the door ajar. Trosper slipped across the threshold, pulling Nancy with him.

"I say," Brattle whispered. "I say . . . I hadn't expected this."

Brattle took the cosmetics bag from Nancy and gave her a hug. "You're all right," he whispered.

"I'm scared as hell," she said, "but I'm sure glad to see you."

"She came to do the makeup," Trosper said. "I think we've brought everything."

"You'll be all right," Brattle said, his arm around her shoulders. "We'll have you out of here in a couple of hours."

The door of the study opened and Aksenov stepped out. His suit, blue button-down shirt, and knit tie were still as immaculate as when Trosper had met him at the cafe. He glanced at Nancy and, turning to Trosper, asked in German, "Who?"

"A technician," Trosper said. "She will handle your disguise."

The Russian nodded. "You call me Grisha," he said as they shook hands. He turned to Trosper. "Plans?"

"We will leave by train in the morning at eleven. Tonight we will do the disguise and change the passport photograph."

"What about that?" He pointed to the body.

"It would be best if we could dispose of it," Trosper said. "I don't see how we can leave it to Kados. If he panics before we are across the border, there could be trouble."

"That will be up to your service, to the local station. Surely they have capabilities. It is not my problem."

"If you could have held your fire," Brattle said, "there wouldn't be any problem."

"And if you had let that hooligan walk out of here, he would have gone straight to the AVO." Aksenov turned to Trosper. "I cannot understand how your service works, what your station can be thinking of to get involved with scum like these two."

"I've told you before," Trosper said. "We have no contact with anyone here in Hungary."

Aksenov turned to Nancy. "Coffee," he said. It was a command. She poured a cup. "Sugar?" Aksenov shook his head.

"You people are worse than amateurs," Aksenov said. "There is no excuse for your failure to provide for contingencies. Contingency planning is fundamental to all operations."

"That's not exactly an original bit of doctrine," Trosper said. "But since you brought it up, perhaps you will enlighten me on *your* contingency plan. Just what will you do if my colleagues and I walk out of here right now?"

The Russian looked from Trosper to Brattle. "At least I can get rid of the body over there."

"Please," Trosper said politely.

"It is quite simple," Aksenov said. "In operations, simple plans are always best." The trace of a smile crossed the Russian's face. "I will telephone Lieutenant Colonel Pokhomov, my man here in Budapest, and instruct him to bring a car."

"A car from the *rezidentura?*" Trosper did not conceal his surprise.

"Exactly so."

37 BUDAPEST

ONLY a few phrases of the stream of Russian that Aksenov barked into the telephone came through to Trosper. " . . . car in thirty minutes . . . your information only . . . top priority . . . bring Lt. Smolenkov . . ." The Russian turned to Trosper. "We've got thirty minutes to clean up this mess and deliver it to Pokhomov." He pointed to Istvan, face down on the carpet. He called to Kados, who with Marta, had been told to stay in the bedroom. "Get me gloves and a roll of tape."

Kados turned away as Aksenov began to work on the corpse. Moving quickly, the Russian cut a square from the bloody towel Kados had thrown over his friend's head, and stuffed the cloth into the wound. With strips of black electrician's tape Aksenov fixed the soggy compress securely in place. He slipped his gloved hand hand under Istvan's chin and lifted the head. He eased the wig free, pulled it into place and secured it with bits of the black tape. The long black hair covered the crude, bulging bandage. Aksenov seized one shoulder of the green tweed jacket and, with an effort, began to pull the thick body over onto its back.

Before rolling face up on the blanket, the body balanced for a moment on one shoulder. Aksenov stepped across the corpse and pushed it lightly with his toe. As Istvan rolled flat onto his back, the last breath was pushed from his lungs in a foul, posthumous cough.

Brattle glanced anxiously at Nancy. She was still seated at the round table, her back to the men in the center of the room. At the sound, she got up and took a few steps toward Brattle. Her face was drawn and her eyes red. She stopped dead still as she saw Istvan's uncovered face. "Christ," she said, stumbling back to the table. "There's nothing like a corpse on the rug to make a room look really tacky."

Trosper glanced at Brattle and shook his head. No doubt about it, Comrade Istvan *was* rather more of a mess than either of them had anticipated.

The protruding eyes had ruptured and blood had seeped along the sides of the Hungarian's nose, broken when he pitched onto his face. Subcutaneous contusions had blackened the area around the cheekbones. Only the wound was neat. About the caliber of a thick pencil, it was perfectly centered—quiet testimony to Aksenov's marksmanship.

Hesitating for a moment, Aksenov attempted to ease the eye lids down over the bulging eyes. He could not do it. He stood up.

"Glasses," he said to Kados. "I need a pair of eyeglasses."

Kados shook his head.

"Reading glasses, sunglasses," Trosper said.

"I haven't any," Kados said. "I don't wear glasses."

"Ski glasses?"

Kados shook his head.

"Your father wore glasses," Brattle said. "You can't have thrown them all out."

"Maybe in the drawer, in the desk over there." He pointed to a breakfront writing desk in the corner.

Aksenov pulled wire-rimmed glasses over the bulging eyes and fastened the frames beneath the black hair with tape.

"Pockets," Aksenov said. "Do his pockets. Everything out."

Trosper began to fish through the green jacket. As he emptied each pocket, he turned it inside out. A crushed box of Winston cigarettes, a clumsy chrome cigarette lighter, greasy comb, shiny fingernail clipper, a sordid handkerchief, and a few coins were Istvan's legacy. With scissors, Trosper cut the labels from the jacket. Seizing the lapels of the green tweed jacket, Brattle lifted the body while Trosper cut the label and laundry marks from the blood-soaked collar.

"This might not be necessary," Aksenov said. "But someone could be tempted to keep to keep a bit of clothing—"

He glanced at Kados. "When they known I've gone, the investigation will shake this city apart. The less evidence we leave, the less chance they'll have to track him back here."

"Then we'd better get rid of the shoes," Trosper said.

The Hungarian's tan shoes were makeshift "elevators," with lifts nailed onto the high heels and fitted with thick insoles. The toes, broad as a platypus bill, were scuffed. Trosper tossed them onto a chair beside the Hungarian's worn wallet. There was, he realized, one bit of luck. Istvan was almost an inch shorter than he had seemed, and probably a few pounds lighter.

Then, struggling to hold the body upright, they pulled Istvan's raincoat over the thick tweed jacket. It was like fitting the coat over a loosely packed sack of potatoes. Trosper pulled the arms of the raincoat into place. Aksenov cut the label from the lining and turned up the collar.

"A hat," the Russian said. "Get a hat."

Brattle rummaged through the cabinet beneath the bar at the side of the room. He took a bottle of barack and splashed it over Istvan's shirt and the raincoat. "Christ," he muttered, "that stuff smells worse than it tastes."

Brattle pulled the shabby broad-brimmed hat over Istvan's head. "You'd better let me help carry him," he said.

"We've only got the stairs and about four blocks to go before we

make the delivery," Trosper grunted. "And you're too easy to identify. Stay here with Nancy, check on the girl in the bedroom, and
go through Istvan's wallet."

With Istvan's arms over their shoulders, and his toes dragging on
the floor, Trosper and Aksenov moved toward the door. From far
enough away, a casual observer might think that two friends were
carrying a pal, very much the worse for drink, home from a night
on the tiles.

Aksenov pointed to the gun bulging in Brattle's pocket. "Don't
hesitate to shoot that little fascist if he starts anything," he said.

Nancy got up from the table and stood staring across the room,
her face puffy with fatigue and her eyes red. As Trosper and Aksenov began to move Istvan toward the door, she said, "You guys
sure know how to take a woman's mind off her troubles."

Brattle eased the door shut behind them.

38   BUDAPEST

THE BLACK Zhiguli was parked fifty meters from the intersection.
The motor was running. Two men were in the front seat. Both wore
hats.

Trosper was breathing heavily. Sweat ran down his face. He did
not attempt to get a glimpse of the license plates.

Neither of the men in the car moved until Aksenov and Trosper
and their burden were abreast of the car. When Aksenov touched
the door, a stocky man jumped from behind the driver's seat, bustled
around the rear, and began to unlock the trunk.

"Not in there, you ass," Aksenov hissed. "Put him on the backseat." The stocky man slammed the lid shut and yanked open the
rear door.

"Give us a hand, Smolenkov," Aksenov said. The young man in
the passenger seat jumped out, took Istvan's arm from over Trosper's shoulder and with Aksenov's help began to push the body onto

the backseat. "Fix him so that he stays upright," Aksenov said. But the body slumped sideways. "Sit in the back. Hold him upright," Aksenov ordered. Smolenkov rushed around the car and slid onto the seat beside Istvan.

Trosper stepped away from the car. Ostensibly keeping watch for pedestrians, he kept his face averted from the Russians. It was after midnight, and the street was deserted.

Aksenov took the stocky man's arm. "Pokhomov, you drive—fast but no accidents. Go straight to Central Group of Forces headquarters at Debrecen. Use your service pass. Go directly to the morturary . . ." Pokhomov made a motion as if to interrupt. Aksenov brushed him aside.

"This is a top secret affair—*sovershenno sekretno*—and all messages are delivered by hand—*lichno v ruki,*" he said sharply. "I want this body cremated at once. No questions to be asked by anyone." Pokhomov interrupted again. Aksenov thrust his face close to Pokhomov. "This is urgent business, these are orders from the Center. I want no fuss made, and no questions from any of those military assholes."

"But it's more than two hundred thirty kilometers. There won't be anyone on duty by the time we get there."

"That's what duty officers are for," Aksenov said. "They wake people up."

Flustered, Pokhomov touched his hat in a token salute and dashed around to the driver's seat. Aksenov followed. "I want everything burned, clothing, hat, everything. Do you understand?"

Pokhonov nodded several times.

"No one on the base is to make any report. Do you understand?"

Pokhonov nodded vigorously and said, "But they will *have* to. . . ."

"They don't have to do a thing but deal with this body. They cremate every enlisted man who dies in this command. There's no reason they can't handle this bit of Moscow business as well. It's got nothing to do with anyone in this command."

"But Colonel Sadovnikov is *rezident.* He will have to be told something. . . ."

"If that fat *zhopa* can't handle this on his own, tell him to get in touch with me in Moscow. I will see that his problem is referred to the Chairman of State Security—I'm sure that Viktor Mikhailovich Chebrikov will be glad to to take the time to answer Colonel Sadovnikov's questions." Aksenov stopped to catch his breath. "If that doesn't satisfy Sadovnikov, he can come back to Moscow and I will see to it that he makes his report directly to Viktor Mikhailovich himself."

Pokhomov touched his hat again. He wedged himself behind the wheel and opened the window. Aksenov leaned down and said, "Be absolutely sure everything is burned, clothing, everything." Pokhonov nodded. "When that is finished, take the ashes and strew them along the road on the way back . . . understood?" Pokhomov nodded. With a glance at the rear seat, he started the motor. Smolenkov had pulled the hat down so that the brim covered the neat red hole beneath the wire frame of Sandor Kados's glasses.

Aksenov stepped back from the car. With an abrupt gesture with his thumb, he signaled Pokhomov to drive off.

Aksenov turned to Trosper. "It will be thirty-six hours before anyone can even begin to try to sort that out."

"I'll settle for twenty-four," Trosper muttered.

As they turned to walk back to Kados's apartment, Aksenov said, "You know I haven't had much to amuse me in the last few days. The only real comedy is to think of Pokhomov, the laziest officer in the service, and Sadovnikov, a bloated drunk, already past retirement, trying to explain to Moscow what happened here." He snorted and began to pick up the pace.

39   BUDAPEST

"*THIS* is a problem for me," Aksenov said. "I really do not like it at all." He spoke in German.

Nancy put down the makeup kit and turned to Brattle. "What *is* he talking about, something wrong with the color?"

"He resents being made up," Brattle said. "It embarrasses him to pose as a woman."

"Tell him that this stuff came from Elizabeth Arden," Nancy said. "I won't even be able to replace it until I get to Paris or London." She began to work the pancake makeup into his cheeks. "I've only got one color—Sun Tan," she said, "so I'll have to put a little rouge under the cheek bone. That will give him the sucked-in look they use on *Vogue* covers."

"He'll appreciate that," Trosper said. "Just don't make it too fancy."

The Russian sat on a straight-backed chair between two floor lamps, near the middle of the room. When Nancy complained about the light, Brattle removed the shades from the lamps.

She began to work on the eyes, adding shadow to the lid, and elongating the corners with a pencil. With a mascara brush, she darkened and lengthened the Russian's eyelashes.

"I don't know what to do about the eyebrows," she said. "His are quite light, but it would be better if I plucked a few. Will he stand for that?"

"How long will it take for them to grow back?"

"I don't know," she said. "But probably quite awhile."

Grigorenko pulled his hands from under the sheet Nancy had tied around his neck. "No eyebrows," he said in English, waving his hands. "I will not have my eyebrows shaved."

"All right, all right," Nancy said. "But I'll still have to trim them, and take out the hair above the nose." She began snipping with a small pair of scissors. "Now, I'll give them a little definition with this pencil."

She turned to Brattle and whispered, "If he's this fussy about his eyes, what is he going to do about the lipstick? It may not be very fashionable, but I've got to give him heavy lipstick."

"It's just for the passport picture," Trosper said. "By the time he shaves again, he'll probably be used to it all."

NANCY pulled the wig out of the tote bag. "This is going to be too small, I just know it."

The hair was short and cut in layers. A feather cut, she explained.

It was almost the same color as her own hair, ash blond, frosted with gray. "If he can't wear it on the train, we'll tie a scarf around his head and put a hat on top of that." She began to pull the wig over Grigorenko's close-cropped hair. Simultaneously, Trosper and Brattle turned and walked away from the harsh light. It was as if they both had decided not to watch the final transformation.

"*YOU'D* better check this," she said. "I'm not a good judge of my own work."

"I'll be damned," Trosper said.

"Well done," Brattle said. "Jolly good."

Aksenov walked to the mirror at the side of the room. He stared at himself, adjusted the wig slightly, and turned to face Trosper. "Your technician does good work," he said softly. "It is forty years now since I wore makeup, and then at the Bolshoi school performances, but I can tolerate this." He nodded to Nancy, and, as if rehearsing, affected a mincing walk back to the chair between the lights.

"Toes straight ahead, do not come down on your heels, knees more together," Nancy said. Brattle translated. Aksenov's walk improved.

"It will be better after he shaves his sideburns above the ears, and we get him into a blouse and cardigan," she said proudly. "The only trouble is the wig, it *is* too small. I'm not sure what we can do about it."

"Now let's take the pictures," Aksenov said. "After that, I'll give myself a very close shave and she can repair the makeup—for the last time."

"*AT LEAST* there's one thing I've had some experience at," Brattle said. "I should be able to lift Mrs. Bristol's passport picture." He rummaged in Kados's equipment box and brought out a small brown bottle. He shook it. "We'd better hope this stuff is still good."

In the kitchen he softened the passport page with the jet of steam that whistled from the spout of the miniature kettle, and wiped the photograph with liquid from the brown bottle. It smelled like a mixture of ether and rubbing alcohol. Then he began to work the paper-thin ivory wedges under each corner of the soggy photograph. He held the passport close to the steam, and smeared more solvent across the photograph. He pushed the four ivory wedges gently toward the center of the picture until it fell free.

"There, by God," Brattle exclaimed. "The chemical is too old, and I used too much steam, but I haven't lost my touch."

Trosper agreed.

Even Kados was impressed.

TROSPER looked at his watch and turned to Nancy, who was dusting Aksenov with a final touch of powder. "We've got to keep an eye on the time. You must be back at the hotel before Jerry reports you missing, Kados has got to glue the photo into the passport and emboss the seal. And, I've . . . " He stopped. It would serve no purpose for Nancy to know he did not know what to do with Marta. She had been in the bedroom—her natural habitat, as Brattle had observed—since a few minutes after Istvan was shot.

Aksenov had finished shaving his legs and had begun on his hands and forearms.

"You'd better cut the hair high up the back of his neck," Nancy said. "There can't be any hair showing at the back."

She took the Russian's hands and examined the nails. "They're too short," she said. "In New York, I could buy false nails in any drugstore, I don't know where to get anything like that here." She glanced nervously at Trosper on the other side of the room. "The best I can do is put on a light polish—no one with nails that short would risk drawing attention to them with darker polish."

"He'll be wearing gloves," Brattle said. "You brought gloves."

"I keep forgetting," she said. "But in case he has to take them off, we'll be all right."

Trosper walked across the room to where Brattle was watching Kados tap the embossing of the seal onto the Polaroid photograph. "Nancy looks as if she's about to pack it in," he said. "You'd better get her back to the hotel."

It was after three. "Damn it," Brattle said. "I should have realized."

Trosper spoke to Nancy. "You've done a terrific job. They

couldn't have done any better in Hollywood."

"I'll see you at the train," she said. 'I don't know where my reservation is, but if there's room in your compartment, I'll come in there."

Trosper took both her hands. "Nancy, you've done enough." He turned to Brattle for support. The Englishman said nothing. "It could be a tricky business tomorrow. I can't be sure what will happen if anything goes wrong. It will be best if you travel in a separate compartment. The train won't be crowded this time of year. There will be plenty of room. It will only take about two hours until we are at the border. As soon as we are through the passport controls and in Austria, you can come in and we'll celebrate."

"Don't you people know *anything?*" she exclaimed. "Two couples look much less conspicuous. Just three Americans and Douglas on a toot in new Buda and old Pest." She smiled brightly. "Besides, before we get to the border, Grisha's makeup may need some touching up. That's something only we girls know about."

Trosper glanced at Brattle. The Englishman shrugged.

"Okay," Trosper said.

THEY were at the door. Aksenov walked toward them, and pointed at Brattle's pocket. "I want my gun," he said. Instinctively Brattle glanced at the bedroom door. "Not likely," he said.

"We've had all of that we can take care of," Trosper added quickly.

"It's not that," Aksenov said. "I will not go out on the street without it."

"You carried that damned corpse without any gun," Trosper said.

"I will not be taken alive." Aksenov spoke slowly. "Not after so many years, not with my record, and not like this." He opened his arms and turned slowly. "Whatever my comrades may come to think of me, at least they will never see me like this."

The gray flannel slacks were too small, but Nancy had opened the seam to allow three more inches around the waist. Because there was no time for careful sewing, she had patched them with a piece cut from panty hose. The slight elasticity of the material helped ease the pressure on the hasty stitches Nancy had used to secure the patch. The blouse was a reasonable fit. From the front, the shape of the bra was normal enough, and the socks Nancy had used for padding could not be seen. But through the sheer material, the back of the brassiere was plainly visible: it was too small to encompass the Russian's chest, and Nancy had tied it together with five inches of string.

It was the makeup that really worked. By accenting Aksenov's eyes, Nancy had softened the firm set of his jaw and exposed the delicate line of his nose. By indirection, she had created the mask of an interesting woman, some twenty years younger than the man it cloaked.

"I can't say that I blame him," Brattle said. "I wouldn't want to be arrested and photographed for a show trial looking like that."

"Let me see the piece," Trosper said.

Gingerly, Brattle pulled the gun from his pocket and handed it to Trosper. It was a 7.62-mm Tul'skii Tokarev. Widely used until about 1950, it was smaller and more easily concealed than the 9-mm Makarova, and much favored by old-timers.

"What if I carry it for you?"

The Russian shook his head. "I will not be taken alive." A faint smile eased his compressed lips. "I know that I can't hope to shoot my way out. But if I am about to be taken, do you think I can trust you Anglo-Saxons to do the necessary? To shoot me, the way I did that Hungarian?" His smile broadened. "And if you did shoot me," he said, "they would try you for murder, as well as everything else they can think of. And there wouldn't be a thing your embassy could do about it."

Trosper handed him the pistol.

40   BUDAPEST

MARTA hitched at her dress and fixed her eyes on Trosper. Her face was carefully made up. She seemed calm.

It was eight-thirty. Trosper and Aksenov had spent the night in Kados's living room. Neither had got much sleep. When Trosper signaled Kados to bring Marta from the bedroom, Aksenov had gone to the kitchen. Marta was not to see him in disguise.

"You have some decisions to make," Trosper said in German. "I don't know how closely either of you is identified with your friend Istvan."

Kados started to speak, but Trosper continued. "Sooner or later, Istvan will be missed and there will be a police investigation. I have no idea how long it will take the police to associate his disappearance with that of the Russian. But when it happens, there will be a very intensive investigation. In my opinion the search will lead directly to you, and in a relatively short time."

Trosper pointed to the bullet hole burned into the rug when Brattle knocked the pistol from Aksenov's hand.

"These are your problems, not mine," Trosper said. "All you can do now is to destroy Istvan's effects, the shoes, his wallet, and anything else that might show he has been here recently." He asked Kados to translate for the girl.

Marta said something in Hungarian.

"She told me not to forget his briefcase," Kados said. "It's in the hall."

"Don't just toss the stuff into a trash can. You must destroy each article, and dump the bits in different places. Don't leave anything intact. Make sure that there is nothing left that the police can possibly associate with Istvan."

Kados translated.

"Are you sure you understand this?" Trosper asked.

Kados nodded and said something in Hungarian to Marta.

Kados and Marta had a choice, Trosper explained. They could try to get out immediately, or stay in Budapest and attempt to bluff it out. The decision was theirs. "But if you stay here," Trosper said, "there is nothing I can do to help you."

"And if we cross the border?"

"I will arrange to have a few dollars made available to help your resettlement."

"How much?"

"Five thousand," Trosper said. "That is more than enough to get you started somewhere."

"It's not much," Kados said.

"It is much more than most refugees have, and it's more than you deserve." And, Trosper realized, if the Firm didn't agree to settle up, it was about five hundred dollars more than he had in his New York checking account.

"At this point," he said, "you are both lucky to be alive." He looked at Marta, who had kept her eyes away from the rug where Istvan's body had fallen. "Or perhaps you have forgotten?"

Kados turned to Marta and spoke rapidly in Hungarian. She answered volubly, tossing her head for emphasis.

"She's been after me for a long time to leave," he said. "She has some idea she can work as a model in Vienna. Her sister is there."

"These are your decisions," Trosper said. "There is nothing I can do to help you."

"She's too lazy to learn a language," Kados said. "A few words of German, some Italian, and not enough English to work as a waitress." He looked at her appreciatively. "But she does have some talent."

"I can only remind you that if you stay here, you will be in terrible trouble if the police find any trace between Istvan and the disappearance of the Russian."

Kados looked slowly around the apartment. "I guess I haven't much reason to stay. Just this apartment, and the housing people have been trying to take it away from me ever since my parents died." He glanced at his high fidelity equipment, but said nothing.

Marta spoke rapidly, she seemed to be urging Kados to leave.

"All right," he said. "I'll accept your offer. We will try to get to Vienna sometime during the Easter holiday. It will cost me a fortune in bribes." Kados stared at the bullet hole in the carpet. "How do we get in touch with you?"

"I'm still not sure you understand just how serious this is," Trosper said. "There is no way you can possibly explain this to the AVO or even the police. The moment the Russians find out that you are involved with the disappearance of their man, they will hang you by your heels—no matter what story you tell them."

"You don't have to tell me all that."

"You saw what happened when my friend thought Istvan was trying to blackmail him," Trosper said.

"Believe me, I understand," Kados said. "Why would I say anything?"

"Tell her," Trosper said. "Tell her that one word about this and she will be lucky if she lands in jail. Ask her if she has any idea what will happen to her in prison and later in a work camp?"

Kados spoke rapidly. Marta nodded several times and said something in Hungarian to Trosper.

"She promises," Kados said.

"Get her into the bedroom," Trosper said. "My friend and I will leave now."

It was almost nine when Trosper scribbled the Vienna telephone number for Kados.

41 BUDAPEST

TROSPER took the canvas bag, heavy with Aksenov's suit, shirt, and shoes, from the front seat of the taxi and offered his hand to the Russian. "Mind your head, dear," he said in English as the Russian struggled free of the cramped rear seat. Taking Aksenov's arm, he brushed past the doorman and pushed through the heavy glass door to the lobby.

The prefabricated Spanish dark wood decor of the brightly lighted lobby of the Flamenco did not disguise the functional design of the crowded, commercial hotel. Near the entrance, three porters pawed through mounds of luggage, separating the belongings of a busload of newly arrived guests from an apparently identical pile destined for a motorcoach of visitors anxiously waiting to leave.

"You'd better stay here while I get my key and see about some breakfast," Trosper said. Gratefully, Aksenov slipped into a tall chair, his back to the hotel entrance. He moved as if to cross his legs, but corrected himself. He brought his knees together and chastely crossed one ankle over the other.

Trosper picked up his hotel key. At the newsstand he bought a week-old *Sunday Observer, Time,* and *Newsweek.* At the IBUSZ office, he inquired about train reservations to Vienna. "No problem today," the chic young woman said. "It's Thursday and *Kar-freitag* —Good Friday—when we'll be crowded." He booked two seats in the first class section of the Orient Express to Vienna.

"By the time we've had breakfast," Trosper said to Aksenov, "the clerk will have our tickets. We can wash in my room, and still have plenty of time to get to the *Westbahnhof*." He looked sharply at the Russian. A trickle of sweat was running from under the wig. "Which is worse," Trosper asked. "The shoes or the wig?" Both were too small.

Aksenov glanced at the low-heeled American loafers that Nancy had supplied. "The shoes," he muttered. "So tight, I'm afraid they will break."

"We'd better have a good breakfast," Trosper said. "It's going to be a long day."

The Russian pulled the front of the beige raincoat Nancy had supplied and got up with the same easy grace Radl had shown in Vienna. The raincoat, designed like an old-fashioned duster, had been made big enough to be worn over Nancy's mink coat. It was the only piece of her clothing that really fitted him.

AKSENOV put down his empty coffee cup. He had eaten only one of the sweet rolls. "Tell me, honestly please, what do you think my chances are?"

"In the States?"

"I can take care of myself once we are out of here . . . what I mean is the border. What are my chances?"

Trosper looked straight into Aksenov's eyes. There was no point in giving the Russian any false confidence. "I would say you have eight chances in ten of getting across. Only two things can trip us up. Kados or that girl could decide to make a deal with the AVO or the police. But even if they do, they don't know when we are leaving, or how. And by the time they make up their mind to sell us out, we should be well on our way. The only other problem is the passport and the exit document. Both look good to me, but it depends on how carefully they examine the papers."

"You are not to interfere if I decide the game is over. Do you understand that?"

If only the wig were larger, Trosper thought, and the shoes less painful, the Russian could concentrate on the part he was playing. It was too much to expect an actor to concentrate if he was worried about his wig falling off.

"You have my word," Trosper said, "but only with one understanding."

The Russian's eyebrows shot up. "Yes?" The makeup Nancy had applied seemed to intensify every facial expression.

"I have never believed in what the newspapers call 'suicide pills.' No matter how desperate a situation may seem, it is very difficult to be sure no hope is left. In my opinion, an agent who thinks he is in extremis cannot be counted on to make the right decision." Trosper stirred his coffee. "All I ask is that if you think something has gone wrong, that you wait a little longer than you think wise."

Aksenov's face brightened. "All right," he said. "I guess you really do know something about our business—what you are worried about actually happened to us in Vienna in 1944. We lost a radio man whose nerves had broken. He bit into the cyanide capsule without reason." Aksenov shook his head. "You might even say that he was frightened to death—he killed himself when one of those uniformed postmen rang the bell of the safe house. The poor devil thought it was the Gestapo . . . we had a terrible time getting rid of the body." He spread jam on a piece of toast. "It was a waste," he said quietly. "We lost so many good men."

"What did you do with the body?" Trosper was making conversation.

Aksenov smiled. "That was before I had a crematorium. We buried him in the cellar. It was a terrible job. We had no tools, and we didn't dig deep enough." He shook his head sadly. "If something happens, I will shoot myself in the heart—twice if I can manage it. I will not take the gun out from under my coat."

Trosper nodded.

"Now that we are alone, I have a question for you," Aksenov said.

"Yes?"

"There is something very wrong with the way you are handling my escape. Franz told your service plainly that Kudrov, in Washington, is a false defector. Someone, I suppose someone high up in your service, didn't believe the story and must have discussed it with Kudrov himself."

Trosper busied himself with a piece of toast.

"That was stupid, completely unprofessional—"

"Damn it, *Barbara,*" Trosper whispered. "Will you please remember that you are in costume? You are acting as if you were back in your office." Trosper glared across the table. "Act a little more feminine and watch your voice. This is a trial run, but if you can't get through breakfast without blowing your disguise, how do you expect to pass the border control?"

Aksenov mumbled an apology, and dabbed at his mouth with a napkin. He looked at the napkin to see if he had wiped off any lipstick.

"What I want to know," Aksenov said quietly, "is why you have gone about my escape the way you have? I can't believe that your service would try to get away with using those two scruffy Hungarians . . . untested and incompetent. It is just a fluke that we have got this far. I know the Firm has better means and better documents than these amateur arrangements you and the Englishman have made."

"It will serve no purpose for me to try to explain things now."

"Then permit me to explain it to you," Aksenov said. He softened his voice, touched the napkin to his lips, and affected a grim smile. "I think you are acting independently of your service. I even think you were told to abandon us, and that for some reason you decided to act on your own." The Russian did not take his eyes off Trosper.

"That is the only possible explanation."

"There is nothing I will say now."

Aksenov nodded, slowly and thoughtfully. "I do not know what will happen at the border," he said. "But I can tell you now, I appreciate what you have tried to do, and the risk that you and the Englishman and your technician have taken. No matter what happens, I am in your debt."

"That's all right," Trosper said. "I appreciate what you're saying."

"If I don't make it," Aksenov said, "and if you or the Englishman get through, I hope you can do something for Franz. He is a good friend, he was loyal to me during the war, and he deserves help." The Russian studied Trosper's face. "Besides, *der Franzl* will be a good source of information for your service." He paused for another moment and said, "If I am killed, he will hate them more than ever."

"I will do my best," Trosper said. "Right now I think we'd better go to my room so I can pack and settle my bill." He glanced at Aksenov's feet. "And you may want to slip out of those shoes for a few minutes."

TROSPER picked up the telephone and dialed the operator. "Vienna, Austria," he said in English, and gave the telephone number. By the time he had finished packing, the operator had called back. He spoke for a few minutes and then said, "Yes, around two o'clock, I think. If you can make a hotel reservation I would appreciate it. A comfortable room with bath."

Mercer said he would take care of the accommodations.

42 BUDAPEST

THEY were early, almost half an hour before train time. Trosper piled his suitcase and the canvas tote bag onto a rusty luggage cart. With the Russian at his side, he moved slowly from the entrance where the taxi left them, through the main hall of the *Westbahnhof* to the platform where the Orient Express waited.

It was a long walk for Aksenov. A bright Hermès silk scarf, tied babushka-fashion over his wig and under his chin, seemed to accent his high forehead, deep-set eyes, and delicate nose. Black leather gloves matched the large leather handbag slung over his left shoulder. His gait, half limping, half imitation of a ballerina who had just stepped off stage, masked the authority with which he usually walked. With his right hand, he held the loose-fitting raincoat tight across his chest.

The early morning trains had pulled out. Aside from a scattering of Hungarians and a few tourists headed for Vienna, the station was empty.

There were two first class cars. Trosper checked their tickets and found the reserved seats in the second wagon. He threw the luggage onto the rack above the window seats and motioned Aksenov to the seat facing west. "At the border," he explained, "the sun will be coming in the window over your shoulder." He laughed. "*Contre-jour,* that's the best light at our time of life." He handed the Russian *Time* magazine.

Aksenov fished in the deep handbag and pulled out the pair of hornrimmed reading glasses Nancy had given him. "Special," he said, "for reading English."

It was the first joke Trosper had heard him make.

There was movement in the corridor and Trosper recognized Brattle speaking in German to the train man. "We reserved these seats with our friends, all the way to Vienna," the Englishman said loudly as he brushed the protesting *Schaffner* aside. As Nancy Cunningham stepped into the compartment, Aksenov stood. She pushed him gently back into the seat, and bussed his cheek. "We girls remain sitting, dear," she whispered. She pulled off her coat and let it fall onto the seat beside Aksenov. "As soon as we get underway, we can change coats," she said. "No one has ever suspected a woman in mink."

Brattle threw Nancy's three bags onto the luggage rack and tossed his worn leather bag on top of Trosper's suitcase.

"What about Jerry?" Trosper asked. "Is everything under control?"

"We had a hell of a row," Nancy said. "But I think he has got over his surprise by now." She tossed her head in an angry gesture. "This is the third time he's pulled something like this. I don't know what it is about American men, but when they hit fifty, either they step out of the closet or start acting like Errol Flynn. In Jerry's case it's as if he had just discovered women."

Embarrassed, Brattle stepped into the corridor. He pulled the window open and peered down the quay. Then he closed the window and sauntered along the corridor before stepping back into the compartment. "There are only about fifteen people in this car," he said. "No problem about our sitting in here with you." He turned to Trosper, "I didn't see any goons at all."

"There are two in the last car," Trosper said. "The others get on at Sopron. We'll be there at least forty-five minutes."

The train began to move.

I THINK it's time to do a little retouching," Nancy said. "Why don't you stand watch at the door to the compartment," she said to Brattle. "This is the sort of thing we usually do by ourselves." She eyed Aksenov critically. "That lipstick is too . . . floozy. It must have been the light last night. We'll have to smarten it up. With those marvelous eyes, only the best will do." Quickly taking her own lipstick out, she bent over Aksenov and with a brush applied the lighter shade.

"The eyes have held up all right, but there's a little problem along the hair line." She began to dab foundation cream where the sweat had run down the sides of Aksenov's face. "That damned wig is not so good," she said. "But I think we'll have to take off the scarf if he's going to stop sweating."

Brattle, his back to the compartment, peered out into the corridor. His bulk blocked the compartment door.

With a small wire brush, Nancy began to tease the wig, pushing the hair back into feathered layers. "It will have to do," she said. "Now get into the coat." Aksenov pulled the handbag from his shoulder, opened it and took the Tokarev. With a furtive glance at

Nancy, he turned toward the window, checked the clip, and jacked a round into the chamber.

Nancy exhaled loudly. "Do you people ever really get used to this?"

"Not really," Trosper murmured. He helped Aksenov into the coat. It was full length, with a shawl collar and deep sleeves. Nancy looked on approvingly. "It will be a while before Jerry can buy one of those for that little tramp."

Nancy knotted the silk scarf loosely around the Russian's neck and pulled the reading glasses down on his nose. "It's only the wig," she whispered to Trosper. "Everything else is perfect."

Aksenov sat down, the collar pulled high around his ears. As the Russian crossed his legs, Trosper saw a trace of blood oozing through the heel of one stocking. The tightfitting shoes had chafed the skin raw and worn a hole the size of a quarter in the light brown pantyhose. Above the hole, the stocking had laddered.

"Damn," Nancy said.

"Cross your feet," Trosper said in German. "See if you can cover the hole that way." The other shoe and stocking were the same.

THE operation had passed the point of possible recall, but Trosper could not keep himself from taking stock.

The Russian's face was so frozen with anxiety that the wig seemed to have risen slightly on his head. It appeared, at least to Trosper in his mood, to be perched unsteadily, and to clash with the expensive fur, casual flannel slacks, silk blouse, and cashmere cardigan. Aksenov's gloved left hand clutched the *Time* magazine. His right hand was thrust under the coat, holding the pistol. He sat with his knees to one side, his feet crossed in a vain attempt to cover the torn stockings and traces of the broken blisters.

Sensing Trosper's concern, Nancy tried to drape the coat to cover Aksenov's feet. It did not work. She fumbled in her handbag and pulled out a vial of perfume. "Here," she said. "Let's add a little more sex appeal. It's *Ma Griffe,* a little bold for you, but I don't think the customs people will mind."

Sitting beside Nancy, who faced the Russian in the window seat, Brattle studied the week-old Sunday *Observer.* Then, putting the paper aside, he looked over the rim of his reading glasses, and murmured, "Steady, steady all around."

It was time, Trosper realized, to give Aksenov more to think about than his disguise and the border crossing. In German, Trosper said, "This morning, you spoke personally to me. May I do the same to you?"

Surprised, the Russian nodded.

"Do you know a General Aleksandr Nikolaevich Chestnoy?"

Aksenov thought for a moment and said, "The one who was commander of the Moscow Military District?"

"Yes."

"I have met him a few times," Aksenov said. "I never really knew him."

"What about his son, Lieutenant Anatoli Chestnoy?"

"Of course," Aksenov said. "The old general insisted that we take him into the service. Yuri Vladimirovich—Andropov—was a fool to agree, but he did. It was just politics. You may not believe it, but even the Center depends on the military for favors. The commander of the Moscow District is particularly important to us. The only trouble was that his son was a drunk. Even worse than some of the other hooligan children of our new elite." Aksenov paused. "Isn't he the one who tried to go over to your people in Berlin?"

"Yes," Trosper said. "He came through the East German checkpoint on his official papers. But he died within a few hours. Heart congestion, our doctor thought."

"I remember the investigation. He had been disciplined two or three times for drinking and had been ordered back to Moscow. The *rezidentura* had him under light control, but he slipped away, took a car from the motor pool, and drove right across our checkpoint and into your sector. It was the devil of a scandal. Later, the security people found he had stopped to drink three or four times in East Berlin. As I recall the investigation showed that he must have consumed more than a liter of vodka before he crossed."

"I suppose that's what killed him," Trosper said. "He died within a few hours of crossing. Our people had the military police return the body and the car."

"That's right," Aksenov said. "We were never sure whether he was on a drunken binge or trying to defect. As it was, we couldn't even make a fuss about it. No one wanted any publicity because of his father's position in Moscow."

"He had some notion of defecting," Trosper said, "but had made no plans. Before he collapsed, he tried to impress our people with how much he knew. But the only thing he could think of to tell us about was a case that had happened some years earlier. He called the case 'Worker'—'*Rabotnik.*' It involved the recruitment of an American soldier, an enlisted man in our military mission in Moscow, maybe in 1945."

The Russian shook his head. "I remember several cases like that, we studied them at the training course I took after the war."

"That could be it."

"You people were so naive," the Russian said. "Your enlisted men had no supervision. You thought because we were allies that we were only interested in the Germans. But we never stopped working against your embassy and the military missions. In 1944, when we knew the war was won, we stepped up our work against you. We signed up half a dozen of your soldiers. As I recall, nothing came of any of the cases. That's why we cleared the files for use in the training courses."

"Can you remember any details?"

The Russian relaxed his grip on the magazine. "They were all about the same. As a rule we supplied the soldier with a girl friend —we call these women *lastochki*—'swallows.' After a few weeks of true love, we would have the girl tell the soldier she was pregnant and ask him to pay for an abortion. Usually the soldier would agree. When they got to the abortionist, our people would break in, pretend to arrest them all, and tell the soldier that abortion was a serious crime in the Soviet Union. After a few threats, one of our men would —in a very friendly way—suggest that the soldier could get out of it by helping us to understand what was going on in your embassy, what the people were really saying about us. In a few weeks the case men would have the soldiers bringing out telegrams and secret files. As far as our people could tell, no one in the embassy or military missions worried much about security in the days when we were such good allies. The cases would run as long as the soldiers were in the Soviet Union."

"Afterwards, what happened afterwards?"

"The scheme was that we would contact them later, when they were out of the army." Aksenov laughed. "The trouble was that we were not yet set up to follow through. We concentrated on Russian speakers, people who might later join your foreign office, or stay in the intelligence service. But as I recall, nothing ever came of any of these cases."

"Do you remember the one known as 'Rabotnik?' "

Aksenov looked closely at Trosper, glanced at Brattle, and began to speak in Russian. "Why do you dig up such ancient history? Is this something personal?"

"In a way it is personal," Trosper said softly. "One day, when I was between assignments, I was leafing through a bundle of files, old material sent us by our G-2 people in Berlin. None of the reports was of any interest except for a short account of the Chestnoy incident. It was a very brief paper, only a few notes on what Anatoli had said about his father, General Chestnoy. The only thing he said of any operational interest came from his training course at your school. He mentioned the operations against the embassy and military mission, but could only remember one case—'Rabotnik,' 'Worker.' "

Aksenov shook his head.

"It involved a very young enlisted man at the military mission. He was from a working-class family and had learned Russian. Your people trapped him, just as you described it."

"I don't understand your interest," Aksenov said.

"I thought there might be enough in the report for me to identify the soldier. When I checked the old military records, I found there were only two or three of the enlisted men in the military mission who spoke any Russian at all. It didn't take long to learn that one of these men was someone whom I had recommended for our service."

"Had he admitted this when you took him in?"

"No," Trosper said, "although our chief always asks each new man if there is anything in the past that might have been overlooked in our background investigations and that might later be uncovered. If my friend had admitted it to the chief, there would not have been any problem. Unfortunately he said nothing."

"But you found Chestnoy's report and identified the man?"

"Yes, it was about two years after my friend had come to work for us."

"I don't remember these cases well. The only one I recall was a man we found in Paris. He denied the entire incident, laughed in my man's face, and threatened to call the police." Aksenov smiled. "That was exactly the right reaction."

"Do you recall his name?"

"No, of course not. Those cases meant nothing at all. It happened before I took over the division. If hc is the man I am thinking of, he died in an accident a few weeks after we approached him. As a matter of fact, we were never even sure he was identical with the young soldier."

And that, Trosper knew, was the end of the Tim Gidding story.

WHAT a ridiculous tableau we make, Trosper thought. Nancy, leafing through a picture magazine and not understanding a word of German. Brattle, as aloof as a retired colonel on a train to London for lunch at his club. And an American, traveling on the passport of a man who died in 1945 and questioning a KGB colonel in full drag. All this on the shabby Orient Express pulling slowly through Györ, fifteen minutes from the showdown at the border control point.

Aksenov reached across and tapped Trosper's knee. "If it makes you fccl any better, I would certainly have known if we had been able to do any business with your friend in Paris."

43   THE ORIENT EXPRESS

"HERE," Trosper said, "We should begin to chat amiably." The train had pulled through Györ and was moving slowly across the open farmland. They were more than halfway to Vienna, and only

a few kilometers from the Hungarian border control.

"When we get to the control point," Trosper said to Brattle, "you'd better hand Mrs. Bristol's passport and exit visa to the customs man along with your own. That way, he won't have two American passports in hand at the same moment, and won't be able to make an immediate comparison."

The Englishman turned to Aksenov beside him. "Mrs. Bristol," he said, "I don't think you will have to say anything, but you might have a handkerchief out, and perhaps act as if you had a cold."

The Russian attempted to smile. It was more nearly a grimace, at odds with the cheerful, bright lipstick. He began to rummage in the leather handbag. When he seemed about to dump the contents onto his lap, Nancy intervened. "What's the matter?"

"There's no . . . no . . ." He groped for the word in English. *"Ich habe kein Taschentuch,"* he said, desperation in his voice.

Nancy took the bag and extracted a package of Kleenex. "Not very elegant," she said, 'but just the thing for travel."

Aksenov pulled several tissues from the package and clutched them in his gloved hand.

"By way of chatting amiably," Brattle said to Nancy, "did you come to Hungary by train?"

"We flew from Vienna," Nancy said, her voice tight. "I don't think Jerry has ever been on a train."

They talked aimlessly until, two hundred and twenty kilometers from Budapest, the train bumped slowly to a halt.

To the west across the platform and an empty line of track, they could see the train from Vienna. Passengers headed for an Easter vacation in Hungary hung out the windows, eager for their first glimpse of the country.

"This is a lay-by," Trosper said. "The trains from Vienna and from Budapest meet here and all the customs control checks are made at the same time."

Across the empty track to the east and behind a chest-high, wire mesh fence, Trosper could see the faded sign "Sopron" in large letters across the front of a shabby cement station house that seemed completely empty. At the rear of the car, the customs and security officials began the passport control. *"Alle Reisepässe bitte. . . ."*

Brattle tossed his newspaper aside and said, "You know, this isn't actually the border. The Hungarians handle the control here, but the border is beyond Hegyeshalom, several kilometers farther along."

"Why?" Nancy asked.

"I think they've built a sort of Potemkin enclave here," Brattle said. "The actual border with all the police state paraphernalia—the plowed fields, barbed wire, machine guns, mines, and the observation towers every few hundred yards—is not the image they want to project. So they moved it a quarter of a mile or so to either side of this train line. They probably have the wire running parallel with the track, but just beyond the view of the capitalists riding on the train." He chuckled, "It makes a better impression on tourists and journalists."

"This isn't even the Sopron rail station," Trosper said with a gesture toward the desolate building. "Sopron is a city of sixty thousand people. Picturesque, according to the guide books. This is a siding, a couple of kilometers west of the city. I suppose they arranged it to keep the international traffic well away from the local trains that use the big station in the city."

Nancy stared at the uniformed guards, machine guns slung across their shoulders, patrolling the space between the trains.

"This arrangement also helps to keep the citizens from jumping aboard," Brattle said.

Aksenov made no small talk, his attention apparently fixed on the low, scudding clouds over head.

"All of which means," Trosper said, "that we keep our celebrating in check until we're sure we are in Austria." Assuming, he told himself, that we get through. Every time he glanced at Aksenov, the wig seemed more awry, the laddered stockings more conspicuous, and the makeup more grotesque. Never again, he promised himself.

There was movement in the corridor, and the clump of heavy boots. The compartment door was thrust aside and a chubby, blue-uniformed customs official touched his cap. He looked pleasantly around the compartment. *"Grenzkontrolle bitte, alle Reisepässe, bitte."* He glanced at Nancy and said, "All passport, please." Behind him stood a sour-faced security man in khaki uniform, and a young soldier with a submachine gun strapped across his back and a flashlight in his hand.

Brattle reached across to Mrs. Bristol and took the passport and exit document. He put it on top of his blue British passport and handed it to the customs man.

"The customs fellow," Brattle said softly, "looks as if he should be playing the violin in one of those gypsy orchestras."

Nancy smiled brightly at the man and said, "From now on, you're the gypsy, our own *Zigeuner.*" He did not understand, but nodded pleasantly.

Trosper pulled a travel agent's envelope from the breast pocket of his tweed jacket and began deliberately to sort through travel folders and brochures until he found his passport. He took Nancy's passport and folded exit permit and held both the documents, politely waiting until the customs man had completed his examination of Mrs. Bristol's papers and Brattle's worn British document.

"You know, Nancy," Trosper said quietly, "this is not the *famous* Orient Express."

"To tell the truth," she said, "I *had* expected something more romantic, like one of those old movies."

"Only one of the great old trains is left," Trosper said, not looking at the guard. "They use it for special runs. During the tourist season, it goes from Paris to Venice." Would he never finish with the damned passport? Trosper wondered. "They serve seven-course meals four or five times a day," he added.

Aksenov sat rigid, pressed back into the seat, his right hand across his chest under the fur coat. He had probably slipped the safety.

Trosper glanced at the blue-uniformed customs officer. He did look a bit like a gypsy. There was a touch of humor about his eyes. Trosper saw it and for a moment he dared to hope.

"What about the wine?" Brattle asked. "All the shaking must be a problem for fine wines on the train."

"I've always wondered about that," Trosper said. "If I remember, I'll ask my friend Mercer. He knows just about everything."

"On ocean liners they say the rolling makes the wine mature more quickly," Brattle said.

"I suppose it's true," Trosper said. "I was served some pretty mature milk on the *Queen Elizabeth* once."

"I think you've both gone crazy," Nancy said.

The gypsy finished his examination of Aksenov's passport, and peered into the Russian's face, checking it against the photograph. He snapped the passport closed, took the exit permit, glanced briefly at Aksenov's picture and handed both documents to the security officer. Behind them, the young soldier fidgeted, bored with the procedure.

The security officer's shiny uniform was creased tightly at the waist and under the shoulders. A worn automatic pistol hung in a holster on the unpolished leather belt cinched across his paunch. He stared at Aksenov's visa, and thumbed back to the photograph. He glanced at Aksenov, and turned back to the Hungarian visa. He flipped the pages, stopping at the place and date of issue. "Barbara Bristol," he read, slowly emphasizing each syllable. "Bar-bar-a Brisshtol," he repeated.

It was a new passport, issued a few days before she left for Europe. Only the photograph and birthdate had been changed. Barbara Bristol was born in 1944. Kados had changed one numeral, to show Aksenov born in 1934.

Trosper watched Aksenov's pistol hand move deeper into the fur coat.

The customs officer asked, "Hungarian money?"

Brattle shook his head. "No Hungarian currency."

Aksenov attempted a smile. "No Hungarian money," he said, and dabbed at his nose with a paper tissue.

"We haven't any money left," Trosper said in German. "We spent every last forint in Budapest."

Nancy smiled and said in English, "Not a dime."

The gypsy smiled amiably.

The security officer had been studying Brattle's worn passport. He checked each page, puzzling over the entry and exit stamps showing the Englishman's many trips in Western Europe. Occasionally he turned the pages back, as if rechecking some particularly interesting stamp.

No one, Trosper knew, could hope to unravel the dozens of cachets this rapidly. At the most, such a hasty examination might reveal a trace of careless forgery or clumsy alteration of the passport. Trosper wasn't comforted by his deduction.

The gypsy handed Nancy's and Trosper's passports to the security man. With a grunt, he brushed the gypsy's hand aside, and turned again to Aksenov's document. He ran his finger over the seal Kados had embossed on the photograph and glanced at Aksenov.

Trosper saw a question in the security man's eyes. He did not dare look at Aksenov's gun hand beneath the black mink coat.

There was another second, and another, before the security man snapped the passport shut.

The gypsy smiled deferentially and said something in Hungarian. The security officer snorted and, spoke sharply in Hungarian. Holding Aksenov's and Brattle's passports in one hand, he tapped the documents lightly against the sleeve of his uniform. Abruptly, he thrust the two passports toward the customs man.

As the gypsy clutched the documents and stepped into the compartment, his heavy boot landed squarely on the polished toe of Trosper's brogue.

As Brattle reached to take the two passports, the distracted official turned to apologize to Trosper. Like a relay runner stumbling at the moment of passing the baton, he dropped both passports inches from Brattle's outstretched hand. They fell to the floor at the Englishman's feet.

The flustered customs man muttered *"Verzeihung,"* and took another step into the compartment. As he ducked down to pick up the documents, his stiff cap brushed Brattle's knee. The hat tumbled to the floor and rolled toward Aksenov.

Cover your feet, Trosper willed silently. Cross your ankles and cover your heels.

But Aksenov never took his eyes from the security officer who had stopped his examination and was watching his colleague.

As the customs man bent forward to reach for his cap, he dropped to one knee. His face was within three feet of Aksenov's polished loafers.

For a moment he remained motionless, cap in one hand, the passports in the other. Then he looked up, raising his eyes from Aksenov's shoes and torn stockings to the wig. Aksenov had begun to perspire. A bead of sweat ran along the Russian's jaw.

Now, Trosper thought. Now, all hell will break lose.

From the doorway, the security officer spoke harshly in Hungarian. He turned and said something in Hungarian to the soldier standing behind him. The young soldier broke into a broad grin. It could not be the first time the security man had mocked the gypsy.

Still clutching the passports in one hand, the gypsy picked up his cap, took a lingering look at Aksenov's shoes and torn stockings, and pushed himself off the floor. His face flushed, he brushed dirt from his knee.

He peered again at Aksenov. Then his glance moved from the Russian to Nancy, to Brattle, and finally to Trosper.

He turned back to the security man. He seemed to be debating what to say when he glimpsed the intensity of the security officer's bullying expression.

There was a burst of Hungarian from the security man. It was as if he were a drill sergeant barking at a recruit. For emphasis andto make sure that the foreigners could understand, he interspersed a few words in German. *"Was für ein Trottel . . . Bloeder Kerl . . . Ungeschicklichkeit . . ."*

Aksenov sat motionless, his eyes open wide.

From the side, Trosper could see the Russian's hand clenched on the pistol butt.

Nancy's face was white. She seemed about to faint.

"Do you have a cigarette, my dear?" Brattle said cheerfully.

Nancy inhaled sharply.

"I stopped . . . I mean I haven't smoked since September fifth," she said, her voice rising. Then, loudly, she added, "But now that you mention it, I suppose this is as good a time as any to begin again." She smiled uncertainly and began to grope in her handbag.

"The trouble is, I don't have any cigarettes."

"Then I'm afraid we'll have to wait until we get to Vienna," Brattle said. "There's no *wagon restaurant* on this train."

The gypsy did not take his eyes off Aksenov.

If it weren't for the shoes, Trosper thought. And that stupid wig.

The security man growled a few more words in Hungarian. The gypsy glanced at his cap and began quickly to wipe the dust from the flat top. With an impatient gesture, the security man motioned the soldier into the compartment.

Hitching at the submachine gun over his shoulder, the soldier dropped to one knee and flashed his light under the seats. Aksenov tucked his feet demurely to one side. Like chorus girls, the others lifted their legs to allow the soldier a clear view of the empty space beneath the worn seats.

The soldier scrambled to his feet, stood on tiptoe, and glanced hurriedly at the luggage piled on the racks above.

He turned to the security man and said something in Hungarian.

The security man touched his cap, muttered *"Gute Reise,"* and strode along the corridor. The soldier followed.

The gypsy wiped the visor of his cap across his sleeve. He glanced at each passenger, slapped his cap squarely on his head, and followed his colleagues along the train corridor.

Trosper could hear the door of next compartment being pushed open.

"Jesus H. Christ," Trosper muttered.

THERE was a long wait before the sound of heavy shoes echoed along the train corridor and the three officials, heading for the rear of the train, strode past the closed compartment door. Last in the line, the customs man broke his stride to stare into the compartment. Trosper nodded politely. The trace of a smile crossed the gypsy's face as he lumbered along after his colleagues.

The rear door of the car clanged shut. On the quay, a uniformed station master raised his arm and blew three shrill blasts on a silver whistle. The train lurched and began to move. Trosper slid the door of the compartment open and stepped into the corridor. The train had gathered speed. He could no longer make out the faded sign above the door of the desolate station. At the end of the corridor, the Austrian customs officials began to make their round.

"IT'S opening time," Brattle said as the Austrians stepped back into the corridor after their perfunctory glance at the passports. "The moment for a restorative." He fished a silver flask from the breast pocket of his blazer. He twisted the cap and offered it to Nancy.

"Malt whiskey," he said. "I'm sorry there's no ice, but it doesn't really go with Glenlivet."

Nancy took the flask, held it in toast to Aksenov, Trosper, and finally to Brattle. She took a sip, made a wry face and passed the flask to Aksenov.

He lifted the flask in a toast and took a long swallow. "When can I change?" he asked.

"When we pass the first Austrian flag," Brattle said, "our Austrian friends will be dropped off." He glanced out the window. "Just about here, I should think."

44   VIENNA

"WELL, Alan," Hamel said, "I don't know what's happened, but you've surer than hell blown the roof off."

They were standing beside the Orient Express at the Vienna *Westbahnhof.* Alerted by Trosper's telephone call from Budapest, Mercer had rushed to Hamel's office. Together they had drafted an urgent cable for Bates—Trosper was crossing out of Hungary with Colonel Grigory Pavlovich Aksenov, First Chief Directorate, Moscow Center. Because of an unexplained difficulty in Budapest, it would be essential that Aksenov and his agent, Franz Radl, be evacuated from Austria soonest.

Trosper had asked Brattle and the others to remain on the train while he made arrangements with Hamel.

"We need a new safe house, the most comfortable and secure that you have," he said. "The old one is blown, or it will be if they ever get around to checking on my phone call to Vienna."

"That's two houses down the drain since you've been here," Hamel said glumly.

"I've got to write some cables."

"I dare say," Hamel replied.

"I want you to make sure Aksenov can relax for a few hours. He's had a rough week, and I'm going to need a couple of hours with him tonight. There are some things to be checked for Bates."

"I should think so."

Trosper knew Hamel was irritated. As office chief, he took his orders from the Controller, not from visiting case men.

"Grisha and Franz are to be handled as a team. They won't accept anything else at this point."

"Okay."

"Both of them are to be out of Austria by mid-afternoon tomorrow. There'll be hell to pay when Moscow realizes their colonel is missing." He stopped for a moment, and then said, "There's also a dead Hungarian AVO agent that someone will have to account for."

"On the train?" Hamel's voice rose to a squeal.

"Don't be silly. If things went right, he has already been cremated in Debrecen."

Hamel groaned. "What else?"

"I need money for expenses."

"How much?"

"I'm not sure now, but Douglas Brattle and Mrs. Cunningham have both had considerable expenses."

"Brattle?"

"Butch Brattle, he was with me."

"Mother of God . . . do you know that Bates has to go to the White House on this stunt of yours? How in hell is he going to explain to the President that you've involved a British agent in it?"

Trosper laughed. "I think he'll have enough to say without going into that."

"Who the devil is Mrs. Cunningham?"

"Aksenov thinks she's one of my many assistants, a disguise specialist."

"Who *is* she?"

"She's an American tourist who volunteered to help us."

Hamel rolled his eyes. "Have you asked for file traces on any of these people? Have they been briefed on security? Have they signed an oath or anything?"

"Certainly not," Trosper said. "I doubt that Colonel Brattle will feel he has to sign anything at all." Trosper laughed. "But I might ask him to brief Mrs. Cunningham on the need for keeping secrets."

"What else?"

Trosper handed Mrs. Bristol's passport to Hamel. "We used this to get Aksenov out. I' not sure when the woman will discover it's lost. But someone in Washington has to cable the consulate in Budapest and instruct them to issue another passport as soon as Mrs. Bristol finds that hers is missing. It is absolutely essential that Mrs. Bristol be far away before the balloon goes up in Budapest."

"Did you steal this from her?"

"That's not the most felicitous way to put it," Trosper said.

Hamel leafed through the passport. He held the page with the Polaroid photograph of Aksenov in the wig and earrings to the light.

"It's beyond belief," he said. "Bates seems to think that your colonel is the hottest defector since World War II, and you bring him across the Hungarian border with a rag like this?"

"I know," Trosper said. "Believe me, I know." He beckoned to Brattle on the train.

"If you've got everything squared away," the Englishman said to Trosper, "I think I might try to find a bit of lunch for Nancy." He shook hands with Trosper. "That was a damned good show," he said. "I'm not sure I'd want to try it again right away, but it was a good stunt."

Brattle began to pile luggage onto a trolley. "Nancy has decided to stay at the Kaiserin Elisabeth for a couple of days. I'll be at Sacher's. Maybe we can have a meal before you shove off?"

"Tomorrow night," Trosper said. He turned and threw his arms around Nancy. "You were terrific, simply terrific," he said. "We couldn't have got him out without you."

Nancy's eyes watered, and she brushed at them with the back of her hand. "I still don't believe any of this. I don't think I will ever understand what has happened to me in the last forty-eight hours."

She took Trosper's hand. "For a moment," she said, "I was sure the gypsy was going to say something about Grisha's shoes. But then the man in khaki was so rude. . . . I think our friend, the gypsy, changed his mind."

"Yes," said Brattle. "But everybody's safe now."

"I hope he doesn't get into any trouble," she said doubtfully. "Anyway, as soon as I catch my breath here, I'm going to go to Salzburg for a few days. Douglas says the food at the *Goldener Hirsch* is better than in Budapest—I'll stay there a few days while I try to work things out."

Brattle finished loading the luggage cart.

Aksenov stepped from the train. With Nancy's help, he had used cold cream to wipe the makeup from his eyes and face and had slipped back into his American suit and shirt on the train. Now, free of the loafers and wig he had regained his confidence.

"This is the Colonel," Trosper said. "Mr. Miller will take over at this point." Hamel stepped forward and shook hands.

Aksenov turned to Trosper. "You leave now?" he asked anxiously.

"No, no, I'll be here for another couple of days, I'll see you tonight."

"Good," Aksenov said. "There are some questions I have."

"There's one more thing . . . "

"What thing?"

"The . . . ah . . . gun," Trosper muttered. "You can't carry it in Vienna. Not even in the United States."

Reluctantly, Aksenov took the gun from his jacket pocket. He snapped the safety and handed the pistol butt first to Trosper.

"Christ almighty," Hamel murmured. "You let him cross the border with a gun in his pocket?"

"He's rather an expert marksman."

Aksenov interrupted, "When do I see Franz?"

"I couldn't keep them away," Hamel said quietly to Trosper. "Mercer's got the little guy in tow, they're in one of the cars, outside." He glanced around the empty quay. "It's time to be moving along."

TROSPER could see Mercer's bulky figure hustling along the sidewalk. Beside him, immaculate as ever, Radl walked with disciplined, short steps. When he spotted Aksenov, he broke into a faster gait. Trosper did not conceal his curiosity. Radl slowed his pace as he approached Aksenov. They shook hands formally. Then, Radl stepped back, murmured a few words of Russian, and threw his arms around Aksenov's shoulders. It was as if the Russian had kicked a soccer goal and was being congratulated by a teammate.

Radl stepped back and turned to Trosper. He pumped his hand several times. "We are in your debt, Mr. Warner. I am sorry for the hard times I gave you before, but there was nothing else I could do. Now we are in your debt." He clasped him around the shoulders. "Thank you for the effort you made."

Trosper smiled encouragingly and nodded to Hamel. "Let's get the hell off the sidewalk."

Hamel held the door of a small Mercedes while Aksenov and Radl slid into the rear seat. Hamel pointed to a shabby Opel across the street. "The driver knows where to take you."

Mercer hurried to keep up with Trosper. "Do you know what day this is?"

"It's Wednesday," Trosper said.

"In Ireland," Mercer said, "they call it 'Spy Wednesday'—the Wednesday before Good Friday, the day Judas made the deal with the Romans."

"I'm glad I didn't know that this morning," Trosper said.

45 VIENNA

"THERE'S only one point we have to clarify tonight," Trosper said. "I must have the details on 'Phoenix.' "

They had finished dinner and were seated around the fireplace in a comfortable villa on the outskirts of the Wienerwald.

Mercer picked up a yellow pad.

"The operation was initiated by Service A, the active measures —disinformation and deception—section of the First Chief Directorate," Aksenov said softly. "It was just a replay of the old Trust operation, the one we ran against you in the twenties."

Mercer chuckled.

"The Politburo and the Secretariat wanted to buy some time, to have your government ease the pressure for negotiations and disarmament. I think they meant it to be a temporary measure, something that might last until they had a new leader, someone healthy enough to take charge and actually run things again."

Mercer's pen flew across the yellow pad.

"It was an ambitious scheme, perhaps too ambitious," Aksenov said. "No one is better at that sort of operation than we are, but it is hard to do long-range planning when no one is sure of policy. The operation was conceived when Yuri Vladimirovich—Andropov— was still in our service. It might have worked, but there was a vacuum at the top. Our people seem lost without a strong chairman."

Aksenov stared into the fire. "Sending Kudrov to Paris to defect to you people was the first active step. We tried to make sure he would go to the Firm, rather than the Agency. That worked better than we thought possible. Your people kept it to themselves. That was a big mistake."

"How did *you* learn about it," Trosper asked.

"I am . . . I was . . . chief of Twelfth Department. That is a section Andropov set up. Most of the officers are old-timers, veterans who have served abroad for years, but who do not fit into our new bureaucratic organization very well. Some of our most experienced and best officers were assigned to the Twelfth. We allow them to work—almost without direct supervision—at the things they do best, in the areas they are most familiar with. They work out of Moscow and usually have little to do with the local residencies. As a result, we run some of the most productive operations in the entire service—Yuri Andropov knew what he was doing when he established the Twelfth Department."

Aksenov gave Trosper an appraising look. "I suppose that is

something like the way you have been working."

"Not quite," said Trosper. "I've had more than my share of supervision."

"Because of his record, we were told to take Mikhail Aleksandrovich Lopatin—the old fellow you know as 'Schneider'—into the Twelfth Division. The decorations he was given and the assignment to our group was all part of a belated effort to make up for the way Stalin treated him after the war."

Aksenov stared into the fire. "It was a mistake to make us take him. But because we knew he had never recovered from the treatment Stalin had given him we kept him busy on low-level things and made sure he was never involved in anything very important."

Aksenov took a sip of cognac. "Then, some idiot from Service A, the active measures group—the people who were running 'Phoenix' —remembered the old fellow had served in Austria for years and told him to establish an agent in Vienna. Someone who could be used when the 'Phoenix' case men needed some special support in Austria."

"You mean they were actually planning to set up an office in Vienna, the way Trust established an office in Finland?"

"I'm not sure what they had in mind," Aksenov said. "But they didn't ask my division about Schneider before they approached him —the operation was 'too secret' for anything like that. So they propositioned Schneider without our clearance. When he got to Vienna, the old fellow told your man Galkin about 'Phoenix.' After Galkin was arrested, he mentioned 'Phoenix' to the interrogators. That was all it took—he was executed a few hours after his interrogation was completed."

"What happened to Schneider?" Trosper asked.

"He was sent to one of the provincial cities—anyone else would have been dismissed and given a jail sentence.

"When did you learn about 'Phoenix?' "

"It was much later. When the Service A people were trying to find out who Schneider might have told about 'Phoenix' they came to me. They thought they were questioning me, but before they were through I had elicited a pretty complete picture of the case from them. that's when I made the big mistake of telling Franz that he could tell you about it."

Aksenov paused and glanced across to Radl. "In the long run, I suppose it worked out best that way—at least we are both out now."

It was midnight before Trosper said, "I think I've got the story now. It's time to call it a night."

"When your service has agreed that Franz and I can have visas and we have worked out the resettlement provisions you mentioned, Franz can empty our box in the Basel bank. We cached my notes on 'Phoenix' and a few rolls of negatives there."

"An insurance policy?"

"Exactly," Aksenov said.

46 WASHINGTON, D.C.

"*I'M GLAD* to see you back," Bates said.

"I wasn't sure whether or not you wanted to see me," Trosper said. He could have done without this graveyard interview, but in view of what happened he did not attempt to avoid it.

"I suppose you've heard about my resignation," Bates said. He was in shirt sleeves, his jacket tossed across the leather chair beside his desk.

Trosper nodded. "Along with everything else, Mercer keeps up with high-level personnel moves. He had the news before we left Vienna."

Bates managed a smile. "That was one hell of a stunt you pulled off."

"I hope they never make the file available for training—there's nothing to be learned from what we did," Trosper said.

"That's as may be," Bates said. "Perhaps I'm the only one who learned anything."

Trosper shrugged.

"I should tell you that after we had that row, just before you went back to Vienna, I broke my promise to you." Bates voice cracked and he took an angry puff of his cigarette. "What I did was stupid and unprofessional." He got up and walked to the window. He stood staring out at the small courtyard below.

"I *told* that damned Kudrov that he had been denounced." Bates turned to face Trosper. "The only reason I did it was because your report from Radl was exactly along the line that Kudrov had told me the Center would use to try to discredit him and the Iskra group." He walked back to the desk and sat down.

"Maybe my judgment was a little clouded because of the pressure I was getting from General Foster. Right at the beginning, I should have told him to leave the details of our work to us. But I didn't do it, and he kept encroaching on us."

Bates managed a smile. "If I make one recommendation to Duff Whyte, it will be for him to keep the amateurs at arm's length." He hunched forward over the desk.

"It must have been the day before you left Vienna for Budapest that I decided to go to the Director, and to ask him to have a couple of agency analysts go over the file." Bates shook his head. "Then the two of us went to the White House and told General Foster to simmer down while we sorted things out. That was quite a session."

"Did the Agency people find anything?"

Bates laughed. "They found everything that our people had turned up. They noted some of the same precedents—the old Trust case and the other operations like it that Moscow has run since World War Two. The really big difference was that no matter how good Kudrov's reports looked, they found that he had not told us very much that was new. This is what our people had missed. By the time we had this in hand, you and the Englishman had left for Budapest." Bates reached for another cigarette.

"What did the Agency people recommend?"

"The DCI himself told me that we should continue to play Kudrov *and* your little pal in Vienna, and that we should tell the White House to buzz off while we sorted things out." He looked closely at Trosper. "*That,* I am sure you will recall, was exactly what you had recommended."

"It wasn't a very profound recommendation," Trosper said.

Bates flipped his unlighted cigarette into the lacquered box. "By the time this had transpired, I knew I had bought a dog and that Kudrov was on a leash."

Trosper shrugged. "If Aksenov turns out to be as valuable as he looks, we will have got more than our own back."

"That's certainly true, but it's not exactly the point," Bates said. "When you got back from Budapest and wrote your first cable from Vienna, I took a copy to General Foster in the White House. He didn't want to believe it, but I insisted that we go right in to the President."

"If I'd known more about the audience," Trosper said, "I might have drafted a more pompous cable."

"I resigned that afternoon, right in the President's office," Bates said. "Much as I wanted this job, and as hard as I worked to try to do it well, I knew I'd made a mess of it and that it was largely my own fault."

"I'm sorry about that."

"So am I," Bates said.

ACROSS the narrow hall from Bates's office, Duff Whyte was, as Mercer put it, "reading in."

Whyte stood up when Trosper came into the office. "Hello, Alan."

"I take it we're still speaking," Trosper said as they shook hands.

Whyte sat down. He was six feet two inches tall and built like a light heavyweight boxer. Although he had spent most of his working life abroad, he affected a completely American look—button-down shirt, knit tie, and Ivy League suit. The suits were so elaborately casual that Trosper had long suspected Whyte had talked a London tailor into making them.

"In the circumstances," Whyte said with a slight smile, "I suppose your stunt can be considered justified. You made it back, we've got a classy defector, and Moscow is missing one rather prominent front tooth."

"It's not anything I'd like to make a habit of," Trosper said. He looked at the pile of files on Whyte's desk. "I'm glad you're taking over—it's past time."

"Next week," Whyte said.

"What's happened to Kudrov?"

"We offered him asylum—once again," Whyte said. "He thought it over for a while, but then he turned himself in to the Embassy. He'll be leaving on Aeroflot in a couple of days."

"I suppose we can expect to see him in a Moscow press conference—denouncing us for having kidnapped and drugged him," Trosper said.

"That's their usual form," Whyte replied, "but they may be too embarrassed to make a fuss this time."

They chatted until Whyte asked, "What about Butch, is he okay?"

"If it hadn't been for him, the best I could have done would have been to dump Aksenov on some embassy and hope that they could smuggle him out," Trosper said. "What with the paprika and all, I think Douglas has a new interest in life."

Whyte looked puzzled.

"He and the American, Nancy Cunningham, rather hit it off."

"I'll be damned," Whyte said. "I always thought Butch was a confirmed bachelor."

"Ther's nothing like a little danger to cement a relationship," Trosper said.

"And your plans?"

"I've got to tidy up a few things in New York and then I have a date to meet a young woman in London."

Whyte looked surprised.

"Emily Gidding promised to introduce me to her daughter—Amanda is eleven, I think."

"I had forgotten about you two," Whyte said with a quizzical look. "Have you thought about coming back?"

"I don't think it's for me anymore, Duff. I've had a long run."

"You don't have to make up your mind now," Whyte said.

"Did the Hungarian ever show up—young Kados?" Trosper asked.

"He and his girl got out during the Easter weekend," Whyte said. "Hamel was rather put out that you had given him the office phone number."

Trosper laughed. "I don't blame him, but it was the only number I had."

"I authorized the . . . ah . . . generous payment you offered him," Whyte said. "It's probably best to leave chaps like that with a smile."

"I agree," Trosper said.

"Let's keep in touch," Whyte said.